LILIAN
JACKSON
BRAUN

THREE COMPLETE NOVELS

Also by Lilian Jackson Braun

The Cat Who... Could Read Backwards
The Cat Who Ate Danish Modern
The Cat Who Turned On and Off
The Cat Who Saw Red
The Cat Who Played Brahms
The Cat Who Knew Shakespeare
The Cat Who Sniffed Glue
The Cat Who Went Underground
The Cat Who Talked to Ghosts
The Cat Who Lived High
The Cat Who Knew a Cardinal
The Cat Who Moved a Mountain
The Cat Who Wasn't There
The Cat Who Went into the Closet
The Cat Who Had 14 Tales
(short story collection)

LILIAN JACKSON BRAUN

THREE COMPLETE NOVELS

The Cat Who Saw Red
The Cat Who Played Brahms
The Cat Who Played Post Office

G. P. PUTNAM'S SONS
New York

G. P. Putnam's Sons
Publishers Since 1838
200 Madison Avenue
New York, NY 10016

ISBN 0-399-13885-4

Printed in the United States of America

Dedicated to
Earl Bettinger, the husband who . . .

CONTENTS

CONTENTS

The Cat Who Saw Red

ONE

Jᴉᴍ Qᴡɪʟʟᴇʀᴀɴ sʟᴜᴍᴘᴇᴅ in a chair in the Press Club dining room, his six-feet-two telescoped into a picture of dejection and his morose expression intensified by the droop of his oversized mustache.

His depression had nothing to do with the price of mixed drinks, which had gone up ten cents. It had nothing to do with the dismal lighting, or the gloomy wood paneling, or the Monday mustiness that blended Friday's fish and Saturday's beer with the body odor of an old building that had once been the county jail. Qwilleran had been stunned by bad news of a more vital nature.

The prize-winning feature writer of the *Daily Fluxion* and the newspaper's foremost connoisseur of sixteen-ounce steaks and apple pie à la mode was reading—with horror and dismay—a list printed on a bilious shade of green paper.

Across the table Arch Riker, the *Fluxion*'s feature editor, said: "What's everybody going to eat today? I see they've got potato pancakes on the menu."

Qwilleran continued to stare at the sheet of green paper, adjusting his new reading glasses on his nose as if he couldn't believe they were telling him the truth.

Odd Bunsen, *Fluxion* photographer, lit a cigar. "I'm having pea soup and short ribs and an order of hash browns. But first I want a double martini."

In silence Qwilleran finished reading his incredible document and started again at the top of the list:

NO POTATOES
NO BREAD
NO CREAM SOUPS
NO FRIED FOODS

Riker, who had the comfortably unholstered contours of a newspaper deskman, said: "I want something light. Chicken and dumplings, I guess, and coleslaw with sour cream. What are you having, Qwill?"

NO GRAVY
NO SOUR CREAM
NO DESSERTS

Qwilleran squirmed in his chair and gave his fellow staffers a vinegary smirk. "I'm having cottage cheese and half a radish."

"You must be sick," Bunsen said.

"Doc Beane told me to lose thirty pounds."

"Well, you're reaching that flaky age," the photographer said cheerfully. He was younger and thinner and could afford to be philosophical.

In a defensive gesture Qwilleran stroked his large black mustache, now noticeably flecked with gray. He folded his glasses and put them in his breast pocket, handling them gingerly.

Riker, buttering a roll, looked concerned. "How come you went to the doctor, Qwill?"

"I was referred by a veterinarian." Qwilleran fumbled for his tobacco pouch and started to fill his voluptuously curved pipe. "You see, I took Koko and Yum Yum to the vet to have their teeth cleaned. Did you ever try to pry open the mouth of a Siamese cat? They think it's an outrageous invasion of privacy."

"Wish I'd been there with a movie camera," Bunsen said.

"When Koko realized what we had in mind, he turned into something like a fur tornado. The vet got him around the neck, an assistant grabbed his legs, and I hung on to his tail, but Koko turned inside out. Next thing we knew, he was off the table and headed for the kennel room, with two vets and a kennel boy chasing him around the cages. Dogs barking—cats having fits—people yelling! Koko landed on top of the air conditioner, eight feet off the floor, and looked down and gave us a piece of his mind. And if you've never been cussed out by a Siamese, you don't know what profanity is all about!"

"I know!" said Bunsen. "That cat's got a voice like an ambulance siren."

"After that episode I was bushed, and the vet said I needed a physical checkup more than the cats needed a dental prophylaxis. I've been short of breath lately, so I took his advice and went to Doc Beane."

"How'd you get the cat down?"

"We walked away and left him there, and soon he came sauntering into the examination room, hopped on the table, and yawned."

"Score another one for Koko," said Riker. "What was the female doing all this time?"

"Yum Yum was sitting in the traveling box waiting her turn."

"And probably laughing like hell," said Bunsen.

"So that's the story," Qwilleran summed up. "And that's why I'm on this miserable diet."

"You'll never stick with it."

"Oh, yes I will! I even bought a bathroom scale with some of my prize money—an antique from a country doctor's office in Ohio."

Qwilleran had won $1,000 in a *Daily Fluxion* writing contest, and the entire staff was waiting to see how the frugal bachelor would spend it.

"What did you do with the rest of the dough?" Riker asked with gentle sarcasm. "Send it to your ex-wife?"

"I sent Miriam a couple of hundred, that's all."

"You chump!"

"She's sick."

"And your in-laws are rich," Arch reminded him. "You should be buying a car for yourself—or some furniture so you can get a decent place to live."

"There's nothing wrong with my apartment in Junktown."

"I mean you should get married again—start buying a house in the suburbs—settle down."

Qwilleran cringed at the suggestion. After lunch, when the three men walked back to the office, he continued to cringe inwardly—for several reasons. In the first place, he loathed cottage cheese. Also, Riker had been goading him gently throughout the lunch hour, and Qwilleran had let him get away with it because they were old friends. The third reason for his discomfort was a summons from the managing editor to attend an afternoon meeting. An invitation from the boss was usually bad news, and the man himself riled Qwilleran; he had a synthetic camaraderie that he turned on and off to suit his purpose at the moment.

Qwilleran reported to the front office at the appointed time, accompanied by Riker, his immediate superior.

"Come in, Arch. Come in, Qwill," said the editor—in the syrupy voice he reserved for certain occasions. "Did you fellows have a good lunch? I saw you at the club living it up."

Qwilleran grunted.

The boss motioned them to seats and settled into his high-backed executive chair, beaming with magnanimity. "Qwill, we've got a new assignment for you," he said, "and I think you're going to like it."

Qwilleran's face remained impassive. He would believe it when he heard the details.

"Qwill, everyone seems to think you're the champion trencherman on the staff, and that fact per se qualifies you for a job we're creating. In addition, we know you can give us the meaty writing we're constantly striving for on this paper. We're assigning you, my friend, to the new gourmet beat."

"What's *that* all about?" The question came out gruffly.

"We want you to write a regular column on the enjoyment of good food and wine. We want you to dine at all the outstanding restaurants—on an expense account, of course. The *Fluxion* will pay expenses for you. You can take a guest." The editor paused and waited for some expression of joy.

Qwilleran merely swallowed and stared at him.

"Well, how does it sound, Qwill?"

"I don't know," Qwilleran replied slowly. "You know, I've been on the wagon for two years . . . and today I started a low-calorie diet. Doc Beane wants me to lose thirty pounds."

The boss was nonplussed for only the fraction of a second. "Naturally there's no need to *eat* everything," he said. "Just sample this and that, and use your imagination. You know the tricks of the trade. Our cooking editor can't boil an egg, but she puts out the best recipe page in the country."

"Well . . ."

"I see no reason why you can't handle it." The managing editor's brief show of goodwill was fading into his usual expression of preoccupation. "We plan to start next Monday and give the column a send-off in Sunday's paper—with your photograph and a biography. Arch tells me you've eaten all over Europe."

Qwilleran turned to his friend. "Did you know about this, Arch?"

The feature editor nodded guiltily. He said, "Better get that mustache trimmed and have a new picture taken. In your old photo you look as if you have bleeding ulcers."

The boss rose and consulted his watch. "Well, that's the story. Congratulations, Qwill!"

On the way back to the feature department Riker said, "Can't you defer that diet a few weeks? This bright idea of Percy's will blow over like all the rest of them. We're only doing it because we found out the *Morning Rampage* is starting a gourmet column in two weeks. Meanwhile, you can live like a king—entertain a different date every night—and it won't cost you a cent. That should appeal to your thrifty nature. You're Scotch, aren't you?"

"Scottish," Qwilleran grumbled. "Scotch comes in bottles."

He went first to the barber and then to the photo lab to have his picture taken and to complain to Odd Bunsen about the new assignment.

"If you need company, I'm available," the photographer volunteered. "I'll eat, and you can take notes." He seated Qwilleran on a stool in a backbreaking position and tilted his head at an unnatural angle.

"Riker says you should make me look like a bon vivant," Qwilleran said with a frown.

Bunsen squinted through the viewfinder of the portrait camera. "With that upside-down mustache you'll never look like anything but a hound dog with a belly-ache. Let's have a little smile."

Qwilleran twitched a muscle in one cheek.

"Why don't you start by eating at the Toledo Tombs? That's the most expensive joint. Then you can do all the roadhouses." Bunsen stopped to twist Qwilleran's shoulders to the left and his chin to the right. "And you ought to write a column on the Heavenly Hash Houses and tell people how rotten they are."

"Who's running the gourmet column? You or me?"

"Okay, now. A little smile."

The muscle twitched again.

"You moved! We'll have to try another . . . Say, wait till your crazy cats hear about the new assignment! Think about all the doggie bags you can take home to those brats."

"I never thought of that," Qwilleran murmured. His face brightened, and Bunsen snapped the picture.

The *Fluxion*'s new gourmet reporter had every intention of starting his tour of duty at the exclusive Toledo Tombs—although not with Odd Bunsen. He telephoned Mary Duckworth, the most glamorous name in his address book.

"I'm so sorry," she said. "I'm leaving for the Caribbean, and I've already declined an invitation to attend a Gourmet Club dinner tonight. Would you like to go in my place? You could write a column on it."

"Where's the dinner?"

"At Maus Haus. Do you know the place?"

"Mouse House?" Qwilleran repeated. "Not a very appetizing name for a restaurant."

"It's not a restaurant," Mary Duckworth explained. "It's the home of Robert Maus, the attorney, *M-a-u-s*, but he uses the German pronunciation. He's a superb cook—the kind who locks up his French knives every night, and whips up a sauce with thirty-seven ingredients from memory, and grows his own parsley. They say he can tell the right wing from the left wing of the chicken by its taste."

"Where is . . . Maus Haus?"

"On River Road. It's a weird building that's connected with a famous suicide mystery. Maybe you can solve it. Wouldn't that be a scoop for the *Daily Fluxion*?"

"When did the incident happen?"

"Oh, before I was born."

Qwilleran huffed into his mustache. "Not exactly hot news."

"Don't discuss it at the dinner table," Mary warned. "Robert is thoroughly weary of the subject. I'll phone and tell him you'll be there."

Qwilleran went home early that afternoon to change into his good suit and to feed the cats, first stopping at the grocery to buy them some fresh meat. With their catly perception they knew he was coming even before he climbed the stairs. Waiting for him, they looked like two loaves of homemade bread. They sat facing the door—two bundles of pale toasty fur with brown legs tucked out of sight. But the brown ears were alert, and two pairs of blue eyes questioned the man who walked into the apartment.

"Greetings," he said. "I'm early tonight. And wait till you kids see what I've brought you."

The two cats rose as one. "Yow!" said Koko in a chesty baritone. "Mmmm!" said Yum Yum in a soprano squeal of rapture.

She leaped on the unabridged dictionary and started scratching its tattered cover for joy, while Koko sailed onto the desk in a demonstration of effortless levitation and stepped on the tabulator key of the typewriter, making the carriage jump.

Qwilleran stroked each cat in turn, massaging Koko's silky back with a heavy hand and caressing Yum Yum's paler fur with tenderness. "How's the little sweetheart?" He spoke to Yum Yum with an unabashed gentleness that his cronies at the Press Club would not have believed and that no woman in his life had ever heard.

"Chicken livers tonight," he told the cats, and Koko expressed his approval by resetting the lefthand margin on the typewriter. His mechanical ability was a new-found talent. He could operate wall switches and open doors, but most of all he was fascinated by the typewriter with its abundance of levers, knobs, and keys.

Qwilleran had mentioned his development to the veterinarian, who had said, "Animals go through phases of interest, like children. How old are the cats?"

"I have no idea. They were both full-grown when I adopted them."

"Koko is probably three or four. Very healthy. And he seems highly intelligent."

At this comment Qwilleran had smoothed his mustache discreetly and refrained from mentioning Koko's outstanding faculty. The truth was that the precocious Siamese seemed to

possess uncanny skills of detection. Qwilleran had recently uncovered a crime that baffled the police, and only his close friends
knew that Koko was largely responsible for solving the case.

Qwilleran chopped chicken livers for the cats, warmed them
in a little broth, and arranged the delicacy on a plate the way
they liked it, with juices puddling in the center and bite-size
morsels of meat around the rim.

"Lucky beggars!" he said. They could eat all they wanted without gaining an ounce. Under their sleek fawn-colored fur they
were lean and muscular. Although they moved with grace and
feather-light tread, there was strength in their hind legs that
carried them to the top of the refrigerator in a single effortless
leap.

Qwilleran watched them for a while and then turned his attention to his new assignment, sitting down at the typewriter to
make a list of restaurants. He always left a fresh sheet of paper in
position around the platen, ready for action—a writer's trick that
made it easier to get started—and as he glanced at his paper, his
fingers halted over the keys. He put on his new glasses and had a
closer look. There was a single letter typed at the top of the
page.

"By golly, I knew you'd learn to operate this machine sooner
or later," he said over his shoulder, and there was a gargled
response from the kitchen, as Koko simultaneously swallowed a
bit of liver and made an offhand comment.

It was a capital *T*. The keyboard was locked in upper case.
Koko had apparently stepped on the shift lock with his left paw
and on the letter key with his right.

Qwilleran added "oledo Tombs" to Koko's *T* and then listed
the Golden Lamb Chop, the Medium Rare Room at the Stilton
Hotel, and several roadhouses, ethnic restaurants, and underground bistros.

Then he dressed for dinner, shedding the tweed sports coat,
the red plaid tie, the gray button-down shirt, and the dust-
colored slacks that constituted his uniform at the *Daily Fluxion*.
In doing so, he caught a glimpse of himself in the full-length
mirror, and what he saw he did not like. His face was fleshed
out; his upper arms were flabby; where he should have been
concave, he was convex.

Hopefully but not confidently he stepped on the antique scale in the bathroom. It was a rusty contraption with weights and a balance arm, and the arm went up with a sharp clunk. He held his breath and moved the weight along the arm, hesitantly adding a quarter-pound, a half-pound, then one, two, three pounds before the scale was in balance. Three pounds! He had eaten nothing but grapefruit for breakfast and cottage cheese for lunch and he was three pounds heavier than he had been that morning.

Qwilleran was appalled—then discouraged—then angry. "Dammit!" he said aloud. "I'm not going to turn into a fat slob for the sake of a lousy assignment!"

"Yow!" said Koko by way of encouragement.

Qwilleran stepped off the scale to take another critical look in the mirror, and the sight sent a wave of determination surging through his flabby flesh. He expanded his chest, sucked in his waistline, and felt a new strength of character.

"I'll write that damn column," he announced to the cats, "and I'll stay on that dumb diet if it kills me!"

"Yow-wow!" said Koko.

"Three pounds heavier! I can't believe it!"

While weighing himself, Qwilleran had failed to notice Koko standing behind him with front paws planted solidly on the platform of the scale.

TWO

As Jim Qwilleran dressed for dinner Monday evening, he was feeling his age. He now needed reading glasses for the first time in his life; his mustache and good head of hair had now reached the pepper-and-salt stage; and his beefy waistline was another reminder of his forty-six years. But before the evening was over, he was a young man again.

He took a taxi to the River Road residence of Robert Maus—out beyond a sprawling shopping center, beyond Joe Pike's Seafood Hut with its acres of parking, beyond a roller rink and lumberyard. Between a marina and a tennis club stood a monstrous pile of stone. Qwilleran had seen it before and guessed it to be the lodge hall of some eccentric cult. It stood back from the highway, aloof and mysterious behind its iron fence and two acres of neglected lawn, resembling an Egyptian temple that had been damaged in transit and ineptly repaired.

Pylons framed a massive door that might have been excavated on the Nile, but other architectural features were absurdly out of character: Georgian chimneys, large factory windows in the upper story, an attached garage on one side and a modern carport on the other, and numerous fire escapes, ledges, and eaves troughs in all the wrong places.

Qwilleran found a door knocker and let it fall with a resounding clang. Then he waited—with an air of resignation, his stomach growling its hunger—until the heavy door opened on creaking hinges.

For the next half-hour very little made sense. Qwilleran was greeted by a slender young man with impudent eyes and ridiculous sideburns, long and curly. Although he wore the white duck coat of a servant, he was carrying a half-empty champagne glass in one hand and a cigarette in the other, and he was grinning like a cat in a tree. "Welcome to Maus Haus," he said. "You must be the guy from the newspaper."

Qwilleran stepped into the dim cavern that was the foyer.

"Mickey Maus is in the kitchen," said the official greeter. "I'm William." He lipped his cigarette in order to thrust his right hand forward.

Qwilleran shook hands with the amiable houseboy or butler or whatever he was. "Just William?"

"William Vitello."

The newsman looked sharply at the young-old leprechaun face. "Vitello? I could swear you were Irish."

"Irish mother, Italian father. My whole family is a goulash," William explained with an ear-to-ear smile. "Come on in. Everybody's in the Great Hall, getting crocked. I'll introduce you around."

He led the way into a vast hall so dark that scores of lamps and candles on torchères and in sconces succeeded in lighting it only dimly, but Qwilleran could distinguish a balcony supported by Egyptian columns and a grand staircase guarded by sphinxes. The floor and walls were inlaid with ceramic tiles in chocolate brown, and voices bounced off the slick surfaces, resounding with eerie distortions.

"Spooky place, if you don't mind my saying so," said Qwilleran.

"You don't know the half of it," William informed him. "It's a real turkey."

In the center of the hall, under the lofty ceiling, a long table was laid for dinner, but the guests were cocktailing under the balcony, where there was some degree of coziness.

"Champagne or sherry?" William asked. "The sherry's a bomb, I ought to warn you."

"You can skip the drink," Qwilleran said, reaching in his

pocket for tobacco and pipe and hoping that a smoke could curb his hunger pangs.

"It's just a small party tonight. Most of the people live here. Want to meet some of the girls?" William jerked his head in the direction of two brunettes.

"*Live* here! What kind of establishment is Maus running?"

The houseboy hooted with delight. "Didn't you know? This is a sort of weird boarding house. It used to be a real art center—studios on the balcony and a big pottery operation in the back—but that was before Mickey Maus took it over. I'm a charity case myself. I go to art school and get room and board in exchange for several kinds of menial and backbreaking labor."

"Of which grass-cutting is not one," Qwilleran said with a nod toward the shaggy front lawn.

William launched another explosive laugh and slapped the newsman on the back. "Come and meet Hixie and Rosemary. But look out for Hixie; she's a husband-hunter."

The two women were standing near a sideboard that held platters of hors d'oeuvres. Rosemary Whiting was a nice-looking woman of indefinite age and quiet manner. Hixie Rice was younger, plumper, louder, and had longer eyelashes.

Hixie was intently busy with her champagne-sipping and canapé-nibbling, all the while chattering in a highpitched monotone: "I'm rabid for chocolate! Chocolate butter creams, chocolate chip cookies, brownies, black-bottom pie, devil's food cake—anything that's made with chocolate and three cups of sugar and a pound of butter." She stopped to pop a bacon-wrapped oyster into her mouth.

There was quite a lot of Hixie, Qwilleran noted. Her figure ballooned out wherever her tightly fitted orange dress would permit, and her hair puffed like a chocolate soufflé above her dimpled dumpling face.

"Caviar?" Rosemary murmured to Qwilleran, offering a platter.

He took a deep breath and resolutely declined.

"It's rich in vitamin D," she added.

"Thanks just the same."

"Mickey Maus," William was saying, "is a nut about butter. The only time he ever lost his cool was when we were having a small brunch and we were down to our last three pounds of butter. He panicked."

"Unfortunately, animal fats—" Rosemary began in a soft voice, but she was interrupted by Hixie.

"I eat a lot because I'm frustrated, but I'd rather be fat and jolly than thin and crabby. You have to admit that I have a delightful disposition." She batted her eyelashes and reached for another canapé. "What's on the menu tonight, Willie?"

"Not much. Just cream of watercress soup, jellied clams, stuffed breast of chicken baked in a crust, braised endive—I hate endive—broiled curried tomatoes, romaine salad and crepes suzette."

"That's what Charlotte would call just a little bite to eat," Hixie observed.

William explained to Qwilleran: "Charlotte never has a meal. Only what she calls 'a bite to eat.' That's Charlotte over there—the old gal with the white hair and five pounds of jewelry."

The woman with hair like spun sugar was talking vehemently to two paunchy gentlemen who were listening with more politeness than interest. Qwilleran recognized them as the Penniman brothers, members of the Civic Arts Commission. It was Penniman money that had founded the *Morning Rampage*, endowed the art school, and financed the city park system.

Moving nervously about the Great Hall was another man who looked vaguely familiar. He had a handsome face and a brooding expression that changed to a dazzling smile whenever a woman glanced his way; the startling feature of his appearance was a shaven head.

Qwilleran, studying the other guests, noted an attractive redhead in an olive green pantsuit . . . and a young man with a goatee . . . and then he saw *her*. For a moment he forgot to breathe.

Impossible! he told himself. And yet there was no mistaking that tiny figure, that heavy chestnut hair, that provocative one-sided smile.

At the same time, she turned in his direction and stared in disbelief. He felt a crawling sensation on his upper lip, and he touched his mustache. She started to move toward him across the tile floor—gliding the way she used to do, her dress fluttering the way it used to do, her melodic voice calling, "Jim Qwilleran! Is it really you?"

"Joy! Joy Wheatley!"

"I can't believe it!" She stared at him and then rushed into his arms.

"Let me look at you, Joy . . . You haven't changed a bit."

"Oh, yes, I have."

"How many years has it been?"

"Please don't add them up . . . I like your mustache, Jim, and you're huskier than you were."

"You mean stouter. You're being kind. You were always kind."

She pulled away. "Not always. I'm ashamed of what I did."

He looked at her closely and felt his collar tighten. "I never thought I'd see you again, Joy. What are you doing here?"

"We've been living here since January. My husband and I operate the pottery at the back of the building."

"You're married?" Qwilleran's rising hopes leveled off.

"My name is Graham now. What are you doing here, Jim?"

"No one calls me Jim anymore. I've been Qwill for the last twenty years."

"Do you still spell Qwilleran with a *w*?"

"Yes, and it still gives typesetters and proofreaders ulcers."

"Married?"

"Not at the moment."

"Are you still writing?"

"I've been with the *Daily Fluxion* for more than a year. Haven't you noticed my byline?"

"I'm not much of a reader—don't you remember? And my husband is mad at the *Fluxion* art critic, so he buys the *Morning Rampage*."

"Tell me, Joy—where have you been all these years?"

"Mostly in California—until Mr. Maus invited us to come here and take charge of the pottery . . . There's so much to talk about! We'll have to—when can we—?"

"Joy," Qwilleran said, lowering his voice, "why did you run away?"

She sighed and looked first to one side and then the other. "I'll explain later, but first I think you should meet my husband . . . before the terrible-tempered Mr. G. throws a tantrum," she added with a wry smile.

Qwilleran looked across the hall and saw a tall, angular man watching them. Dan Graham had faded carrot hair, a prominent Adam's apple, and freckled skin stretched taut across prominent bones in his face and hands. His worn corduroy jacket, unpressed shirt, and barefoot sandals evidently were intended to express the free artistic spirit, Qwilleran thought, but instead they made the man look seedy and forlorn. But terrible-tempered? . . . No.

Graham's nod of acknowledgment was curt when Joy introduced Qwilleran as "an old flame." There was something pointed about the way she said it—not with mischief but with spite—and Qwilleran thought, All is not well between these two. And he felt guilty about feeling glad.

He said to Dan Graham, "I knew your wife in Chicago when we were kids. I was the boy next door. I'm with the *Daily Fluxion* now."

Graham mumbled something. He spoke rapidly and swallowed his words.

"Beg your pardon?" Qwilleran said.

"Gettingreadyforanexhibition. Maybeyoucangetmesomepublicity."

Joy said, "It's going to be a husband-and-wife show. We work in quite different styles. I hope you'll attend the opening, Jim."

"Don'tthinkmuchofyourartcritic," her husband mumbled. "Hisreviewsaren'tworthahillofbeans."

"Nobody loves an art critic," Qwilleran said. "That's one newspaper job I wouldn't want. Otherwise, how do you like it here in the Midwest, Mr. Graham?"

"Wouldn't give you two cents for this town," said the potter. Qwilleran's ear was becoming attuned to his rapid delivery and his liberal use of outdated expressions and clichés. "Expect to work in New York eventually—maybe Europe."

"Well, I like this part of the country very much," Joy said defiantly. "I'd like to stay here." She had always liked everything very much. Qwilleran remembered her boundless enthusiasms.

Graham glanced testily at the dinner table. "Jeepers creepers! When do we get some chow? I could eat a horse." He waved an empty champagne glass. "This stuff gives you an appetite and no buzz."

"Do you realize," Qwilleran said, "that I haven't met our host?"

Joy seized his hand. "You haven't? I'll take you to the kitchen. Robert Maus is a real lamb pie."

She led him through a low-ceilinged corridor at the rear of the Great Hall, gripping his fingers and staying closer to him than was necessary. They walked in self-conscious silence.

The kitchen was a large picturesque room, fragrant with herbs and cooking wine. With its ceramic tile floor, beamed ceiling, and walk-in fireplace, it reminded Qwilleran of kitchens he had seen in Normandy. Copper pots and clusters of dried dill and rosemary hung from an overhead rack, while knives and cleavers were lined up in an oak knife block. On open shelves stood omelet pans, soufflé dishes, copper bowls, a fish poacher, salad baskets, and a few culinary objects that remained a mystery to the uninitiated.

Dominating the scene was a towering, well-built man of middle age, immaculate in white shirt, conservative tie, and gold cuff links. He had the dignity of a Supreme Court justice, plus a slight stoop that gave the effect of a gracious bow. A towel was tied around his waist, and he was kneading dough.

When Joy Graham made the introduction, Robert Maus exhibited his floured hands in apology and said in measured tones, after some consideration, "How . . . do you do."

He was assisted by a woman in a white uniform, to whom he gave brief orders in a deferential tone: "Refrigerate, if you please . . . Prepare the sauteuse, if you will . . . And now the chicken, Mrs. Marron. Thank you."

He started boning chicken breasts with deft slashes of a murderous knife.

Qwilleran said, "You handle that weapon with a vengeance."

Maus breathed heavily before replying. "I find it most . . . satisfying." He whipped the knife through the flesh, then gave the quivering breast a whack with the flat of the blade. "Shallots, if you please, Mrs. Marron."

"This is an extraordinary building," Qwilleran remarked. "I've never seen anything like it."

The attorney considered the comment at length before rendering his verdict. "It would not be unreasonable to describe it . . . as an architectural horror," he said. "With all due respect to the patron of the arts who built it, one must concede . . . that his enthusiasm and resources outweighed his . . . aesthetic awareness."

"But the apartments upstairs are adorable," Joy said. "May I take Jim to the balcony, Mr. Maus?"

He nodded graciously. "If it is your pleasure. I am inclined to believe . . . that the door to Number Six . . . is unlocked."

Qwilleran had never seen anything to equal Number Six. The studio apartment they entered was a full two stories high, and half the outer wall was window, composed of many small panes. The orange glow from a spring sunset was flooding the room with color, and three small leaded-glass windows above the desk were making their own rainbows.

Qwilleran blew into his mustache. "I like this furniture!" It was massive, almost medieval in appearance—heavily carved and reinforced with wrought iron.

"It belongs to Ham Hamilton," Joy told him. "Sexy, isn't it? He'll be sending for it as soon as he knows where he's going to be situated."

"You mean he's moved out?"

"He was transferred to Florida. He's a food buyer for a grocery chain."

Qwilleran eyed the apartment avidly—particularly the big loungy chair in bold black-and-white plaid, the row of built-in bookcases, and—wonder of wonder—a white bearskin rug. "Is this place for rent?" he asked.

The question made Joy's eyes dance. "Oh, Jim! Are you interested? Would you like to live here?"

"It would depend on the rent—and a couple of other things." He was thinking about Koko and Yum Yum.

"Let's ask Mr. Maus right away."

That was the Joy he remembered—all instant decision and breathless action.

"No, let's wait until after dinner. Let me think about it."

"Oh, Jim," she cried, throwing her arms around him. "I've thought about you so much—throughout the years."

He felt her heart beating, and he whispered, "Why did you disappear? Why did you leave me like that? Why didn't you ever write and explain?"

She drew away. "It's a long story. We'd better go down to dinner now." And she gave him the half-smile that never failed to make his heart somersault.

The table was laid with heavy ceramic plates and pewter serving pieces on the bare oak boards, and it was lighted by candles in massive wrought-iron candelabra. Qwilleran found his place card between Hixie Rice and the white-haired woman, who introduced herself as Charlotte Roop. Joy sat at the far end of the table between Basil and Bayley Penniman, and the only way she could communicate with Qwilleran was with her eyes.

Opposite him sat the bald brute with the facile smile. The man half rose and bowed across the table with his right hand over his heart. "I'm Max Sorrel."

"Jim Qwilleran of the *Daily Fluxion*. Haven't I met you somewhere?"

"I have a restaurant. The Golden Lamb Chop."

"Yes, I had dinner there once."

"Did you order our rack of lamb? That's our specialty. We lose money on every one we serve." As the restaurateur spoke, he was industriously polishing his silverware with his napkin.

Spoons were raised. Qwilleran tasted the watercress soup and found it delicately delicious, yet he had no overwhelming desire to finish it. A sense of elation had banished his appetite. His thoughts, and his eyes, kept turning to Joy. Now he knew why he had always been attracted to women with translucent skin and long hair. Tonight Joy's luxuriant brown hair was braided and coiled around her head like a crown. Her dress had the same filmy quality he used to tease her about when she bought curtain remnants and made them into romantic, impractical clothes. What a crazy kid she had been!

William removed the soup bowls from the right, served the clams from the left, and poured a white wine, while whistling a tune off-key. When he had finished serving, he joined the guests at the table, white coat and all, and monopolized the conversation in his immediate vicinity.

"Unorthodox arrangement," Qwilleran mentioned to Hixie.

"Robert is very permissive," she said. "He seems stuffy, but he's a doll, really. May I have some more butter, please?"

"How do you happen to be living here?"

"I'm a copywriter at an agency that handles food accounts. You have to have some special interest in food, or Robert won't rent to you. Miss Roop manages a restaurant."

"Yes, I manage one of the Heavenly Hash Houses," said the woman on Qwilleran's left, twisting her several bracelets. She was a small, sprightly woman, probably nearing retirement age, and she wore an abundance of nondescript costume jewelry. "I went to work for Mr. Hashman almost forty years ago. Before that I was secretary to the late Mr. Penniman, so I know something about the newspaper business. I admire newspaper people! They're so clever with words . . . Maybe you can help me." She drew a crossword puzzle from the outer pocket of her enormous handbag. "Do you know a five-letter word for *love* that begins with *a*?"

"Try *a-g-a-p-e*," Qwilleran suggested.

Miss Roop frowned. "Agape?"

"It's a Greek word, pronounced *ag-a-pe*."

"Oh, my!" she said. "You are brilliant!" Delightedly she penciled the word in the vertical squares.

The chicken was served, and again Qwilleran found it easy to abstain. He toyed with his food and listened to the voices around him.

"Do you realize truffles are selling for seventy-five dollars a pound?" Sorrel remarked.

The redhead was saying, "Mountclemens was a fraud, you know. His celebrated lobster bisque was a quickie made with *canned* ingredients."

"I'm having so much fun in the attic of this building. I've found some old letters and notebooks stuffed away in a dusty jardiniere," Joy told Basil Penniman.

Rosemary Whiting said, "You can put a sprinkle of wheat germ in almost anything, and it's so good for you."

"Everyone knows shrimp cocktail is déclassé!" Hixie announced.

The redhead went on talking: "I know of one cassoulet that cooked for thirty years."

And Joy added, "You'd be surprised what I've found in the attic. It would upset quite a few people."

The man with the goatee was revealing a cooking secret: "I

always grate cheese by hand; a little grated knuckle in the Asiago improves the flavor."

Maus himself, at the head of the table, was speechless in a world of his own making, as he tasted each dish critically, gazing into space and savoring with lips and tongue. Once he spoke: "The *croûte*, in my opinion, is a trifle too short."

"On the contrary, it's exquisite," Miss Roop assured him. She turned to Qwilleran. "Mr. Maus is a brilliant cook. He's discovered a way to roast a suckling pig without removing the eyeballs. Imagine!"

"Are you people aware," Qwilleran asked, raising his voice to attract general attention, "that Mrs. Graham also is an excellent cook? She invented a banana split cake when she was seventeen and won a statewide baking contest."

Joy blushed attractively. "It was an adolescent's delight, I'm afraid—with bananas, coconut, strawberries, chocolate, walnuts, marshmallows, *and* whipped cream."

"I don't know about her cooking," said Max Sorrel, "but she's a helluva good potter. She made this dinner service." He tapped his plate with his fork.

"It was very generous of Mr. Maus to give me such a wonderful commission," Joy said.

Qwilleran looked at the thick-textured plates of silvery gray, flecked and rimmed with brown. "You mean you made all these dishes? By hand? How many?"

"A complete service for twenty-four."

Sorrel flashed his winning smile at her. "They're terrific, honey. If I were a millionaire, I'd let you make all the dishes for my restaurant."

"You're very sweet, Max."

"How long did the job take?" Qwilleran asked.

"Hmmm . . . it's hard to say—" Joy began.

"That's nothing," Dan Graham interrupted in a voice that was suddenly loud. "Out on the Coast I did a six-hundred-piece set for one of the movie big shots."

His pronouncement had a dampening effect on the conversation. All heads immediately bent over salads. Suddenly everyone was intent on spearing romaine.

"Tell you something else," Graham persisted. "Wedgwood

made nine hundred and sixty-two pieces for Catherine of Russia!"

There was silence at the table until William said, "Anyone for bridge after dinner? It'll take your mind off your heartburn."

THREE

WHEN QWILLERAN WENT home and told his widowed landlady he was moving, she cried a little, and when he gave her a month's rent in lieu of notice, Mrs. Cobb shed a few more tears.

The rent at Maus Haus was higher than he had been paying on Zwinger Street, but he told himself that the sophisticated cuisine was appropriate to his new assignment and that the cats would enjoy the bearskin rug. Yet he was fully aware of his real reason for moving.

The cats were asleep on the daybed when he went into his old apartment, and he waked them with stroking. Koko, without opening his eyes, licked Yum Yum's nose; Yum Yum licked Koko's right ear; Koko licked a paw, which happened to be his own; and Yum Yum licked Qwilleran's hand with her sandpaper tongue. He gave them some jellied clams from Maus Haus, and then he phoned Arch Riker at home.

"Arch, I hope I didn't get you out of bed," he said. "You'll never guess who walked back into my life again tonight . . . Joy!"

There was an incredulous pause at the other end of the line. "Not Joy Wheatley!"

"She's Joy Graham now. She married."

"What's she—? Where did you see—?"

"She and her husband are artists, and they've come here from California."

"Joy's an *artist?*"

"They do ceramics. They live in a pottery on River Road, and I'm taking an apartment in the same building."

"Careful," Arch warned.

"Don't jump to conclusions. It's all over as far as I'm concerned."

"How does she look?"

"Fine! Cute as ever. And she's the same impetuous girl. Act now, think later."

"Did she explain what—or why—?"

"We didn't have that much time to talk."

"Well, that's a bombshell! Wait till I wake up Rosie and tell her!"

"See you tomorrow around noon," Qwilleran said. "I want to stop at Kipper and Fine on my way to the office and look at their spring suits. I could use some new clothes."

He whipped off his tie and sank into an easy chair and dredged up whimsical memories: Joy baking bread in her aunt's kitchen and losing a Band-Aid in the dough; Joy getting her long hair caught in the sewing machine. As a boy he had written poems about her: Joy . . . coy . . . alloy. Qwilleran shook his head. It was incredible.

On Tuesday morning—a day that smelled joyously of spring— he spent some of his prize money on a new pair of shoes and a suit in a cut more fashionable than he had owned for some time. At noon he lunched with Arch Riker, reminiscing about old times in Chicago when they were both cub reporters, double-dating Joy and Rosie. In the afternoon he borrowed a station wagon from an antique dealer and moved his belongings to Maus Haus.

Koko and Yum Yum traveled in a canned soup carton with air holes punched in the sides, and all during the journey the box rocked and thumped and resounded with the growls and hisses of feline mayhem. Koko, a master of strategy, went through the motions of murdering Yum Yum whenever he wanted to attract urgent attention, and the little female was a willing accomplice, but Qwilleran knew their act and was no longer deceived.

Mrs. Marron, the housekeeper, admitted Qwilleran and the

soup carton to Maus Haus. She was a sad-faced woman with dull eyes and a sallow complexion. With weary step she led the way across the Great Hall, now flooded with daylight from a skylight three stories overhead.

"I gave Number Six a good cleaning," she said. "William washed the walls last week. He'll bring your things up when he comes home from school."

The afternoon sun was streaming through the huge studio window as if to prove the spotlessness of the premises. The floor of brown ceramic tile gleamed with an iridescent patina; the dark oak furniture was polished; the windowpanes sparkled. Mrs. Marron lowered the Roman shade—a contraption of pleated canvas favored by artists in earlier days—and said, "Mr. Maus didn't tell me what meals you'd be taking. Everybody works different hours. They come and they go. They eat or they don't eat."

"I'll have breakfast and notify you from day to day about the other meals," Qwilleran said. "Count me in for dinner tonight . . . How about this telephone? Is it connected?"

"I'll tell the phone company to start service." She suddenly jumped back. "Oh! What's in that box?"

The soup carton, which Qwilleran had placed on the desk, had gone into convulsions, quaking and rocking and emitting unearthly sounds.

"I have two Siamese cats," the newsman explained, "and I want to be sure they don't get out of the apartment, Mrs. Marron."

"Are they expensive?"

"They're extremely important to me, and I don't want anything to happen to them. Please be careful when you come in to clean."

When the housekeeper left, Qwilleran closed the door, first testing the lock and the latch. He also investigated the catches on the three small casement windows over the desk. He checked the bathroom window, heat registers, air vents, and anything else that might serve as an escape hatch for a determined cat. Only then did he open the soup carton.

The cats emerged cautiously, swinging their heads from side to side. Then with one accord they crept toward the white bear rug, stalking it with tails dipped and bellies close to the floor.

When the beast made no move to attack or retreat, Koko bravely put his head inside the gaping jaws. He sniffed the teeth and stared into the glass eyes. Yum Yum stepped daintily on the pelt, and soon she was rolling over and over on the white fur in apparent ecstasy.

Qwilleran's practiced eye perused the apartment for trouble spots and found it catproof. His inquisitive roommates would not be able to burrow into the box spring; the bed was a captain's bunk, built in between two large wardrobes. There were no plants for Yum Yum to chew. The lamp on the desk was weighty enough to remain upright during a cat chase.

For entertainment there were pigeons on the ledge outside the windows, and an oak dining table in a sunny spot would hold the cats' blue cushion.

"I think this place will do," Qwilleran said to the cats. "Don't you?"

The answer came from the bathroom, where Koko was crowing in exultation, enjoying the extra resonance that tile walls gave to his normally loud and penetrating voice.

The man felt exhilarated, too. In fact, his elation had acted as a substitute for calories at lunchtime. Since meeting Joy the night before, his hunger pangs had vanished, and already he felt thinner. He wondered whether Joy was in the pottery—and whether it would be discreet to go looking for her—and whether he would see her at the dinner table.

Then he remembered the can of boned chicken in his topcoat pocket. He found a can opener in the tiny kitchenette and was arranging morsels of chicken on a handmade stoneware plate when he heard a knock at the door. It was a playful knock. Was it Joy? Hastily he placed the dish on the bathroom floor, summoned the cats, and closed the door on them. Before answering the knock, he took time to glance in the bathroom mirror, straighten his tie, and run a hand over his hair. With his face pleasantly composed, he flung open the door.

"Hi!" said William, who stood there grinning and carrying a suitcase and a carton of books.

"Oh, it's you," said Qwilleran, his face relaxing into its usual sober lines. "Thanks. Just drop them anywhere."

"You've got the best setup in the whole building," the houseboy said, walking around the room with a proprietary swagger. "How much rent is Mickey Maus charging you?"

"There are some more boxes in the wagon," Qwilleran told him. "And a scale, and a big wrought-iron coat of arms. Do you mind bringing them up?" He started unpacking books, stacking them in the row of built-in bookcases at one end of the room.

William walked to the window. "You've got a good view. You'll be able to watch all the wild parties down at the marina . . . Do you play bridge?"

"I'm no asset to the game," Qwilleran mumbled.

"Hey, do you really read all this heavy stuff?" The houseboy had picked up a volume of Toynbee that Qwilleran had bought for a dime at a flea market. "All I ever read is whodunits . . . Jeez! What's that?"

An earsplitting shriek came from the bathroom.

"One of the cats. Their litter pan is in the car, too, and a sack of gravel. Better bring those up first."

"Mind if I take a look at them?" William moved toward the bathroom.

"Let's wait till everything's moved in," Qwilleran said with a touch of impatience. "They might dart out into the hall. They're edgy in a strange place."

"It must be great—working for a newspaper. Do you cover murder trials?"

"Not anymore. That's not my beat."

"What do you do, then?"

Qwilleran was half irritated, half amused. The houseboy's curiosity and persistence reminded him of his own early days as a copyboy. "Look, I'll tell you the story of my life tomorrow," he said. "First let's get my things moved in. Then I'd like to visit the pottery."

"They don't like visitors," William said. "Not when they're working. Of course, if you don't mind getting thrown out on your ear . . ."

Qwilleran did not see Joy until dinnertime. The meal was served at a big round table in a corner of the kitchen, because there were only six sitting down to dinner. Robert Maus was absent, and Miss Roop and Max Sorrel were on duty at their restaurants.

The room was heady with aromas: roast beef, cheese, logs burning in the fireplace, and Joy's spicy perfume. She looked more appealing than ever, having rouged her cheeks and darkened her eyelids.

Qwilleran merely sampled the corn chowder, ate half of his portion of roast beef and broccoli parmigiana, declined a Parker House roll, and ignored a glob of mush flecked with green.

"Everything's good," he assured Mrs. Marron, who had prepared the meal, "but I'm trying to lose weight."

Rosemary, the quiet one, glanced at the untouched glob on Qwilleran's salad plate. "You should eat the bulgur. It's highly nutritious."

"Do you cook, Mr. Qwilleran?" Hixie asked.

"Only a few gourmet dishes for my cats."

The conversation at the table was lagging; the Grahams were moody, and William was eating as if he might never have another meal. Qwilleran tried to entertain the group with tales about Koko and Yum Yum. "They can smell through the refrigerator door," he said. "If there's lobster in there, they won't eat chicken, and if there's chicken, they won't eat beef. Salmon has to be a nationally advertised brand; don't ask me how they know. In the morning Koko rings for his breakfast; he steps on the tabulator key of the typewriter, which jerks the carriage and rings the bell. One of these days I think he'll learn to type."

With Joy in the audience he was feeling at his best, and yet the more he talked, the more he sensed her melancholy.

Finally she said, "I had a cat, but he disappeared a couple of weeks ago. I miss him terribly. His name was Raku."

Her husband spoke for the first time that evening. "Somebody probably stole the Blimp. That's what I called him. The Blimp." He looked pleased with himself.

"What kind of cat?" Qwilleran asked Joy. "Did you let him go out?"

"No, but cats have a way of sneaking out. He was a big smoky brown longhair."

Her husband said, "People steal cats and sell them to labs for experiments."

Joy gritted her teeth. "For God's sake, Dan, must you bring that subject up again?"

"It's getting to be big business," he said. "*Kit*napping." Dan looked hopefully around the table for appreciation of his bon mot.

"That's not funny!" Joy had put down her fork and was sitting with clenched fists. "It's not funny at all."

Qwilleran turned to her husband. "By the way, I'd like to have a tour of the pottery when you have time."

"Not before the exhibition," said the potter, shaking his head gravely.

"Why not?" his wife snapped.

"Cripes, you know it's nerve-racking to have somebody around when you're working." To Qwilleran he said, "Can't afford any interruptions. Busy as a one-armed paperhanger with the itch, if you know what I mean."

Joy turned to Qwilleran, her voice icy. "Anytime you want to see the pottery, let me know. I'd love to show you my latest work." She shot a venomous glance at her husband.

To cover the embarrassed silence that followed, the newsman addressed Graham again. "You were telling me you didn't like the *Fluxion* critic. What's your complaint?"

"He doesn't know beans about pottery, if you know what I mean."

"He was a museum curator before he started writing for us."

Graham snorted. "Doesn't mean a thing. He may know Flemish painting and African sculpture, but what he doesn't know about contemporary pots would fill a book, if you know what I mean. When I had my last one-man show in L.A., the leading critic said my textures were a treat for the eye and a thrill for the fingertips. And I quote."

Joy said to Qwilleran with a disdainful edge to her voice, "Dan put a couple of old pots in a group show when we first came here, and your critic was unkind."

"I don't expect a critic to be kind," her husband said, his Adam's apple moving rapidly. "I expect him to know his business."

William spoke up. "He calls 'em the way he sees 'em. That's all any critic can do. I think he's pretty perceptive."

"Oh, William, shut up," Joy snapped. "You don't know anything about pots either."

"I *beg* your pardon!" said the houseboy with mock indignation.

"Anyone who gets the cones mixed up and puts cracked biscuit shelves away with the good ones is a lousy potter," she said curtly.

"Well, Dan told me to—"

"Don't listen to Dan. He's as sloppy as you are. What do they teach you at Penniman Art School? How to make paper flowers?"

Qwilleran had never seen that side of Joy's nature. She had been moody as a girl but never sharp-tongued.

Hixie said to the houseboy in a bantering tone, "Don't let it burn you, Willie dear. Your personal charm makes up for your stupidity."

"Gee, thanks."

"This bickering," Rosemary murmured, "is not very good for the digestion."

"Don't blame it on me," said William. "She started it."

Dan stood up and threw his napkin on the table. "I've had it up to the ears! Lost my appetite." He strode away from the table.

"The big baby!" his wife muttered. "I noticed he finished his apple pie before he made his temperamental exit."

"I don't blame him," said Hixie. "You were picking on him."

"Why don't you mind your own business and concentrate on stuffing your face, dear? You do it so well!"

"See?" Hixie said, batting her eyelids. "The skinny ones always have miserable dispositions."

"Really!" Rosemary protested in her gentle voice. "Do we have to talk like this in front of Mr. Qwilleran?"

Joy put her face in her hands. "I'm sorry, Jim. My nerves are tied in knots. I've been . . . working too hard. Excuse me." She left the table hurriedly.

The meal ended with stilted scraps of conversation. Hixie talked about the cookbook she was writing. Rosemary extolled the healthful properties of blackstrap molasses. William wondered who had won the ball game in Milwaukee.

After dinner Qwilleran called Arch Riker at home, using the public telephone in the foyer. "I've sure walked into something at Maus Haus," he said, speaking in a low voice. "The tenants are all one big scrappy family, and Joy is definitely upset. She says she's overworked, but it looks like domestic trouble to me. I wish I could get her away for a visit with you and Rosie. It might do her some good."

"Don't take any chances until you know the score," Riker warned him. "If it's marital trouble, she might be using you."

"She wouldn't do that. Poor kid! I still think of her as twenty years old."

"How do you size up her husband?"

"He's a conceited ass."

"Ever meet an artist who wasn't? They all overrate themselves."

"But there's something pitiful about the guy. For all I know, he may have talent. I haven't seen his work. Someone said he was a slob potter, whatever that means."

"It doesn't sound good . . . How about your new column? Are you going to do a story on Maus?"

"If I can pin him down. He's gone to an MSG meeting tonight."

"What's that?"

"Meritorious Society of Gastronomes. A bunch of food snobs."

"Qwill," said Riker in a serious voice, "watch your step, will you? About Joy, I mean."

"I'm no kid, Arch."

"Well, it's spring, you know."

FOUR

WHEN QWILLERAN RETURNED to Number Six, he found Koko and Yum Yum locked in mortal combat with the bearskin rug, which they had chased into a corner. The poor beast, powerless against two determined Siamese, had skidded across the glossy tile floor and was cowering, with back humped and jaws gaping, under the massive carved desk.

Qwilleran was haranguing the cats and dragging the rug back to its rightful position in front of the captain's bed when there was a knock on the door, and—despite a promise he had made to himself—his heart flipped when he saw Joy standing there. Her hair was hanging down to her waist, and she was wearing something filmy and apple green. Although her eyes looked puffed, her composure had returned.

She smiled her funny little smile and peeked into the apartment hesitantly. "Do you have company? I thought I heard you talking to someone."

"Just the cats," Qwilleran said. "When you live alone, it's sometimes necessary to hear the sound of your own voice, and they're good listeners."

"May I come in? I tried to call you, but your phone isn't connected."

"Mrs. Marron said she'd call the phone company."

"Better do it yourself," Joy said. "There's been a tragedy in her family, and she's still in a daze. Forgets to put potatoes in the potato pancakes. Puts detergent in the soup. She may poison us all before she gets back to normal."

She and her gauzy gown fluttered into the apartment, accompanied by a zephyr of perfume, suggesting cinnamon.

"Look at those beautiful cats!" She gathered Koko in her arms, and he permitted it, much to Qwilleran's surprise and pleasure. Koko was a man's cat and not used to being cuddled. Joy scratched the sensitive zone behind his ears and massaged the top of his head with her chin, while Koko purred, crossed his eyes, and turned his ears inside out.

"Look at him! The old lecher!" Qwilleran said. "I think he likes your green dress . . . So do I!"

"Cats can't distinguish colors," Joy said. "Did you know that? Raku's vet told me." She sighed and hugged Koko tightly, burying her face in the ruff around his neck. "Koko's fur smells like something good to eat."

"That's the aroma of the old house we just moved out of. It always smelled like baked potatoes when the furnace was on. Cats' fur seems to pick up house odors."

"I know. Raku's fur used to smell like wet clay." Joy squeezed her eyes shut and gulped. "He was such a wonderful little friend. It kills me not to know what's happened to him."

"Did you advertise?"

"In both papers. I didn't get a single call—except from one crackpot—some fellow trying to disguise his voice . . . Be sure to keep your cats indoors, won't you?"

"Don't worry about that. I keep them under lock and key. They mean a lot to me."

Joy looked out the window. The river flowed black between two lighted shorelines, and she shuddered. "I hate water. I was in a boat accident a few years ago, and I still have nightmares of drowning."

"It used to be a beautiful river, they tell me. It's polluted now."

"In our apartment I'm always dropping the blinds to shut out the river, and Dan's always raising them."

Qwilleran took the hint and lowered the Roman shades.

Still carrying Koko over her shoulder, Joy moved about the

apartment as if looking for clues to Qwilleran's personal life. She touched his red plaid bathrobe draped over one of the carved Spanish dining chairs. She admired the Mackintosh coat of arms propped on top of the bookcase. She glanced at titles on the shelves. "Have you read all these books? You're such a brain!" At the desk she examined the antique ebony book rack, the ragged dictionary, the typewriter, and the sheet of paper in the machine. "What does this mean? These initials—BW."

"That's Koko's typing. He's ordering his breakfast, I think. Beef Wellington."

Joy laughed—a long, musical trill. "Oh, Jim, you've got a wild imagination."

"It's good to hear your laughter again, Joy."

"It's good to laugh, believe me. I haven't done it for so long . . . Listen! What's the matter with the other cat?"

Yum Yum had retreated to a far corner and was calling in a piteous voice, until Koko jumped from Joy's arms and went to comfort her.

"Jealous," Qwilleran said.

The cats exchanged sympathetic licks. Yum Yum squeezed her eyes shut while Koko passed a long pink tongue over her eyes, nose, and whiskers, and then she returned the compliment.

Joy stopped circling the apartment and draped herself over the arm of the big plaid chair.

"Where's Dan tonight?" Qwilleran inquired.

"Out. As usual! . . . Would you like a tour of the pottery?"

"I don't want to cause trouble. If he doesn't want—"

"He's being ridiculous! Ever since we arrived here, Dan's been mysteriously secretive about our new work. You'd think we were surrounded by spies, trying to steal our ideas!" Joy jumped off the arm of the chair impulsively. "Come on. Our exhibition pots are locked up, and Dan's got the key, but I can show you the clay room and the wheel and the kilns."

They went downstairs to the Great Hall and along the kitchen corridor to the pottery. A heavy steel door opened into a low-ceilinged room filmed with dust. Like a veil, the fine dust covered the floor, worktables, shelves, plaster molds, scrapbooks, broken pots, and rows of crocks with cryptic labels. Dust gave the room a ghostly pallor.

"What's the old suicide mystery connected with this place?" Qwilleran asked.

"An artist was drowned—a long time ago—and some people thought it was murder. Remind me to tell you about it later. I have an interesting new angle on it." She led the way into a large, dismal area that smelled damp and earthy. Everything seemed to be caked with mud. "This is the clay room, and the mechanical equipment is all very old and primitive. That big cylinder is the blunger that mixes the clay. Then it's stored in a tank under the floor and eventually formed into big pancakes on the filter press over there . . . after which it's chewed up by the pug mill and formed into loaves, which are stored in those big bins."

"There must be an easier way," Qwilleran ventured.

"Every step has its purpose. This used to be a big operation fifty years ago. Now we do a few tiles for architects and some garden sculpture for landscape designers—plus our own creative work." Joy walked into a smaller room. "This is our studio. And this is my kick-wheel." She sat on a bench at the clay-coated machine and activated a shaft with a kick-bar, spinning the wheel. "You throw a lump of clay on the wheel and shape it as it spins."

"Looks pretty crude."

"They had wheels of this type in ancient Egypt," Joy said. "We also have a couple of electric wheels, but the kick-wheel is more intimate, I think."

"Did you make that square vase with the blobs of clay on it?"

"No, that's one of Dan's glop pots that your critic didn't like. Wish I could show you my latest, but they're locked up. Maybe it's just as well. Hixie came in here one day and broke a combed pitcher I'd just finished. I could have killed her! She's such a clumsy ox!"

The next room was dry and warm—a large, lofty space with windows just under the ceiling and an Egyptian-style mural running around the top of all four walls. Otherwise, it looked like a bakery. Several ovens stood around the room, and tables held trays of dun-colored tiles, like cookies waiting to be baked.

"These tiles are bone dry and ready for firing," said Joy. "The others are bisque, waiting to be glazed. They'll be used in the chapel that the Pennimans are donating to the university . . .

And now you've seen the whole operation. We live in the loft over the clay room. I'd invite you up, only it's a mess. I'm a terrible housekeeper. You should be glad you didn't marry me, Jim." She squeezed Qwilleran's hand. "Shall we have a drink? I've got some bourbon, and we can drink in your apartment, if you don't mind. Is bourbon still your favorite?"

"I'm not drinking. I've signed off the hard stuff," he told her. "But you go and get your bottle, and I'll have a lemon and seltzer with you."

Qwilleran returned to Number Six and found the cats lounging on top of the bookcase. "Well, what do you think of her?" he asked them.

"Yow!" said Koko, squeezing his eyes shut.

When Joy arrived with her bourbon, she said, "You can make yourself very popular in this house by keeping a bottle handy. Mr. Maus doesn't approve of hard liquor—it paralyzes the taste buds—but most of us like to sneak a cocktail now and then."

"How does anyone live here and stay thin?"

"Mr. Maus says a true gourmet never stuffs himself."

Qwilleran poured the drinks. "You were a great cook, Joy. I still remember your homemade raisin bread with honey and lemon frosting."

"Potting is not far removed from baking," she said, curling up comfortably on the built-in bunk. "Wedging clay is like kneading dough. Applying a glaze is like frosting a cake."

"How did you happen to take up potting?"

Joy gazed wistfully into the past. "When I left Chicago so suddenly, Jim, it had nothing to do with you. I adored you—I really did. But I wasn't satisfied with my life . . . and I didn't know what I wanted."

"If you had only explained—"

"I didn't know how. It was easier just to . . . disappear. Besides, I was afraid you'd change my mind."

"Where did you go?"

"San Francisco. I worked in restaurants for a while and then supervised the kitchen on a large ranch. It was operated as a pottery school, and eventually they let me handle some clay. I learned fast, won prizes, and I've been potting ever since."

Qwilleran, relaxing in the big plaid arm chair, took time to light his pipe. "Is that how you met Dan?"

She nodded. "Dan said there was too much competition in California, so we moved to Florida, but I hated that state! I couldn't create. I felt a hundred years old in Florida, so we went back to the Coast until we got the offer to come here."

"No kids?"

Joy took a long, slow sip of her drink. "Dan didn't—that is, he wanted to be free to be poor. And I had my work, which was time-consuming and fulfilling. Did you ever marry, Jim?"

"I gave it a try. I've been divorced for several years."

"Tell me about her."

"She was an advertising woman—very successful."

"But what did she look like?"

"You." Qwilleran allowed himself to look at Joy fondly. "Why are we talking in the past tense? She's still alive—though not well and not happy."

"Are you happy, Jim?"

"I have good days and bad days."

"You look marvelous! You're the type that improves with age. And that mustache makes you look so romantic. Jim—I've never forgotten you—not for a single day." She slid off the bunk and sat on the arm of his chair, leaning toward him and letting her hair fall around them in a thick brown curtain. "You were my first," she whispered, close to his lips.

"And you were my first," he replied softly.

"Yow!" said an imperious voice from the top of the bookcase. A book crashed to the floor. Cats flew in all directions, and the spell was broken.

Joy sat up and sighed deeply. "Forgive me for that silly outburst at dinner tonight. I'm not like that—really I'm not. I'm beginning to hate myself."

"Everyone flies off the handle once in a while."

"Jim," she said abruptly. "I'm going to get a divorce."

"Joy, you shouldn't— I mean, you must think it through carefully. You know how impulsive you are."

"I've been thinking about it for a long time."

"What's the trouble between you and Dan? Or don't you want to talk about it?"

She glanced around the room, as if searching for the words. "I don't know. It's just because . . . well, I'm *me* and he's *himself*. I won't bore you with details. It may be selfish of me, but I know I could do better on my own. He's dragging me down, Jim."

"Is he jealous of your work?" Qwilleran was thinking of the six-hundred-piece table service.

"I'm sure of it, although I try to keep a low profile. Dan has never been really successful. I've had better reviews and bigger sales—and without even trying very hard." Joy hesitated. "No one knows it, but I have fantastic ideas for glazes that I've been holding back. They'd be a sensation, I guarantee."

"Why have you held them back?"

She shrugged. "Trying to play the good wife, trying not to surpass my husband. I know that's old-fashioned. The only way I can shake loose and be honest with myself as an artist is to get out of this marriage. I tell you, Jim, I'm wasting my life! You know how old I am. I'm beginning to want comforts. I'm tired of making my own clothes out of remnants and driving an ancient Renault without a heater . . . Well, it *does* have a heater, but there's this big hole in the floor—"

"You'd better get some legal advice," Qwilleran suggested. "Why don't you discuss it with Maus?"

"I did. His firm doesn't handle divorces—only very dignified corporate stuff—but he referred me to another attorney. And now I'm stymied."

"Why?"

She smiled her pathetic smile. "No money."

"The eternal problem," Qwilleran agreed.

"I had a little money of my own before we were married, but Dan has it tied up somehow. You know I was always bored with financial matters, so I didn't question him about it. Wasn't that dumb? I was too busy making pots. It's an obsession. I can't keep my hands out of clay." She pondered awhile and then added in a low voice, "But I know where I could raise some cash . . . with a little polite blackmail."

"Joy!" Qwilleran exploded. "I hope you're kidding."

"I'd be discreet," she said coolly. "I've found some documents in the attic of the pottery that would embarrass a few people . . . Don't look so horrified, Jim. There's nothing sinister about it—simply a business transaction."

"Don't you dare! You could get into serious trouble." Qwilleran stroked his mustache reflectively. "What, uh . . . how much money would you need?"

"Probably—I don't know—maybe a thousand, to begin with . . . Oh, Jim, I've got to get out of this suffocating situation. Sometimes I just want to jump into that horrid river!"

Joy was still sitting on the arm of his chair, but she was straight-backed and tense now. The lamplight, hitting her face in a certain way, revealed wrinkles around her eyes and mouth. The sight of his childhood sweetheart with signs of age in her face filled Qwilleran with sadness and affection, and after a moment's silence he said, "I could lend you something."

Joy showed genuine surprise. "Would you really, Jim? I don't know what to say. It would save my life! I'd sign a note, of course."

"I don't have much savings," he said. "I've had some rough sledding in recent years, but I won a cash prize at the *Fluxion* in January, and I could let you have—about seven hundred and fifty."

"Oh, Jim! How can I thank you?" She swooped down to kiss him, then jumped up, grabbed Koko from his blue cushion, and whirled around the room with the surprised cat.

Qwilleran went to the desk to write a check, automatically reaching for his glasses, then changing his mind out of sheer vanity.

Joy leaned over his shoulder to watch and gave his temple another kiss, while Koko struggled to get out of her enthusiastic embrace.

"Why don't you pour yourself another drink—for good luck," Qwilleran suggested, fumbling with the checkbook and concealing the figure that represented his meager balance. He was lending this money against his better judgment, and yet he knew he could not have done otherwise.

After Joy had gone back to her own apartment, he deducted the amount of the check and wished he had not bought the new suit or the antique scale. He looked at the note she had signed, written in the absurd hand he remembered so well—all *u*'s and *w*'s.

"I oww Juu Qwwww $750," it read, and it was signed "Jww Gwww." She had never been willing to take time to cross *t*'s and loop *h*'s. Funny, lovable, exhilarating, capricious Joy, Qwilleran thought. What would the future hold for both of them?

The cats had behaved themselves, more or less; that was not always the case when Qwilleran had a woman visiting his living quarters. Koko was a self-appointed chaperon with his own ideas of social decorum.

"Good cat!" said Qwilleran, and in his mood of reckless indulgence he gave them their second dinner. He opened a can of lobster—the last of their Christmas present from the affluent Mary Duckworth. Koko went wild, racing around the apartment and singing in a falsetto interspersed with chesty growls.

"Do you think I did the right thing tonight?" Qwilleran asked him. "It leaves me right back where I was before. Broke!" And the man was so preoccupied with his own wonderment that he failed to notice Koko's sudden silence.

After their feast, the cats went to sleep in the big chair, and Qwilleran spent his first night in the new bed. Lying on his side and staring out of the studio window, he had a full view of the navy-blue sky and a string of lights marking the opposite bank of the river. For several hours sleep evaded him. This time it was not his past that kept him awake but his future.

He heard and identified all the sounds of a new habitat: the hum of traffic on River Road, a lonely boat whistle, a radio or stereo somewhere in the building, and eventually the crunch of tires on the crushed stone of the driveway. He guessed it would be Maus returning from his gourmet meeting, or Max Sorrel coming home from his restaurant, or Dan Graham in the old Renault, returning from some rendezvous. The garage door creaked, and soon there were footsteps tapping on the tiles of the Great Hall. Somewhere a door closed. After that there was the distant rumble of an approaching storm, and occasionally the sky flashed lavender.

Qwilleran had no idea at what hour he fell asleep—or how long he had slept when he was startled awake by a scream. Whether it was the real thing or a fragment of his dream, it was impossible to say. He had been dreaming intensely—a silly dream about mountain climbing. He was standing triumphantly on the summit of a snow-white mountain of mashed potatoes, gazing across a sea of brown gravy. Someone shouted a warning, and there was a scream, and he waked.

He raised his head and listened sharply. Silence. The scream, Qwilleran decided, had been part of the sound effects of his dream. He switched on the bed lamp to check the time, and that was when he noticed the cats. They had raised their heads and were listening, too. Their ears were pointed forward. Both heads rotated slowly as they scanned the soundscape in every direction. The cats had heard something. It had not been a dream.

Still, the man told himself, it could have been squealing tires on River Road, or the garage door creaking again. Noises magnified themselves on the threshold of waking. At that moment he heard the sound of creaking hinges quite plainly, followed by the rumble of a car engine, and he jumped out of bed in time to see a light-colored convertible pulling away from the building. He glanced at his watch. It was three twenty-five.

The cats laid their ears back and their chins on their paws and settled down to sleep, and Qwilleran closed the ventilating panes in the big studio window as the first drops of rain splashed on the glass like enormous tears.

FIVE

WHEN QWILLERAN AWOKE Wednesday morning, it took him a few seconds to get his bearings in the strange apartment. He looked at the sky through the studio window—a vast panorama of blue, broken only by a single soaring pigeon. He stared up at the beamed ceiling two stories overhead, noted the big plaid chair, remembered the white bearskin rug. Then the events of the previous day came rushing into his mind: his new home in a pottery . . . the nearness of Joy after all the years of separation . . . her marital trouble . . . the $750 loan . . . and the sound he had heard in the night. In daylight the recollection of it seemed considerably less alarming. He stretched and yawned, disturbing Yum Yum, who was huddled in his armpit, and then he heard a bell ring. Koko was standing on the desk with one paw on the typewriter.

"Coming right up!" Qwilleran said, hoisting himself out of bed. He put on his red plaid bathrobe and went to the tiny kitchen to open a can of food for the cats. "I know you ordered beef Wellington," he told Koko, "but you'll have to settle for red salmon. This is two dollars a can. *Bon appétit!*"

The prospect of breakfast touched off a joyous scuffle. Yum Yum kicked Koko with her hind leg like a mule, and he gave her a push. They went into a clinch, pummeling each other until

Koko played too rough. Then Yum Yum sprang back and started to circle, lashing her tail. Suddenly she pounced and grabbed him by the throat, but Koko got a hug-hold, and they rolled over and over, locked together. By secret signal both cats quit the fight at the same instant and licked each other's imaginary wounds.

When Qwilleran dressed and went downstairs, he followed the aroma of bacon and coffee into the kitchen. At the big round table Robert Maus was solemnly breakfasting on croissants and marmalade and French chocolate, while Hixie waited for Mrs. Marron to make French toast.

Qwilleran helped himself to orange juice. "Where's everybody this morning?"

"Max never gets up for breakfast," Hixie reported promptly, as she spooned sour cream into her coffee. "William's gone to an early class. Rosemary always has wheat germ in her apartment. Charlotte came early and had 'a bite to eat' big enough to choke a horse, and now she's gone to the Red Cross to roll bandages, or whatever she does there on Wednesday mornings."

"Miss Roop," Maus explained in his pedantic manner, "devotes a generous amount of time to . . . volunteer clerical work at the blood bank, for which she must be . . . admired."

"Do you suppose she's atoning for something wicked in her past?" Hixie asked.

The attorney turned to her in solemn disapproval. "You are, to all appearances, a nasty young lady. Furthermore, I find the use of . . . *sour cream* in coffee an extremely . . . revolting habit."

"Hurry up with the toast, Marron baby," said Hixie. "I'm starving."

"Do the Grahams come down to breakfast?" Qwilleran asked.

"They haven't shown up this morning." She was heaping gooseberry jam on a crusty French roll. "I wish I had a job like theirs, so I could be my own boss and set my own hours."

"My dear young woman," Maus told her gravely, "you would be bankrupt within six months. You are entirely without . . . self-discipline." Then he turned to Qwilleran. "I trust you are sufficiently . . . comfortable in Number Six?"

As he spoke, Qwilleran noticed for the first time a slight discoloration around the attorney's left eye. "Everything's fine," the newsman said, after a barely perceptible pause, "but I heard something strange in the night. Did anyone else hear an outcry about three-thirty this morning? It sounded like a woman's scream."

There was no reply at the table. Hixie opened her eyes wide and shook her head. Maus calmly went on chewing with the kind of concentration he always gave to the process.

It was characteristic of members of the legal profession never to show surprise, Qwilleran reminded himself. "Maybe it was the garage door that I heard," he suggested.

Maus said, "Mrs. Marron, kindly ask William to . . . lubricate the garage doors when he returns."

"By the way," said the newsman, pouring himself a cup of the excellent coffee, "I'd like to write a column on your cooking philosophy, Mr. Maus, if you're agreeable." He waited patiently for the attorney's response.

After a while it came, accompanied by a gracious nod. "I cannot, at this time, see any . . . objection."

"Perhaps you could have dinner with me tonight at the Toledo Tombs—as the guest of the *Daily Fluxion*."

At the mention of the epicurean restaurant Maus brightened noticeably. "By all means! We shall have their . . . eels in green sauce. They also prepare a superb veal dish with tarragon and Japanese mushrooms. You must allow me to order."

They set a time and place to meet, and Maus left for his office, carrying an attaché case. Qwilleran had seen Mrs. Marron stock it with some small cartons, a thermos bottle, and a cold artichoke. Hixie left soon afterward, having finished a plate of bacon and French toast, swimming in melted butter and maple syrup and sprinkled with chopped pecans. Qwilleran remained alone, wondering about his landlord's black eye.

When Mrs. Marron came to the table to remove the plates, she said, "You should eat something, Mr. Qwilleran—something to stick to the ribs."

"There's too much sticking to my ribs already."

The housekeeper lingered at the table, slowly piling dishes on a tray and slowly rearranging them. "Mr. Qwilleran," she said, "I heard something last night, and it wasn't the garage door."

"What time did you hear it?"

"It was after three o'clock. I know that much. My room is in the back, and I don't sleep very good lately, so I watch television in bed. I use the earphone, so I don't disturb anybody."

"Exactly what did you hear?"

"I thought it was tomcats scrapping down at the boat docks, but it could've been somebody screaming."

"I hope everyone in the house is all right," Qwilleran said. "Why don't you check on Mrs. Whiting and the Grahams?"

"Do you think I should?"

"Under the circumstances, Mrs. Marron, I think it would be advisable."

I'm beginning to sound like Robert Maus, he told himself as he sipped black coffee and waited for the housekeeper's return.

"Mrs. Whiting is all right; she's doing her exercises," Mrs. Marron reported. "But I couldn't get ahold of the Grahams. The door to the pottery is locked. I knocked three, four times, but nobody answered. If they're upstairs in their apartment, they can't hear."

"You don't have a key to the pottery?" He glanced at a key rack on the kitchen wall.

The housekeeper shook her head. "Those are only the apartment keys, so I can clean. Shall I go around the backyard and up the fire escape?"

"Let's try telephoning," Qwilleran suggested. "Do you know the Grahams' number?"

"What shall I say to them?"

"I'll do the talking."

Mrs. Marron dialed a number on the kitchen phone and handed the receiver to Qwilleran. A man's voice answered.

"Mr. Graham? Good morning! This is Jim Qwilleran, your new neighbor. Is everything under control at your end of the building? We thought we smelled smoke . . . That's good. Just playing safe. By the way, you're missing a fine breakfast. Mrs. Marron is making French toast . . . Can't tempt you? Too bad. I really wanted to discuss the pottery operation. The *Fluxion* might run a feature story to tie in with your exhibition . . . You will? Good! I'll wait."

"Smoke?" said Mrs. Marron when Qwilleran had handed back the receiver. "I didn't smell any smoke."

A few minutes later Dan Graham walked into the kitchen, looking thinner and more forlorn than ever. He dropped gracelessly into a chair and said he would have coffee and a roll, that's all.

Mrs. Marron said, "I can make some of those cornmeal johnnycakes you like."

"Just a roll."

"Or a stack of wheatcakes. It will only take a minute."

The potter scowled at her, and she went back to the sink and started stacking plates in the dishwasher.

Qwilleran resisted an impulse to ask the man about his wife. Instead he hinted at vast possibilities for free publicity, and Dan warmed up.

"The newspapers ought to print more articles like that," he said, "instead of tearing us down all the time. Hell, they don't pan the new model cars or those stupid clothes they design in Paris. Why do they pick on artists? The papers hire some nincompoop as a critic and let him air his private beefs and chase people away from the exhibitions. A lot of people would like contemporary art if the local newspapers didn't keep telling them how bad it is. They should be explaining to the public how to appreciate what they see."

"I'll speak to our feature editor," Qwilleran said. "It's not my beat and I can't make the decision, but I'm sure Arch Riker will send a photographer over here. He'll probably want to take some shots of you and your wife, as well as your new pottery. A good human interest story might make a spread in the Sunday supplement. In color!"

Dan hung his head and looked deep into his coffee cup. "There's the hitch," he said firmly. "I know you fellows on the paper like cheesecake and all that kind of stuff, but you'll have to settle for a broken-down he-potter with freckles." He said it with a twisted smile.

"Why? Doesn't Mrs. Graham like to be photographed? She's very attractive."

Dan glanced toward the sink, where Mrs. Marron was peeling apples, and lowered his voice. "The old girl's cleared out."

"She's what? She's left you?" Qwilleran had not expected anything to happen so soon, and yet he should have known that Joy would fly into action.

"Yes, she's decamped—vamoosed—flown the coop, if you know what I mean. It's not the first time, either." Again there was the brave one-sided smile, and Qwilleran realized—partly with pity and partly with scorn—that the grimace was an unconscious imitation of Joy's appealing mannerism.

"Once when we were in Florida," the potter went on, "she ran off. No explanation, no note, no nothing. She really left me standing on my ear that time, but she came back, and everything straightened out. Women don't know what they want . . . So I'll just sit tight like a bug in a rug and wait for her to have her fling and get over what's eating her. She'll be back, don't worry. Too bad she had to go right before the exhibition, that's all."

Qwilleran, who was seldom at a loss for words, hardly knew what to say. It was obvious he knew more than the husband about Joy's intentions. "When did you first realize she'd gone?" he asked, trying to appear sympathetic but not personally involved.

"Woke up this morning and couldn't find hide nor hair of the woman! Might as well tell you that we had a little argument last night, but I didn't think it was anything serious." Dan stroked his unshaven jaw thoughtfully and looked hurt and dejected.

Qwilleran noticed that the potter's right thumb was missing up to the first joint, and for a moment his loyalties were divided. A hand injury would be the worst thing that could happen to a potter; was that the reason for his declining success? He could also sympathize with a husband deserted by an ambitious wife; he had gone through the same humiliating experience.

"Did she take the car?" Qwilleran asked.

"No, she left it here. I'd be in a fix if she'd run off with the old jalopy. It's not much, but it gets me there and back."

"Then what did she use for transportation in the middle of the night?"

Dan's mouth fell open. "The bus, I reckon. They run up and down River Road all night."

Or, thought Qwilleran, did she drive away with the owner of the light-colored convertible at three in the morning? . . . Then the dismal possibility flashed into his mind. It could be that his $750 had financed Joy's elopement with another man.

No! He refused to believe that! Still, his face felt hot and cold by turns, and he ran a hand over his forehead. Was he an accomplice or a victim, or both? He was a fool, he decided, either way. His first impulse was to stop payment on the check. As a newsman and a professional cynic he suspected he had been duped, but a better instinct told him to have faith in Joy—if he loved her, and he privately admitted it now: He had never really stopped loving Joy Wheatley.

I know Joy, he told himself. No matter how desperate she was, she would never do that to *me*. Then he remembered the scream.

"I don't want to alarm you, Dan," he said in a calm voice that belied his confusion, "but are you sure she left the premises voluntarily?"

Dan, who had been staring gloomily into his coffee cup, looked up sharply. "How do you mean?"

"I mean . . . I thought I heard a woman scream last night, and shortly after that, I heard a car drive away."

The potter gave a short, bitter laugh. "Did you hear that ruckus? Crazy woman! Tell you what happened. When I came home last night, it was sort of late. I know these guys downtown —all artists, more or less—we play poker, drink a few beers. Well, it was sort of late, and Joy was sitting up waiting. Miffed, I guess. There she was—sitting at the wheel and throwing a pot and looking daggers at me when I came in. And you know what? She was working at the wheel with her hair hanging down a mile! I've warned her about that, but she's cocky and never pays any attention to what I say."

Dan brooded over the situation, staring into his empty coffee cup until Qwilleran poured a refill and said, "Well, what happened?"

"Oh, we had the usual scrap about this and that, and she started tossing her head around—the way she does when she gets on her high horse. And then—dammit if she didn't get her hair caught in the wheel, just as I was afraid. Could've scalped her! Could've broken her neck if I hadn't been there to throw the switch and stop the thing. Crazy woman!"

"And you say she screamed?"

"Woke up the whole house, probably. I tell you it gave me a holy scare, too. I don't know what I'd do if anything happened to that old girl."

Qwilleran wore a frown that passed for sympathy, although it stemmed from his own dilemma.

"I'm not worried. She'll be back," Dan said. He pushed his

chair away from the table and stood up, stretching and patting his diaphragm. "Gotta get to work now. Gotta start setting up the exhibition. See if you can do anything for me at the paper, will you?" He reached in his hip pocket and found his wallet, from which he carefully withdrew a folded clipping. He handed it to Qwilleran with poorly concealed pride. "Here's what the top-drawer critic in L.A. said about my one-man show. This guy really knew his onions, I'm not kidding."

It was a very old clipping, the newsprint yellow and disintegrating where it had been folded.

After Dan had left, patting the rear pocket where he had stowed the wallet and the worn clipping, Qwilleran asked the housekeeper, "Who drives a light-colored convertible around here?"

"Mr. Sorrel has a light car. Kind of—baby blue," she added with a catch in her voice.

"Have you seen him this morning?"

"No, he never gets up early. He works late every night."

"I think I'll take a stroll around the grounds," Qwilleran told her. "I want to put my cat on a leash and give him a little exercise. And if you'll tell me where to find the oilcan, I'll fix that garage door."

"You don't have to do that, Mr. Qwilleran. William is supposed to—"

"No trouble, Mrs. Marron. I'll oil the hinges, and William can cut the grass. It needs it."

"If you walk down to the river," she said in a shaking voice, "be careful of the boardwalk. There might be some loose boards."

Back in his apartment Qwilleran found the cats bedded down for their morning nap on the bunk, their legs and tails interwoven to make a single brown fur mat between them. He lifted the sleeping Koko, whose body had the limp weight of a sack of flour, and coaxed his yawning head through the collar of a blue leather harness. Then, using a piece of nylon cord as a leash, he led the reluctant cat out the door—still yawning, stretching and staggering.

They circled the balcony before going downstairs. Qwilleran wanted to read the nameplates on the doors. Adjoining his own was Rosemary Whiting's apartment from which he could hear the sound of music—then that of Max Sorrel, where guttural snoring could be heard behind the closed door. On the opposite side of the balcony were the nameplates of Hixie Rice, Charlotte Roop, and Robert Maus. Why nameplates? Qwilleran started to wonder, but he dropped the question; there were too many other things on his mind.

He led Koko down the stairs, across the slick brown tiles of the Great Hall, and out into the side yard of Maus Haus. For Koko, an apartment dweller all his life, grass was a rare treat. On the lawn, still wet from the night's rain, he tried to inspect each blade personally, rejecting one and snapping his jaws on the next, with a selectivity understood only by his species. After each moist step through the grass he shook his paws fastidiously.

There was an open carport on the east side of the building, obviously a new addition. It sheltered a dark blue compact and an old dust-colored Renault. The latter did indeed have a hole in the floor, large enough for a size 12 shoe, the newsman estimated.

From there a gravel path led down to the river, where two weathered benches stood on a rotting boardwalk. The water— brown as gravy in daylight and with an indefinable stench— riffled sluggishly against the old piling.

Koko did not care for it. He wanted nothing to do with the river. He pulled away from the boardwalk and stayed on the wet grass until they started back up the path. Once he stopped to sniff a bright blue-green object on the edge of the gravel, and Qwilleran picked it up—a small glazed ceramic piece the size and shape of a beetle. Scratched on the underside were the initials J. G. He dropped it in his pocket, tugged on the leash, and led Koko back toward the house.

From the rear, the misshapen building looked like a grotesque bird with a topknot of chimneys, its carport and garage like awkward wings, its fire escapes and ledges like ruffled feathers. For eyes there were the two large staring windows of the Grahams' loft, and as Qwilleran looked up at them, he saw a figure inside move hastily away.

Coming to the three-stall garage, he opened the lift-doors. Only one of them creaked, and only one of the stalls were occupied. The car was a light blue convertible. Closing the garage door, Qwilleran examined the car carefully, inside and out—the floor, the upholstery, the instrument panel. It was very clean.

"What about this, Koko?" he muttered. "It's almost too clean."

Koko was busy sniffing oil stains on the concrete floor.

When the two returned to Number Six, Koko allowed Yum Yum to wash his face and ears, and Qwilleran paced the floor, wondering where Joy had gone, whether she had gone alone, when (if ever) she would get in touch with him, and whether he would ever see his money again. He had been unemployed for so long, before being hired by the *Daily Fluxion,* that $750 was a small fortune.

He wondered if Kipper & Fine had started alterations on his new suit, and he was tempted to call them and cancel the order. Today he felt no desire for a new suit. It had been a short spring. And now—added to his mental discomforts—he realized that he was desperately hungry.

There was a sudden disturbance on the desk—a shuffling of papers, a clicking of typewriter keys, some skidding of pencils and pens, and then a light clatter as Qwilleran's new reading glasses fell to the floor.

Qwilleran sprang to the desk as Koko made a head-long dive into the big chair. "Bad cat!" the man shouted at him. Fortunately the glasses had been saved by their heavy frames. But Qwilleran felt a tremor in the roots of his mustache when he noticed the sheet of paper in the typewriter. He put on his glasses and looked more closely.

Koko had discovered the top row of keys. He had put one paw on the numeral three and the other on zero.

SIX

SHORTLY AFTER NOON Qwilleran hurried into the Press Club and joined Arch Riker at a table for two, where the feature editor was passing the time with a martini.

"Sorry to be late," Qwilleran said. "I had to rush Koko to the vet."

"What's wrong?"

"I had him out in the backyard at Maus Haus, and he ate a lot of grass. When we got back to the apartment, he threw up, and I thought he'd eaten something poisonous."

"All cats eat grass and throw up," said Riker. "That's how they get rid of hair balls."

"Now I know. They told me at the pet hospital. But I wasn't taking any chances. Too bad he had to select my new shoes as a receptacle. *Both* shoes!"

"You should brush the cats. The kids brush ours every day, and we never have any trouble."

"Why don't people tell me these things? I just paid fifteen dollars for an office call." Qwilleran lighted a pipeful of tobacco and signaled the waitress for coffee.

"Well, what's the big news you mentioned on the phone?" Riker asked.

Qwilleran puffed his pipe intently and took his time about answering. "History repeats itself. Joy has disappeared—again."

"You're kidding!"

"I'm not kidding."

"So she's up to her old tricks."

"I don't know what to believe," Qwilleran said. He told Riker about Joy's visit to his apartment and her plans for a divorce, but not about the $750 check.

Riker said: "Rosie was going to call her up and invite her over for some girl talk. She thought it might help."

"Too late now."

"What does her husband say about it?"

"He says she's done it before. He says she always comes back. But he doesn't know what I know."

"What does he look like, anyway? Rosie told me to find out. You know how women are."

"He looks and talks like a hayseed. Not Joy's type at all. Tall and gangling. Washed-out red hair and freckles. Talks like a hayseed, too. He thinks he's got such a colorful vocabulary, but his clichés are pathetic, and his slang is out of date by about thirty years. If you ask me, he's a guy who wants desperately to be somebody and never will."

"The man who loses the girl never thinks highly of the winner, I might point out," said Riker, looking smug and enjoying his own trenchant observation.

"Joy said it herself. She said he's no crashing success as a potter."

"Why would a classy girl like Joy pick someone like that?"

"Who knows? She always liked tall men. Maybe he's a great lover. Maybe his freckles appealed to her maternal instinct."

Riker ordered another martini, and Qwilleran went on: "Now that you've had a drink, I'll tell you the rest of the story. I lent Joy some money just before she vanished."

The editor choked on an olive. "Oh, no! How much?"

"Seven-fifty."

"Seven *hundred* and fifty? Your prize money?"

Qwilleran nodded sheepishly.

"What a pushover! Cash?"

"I wrote a check."

"Stop payment, Qwill."

"She may need it—badly—wherever she is. On the other hand," he said reluctantly, "she may have run off with another guy. Or . . . something may have happened to her."

"Like what? Where did you get that idea?" Riker was familiar with Qwilleran's hunches; they were always totally correct—or totally unfounded.

"Last night I heard a scream—a woman's scream—and shortly afterward a car pulled out of the garage." He tamped his mustache nervously.

Riker recognized the gesture. It meant that his friend was on the scent of another misdeed, great or small, real or imagined. Qwilleran's early years on the police beat had given him a sixth sense about crime. What Riker did not know—and would not have believed—was the unique sensitivity in that oversized mustache. Qwilleran's hunches were usually accompanied by a prickling sensation on the upper lip, and when this happened he was never wrong.

Riker said, "Got any theories?"

Qwilleran shook his head. He said nothing about the numbers that Koko had typed, although the recollection made his hair stand on end. "I told Dan about hearing the scream, and he had an explanation. He said Joy got her long hair caught in the wheel."

"What wheel?"

"The potter's wheel. They use it to throw pots. Dan says she screamed and he came to the rescue. I don't know whether to believe it or not."

"I think you're worrying without any cause. She's probably on her way to Chicago to see her aunt, if the old lady's still living."

Qwilleran persisted. "At dinner last night Joy was snapping at everyone. There was something in the air."

"Who else lives in that weird establishment?"

"There's Robert Maus, the lawyer, who owns the place. He can't make a statement on any subject, including the weather, without first considering the pros, cons, legal implications, and tax advantages. Very dignified gent. But here's a curious development: This morning he was nursing a black eye . . . Then there's Max Sorrel, who owns the Golden Lamb Chop. He comes on strong as a ladies' man, and it was his car that drove out of the garage shortly after I heard the scream."

"But you aren't positive he was in it," Riker said. "Joy may have been driving."

"If she was, she gave the car a pat on the rump and sent it home again; it was back in the garage this morning. Dan said she probably went on the River Road bus. If so, she picked a fine time; it was pouring rain."

"Who else lives there?"

"Three women. And a houseboy who's nosy but likeable. And a housekeeper." Qwilleran leaned his elbows on the table and massaged his mustache. He remembered Joy's remark about a "discreet" extortion scheme and decided not to mention it.

Riker said, "You're letting your imagination run away with you, Qwill. Nothing's happened to Joy. You wait and see."

"I wish I could believe it."

"Well, anyway, I've got to eat and get back to the office. A syndicate salesman's coming in with some comic strips at two o'clock." He hailed a waitress. "Bowl of bean soup, meatballs and noodles, salad with Roquefort, and let's have some more butter at this table."

"And what'll you have, Skinny?" she asked Qwilleran. "You want cottage cheese again?"

"I'm starving. Quips are not appreciated."

"You want a cheeseburger with french fries? Macaroni and cheese? Ham and sweets?"

"No, I'll take a poached egg," he decided with firm resolve, "and all the celery they've got in the kitchen. I can burn up more calories chewing celery than I get from eating the damn stuff."

"Where are you eating tonight?" Riker asked.

"I've invited Maus to go with me to the Toledo Tombs, and it's going to be a heroic test of willpower on my part. I hear the food's the best in town."

"That's the place where you get a fresh napkin every five minutes. Rosie and I went there for our anniversary, and the waiters made me nervous. After they brought the seventeenth clean ashtray, I started flicking my ashes on the floor under the table."

That afternoon Qwilleran went to the public library to get a book on French food. He also picked up a book on the art of ceramics, without knowing exactly why. At the liquor store he bought a bottle of sherry and some bourbon in preparation for possible visitors to his apartment. He bought a brush at the pet shop. Finally he stopped at a supermarket to buy food for the cats. Goaded by his own unsatisfied appetite and his financial setback, he was hardly in a generous mood.

They're spoiled brats, he told himself. Lobster—red salmon—boned chicken! Other cats eat cat food, and it's about time they faced reality.

He bought a can of Kitty Delight (on sale), some Pussy Pâté (two for the price of one), and a jumbo-size box of Fishy Fritters (with a free offer on the back).

When he arrived home, Koko and Yum Yum were sitting in compact bundles on the windowsill, and their behavior indicated that they sensed the nature of the situation. Instead of chirping and crowing a welcome, they sat motionless and gazed through Qwilleran as if he were invisible.

"Soup's on!" he announced, after smearing a dime's worth of Pussy Pâté on a plate and placing it on the floor.

Neither of the cats moved a whisker.

"Try it! The label says it's delicious."

They seemed totally deaf. There was not even the flicker of an ear. Qwilleran picked Koko up bodily and plumped him down in front of the pâté, and Koko stood there with legs splayed, frozen in the position in which he had landed, glaring at the evil-looking purple smear on the plate. Then he shuddered exquisitely and walked away.

Later that evening Qwilleran described the incident to Robert Maus. "I'm convinced they can read price tags," he said, "but they'll eat the stuff if they get hungry enough."

Maus deliberated a few seconds. "A béarnaise sauce might make it more palatable," he suggested, "or a sprinkling of freshly grated Romano."

The two men had met in the lobby of a downtown building, where an elevator descended to unknown depths and deposited them in a cellar. The subterranean restaurant consisted of a series of cavernous rooms, long and narrow, vaulted in somber black masonry. It had been a sewer before the city installed the new disposal system.

The attorney was greeted with deference, and the two men were conducted to a table resplendent with white napery. Seven wine glasses and fourteen pieces of flat silver glittered at each place. Two waiters draped napkins, lightly scented with orange flower water, across the guests' knees. A captain presented menus bound in gold-tooled Florentine leather, and three bus-boys officiated at the filling of two water glasses.

Maus waved the chlorinated product away with an imperious gesture. "We drink only bottled water," he said, "and we wish to consult the sommelier."

The wine steward arrived, wearing chains and keys and a properly pompous air, and Maus selected a champagne. Then the two diners perused the menu, which was only slightly smaller than the Sunday edition of the *Fluxion,* offering every-thing from aquavit to zabaglione, and from avocado suprême rémoulade to zucchini sauté avec hollandaise.

"I might note, in passing," said the attorney sadly, "that the late Mrs. Maus inevitably ordered chopped sirloin when we dined here."

Qwilleran had not realized that Maus was widowed. "Didn't your wife share your interest in *haute cuisine?*"

After some studied breathing Maus replied: "Not that I can, with any good conscience, admit. She once used my best omelet pan for, I regret to say, liver and onions."

Qwilleran clucked his sympathy.

"I suggest we start, if it meets with your approval, Mr. Qwil-leran, with the 'French bunion soup,' as it was called in our ménage. Mrs. Maus, as it happened, was a chiropodist by profes-sion, and she had the . . . unfortunate habit of discussing her practice at the dinner table."

Onion soup was served, crusted with melted cheese, and Qwil-leran manfully limited himself to three sips. "How did you hap-pen to buy the pottery?" he inquired.

Maus considered his answer carefully. "It was an inheritance," he said at length. "The building was a bequest from my wife's uncle, Hugh Penniman, a patron of the arts and collector of ceramics in particular, who conceived the building as an art cen-ter . . . in which capacity it functioned—at great expense to the philanthropist himself—until his death . . . after which it passed to his two sons, who declined the bequest, considering it a white elephant (under the terms imposed by the will) . . . whereupon it fell to my wife and subsequently to me."

"What were the terms of the will?"

"The old gentleman stipulated that the building must continue to serve the arts, as it were—a proviso synonymous with economic folly in the opinion of my wife's cousins, and not without reason, artists being largely insolvent, as you must be aware. However, I devised the . . . not uninspired expedient of renting the studios to gourmets (since gastronomy is viewed, in the eyes of its practitioners, as an art). At the same time I chose to . . . reactivate the pottery operation, which—I surmised—would prove to be a financial liability with favorable tax consequences, if you follow me."

This recital of facts was terminated by the arrival of the eels in green sauce.

"I've been hearing about a drowning scandal in connection with the pottery," Qwilleran remarked. "When did it happen?"

The attorney drew a slow breath of exasperation. "That unhappy incident is, I assure you, ancient history. Yet time and time again *your newspaper*—a publication for which I entertain only limited admiration, if you will pardon my candor—*your newspaper* disinters the episode and publishes unsavory headlines designed, one can only infer, to titillate a readership of less than average intellect. Now that the building has fallen under my aegis, it is to be hoped there will be no further publicity on the subject. If you are in a position to exert any influence to this end, I shall be indeed . . . grateful."

"By the way," Qwilleran said, "I don't think you should lock the door between the pottery and the apartments. The fire marshal would take a dim view of that."

"The fire door has not, to my knowledge, been locked at any time."

"It was locked this morning—from the inside."

Maus, intent on savoring a morsel of eel, made no reply.

"Is Graham considered a good potter?" Qwilleran asked.

"He is, I am inclined to believe, an excellent technician, with a thorough knowledge of materials, equipment, and the operation of a pottery. The creative talent belongs chiefly, it appears to me, on the distaff side of the family."

"You may not have heard the news," Qwilleran said, "but Mrs. Graham has left her husband. I believe she consulted you about getting a divorce. Well, last night—in the small hours—she cleared out."

Maus continued chewing thoughtfully and then said, "Unfortunate, to say the least."

Qwilleran searched the attorney's face for some revealing reaction but saw only an imperturbable countenance and preoccupied eyes, one of them ringed with a bruise, now turning purple.

The distinguished epicure was engrossed in evaluating the green sauce. He said, "The parsley, it is safe to say, was added a trifle too soon . . . although, as you must know, much controversy can be generated on the subject of herbs. At the Meritorious Society of Gastronomes last evening we enjoyed a stimulating symposium on oregano. The discussion, it eventuated, grew quite . . . stormy."

"Is that how you got that mouse?" Qwilleran asked.

The attorney tenderly touched his left eye. "In the heat of argument, I regret to report, one of our members—an impetuous individual—thrust his fist in my direction at an inopportune time."

The main course and a bottle of white wine were now served in a flurry of excitement by seven members of the restaurant staff. Maus tasted the wine and sent it back, complained about a cigar at the next table, and detected a *soupçon* too much tarragon in the sauce.

Qwilleran viewed with mounting hunger the dish of veal and mushrooms, aswim in delicate juices. He determined, however, to adhere to his regimen: three bites and quit. After the first bite he said to Maus, "Do you think Max Sorrel would make a good personality story for my column?"

The attorney sagely nodded approval. "His restaurant is experiencing certain—shall we say?—difficulties at this time, and it is undoubtedly true that some manner of . . . favorable comment in the press would not go unappreciated. I deem it inadvisable to elucidate, but Mr. Sorrel, I am sure, will be happy to discuss the matter with you, if you so . . . desire."

"And what about Charlotte Roop?"

Maus laid down his knife and fork, which he was manipulating in the European manner. "Ah, there is a jewel! Do not allow yourself to be misled by the fluttering spinster facade. Miss Roop is a successful career woman with remarkable executive ability and integrity of the highest order. If she suffers from certain character defects, it behooves us to leave them unmentioned."

Qwilleran took his second bite. "Rosemary Whiting seems to be very nice. A perfect lady."

"A Canadian," Maus said. His face was beatific as he savored the veal, having come to terms with the excess of tarragon.

"What's her special interest in food?"

"Mrs. Whiting, it pains me to say, is a purveyor of health foods. You may have heard her panegyrics to soybeans and sunflower seeds."

"And Hixie Rice, I understand, is a food writer."

Maus raised his hands in a dignified gesture of resignation. "The young lady writes, in the course of duty, those appalling menus for third-rate restaurants: 'Today's special—a delectable ragout blending tender tidbits of succulent baby lamb with garden-sweet carrots, pristine cubes of choice Michigan potato, and jewellike peas—all in a tasty sauce redolent of the Far East.' That effusion of baroque prose indicates, as you may be aware, yesterday's leftovers drowning in canned gravy . . . with sufficient curry powder to camouflage the rancidity."

Qwilleran took his third bite. "William is an interesting character, too."

"He prattles to excess, alas, and boasts no useful skills, but he is congenial, and his bridge game is not without merit."

The captain and the waiters had been observing, with increasing alarm, Qwilleran's dilatory attitude toward the food, and now there was a stir among the staff as the head chef came storming from the kitchen.

He walked directly toward Qwilleran and demanded, "You no like my cooking?"

"A true gourmet never stuffs himself," the newsman replied calmly. "The food is excellent, rest assured. I'd like to take the rest of this veal home to my cats."

"*Gatti!* Santa Maria! So now I cook for *gatti!*" The chef threw up his hands and charged back to the kitchen.

After the braised fennel amandine and the tossed salad with nasturtium seeds, and the chestnut puree in meringue nests, and the demitasse, Qwilleran reached in his pocket for his pipe and drew forth the turquoise beetle that Koko had found near the waterfront. "Ever see that before?"

Maus nodded. "Mrs. Graham had the charm to present to each of us a scarab—as a token, so to speak, of good fortune.

Mine has, unhappily, disappeared—an omen that bodes no good, one would imagine."

Qwilleran paid the check, thankful that the *Fluxion* was footing the bill; he could have lived for a week on the tip alone. And now he was eager to go home. He had made no notes during the dinner interview, as Maus expounded his culinary tenets. The newsman knew that cautious subjects speak more freely when their words are not being recorded. But he had accumulated plenty of material for a column on Robert Maus, and now it was necessary to collect the piquant quotes from the corners of his mind and get them down on paper before they faded from memory. As soon as the waiters brought the cats' veal to the table, wrapped in a linen napkin, the two men departed—Maus radiating gustatory satisfaction and Qwilleran feeling vaguely hungry and a trifle sorry for himself.

When they arrived at Maus Haus, the attorney took his attaché case to the kitchen and Qwilleran climbed the grand staircase, but at the landing he turned right instead of left. A sudden impulse led him to Hixie's apartment.

Just as he raised his hand to knock on the door, he heard a man's voice, and he hesitated. Through the thick oak panel he could hear only the rumble of the masculine voice without distinguishing the words, but the inflections indicated that the man was coaxing and gently arguing. At first it sounded like television drama, but then Qwilleran recognized the second voice in the dialogue.

Hixie was saying, "No! That's final! . . . Thanks a lot but no thanks!" The high pitch of her voice made the words distinguishable.

There was a wheedling reply from the man.

"That doesn't make any difference. You know my terms." She lowered her voice in answer to a question. "Of course I do, but you shouldn't have come here. We agreed you'd never come here . . . All right, just one drink, and then you've got to leave."

Qwilleran knocked on the door.

There was an abrupt silence and a long wait before Hixie's heels could be heard clicking on the floor and approaching the door. "Who is it?" She opened the door cautiously. "Oh, it's you!" she said with a nervous smile. "I was on the telephone. Sorry to keep you waiting." She did not invite him in.

"I just wondered if you'd like to go to a cheese-tasting tomorrow afternoon. It's a press party."

"Yes, I'd love it. Where shall I meet you?"

"How about the lobby of the Stilton Hotel?"

"That's fine. You know me! I love to eat."

"There'll be drinks, of course."

"Love to drink, too." She batted her long false eyelashes.

Qwilleran tried to glance over her shoulder, but the door was only partially open, and the room was in shadow. He saw only a flutter of movement—a bird hopping about in a cage. "See you tomorrow," he said.

Qwilleran preferred to date women with figures more svelte and clothes more tasteful, but he wanted to ask questions, and he was sure that Hixie liked to babble answers. As he walked around the balcony to Number Six, he was determined to keep an ear tuned for activity across the hall. After "just one drink," who would slip out of Hixie's apartment and where would he go? Why, he asked himself, am I such a nosy bastard? But when he unlocked his own door and stepped into the apartment, he forgot his curiosity. The place was a scene of havoc.

All the pictures on the wall over the bookcase were hanging askew. Several books were on the floor with covers spread and pages rumpled. The wastebasket had been overturned, and its contents were strewn about the tile floor. Cushions had been thrown on the floor, and the desktop was swept clean of all but the typewriter. Burglary? Vandalism? Qwilleran glanced swiftly about him before he took a further step into the room. His foot came down on a small object that crunched and pulverized. He stepped quickly aside. Crunch! There were scores of small brown balls scattered about the floor, and the bearskin rug was missing . . . No, it was huddled under the desk.

"You devils!" Qwilleran bellowed. Those brown balls were Fishy Fritters! The open carton lay on the kitchen floor, empty, and beside it was the plate on which the untouched Pussy Pâté had dried to a nauseating crust. Now it was clear: The devastation was a protest demonstration staged by two militant cats.

The culprits themselves were asleep on the bunk, Yum Yum curled up in a tight ball and Koko stretched full length in a posture of complete exhaustion. When Qwilleran unfolded the linen napkin, however, noses were twitching and ears were alerted, and the two reprobates reported to the kitchen to claim —in a bedlam of baritone and soprano yowls—their escalopes de veau sautées à l'estragon.

"Only a complete sucker would give you a feast after a performance like that," Qwilleran told them.

After straightening the pictures and shoveling up the Fishy Fritters from the four corners of the room, he put on his slippers, lit a pipeful of tobacco, and sat down at his typewriter to list his impressions of the Toledo Tombs and the food foibles of the meritorious gastronome.

Not without apprehension he glanced at the sheet of paper that he regularly left in the machine, and there he saw one word, neatly typed. He adjusted his glasses and leaned closer. It was in lower case this time . . . a single incredible word: *dog!*

In astonishment Qwilleran turned to look at the cat who was industriously licking his paw and washing his face. "Koko!" he said. "This is *too much!*"

SEVEN

Qwilleran intended to set the alarm clock Wednesday night, but he forgot, and on Thursday morning he was awakened instead by a rasping noise at the window. Koko and Yum Yum were sitting on the sill, chattering like squirrels at the pigeons outside the glass, while the birds had the effrontery to strut up and down the outer ledge within inches of the two quivering black noses.

Qwilleran awoke with a sense of loss. Did it mean that Joy had gone for good? Or was it merely coincidence that Koko had typed "30," the old newspaper symbol for the end of a story?

Suddenly he recalled the latest message in the typewriter. Co-incidence or not, it was fantastic!

"D-O-G," he said aloud, and he leaped out of bed with an urgent question on his mind.

He intended to ask Robert Maus at the breakfast table but missed him. He asked Mrs. Marron; she was of no help. He asked Hixie when she reported for ham and eggs and country fries with cinnamon toast, but she had not had the faintest idea. Dan Graham failed to appear for breakfast, and when Qwilleran telephoned the pottery later, there was no answer. Finally he called Robert Maus at his office.

"I regret to say that . . . it escapes my memory," the attorney said, "but allow me to consult a copy of the contract."

Qwilleran mumbled an excuse about writing something and needing the information in a hurry.

"No," said Maus after consulting the files. "I see no evidence of a middle name or initial."

Qwilleran phoned Arch Riker at the office and told him about the three-letter word in the typewriter. He said, "I was sure Dan Graham was the type who'd have a middle name like Otho or Oglebert, and I thought Koko might have been trying to tell me something. He's come up with some clues in the past that were no less fantastic."

"I'm glad he's learning to spell," Riker said. "In another six months he should be able to take over your column. How was your dinner last night?"

"Fine, but I didn't learn much. Maus gave me an unlikely story about how he got his black eye."

"Coming downtown for lunch?"

"No, I want to stay home and write my review of the Toledo Tombs. This gourmet racket is full of absurdities, and it's going to be hard to strike the right note—halfway between adulation and a horse laugh."

"Don't offend any restaurant owners," Arch warned him, "or the advertising department will be on my neck . . . Any news about Joy?"

"No. Nothing."

Qwilleran had another reason for wanting to stay home: to be near the phone in case she called. He knew it was too soon to expect a message in the mail; she had been gone hardly more than twenty-four hours. And yet he rushed downstairs when the mail delivery came at eleven o'clock and was disappointed to find nothing in his slot in the foyer. Then he convinced himself that any communications from Joy would be addressed to his office; she would be smart enough for that! A letter in her handwriting would be too easily recognized at Maus Haus. He wondered if the post office was equipped to cope with a letter addressed to "Juu Qwwww" at the "Duuy Fwxwu."

He spent the next hour at his typewriter, trying to write a slyly objective report on the Toledo Tombs. After several fruitless starts, he abandoned that subject and began a profile of Robert

Maus—with his pride (sharp knives, lots of butter) and his numerous prejudices. Maus abhorred tea bags, pressure cookers, canned fruit cocktail, bottled mayonnaise, instant coffee, iceberg lettuce, monosodium glutamate, eggs poached in geometric shapes, New England boiled dinners, and anything resembling a smorgasbord, salad bar, or all-you-can-eat buffet

Once or twice Qwilleran stopped and listened. He thought he could hear someone singing. It was rare to hear live song—not radio and not television. Somewhere a man was singing a Scottish air, and the newsman's Mackintosh blood responded.

Qwilleran was poking at the keys, quoting Maus on the horror of potatoes baked in foil, when there came a knock on the apartment door. Standing in the hall was his elderly neighbor with her white hair and floury face powder, her crossword puzzle and abundance of costume jewelry.

"Forgive me for intruding," Miss Roop said, fingering her three strands of beads, "but this puzzle has me stumped, and I thought you might have a good dictionary, being a writer and all. I need an eleven-letter word for a kind of orchid. The first letter is *c*, and it ends in *m*."

"Cypripedium," said Qwilleran. He spelled it for her.

Miss Roop gasped, and a look of adoration crept into her small blue wrinkle-framed eyes. "Why—why—why, you are remarkable, Mr. Qwilleran!"

He accepted the compliment without revealing the truth. He had learned the word while playing a dictionary game with Koko a few months before. "Will you come in?" he asked.

She started to back away. "Oh, you're probably busy writing one of your wonderful columns." But her eyes seemed eager.

"It's about time I took a breather. Come on in."

"You're sure it's all right?" She glanced down the hall in both directions before stepping quickly into the apartment with a guilty little shrug.

Qwilleran closed the door behind her, and when she looked apprehensive he explained that he must keep the cats from running into the hall. Koko and Yum Yum were sunning themselves on the blue cushion atop the dining table. Miss Roop glanced at them and stiffened perceptibly.

Koko was stretched full length, and Yum Yum was playing with his tail. He tantalized her by slapping it this way and that, and she grabbed it whenever it came within reach. Airborne cat hairs could be seen glistening in the shaft of sunlight that slanted through the studio window.

The relentless daylight also emphasized the two sets of wrinkles on Miss Roop's forehead, caused by the habit of raising her eyebrows.

Koko caught her disapproving stare and stopped playing games. He rolled over, lifted one hind leg and proceeded to lick the base of his tail. The visitor quickly turned away.

"Will you have a chair?" Qwilleran offered her one of the dining chairs, guessing that she liked to sit up straight. He also offered to make a cup of instant coffee, but she declined hastily as if he had made an indecent suggestion.

Mischievously he asked, "Something stronger?"

"Mr. Qwilleran," she said firmly, "I might as well tell you right now that I disapprove of drinking."

"I don't drink either," he admitted in his best chummy tone, without adding the grim reason why.

Again she beamed at him with so much warmth that she embarrassed herself and began to talk self-consciously—too much, too loud, and too fast. "I love my work. Mr. Hashman was a brilliant man, rest his soul. He taught me everything I know about restaurant management. He sold out a long time ago, and now the Heavenly Hash Houses are a very big fast-food chain; you probably know that. They're owned by three brilliant businessmen—"

"Perhaps I should write a column on the history of the Hash Houses, since they originated in this city." Qwilleran told himself it would be a neat way of sidestepping the quality of the food. "Would you be willing to be interviewed?"

"Oh, dear, no! Don't mention me! I'd rather you would write about the three brilliant men who expanded the chain from three restaurants to eighty-nine."

All uniformly mediocre, thought Qwilleran. He reached for his pipe and then changed his mind, convinced that his visitor would disapprove. With circumspection he attempted to pump her for information. "I'm hoping to write several stories on the gourmets who live at Maus Haus. Do you have any suggestions as to where I should start?"

"Oh, they're all interesting individuals, take my word for it," she said enthusiastically.

"Certainly a varied group. Do they all get along well?"

"Oh, yes, they're lovely people, all very agreeable."

"How about Max Sorrel? Is he a success as a restaurateur?"

"Oh, he's an excellent businessman. I admire Mr. Sorrel greatly."

"Seems to have an eye for the ladies."

"He's a handsome man, with a charming personality, and very fastidious."

Qwilleran felt he was holding a conversation with a computer. He cleared his throat and tried another approach. "You weren't at dinner Tuesday night, but there was a flare-up at the table. William was scolded for incompetence."

"We should all make allowances for youth," Miss Roop said firmly. "He's a nice boy—very friendly. I'm an old lady with white hair, but he talks to me as if we were the same age."

Qwilleran had always had a faculty for inducing people to talk frankly. The look of concern in his eyes and the downward curve of his heavy mustache combined to make him appear sympathetic and sincere, even when he was purely inquisitive, but his technique failed to work with Charlotte Roop. He merely learned that Rosemary was attractive, Hixie amusing, and Robert Maus brilliant—absolutely brilliant.

"I suppose you know," he said, attacking the subject with less delicacy, "that we've lost one of our dinner companions. Mrs. Graham has left her husband—rather suddenly and mysteriously."

Miss Roop raised her chin primly. "I never listen to gossip, Mr. Qwilleran."

"I hope nothing unfortunate has happened to her," he persisted. "I heard a scream the night she disappeared, and it worries me."

"Mrs. Graham is perfectly all right, I'm sure," said Miss Roop. "We must always maintain an optimistic attitude and think constructive thoughts."

"Do you know her well?"

"We've had many friendly conversations, and she has taught me a great deal about her art. I admire her tremendously. A clever woman! And her husband is such a sweet man. They're a lovely couple."

A peculiar noise came from Koko, who had jumped from the table and was looking for an empty shoe. Qwilleran scooped him up and rushed him into the bathroom.

"Excuse me," he said to his guest when the crisis was past. "Koko just chucked his breakfast. He must have a hair ball."

Miss Roop gave Koko a look of faint distaste.

"I wonder what happened to Mrs. Graham's cat," Qwilleran remarked. "She was all broken up about losing him."

"She will rise above it. She is a sensible woman, with remarkably strong character."

"Is that so? I've been told she is capricious and a little scatter-brained."

"I beg to differ! I have seen her at work. She knows what she wants, and she takes endless pains to achieve it. One day she was sitting at the wheel, spinning a pot, as they say—or should I say *casting* a pot?"

"Throwing a pot," Qwilleran corrected her.

"Yes, she was throwing a pot on the wheel, pumping the machine with her dainty little foot, and I asked her why she did not use the electric wheel. It would be so much easier and more efficient. She said, 'I'd rather work harder and produce an object that has my own personality in the clay.' That was a beautiful thought. She is a real artist." Miss Roop rose to leave. "I have stayed too long. I'm keeping you from your work." And when Qwilleran remonstrated, she added, "No, I must go downstairs and get a bite to eat."

When Charlotte Roop was gone, Qwilleran said to Koko, "Did you hear what she said about the wheel?"

"Yow!" said Koko, who was back on the table, washing himself in the sunlight.

"Dan said he saved Joy from a serious injury by throwing *the switch*. A slight discrepancy, don't you think?"

Koko nodded in agreement, it seemed, or was he merely licking the pale patch of fur on his breast?

"I'd like to figure out a way to sneak you into that pottery," Qwilleran said. "I'll bet you could sniff out some clues."

More than once in the past Koko had led the way into a highly revealing situation, but if the cat had a sixth sense about suspicious behavior, Qwilleran's sensitive mustache had an equal awareness. Many a time it had alerted him to bad news, hidden danger, and even unsuspected crime.

Now he was experiencing the same disturbing quiver on his upper lip. It was telling him that something dire had happened to Joy. It was telling him that Joy was not alive. He didn't want to believe his hunch. He *refused* to believe his hunch.

EIGHT

FOR QWILLERAN THE day seemed interminable. He skipped lunch. At noon Rosemary stopped at his door with a ball of yarn; she had been tidying her knitting basket and thought the cats would enjoy some exercise with a ball of yarn. Qwilleran invited her to come in, but she was on her way to work. In the afternoon the sun disappeared behind a bank of gray clouds, and the cold light flooding through the huge studio window drenched the apartment in gloom. The cats felt the chill. Ignoring the yarn, they crept behind the books in the bookcase and found a cozier place for their afternoon nap.

Qwilleran was thankful when the time came to leave for the Stilton Hotel. He needed a change of scene and a change of thought, and he was glad, somewhat, that he had invited the babbling Hixie Rice. On the way to the hotel he stopped at the office to open his mail, and a fleeting impulse sent him to the *Fluxion* library to pick up an old clip file on the River Road pottery . . . the Penniman Pottery, as it was originally known.

He met Hixie in the hotel lobby. It seemed to the newsman that she was exhibiting desperate gaiety with her cherry red suit and shrimp pink hat laden with straw carrots, turnips, and radishes.

"That's a tasty *chapeau*," Qwilleran remarked.

"Merci, monsieur." She fluttered her double set of eyelashes. "I'm glad you like it."

"I didn't say that."

"Oh, you're a kidder!" Hixie gave him a playful shove. "I couldn't resist the straw *légumes*. You know me! . . . Do you speak French?"

"Only enough to keep out of trouble in Paris."

"I'm taking a Berlitz course. Say something in French."

"Camembert, Roquefort, Brie," said Qwilleran.

The annual Choose Cheese celebration was being hosted by the cheese industry in the hotel ballroom. The hundred or more guests, however, were patronizing the free bar and ignoring the long table of assorted cheeses.

"This is a typical press party," Qwilleran explained. "About six of the guests are members of the working press, and nobody knows who the others are or why they were invited."

He smoked his pipe and sampled a Danish cheese made with skim milk. Hixie sipped a Manhattan and sampled the Brie, Camembert, Chesire, Edam, Gorgonzola, Gouda, Gruyére, Herkimer, Liederkranz, Mozzarella, Muenster, Parmesan, Port du Salut, and Roquefort.

"Is that all you're going to eat, for gosh sake?" she asked.

"I might take a little Roquefort home to Koko," Qwilleran said and then added, "We had an unexpected visitor today—Miss Roop. I sense that she disapproves of cats. Koko didn't approve of her, either."

"Charlotte disapproves of *everything*," said Hixie. "Smoking, drinking, gambling, divorce, short skirts, shaggy dog stories, foreigners, motorcycles, movies with unhappy endings, politicians, gum-chewing, novels written after 1910, overtipping of waiters, and sex."

That kind always has a skeleton in the closet, Qwilleran thought. "Has there ever been any romance in her life?" he asked his well-informed companion.

"Who knows? I suspect she was secretly in love with Hash House Hashman. He's been dead for fifteen years, but she still talks about him all the time."

Qwilleran chewed his pipe stem thoughtfully. "Did you ever wonder what happened to Joy Graham's cat?"

Hixie shrugged. "Ran away, I suppose. Got picked up. Got run over by a bus. Fell in the river. Choose one of the above."

"Do you like pets?"

"If they don't cause trouble or tie you down too much. I bought myself a canary, but he seems to be a deaf-mute. That's just my luck. I'm a born loser."

Qwilleran sliced a wedge of Norwegian Gjetost and presented it to her on a cracker. "I suppose you know that Joy has disappeared."

"Yes, I heard she left him." For a moment Hixie's jovial expression changed to one Qwilleran could not identify, but her face quickly brightened again. "Try this Westphalian Sauermilch, *mon ami. C'est formidable!*"

Qwilleran obliged and remarked that it was a little immature. It had not quite achieved total putrefaction. He was determined, however, not to let her change the subject. "Did you ever see Joy throw a pot on the wheel?" he asked.

"No, but she almost threw a pot at my head once. I accidentally broke a dumb-looking pitcher she'd made, and after that I wasn't exactly welcome in the pottery."

"We've got a colorful tribe at Maus Haus. What kind of guy is Max Sorrel?"

"A confirmed bachelor," Hixie groaned. "His only love affair is with that big fat restaurant . . . Poor Max! He's got the legendary heart of gold, and he doesn't deserve the trouble he's having."

"What kind of trouble?"

"Don't you know? He may lose his restaurant. He's even had to sell his boat! He has—or he *did* have—a gorgeous thirty-six-foot cruiser that he used to tie up behind Maus Haus."

"What's the problem?"

"You mean you haven't heard the rumors?"

Qwilleran scowled and shook his head, professionally humiliated because rumors were circulating and he, a member of the Press Club, was in the dark.

"People are saying all kinds of absurd things. Like, Max's head chef has a horrible disease. Like, a customer found something unspeakable in his soup. Sick jokes."

"Sounds like a poison tongue campaign."

"It's rotten, because Max runs a meticulously clean restaurant.

And yet the rumors have mushroomed, and the customers are staying away in droves."

"I thought the Golden Lamb Chop had a sophisticated clientele. They should know that the Board of Health—"

"Nobody *believes* the rumors, but café society and the gambling crowd won't patronize a spot that's being laughed at. And they've been Max's best customers."

"Does he have any idea how the thing started?"

She shook her head. "He's very well liked all over town. I told him he ought to get one of the papers to print a story about it, so he could deny everything publicly, but he said that would only attract more unwelcome attention. He's hoping it will blow over before he goes completely broke."

"It's slander," Qwilleran said. "He's got a case if he can find out who's behind it."

"That's what Robert says, but Max can't trace a thing."

Qwilleran had considered inviting Hixie to dinner—even after all the cheese—but he changed his mind. He wanted to go to the Golden Lamb Chop, and he wanted to go alone. Taking her home in a taxi, he sensed her disappointment.

"Do you like baseball?" he asked. "I can get seats in the press box some weekend, if you'd like to go." He was being noble. If his friends in the press box saw him with this overweight, overdressed, overexpressive date, they'd never let him live it down.

"Sure, I like baseball. Especially the hot dogs."

"Any particular team you'd like to see?"

"Whoever's at the bottom of the league. I like to root for the underdog."

When Qwilleran returned to Number Six to give the cats some turkey with a garnish of Roquefort, he was greeted by a scene of incredible beauty. The apartment had been transformed into a work of art. The cats had found Rosemary's ball of gray yarn and had spun a web that enmeshed every article of furniture in the room. They had rolled the ball across the floor, tossed it over chairs, looped it around table legs, carried it up to the desk and around the typewriter and down again to the floor, hooking it in the jaws of the bear before repeating the same basic design with variations. Now the cats sat on the bookcase, as motionless as statuary, contemplating their creation.

Qwilleran had seen string sculpture at the museum that was

less artful, and it was a shame to destroy it, but the crisscrossing strands made it impossible to move about the room. He found the end of the yarn and rewound it—an athletic performance that took half an hour and burned off an ounce of his avoirdupois. This time he put the ball of yarn away in the desk drawer. Then he went to dinner—alone.

The Golden Lamb Chop occupied a prominent corner where State Street, River Road, and the expressway converged. The building was a nineteenth-century landmark, having been the depot for interurban trolleys before the automobile came on the scene. Now the interior had a golden glow, like money: gold damask on the walls, gold silk shades on the table lamps, ornate gilt frames on the oil paintings. The floor was thickly carpeted in a gold plush, spongy enough to turn an unwary ankle and uniquely patterned with a lamb chop motif in metallic gold threads.

At the door to the main dining room Qwilleran was greeted by Max Sorrel—hand on heart. His well-shaped head was freshly shaved; his dark suit and candy-striped shirt were crisp as cornflakes.

"You alone?" the restaurateur asked, flashing a professional smile with the minty fragrance of toothpaste and mouthwash. "Just hang your coat in the checkroom. We don't have a hat-check girl tonight." He seated the newsman at a table near the entrance. "I want you to be the guest of the house. Understand?"

"No, this is on the *Daily Fluxion*. Let them pay for it."

"We'll argue about that later. Mind if I join you—in between seating customers? We're not very busy on weeknights, and I've given my maître d' a little vacation."

The proprietor took a seat where he could keep a hopeful eye on the entrance. Thirty empty tables stood waiting in their gold tablecloths, with gold napkins folded precisely and tucked into the amber goblets.

"How many can you seat?" Qwilleran asked.

"Two hundred, counting the private dining room upstairs. What'll you have to drink?"

"Just tomato juice."

Sorrel called a waiter. There was only one of them in evidence. "One tomato juice and one rye and soda, Charlie, and get

me a clean glass, will you?" He handed over a goblet on which a
drop of detergent had left a spot. "If there's anything I can't
stand," he told Qwilleran, "it's spots on the glassware. What'll
you have to eat? I recommend the rack of lamb."

"Sounds good," Qwilleran said, "but I may have to take some
of it home in a doggie bag. I'm on a diet."

"What for a first course? Vichyssoise? Herring in sour cream?"

"Better make it a half-grapefruit."

Qwilleran started to light his pipe, and Sorrel pushed an am-
ber glass ashtray toward him, after examining it for blemishes.
"Know how we clean ashtrays here?" he said. "With wet teabags.
It's the best way . . . Excuse me a moment."

A couple had entered the empty dining room, looking bewildered, as if they had come on the wrong night.

"You don't have a reservation?" Sorrel asked them with a
frown. He hesitated. He consulted a ledger. He did some crossing out and some writing in. Finally—with a convincing show of
magnanimity and a buttery smile for the lady—he consented to
give them a table, seating them in a large front window in full
view of passing traffic. He explained to them that the regular
crowd was late because of the ball game, as he removed from
their table a gold tent-card that said "Reserved."

When the grapefruit was served, Sorrel watched Qwilleran
spoon it out of the rind. "You unhappy about something?" he
asked the newsman.

Qwilleran gave him a questioning frown.

"I can tell by the way you eat your grapefruit. You're going
around it counterclockwise. Did you ever watch people eat
grapefruit? The happy ones eat clockwise."

"Curious theory."

"Do you secretly wiggle your toes inside your shoes when you
eat something good?"

"I don't know, and I'm not sure I want to know."

"I can tell a lot about people by watching them eat—how they
break their rolls, spoon their soup, cut their meat—even the way
they chew."

"How do you size up the motley crew at Maus Haus?" Qwilleran asked.

"Interesting bunch. Hixie—she's got a lot of ginger, but she's
getting panicky. She wants to get married in the worst way.

Rosemary—she looks like a perfect lady, but don't be too sure. William—there's something weasely about that boy. He's not on the up-and-up. I can tell by the way he holds his fork. How do you size him up?"

"He's okay. Strikes me as an amusing kid, with a lot of healthy curiosity."

"Maybe I shouldn't tell you this," Sorrel confided, "because I don't want to stir up trouble, but I saw him letting himself into your apartment last night around eight o'clock, and he was looking kind of sneaky. Did you authorize him to go into your apartment?"

"How did you happen to see him?" Qwilleran wanted to know. "I thought you worked every night."

"Well, we had an accident in the kitchen, and some cocktail sauce got splashed on my shirt. I rushed home to change. . . . Excuse me."

The restaurateur jumped up to seat a party of four, obviously tourists, while Qwilleran said to himself, Wouldn't a fastidious guy like Sorrel keep an extra shirt on hand at his place of business?

When the lamb was served, looking like the Rock of Gibraltar, Qwilleran remarked, "Do you know Joy Graham has left her husband?"

"No! When did that happen?"

"Early yesterday morning."

"Is she getting a divorce?"

"I don't know. She left no explanation, according to Dan. Just disappeared."

"I'm not surprised," Sorrel said. "I wouldn't blame her for unloading that ape. She's got a lot on the ball." His eyes glowed with appreciation. "I'm not strongly in favor of marriage myself. There are better ways to live. People marry, divorce, marry, divorce. It's not respectable."

"Did you ever watch her work with clay?"

"Me? No, sir! I've never set foot in that pottery. I took one look at all the dust and mud, and I knew that wasn't for me." His expression changed from one of distaste to one of approval. "So the little cabbage got the hell out, did she? Good for her!"

"It mystifies me why she'd depart in the middle of the night— in a violent rainstorm," Qwilleran said.

"Sure you don't want a baked potato with sour cream and chives?" his host urged.

"Thanks, no . . . And another mystery," Qwilleran went on, "is what happened to her cat. He was a neutered longhair, and they don't go roaming the countryside in search of adventure; they sit around like sofa pillows. Do you have any ideas about what happened to that cat?"

Sorrel turned the color of borscht, and the veins in his temples seemed ready to burst.

"What's the matter?" Qwilleran asked in alarm. "Are you all right?"

The restaurateur mopped his brow with a gold napkin and lowered his voice. "I thought for a minute you were riding me— about that ugly story that's going around town." He gave the newsman a wary glance. "You haven't heard?"

Qwilleran shook his head.

"I'm being persecuted. A lot of dirty rumors are drifting around, and I don't mind telling you they're hurting my business. This place should be three-quarters full on Thursday night. Look at it! Six customers!"

"What kind of rumors?"

Sorrel winced. "That I use cat meat in the twelve-ounce chopped sirloin—and all that kind of rot. I could tell you worse, only it would spoil your dinner. Why don't they say I've got a gambling den in the back room? Why don't they say I keep girls upstairs? *That* I could take! But they're getting me where it hurts. Me! The guy who's known for keeping the cleanest kitchen in the city!"

"Any idea who could be circulating these rumors?" Qwilleran asked. "What would their motive be?"

Sorrel shrugged. "I don't know. Nobody seems to know. But it looks like a plot—especially after what happened Tuesday night."

"What happened?"

"My kitchen caught fire in the middle of the night. The police called me, and I came back downtown. It had to be arson. I don't leave grease around. I don't use any inflammable cleaners . . . Let me tell you: If anything happened to this place I'd crack up! I love this restaurant! The drapes cost forty dollars a yard. The carpet was custom-woven. Where did you ever see a carpet with a lamb chop design?"

Qwilleran had to admit the floor-covering was unusual. "Does anyone have a grudge against you—personally?"

"Me? I've got a million friends. Ask anybody. I couldn't think of an enemy if you paid me."

"How about your employees? Have you fired anyone who might be out for revenge?"

"No, I've always treated my people right, and they like me. Ask any one of them. Ask Charlie." The waiter was bringing the coffee. "Charlie, do I treat you right? Tell this man—he's from the newspaper. Do I treat everyone right?"

"Yes, *sir*," said Charlie in a flat voice.

Qwilleran declined Sorrel's offer of a dessert from the cart, which offered rum cream pie, banana Bavarian, pecan caramel custard, strawberry shortcake, and chocolate mousse, and he left the restaurant with the rest of his lamb wrapped in aluminum foil. He crossed River Road to hail a westbound taxi, but a bus came along and he climbed aboard.

It was one of the slow evening buses, and the leisurely speed and the drone of the engine were conducive to meditation . . . Why were women attracted to men with shiny bald heads? Max Sorrel was obviously attractive to the opposite sex. Had he incurred the enmity of a jealous rival? A jealous husband? . . . Had there been something between Joy and Max? If Dan resented it, would he have the wit to conduct a successful smear campaign against the Golden Lamb Chop? . . . Max had seemed surprised to learn of Joy's disappearance, but he was a good actor. He might have been lying . . . And how about the departure of Max's convertible at three in the morning? The restaurant fire would account for that—if the story of the fire happened to be true. Qwilleran made a mental note to verify it . . . As for William's surreptitious visit to Number Six, Qwilleran was not unduly concerned. The key rack in the kitchen was readily accessible, and the houseboy had probably wanted to see the cats. William had a healthy curiosity—a virtue, from a newsman's point of view. He also had brash nerve and a glib tongue and an easygoing personality. Qwilleran and Riker had been the same way when they were in their twenties, before their exuberance was curbed by disappointments and compromises and the old newsman's realization that there is never anything really new.

Wrapped in his thoughts, Qwilleran rode a mile beyond Maus Haus and had to wait for another slow bus traveling in the opposite direction.

When he finally arrived home, he found some changes in the Great Hall. The long dining table and the high-backed chairs had been moved aside, and the area was dotted with pedestals of various heights. In the center of the room a few railroad ties had been arranged on the floor to form a large square, and Dan Graham was down on hands and knees filling the square with pebbles. Alone in the vast hall, pushing the pebbles this way and that as if their placement mattered profoundly, he made a sad picture of insignificance, Qwilleran thought.

"How's it going, Mr. Graham?" he asked.

"Slow," said the potter. "It's not much fun, doing the setup alone." He stood up and massaged his back, while viewing the pebbles critically. "My best pieces will be displayed on pedestals in this square. I'm gonna surprise this city, you can betcha boots."

"How soon are we going to see the new pots?"

"Maybe Monday or Tuesday. I've got some sweet patooties cooling in the kiln right now. Did you talk to anybody at the paper?"

"Everything is under control. Don't worry about it," Qwilleran said, although he had forgotten to tell Riker about anything but Joy's disappearance. "Any news from your wife?"

"Nope. Not a word. But it wouldn't surprise me if she came back in time for the hoopla on Wednesday. We sent out three hundred invitations last week. Should be a swell party. I'm shooting the works—bubble water, horses' duvvers, the right stuff, if you know what I mean. The critics better come, that's all I've got to say . . . Here, let me show you something." Graham reached around to his hip pocket and once more brought forth the yellowed clipping about his past glories.

When Qwilleran went upstairs to Number Six, he found the cats waiting for him, with anticipation in the cock of their ears.

"Koko, where is that guy getting the money to buy champagne for three hundred guests," Qwilleran asked him.

The cat's eyes were like large black cherries in the lamplight—

expressionless, yet holding all the answers to all the questions ever asked.

Qwilleran arranged his coat over the back of a chair and whipped off his tie. Yum Yum watched the tie with bright, hopeful eyes. He usually switched it through the air for her to jump at and catch, but tonight he was too preoccupied to play. Instead he sat in the big chair, put on his glasses, and opened the packet of clippings from the *Fluxion* library.

Robert Maus had not exaggerated. Every five years the *Fluxion* had resurrected the story of the mysterious deaths at the pottery, most likely to embarrass the *Morning Rampage*. The rival newspaper was still financed by the Penniman family. It had been old Hugh Penniman who built the strange art center and hobnobbed with its arty residents.

The stories, written in the old-fashioned Sunday supplement style, related how "a handsome young sculptor" by the name of Mortimer Mellon had fallen in love with "the lovely Helen Maude Hake," a lady potter. She, alas, happened to be the "protégée" of Hugh Penniman, "the well-known philanthropist." Following a "wild party" at the pottery, the body of the "lovelorn sculptor" was found in the river, and a verdict of accidental death was pronounced by the coroner. Not satisfied with the disposition of the case, reporters from the *Fluxion* attempted to interview other artists at the pottery, but the "slovenly Bohemians" showed "an insolent lack of cooperation." Soon afterward the episode came to "its final tragic end" when "the lovely Helen" took her own life, following Mortimer "to a watery grave." She left a suicide note that was never made public.

Just as Qwilleran finished reading, he heard a thud at the opposite end of the room, and he turned to see a book with a red cover lying open and face down on the floor. With a softer thump Koko landed on the floor beside it and started nosing it across the slippery tile floor.

"Bad cat!" Qwilleran scolded. It was a library book—an old one, none too solid in the spine. "The librarian will have you shot! Bad cat!" Qwilleran repeated.

As he scowled his displeasure, he saw Koko slowly arch his back and flatten his ears. The cat's brown tail stiffened, and he began to step around the book in a strange long-legged dance. He circled the book once, twice, three times, and Qwilleran felt a chill in the pit of his stomach. Once before, in an icy courtyard, he had seen Koko perform that ritual. Once before, the cat had walked around and around and around, and the thing he circled was a body.

Now it was a book he was circling—an old red book titled *The Ancient Art of Potting*. The silence was broken only by the mournful sound of a boat whistle on the river.

NINE

BEFORE GOING TO bed Thursday night Qwilleran telephoned the *Fluxion*'s night man at police headquarters and asked him to check for unidentified bodies dragged from the river in the last forty-eight hours.

Kendall called back with the information. "There was one," he said. "Male. Caucasian. About sixty years old. Is that your boy?"

Qwilleran slept fitfully that night, and between his restless moments he dreamed about seaweed—great curtains of seaweed undulating with the motion of the waves. Then it became a head of green hair swirling in dirty brown water.

When he awoke in the morning he had a feeling that his bones had turned to jelly. He dressed wearily, ignoring the cats, and they seemed to sense that he was preoccupied; they kept out of his way. It was when he started downstairs for a steadying cup of coffee that he walked into the situation that stiffened his spirit. He met Robert Maus on the stairs.

The attorney stopped and faced him squarely, and the newsman saw that the black eye had faded to a banana-peel yellow. Maus gave the impression that he was about to say something momentous, and after a few long seconds it came out: "Mr. Qwilleran, do you, by any chance, have a moment of your valuable time to spare?"

"I guess so."

They went to Maus's apartment, a comfortable place done in English antiques and broccoli-green leather, with much polished brass and steel.

The attorney bowed and motioned Qwilleran to a Bank of England chair. "The matter I have to discuss," he said, "concerns Mrs. Graham. I find it somewhat, shall I say, painful to approach you in this manner, and you must not, under any circumstance, consider this an accusation or even a reproach. However . . . a matter has been brought to my attention, signifying that a word with you at this time would not be amiss—in consideration of the apprehensions I entertain concerning what I humbly describe as . . . the respectability of this establishment."

"What the devil is the problem?" Qwilleran demanded.

The attorney raised a protesting hand. "Nothing that could be termed—in any real and active sense—a problem, I assure you, but rather a situation that has been brought to my cognizance . . . and in apprising you of the fact I am seeking neither confirmation nor denial . . . my only interest being to maintain good relationships . . ."

"Okay, what's this all about?" Qwilleran snapped. "Let's have it!"

Maus paused as if counting to ten and then stated slowly and carefully, "Mr. Graham, whom you have met . . . is under the impression . . . that his wife received considerable financial aid from you . . . to make her departure possible. I am not, I repeat—"

Qwilleran jumped to his feet and walked impatiently across the Oriental rug. "How did I know she was going to run off? She was going to get a divorce. You know that as well as I do. And one of your legal buddies had his hand out for more than she could afford. And if Dan has a complaint, why doesn't he come and see me about it?"

Maus lowered the pitch of his voice and spoke apologetically. "He fears—whether with or without cause, I do not know—that a confrontation might, shall we say, impair his chances of favorable comment in the . . . publication you represent."

"Or—to put it more honestly—he's hoping his accusation will make me feel so guilty that I'll knock myself out to get a picture of his pots on the front page. It's not the first time I've run up against that simple-minded strategy. It's a stupid move, and I may get mad enough to forget the free publicity entirely. You can tell him that!"

Maus raised both hands. "Let us preserve our equanimity, at all costs, and bear in mind that my only motive in intervening is to prevent any taint of . . . scandal."

"You're apt to have something worse than scandal on your hands!" Qwilleran roared as he stormed out of the apartment.

He was still irritable when he arrived at the *Fluxion* to pick up his paycheck and open his mail. He went through his mail hopefully each day, and his pulse still skipped a beat every time the telephone jangled, although instinct told him there would be no word from Joy.

In the feature department he said to Riker, "Come on down to the coffee shop. I've got a few things to tell you."

"Before I forget it," the feature editor said, "would you attend a press luncheon this noon and write a few inches for tomorrow's paper? They're introducing a new product."

"What kind of product?"

"A new dog food."

"Dog food! Isn't that stretching my responsibilities as gourmet reporter?"

"Well, you haven't done anything else to earn your paycheck this week—not that I can see . . . Come on. What's on your mind?"

The *Fluxion* coffee shop was in the basement, and at midmorning it was the noisiest and therefore the most private conference room in the building. Newspaper deadlines being what they were, the compositors were having their dinner, the pressmen were having their lunch, the advertising representatives were having their first coffee break. The concrete-walled room shook with the roar of nearby presses; customers were shouting at one another; counter girls yelled orders; cooks barked replies; busboys slammed dishes; and a radio was bleating without an audience for the reason that it could not possibly be heard. The resulting din made the coffee shop highly desirable for confidential conversations; only mouth-to-ear shouts were audible.

The two men ordered coffee, and the feature editor asked for a chocolate-frosted doughnut as well. "What's up?" he shouted in Qwilleran's ear.

"About Dan Graham! That story he told!" Qwilleran shouted back. "I think it's a lie!"

"What story?"

"About Joy's hair getting caught in the wheel."

"Why would he lie?"

Qwilleran shook his head ominously. "I think something's happened to Joy. I don't think she ran away."

"But you saw a car—"

"Max Sorrel's! Fire at his restaurant!"

The waitress banged two coffees on the counter.

"This hunch of yours—" Riker yelled.

"Wretched thought!"

"Wretched *what?*"

"Wretched *thought!*"

"You don't mean . . ." The editor's face was pained.

"I don't know." Qwilleran touched his mustache nervously. "It's a possibility."

"But where's the body?"

"Maybe in the river!"

The two men stared into the depths of their coffee cups and let the deafening cacophony of the coffee shop assault their numb eardrums.

"Another thing!" Qwilleran shouted after a while. "Dan knows about my check! The seven-fifty!"

"How'd he find out?"

Qwilleran shrugged.

"What are you going to do?"

"Keep asking questions!"

Riker nodded gravely.

"Don't tell Rosie!"

"What?"

"*Don't tell Rosie!* Not yet!"

"Right!"

"Upset her!"

"Right!"

Qwilleran survived the dog food luncheon and wrote a mildly witty piece about it for the feature page, comparing the simplicity of canine cuisine with the gustatory demands of catdom.

Then he went home to feed Koko and Yum Yum, but first he stopped at a delicatessen. He hungrily eyed the onion rolls, chopped chicken livers, and pickled herring, but he steeled himself and bought only a chub for the cats. He had abandoned once and for all his experiment with canned cat food.

He had slipped a note under William's door that morning, inviting the houseboy to have dinner with him at a new restaurant called the Petrified Bagel, and now the young man met him in the Great Hall and accepted with glee.

"Let's leave about six-thirty," Qwilleran suggested. "Is that too early?"

"No, that's good," said William. "I have to go over to my mother's house after. You don't have a car, do you? We can take mine."

Qwilleran went upstairs, taking three of the stone steps at a time. Suddenly he was filled with an unwarranted exhilaration. The bewilderment was over; he had a job to do. Now that he felt certain his hunch was correct—now that he could proceed with his unofficial investigation—his spirit rose to the challenge. Instead of grief for Joy he felt a fierce loyalty to her memory. And it was the *memory* that he loved, he had to confess. It was Joy Wheatley, age nineteen, who had made his heart beat fast on Monday night—not Joy Graham. Two decades of separation made a difference, he now admitted, even though he had convinced himself for a few days that nothing had changed.

The cats caught his high-key mood and raced about the apartment—up on the bookcase, down to the floor, around the big chair, under the table, up on the captain's bunk—with Yum Yum in the lead and Koko following so close behind that they made a single blur of blond fir. Rounding a curve, she slowed for a fraction of a second, and Koko ran over her. Then she was chasing him.

Qwilleran dodged the hurtling bodies, removed his shoes, and stepped on the scale. He stepped off with a smile of satisfaction. It was a fine spring night. The ventilating panes in the big studio window were open, and the breeze was gentle. Somewhere in or around the building a man's voice could be heard, singing "Loch Lomond," and it gave Qwilleran a moment of nostalgia; it had been his father's favorite.

He met William in the Great Hall; the houseboy had dressed

for the occasion in a wrinkled sports coat the color of gravy. A long black limousine of ancient vintage stood quietly rumbling at the front door.

"Looks like a hearse," Qwilleran remarked.

"Best I could get for fifty dollars," William apologized. "I've been warming her up, because she takes a little coaxing before she starts to roll. Open the door easy, or it'll come off."

"Must cost you a fortune in gas."

"I don't use her that much, but she comes in handy for dates. Would you like to drive? Then I can hold the passenger door on."

With Qwilleran behind the wheel, Black Beauty moved majestically down the drive with the authoritative rumbling of a car with a defective muffler. Several times when he glanced in the rearview mirror, he thought he was being followed, but it was only the tail of the limousine looming up in the distance.

The restaurant was in that part of the city known as Junktown, a declining neighborhood that a few enterprising preservationists were trying to restore. A former antique shop on Zwinger Street was now making a brave comeback as a restaurant, and the Petrified Bagel was furnished, appropriately, with junk. Old kitchen chairs and tables, no two alike, were painted in mismatched colors, and the burlap-covered walls were decorated with relics from the city dump, while the waiters appeared to be derelicts recruited from Junktown's bars and alleys.

"The food may not be the greatest," Qwilleran told William, "but it should make a colorful story for my column."

"Who cares, when it's free?" was the houseboy's attitude.

They took a table against the wall, beneath an arrangement of rusty plumbing fixtures, and hardly had they pulled up their chairs when their waiter was upon them.

"What wudjus like?" he asked. "Wudjus like a drink from the bar?" He wore a black suit, a few sizes too large, and a crooked bow tie, and if he had shaved, he had done so with a butter knife.

William said he'd like a beer, and Qwilleran ordered a lemon and seltzer.

"Wudjus say that again?"

"A beer for the gentleman," Qwilleran said, "and I'll have some soda water with a squeeze of lemon." To William he said,

"I know this neighborhood. I used to live in the old Spencer mansion on this block—a historic house with a ghost."

"Honest? Did you ever see the ghost?"

"No, but some strange things happened, and it was hard to sort out the pranks of the disembodied lady from the pranks of my cats."

The waiter returned empty-handed. "Wudjus like sugar in that?"

"No, just lemon and soda water."

William said, "How are the cats doing with their typing lessons?"

"You'd never believe it, but Koko actually typed a word the other day. A rather elementary word, but . . ." Qwilleran looked up and caught the Irish twinkle in the houseboy's eye. "You *dog!*" Qwilleran said. "Is that what you were doing in my apartment Wednesday night? My spies saw you sneaking in."

William guffawed loudly. "I wondered how long it would be before you got the picture. I found some caviar in Mickey Maus's refrigerator and took it up to your cats. They liked it."

"Who wouldn't?"

The waiter brought the drinks. "Wudjus like something to go with it?"

Qwilleran shook his head. To William he said, "How did you hit it off with Koko and Yum Yum?"

"The little one ran away, but the big one came out, and we had a lengthy conversation. He talks even more than I do. I like cats. You can't boss them around."

"And you can't win, either. You may think you've put one over on them, but they always come out ahead."

"Wudjus like to see the menu?" The waiter was offering a grease-spotted folder covered in burlap.

"Later," said Qwilleran . . . "How's everything going at art school?"

William shrugged. "I'm going to quit. It's not my bag. My girl's an artist, and she wanted me to go there, but . . . I don't know. After I got out of the service I tried college, but it wasn't for me. You had to *study!* I'd sort of like to be a bartender. Or a waiter at a good place where you get king-size tips."

"Didjus want something?" asked the waiter, who was never out of earshot.

Qwilleran waved him away, but before the man left he re-arranged the sticky salt and pepper shakers and whisked an imaginary crumb off the plastic tablecloth.

"What I'd really like," William went on, "I'd like to be a private operator. I read a lot of detective stories, and I think I'd be pretty good at it."

"Investigative work fascinates me, too," Qwilleran confided. "I used to cover the crime beat in Chicago and New York."

"You did? Did you cover any big cases? Did you cover the Valentine's Day massacre?"

"I'm not *that* old, sonny."

"Didn't you ever want to be a detective yourself?"

"Not really." Qwilleran preened his mustache. "But a reporter sharpens his faculty for observation and gets in the habit of asking questions. I've been asking myself questions ever since I came to Maus Haus."

"Like what?"

"Who screamed at three-thirty Wednesday morning? Why was the pottery door locked? How did Maus get his black eye? What happened to Joy Graham's cat? What's happened to Joy Graham?"

"You think something's happened to her?"

The waiter was hovering around the table. "Wudjus like to order now?"

Qwilleran took a deep breath of exasperation. "Yes, bring me some escargots, vichyssoise, boeuf Bourguignon, and a small salade Niçoise."

There was a long silence, then, "Wudjus say that again?"

"Never mind," said Qwilleran. "Just bring me a frozen hamburger, gently warmed, and some canned peas."

William ordered cream of mushroom soup, pot roast with mashed potatoes, and salad with Thousand Island dressing. "Say, is it true you used to be engaged to her?" he asked Qwilleran.

"Joy? That was a long time ago. Who told you?"

William looked wise. "I found out, that's all. Do you still like her?"

"Of course. But not in the same way."

"A lot of people at Maus Haus like her. Ham Hamilton was

nuts about her. I think that's why he had himself transferred—to stay out of trouble."

Qwilleran groomed his mustache; another possible clue was gnawing at his upper lip. "Did you hear anything or notice anything unusual the night she disappeared?"

"No, I played gin with Rosemary until ten o'clock. Then she had to take her beauty treatment on her slant board, so I tried to find Hixie, but she was out. I watched TV for a while. Once I heard Dan's car pull out of the carport, but I was in bed by midnight. I have an early class on Wednesdays."

The waiter brought the soup. "Wudjus like some crackers?"

"By the way," Qwilleran asked the houseboy, "do you know what they mean by a 'slob potter'? I've heard Dan called a slob potter."

William's explosive laugh rang through the restaurant. "You mean *slab* potter, although you're not so very far off base. Dan rolls out the clay in flat slabs and builds square and rectangular pieces that way."

"Do you think he's good?"

"Who am I to say? I'm *really* a slob potter . . . This is crummy soup."

"Is it canned?"

"No, worse! It tastes like I made it."

"Dan says he's aiming for big things in New York and Europe."

"Yeah, I know. And I guess he means it. He got a passport in the mail last week."

"He did? How do you know?"

"I was there when the mail came. I *guess* it was a passport. It was in a thick brown envelope that said 'Passport Office' or something like that in the corner."

The waiter served the main course. "Wudjus like ketchup?"

"No ketchup," said Qwilleran. "No mustard. No steak sauce. No chili sauce."

William said, "If you want to see Mickey Maus have a cat fit, just mention ketchup."

"I hear Maus is a widower. What happened to his wife?"

"She choked to death a couple of years ago. They say she choked on a bone in the chicken Marengo. She was a lot older than Mickey Maus. I think he likes older women. Look at Charlotte!"

"What about Charlotte?"

"I mean, the way he butters her up all the time. At first I thought Charlotte was his mother. Max thinks she's his mistress. Hixie says Mickey Maus is the illegitimate son of Charlotte and that old guy who started the Heavenly Hash business." William howled with merriment.

"I hear Max is having a rough time at the Golden Lamb Chop."

"Too bad. I've got my theories about that, too."

"Like what?"

"Like he goes for chicks, you know, on a wholesale scale. And he doesn't bother to play by the rules."

"You think there might be a jealous husband in the picture?"

"It's just a guess. Hey, why don't you and I open a detective agency? It wouldn't take much capital . . . Look out! Here comes Professor Moriarty again."

"Wudjus like some more butter?" asked the waiter.

For a while Qwilleran concentrated on his hamburger, which had been grilled to the consistency of a steel-belted radial tire, and William concentrated on satisfying his youthful appetite.

"I have to get up at six tomorrow morning," he remarked. "Gotta go to the farmers' market with Mickey."

"I wouldn't mind going along," Qwilleran said. "It might be a story."

"Never been there? It's a gas! Just meet us in the kitchen at six-thirty. Want me to call you?"

"Thanks, but I've got an alarm clock. Three of them, counting the cats."

William ordered strawberry cheesecake for dessert. "Best wallpaper paste I've ever eaten," he said.

Qwilleran ordered black coffee, which was served in a mug with the flavor of detergent lingering on the rim. "By the way," he said, "did you ever watch Joy Graham when she was using the wheel?"

His guest nodded, his mouth full of cheesecake.

"Which wheel did she use?"

"The kick-wheel. Why?"

"Never the electric?"

"No, she has to do everything the hard way, when it comes to pottery. Don't ask me why. I know she's a friend of yours, but she does some wacky things."

"She always did."

"Know what I overheard at the dinner last Monday? She was talking to Tweedledee and Tweedledum—"

"The Penniman brothers?"

William nodded. "She was trying to sell them some old papers she found in the pottery somewhere. She said they could have them for *five thousand dollars!*"

"She was kidding," Qwilleran said, without conviction.

They left the Petrified Bagel after the waiter's final solicitation: "Wudjus like a toothpick?"

Qwilleran went home on the bus. William was going to visit his mother.

"It's her birthday," the houseboy explained, "and I've bought her some cheap perfume. It doesn't matter what you give her; she makes insulting remarks about everything, so what's the use?"

In the Great Hall at Maus Haus, Dan was again working on the exhibit, pushing and pulling massive tables and benches into position for the display of pots. He was humming "Loch Lomond."

Qwilleran forgot his morning irritation with the publicity-seeking potter. "Here, let me help you," he offered.

Dan looked at Qwilleran warily, and his mouth dropped open. "Sorry if I said anything to get you riled up. I didn't know Maus would go blabbing it around."

"No harm done."

"It's your money. It's your business what you do with it, I guess."

"Forget it."

"Got a postcard today," Dan said. "Mailed from Cincinnati."

Qwilleran gulped twice before answering. "From your wife? How's everything?" He tried to speak casually. "Will she be back for the champagne party?"

"Guess not. She wants me to mail her summer duds to her in Miami."

"Miami!"

"Yep. Guess she's going to soak up some sunshine before she

comes home. Do her some good. Give her a chance to think things over."

"No bad feeling, then?"

Dan scratched his head. "Husband and wife have to keep their identity, especially when they're artists. She'll get rid of that fuzzy feeling and come back, sassy as ever. We have our blowups; what couple doesn't?" He smiled his twisted smile, so much an imitation of Joy's smile that Qwilleran felt his flesh crawl. It was grotesque.

"It's a funny thing," Dan went on. "I used to ride her all the time about shedding hair all over the place. If it wasn't cat hairs floating around, it was her own—long ones—turning up in the clay and everywhere else. But you wanta know something? I kinda miss those aggravations when she's away. You ever been married?"

"I had a go at it once."

"Why don't you come up for a drink tomorrow night? Come on up to the loft."

"Thanks. I'll do that."

"Might give you a sneak preview of the exhibition. Don't mind telling you I've come up with some dandies that'll rock 'em back on their heels. When you see your art critic, put a bug in his ear, if you know what I mean."

Qwilleran went up to Number Six, massaging his mustache as he climbed the stairs. The cats were alert and waiting for him.

"Well, what do you think of *that* development, Koko?" he said. "She's off to Miami."

"Yow!" Koko replied—ambiguously, Qwilleran thought.

"She hates Florida! She told us so, didn't she? And she's always been allergic to sunlight."

And then Qwilleran had a second thought. Perhaps his $750 check had financed a vacation with that food buyer—Fish, Ham, or whatever his name was—in the Sunshine State! Once again Qwilleran felt like a fool.

TEN

When Qwilleran's alarm went off on Saturday morning, it was still dark and chill, and he debated whether to fulfill his intentions or forget about the farmers' market and go back to sleep. Curiosity and a newsman's relish for an unfamiliar situation convinced him to get up.

He showered and dressed hastily and diced round steak for the cats, who were asleep in the big chair, stretched out in do-not-disturb postures.

By six-thirty Qwilleran was downstairs in the kitchen, where Robert Maus was breaking eggs into a bowl. "Hope you don't mind," Qwilleran said. "I've invited myself to go to the farmers' market with you."

"Consider yourself more than welcome, to be sure," the attorney said. "Please be good enough to help yourself to orange juice and coffee. I am preparing . . . an omelet."

"Where's William?"

Maus took a deep breath before replying. "With William, I regret to say, it is a point of honor to be late for any and all occasions."

He poured the beaten eggs into the omelet pan, shook it vigorously, stirred with a fork, folded the shimmering yellow creation, flipped it onto a warm plate, grated some white pepper over the top, and glazed it with butter.

It was the best omelet Qwilleran had ever tasted. With each tender, creamy mouthful he recalled the dry, brown, leathery imitations he had eaten in second-class restaurants. Maus prepared another omelet for himself and sat down at the table.

"I hate to see our friend William missing this good breakfast," said Qwilleran. "Maybe he overslept. Maybe I should hammer on his door."

He found William's room at the end of the kitchen corridor and knocked once, twice, then louder, without getting any response. He turned the knob gently and opened the door an inch or two. "William!" he shouted. "It's after six-thirty!" There was no sound from within. He peered into the room. The built-in bunk was empty, and the bedspread was neatly tucked under the mattress.

Qwilleran glanced around the room. The bathroom door stood open. He tried another door, which proved to be a small, untidy closet. The entire place was in mild disorder, with clothes and magazines scattered in all the wrong places.

He returned to the breakfast table. "Not there. His bed looks as if he hasn't slept in it, and the alarm clock hasn't been set. I took him out to dinner last night, and he was going to his mother's house afterward. Do you suppose he stayed there?"

"Basing an opinion on what I know about the relationship between William and his mother," said Maus, "I would . . . deem it more likely that he spent the night with the young lady to whom he appears to be . . . engaged. I suggest you wear boots this morning, Mr. Qwilleran. The market manufactures an exclusive brand of . . . mud, composed of wilted cabbage leaves, rotted tomatoes, crushed grapes, and an unidentifiable liquid that binds them together in a slimy black . . . amalgam."

The men started for the market in the attorney's old Mercedes, and as they circled the driveway, Qwilleran thought he saw the enormous tail fins of William's limousine protruding from the carport on the other side of the house.

"I think William's car is there," he remarked. "If he didn't come home last night, how did his car get back?"

"The ways of the young," said Maus, "are incomprehensible. I have ceased all attempts to understand their behavior."

It was true about the mud. A black ooze filled the gutters and splashed up over the sidewalks of the open-air market. There were several square blocks of open sheds where farmers and other vendors sold directly from their trucks. Rich and poor streamed through the cluttered aisles, carrying shopping bags, pushing baby buggies loaded with pots of geraniums, pulling red express wagons filled with produce, or maneuvering chrome-plated, rubber-tired shopping carts through the crowded aisles.

A pickpocket's heaven, Qwilleran thought.

There were women with rollers in their hair, children riding piggyback, distinguished old men in velvet-collared coats, Indian girls with tweed jackets over their filmy saris, teenagers wearing earphones, suburban housewives swaddled in fun furs, and more than the average number of immensely fat women.

Maus led the way between mountains of rhubarb and acres of fresh eggs, past the gallon jugs of honey, the whole pigs, bunches of sassafras, pillows filled with chicken feathers, carrots as big as baseball bats, white doves in cages, and purple cauliflower.

It was a nippy morning, and the vendors stamped their feet and warmed their hands over coke fires burning in oil drums. The smoke mingled with the aromas of apples, livestock, lilacs, and market mud. Qwilleran noticed a blind man with a white cane standing near the lilacs, sniffing and smiling.

Maus bought mushrooms, fern shoots, scallions, Florida corn, and California strawberries. It amazed the newsman to hear him haggling over the price of a turnip. "My dear woman, if you can afford to sell a dozen for three dollars, how can you—in all decency—ask thirty cents for one?" asked the man who served a ten-dollar bottle of wine with the jellied clams.

At one stall Maus selected a skinned rabbit, and Qwilleran turned away while the farmer wrapped the red, stiffened carcass in a sheet of newspaper and the white-furred relatives of the deceased looked on with reproach.

"Mrs. Marron, I must admit, makes an excellent hasenpfeffer," Maus explained. "She will prepare the . . . viands this weekend while I attend a gourmet conclave out of town . . . for which I happen to be the . . . master of ceremonies."

From the open-air market they went into the general market,

a vast arena with hundreds of stalls under one roof and a soft carpet of sawdust underfoot. Hucksters with hoarse voices offered spiced salt belly, strudel dough, chocolate tortes, plaster figures of saints, quail eggs, voodoo potions, canned grape leaves, octopus, and perfumed floor wash guaranteed to bring good luck. A nickel-plated machine ground fresh peanut butter. A phonograph played harem music at a record stall. Maus bought snails and some Dutch mustard seed.

For a moment Qwilleran closed his eyes and tried to sort out the heady mix of smells: freshly ground coffee, strong cheese, garlic sausage, anise, dried codfish, incense. A wave of cheap perfume reached his nostrils, and he opened his eyes to see a Gypsy woman looking at him from a nearby stall. She smiled, and he blinked his eyes. She had Joy's smile, Joy's tiny figure, and Joy's long hair, but her face was a hundred years old. Her clothes were soiled, and her hair looked as if it had never been washed.

"Tell the fortune?" she invited.

Fascinated by this cruel caricature, Qwilleran nodded.

"You sit."

He sat on an upended beer case, and the woman sat opposite, shuffling a deck of dirty cards.

"How much?" he asked.

"Dollar. One dollar, yes?"

She laid out the cards in a cross and studied them. "I see water. You take long trip—boat—soon, yes?"

"Not very likely," Qwilleran said. "What else do you see?"

"Somebody sick. You get letter . . . I see money. Lotsa money. You like."

"Don't we all?"

"Young boy—your son? Some day great man. Big doctor."

"Where is my childhood sweetheart? Can you tell me that?"

"Hmmm . . . she far away—happy—lotsa children."

"You're phenomenal. You're a genius," Qwilleran grumbled. "Anything else?"

"I see water—so much water. You no like. Everybody wet."

Qwilleran escaped from the Gypsy's booth and caught up with his landlord. "Better fix the roof," he told him. "There's going to be another biblical-type flood." He shook himself, as if he might have picked up fleas.

When the two men carried their market purchases into the kitchen at Maus Haus, Mrs. Marron said to Qwilleran, "A man from the newspaper called. He said you should call him. Mr. Piper. Art Piper."

"Where've you been?" Arch Riker demanded when Qwilleran got him on the phone. "Out all night?"

"I've been to the farmers' market, getting material for a column, and I expect to collect time-and-a-half for getting up at an ungodly hour on my day off. What's on your mind?"

"I wish you'd help me out, Qwill. Would you drive to Rattlesnake Lake to act as one of the judges in a contest?"

"Bathing beauties?"

"No. Cake-baking. It's the statewide thing sponsored by the John Stuart Flour Mills. They do a lot of advertising, and we promised we'd send one of the judges."

"Why can't the food editor do it?" Qwilleran snapped.

"She's in the hospital."

"Been eating her own cooking?"

"Qwill, you're crabby today. What's wrong with you?"

"To tell you the truth, Arch, I'd like to stick around here this weekend—to see what I can dig up. Joy's husband invited me in for a drink tonight. I don't want to talk about it on the phone, but you know what we discussed in the coffee shop."

"I know, Qwill, but we're in a jam. You can take some time off next week."

"Can't the women's department handle this contest?"

"They've got a lot of spring weddings to cover. You could make a nice weekend of it, take a company car and drive up this afternoon. You could have a nice dinner at the Rattlesnake Inn —they're famous for their food—and come back tomorrow night."

"They're famous for their bad food, not famous for their good food," Qwilleran objected. "Besides, how can I enjoy a dinner anywhere and stay on my diet? How can I judge a cake contest and lose any weight?"

"You'll figure something out. You're an old pro," said Riker.

"I'll make a deal with you," Qwilleran said after a moment's hesitation. "I'll go to Rattlesnake Lake if you'll send me Odd Bunsen on Monday to shoot pictures in the pottery."

"You think it's a story? We've done potteries before. They all look alike."

"It may not make a story, but I want an excuse to get in there and prowl around." The newsman smoothed his mustache with his knuckles. "We've had another mysterious disappearance, Arch. This time it's the houseboy."

There was silence from Riker as he weighed the alternatives. "Well . . . I'll requisition a photographer, but I can't guarantee you'll get Bunsen."

"I don't want anyone else. It's got to be a nut like Bunsen."

At noon, when Qwilleran reported downstairs for lunch, he asked if anyone had seen William.

Hixie, who was busy chewing, shook her head.

Dan said, "Nope."

Rosemary remarked that it was unusual for William to miss market day.

Mrs. Marron said, "He was supposed to wax the floors today."

Charlotte Roop was engrossed in her crossword puzzle and said nothing.

Mrs. Marron was serving home-baked beans with brown bread and leftover ham, and Dan looked at the fare with distaste. "What's for dinner?" he demanded.

"Some nice roast chicken and wild rice."

"Chicken *again?* We just had it on Monday."

"And a nice coconut custard pie."

"I don't like coconut. It gets in my teeth," he said, making a sandwich of brown bread and ham.

"And tomorrow a nice rabbit stew," the housekeeper added.

"Ecch!"

"Mrs. Marron," Qwilleran interrupted, "these baked beans are delicious."

She gave him a grateful glance. "It's because I use an old bean pot. Forty years old, Mr. Maus says. It was made right here in the pottery, and it's signed on the bottom—H.M.H."

"That must have been about the time the sculptor was murdered," Qwilleran remarked.

"It was an accidental drowning," Miss Roop corrected him, looking up briefly from her puzzle.

"Nobody really believes that," said Hixie, and then she recited in a singsong voice:

> *"A potty young sculptor, Mort Mellon,*
> *Fell in love with a pottress named Helen,*
> *But the pottery gods frowned*
> *And he promptly got drowned.*
> *Who pushed him the potters ain't tellin'."*

Miss Roop lifted her chin. "That's very disrespectful, Miss Rice."

"Who cares?" Hixie retorted. "They're all dead."

"Mr. Maus would not like it, if he were here."

"But he's not here. By now he's halfway to Miami."

"*Miami?*" Qwilleran echoed.

Mrs. Marron brought him some more ham, which he regretfully declined, although he accepted some scraps for his roommates. "By the way," he said to her, "I'm going to be out of town overnight. Would you be good enough to feed my cats tomorrow morning?"

"I don't know much about cats," she said. "Is there anything special I have to do?"

"Just dice some meat for them and give them fresh water. And be absolutely sure they don't get out of the apartment." To the others at the table he said, "I have an assignment at Rattlesnake Lake. Dan, I'll have to take a rain check on your invitation, but we might be lucky enough to get a photographer here on Monday."

Dan grunted and nodded.

Qwilleran went on: "I hate the thought of the long drive up to the lake in a company car. The *Fluxion* seems to have bought a whole fleet of lemons."

A soft voice at his left said, "Would you like company? I'd be happy to go along for the ride. You could drive my car." The newsman turned and looked into the eyes of Rosemary Whiting —the quiet one, the thoughtful one who had brought the cats a ball of yarn. Her brown eyes were filled with an expression he could not immediately identify. He had not realized she was so attractive—her eyes dancing with health, her skin like whipped cream, her dark hair glossy.

Having hesitated too long, he said hurriedly, "Sure! Sure! I'd be grateful for your company. If we leave right after lunch, we'll have time for a leisurely drive and a good dinner at the inn. I have to judge a contest, but it doesn't take place until tomorrow afternoon, so we can sleep late tomorrow and stop somewhere for a bite to eat on the way home."

Miss Roop went on working her crossword puzzle with her lips frozen in a thin, straight line.

ELEVEN

"KOKO DIDN'T WANT me to make this trip," Qwilleran told Rosemary, as they drove away from Maus Haus in her dark blue compact. "As soon as I got out my luggage, he started to scold."

He glanced at his passenger. At Maus Haus he had guessed her age to be about thirty, but seeing her in daylight he increased his estimate to forty—a young forty.

"You look wonderful," he said. "That wheat germ you sprinkle on everything must agree with you. How long have you had your health food shop?"

"Two years," she said. "After my husband died, I sold the house and moved downtown and invested the money in the business."

"Any children?"

"Two sons. They're both doctors."

Qwilleran sneaked another look at his passenger and did some simple arithmetic. Forty-five? Fifty?

"Tell me," Rosemary said. "What brought you to Maus Haus?"

He told her about his new assignment, the invitation to attend a gourmet dinner given by Robert Maus, and his unexpected reunion with Joy Graham, an old friend.

She said, "I guessed it was more than a casual acquaintance."

"You're very discerning. Joy and I were planning to marry at one time, many years ago." He jammed on the brakes. "Sorry," he apologized. "Did you see that stupid cat? It strolled casually across the highway, and as soon as it reached safety, it ran like the devil."

"I hope you didn't think I was awfully bold to invite myself on this trip, Mr. Qwilleran."

"Not at all. I'm delighted. I wish I'd thought of it first. And please call me Qwill. I'm certainly not going to call you Mrs. Whiting all weekend."

"I had a reason for wanting to come. There's something I want to discuss with you, but not right now. I'd like to enjoy the scenery."

As they drove through the countryside, Rosemary observed and remarked about every cider mill, gravel pit, corn crib, herd of cattle, stone barn, and split-rail fence. She had a pleasant voice, and Qwilleran found her company relaxing. By the time they reached Rattlesnake Inn, he was experiencing a comfortable contentment. She remarked that it would be nice if they could have adjoining rooms. It was going to be a good weekend, he told himself.

The inn was a rickety frame structure that should have burned down half a century before. Weeping willows drooped over the edge of the lake, and canoes glided over its glassy surface. Before dinner Qwilleran rented a flat-bottomed boat and rowed Rosemary across the lake and back. During the cocktail hour they danced—Qwilleran's nameless, formless, ageless dance step that he had invented twenty-five years before and had not bothered to update.

"I think I'll celebrate," he said. "I'm going off my diet tonight."

Although Rattlesnake Inn was not celebrated for the quality of its food, it was unsurpassed in terms of quantity. The hors d'oeuvre table presented thirty different appetizers, all of them mashed up and flavored with the same pickle juice. The menu offered a choice of ten steaks, all uniformly tender, expensive, and flavorless. The shrimp cocktails were huge and leathery. An impressive assortment of rolls, biscuits, and muffins came to the table in bun-warmers that were ice cold. The baked potatoes wore foil jackets firmly glued to the skin, except for minute fragments of foil mashed into the interior. The Rattlesnake Inn served asparagus that tasted like Brussels sprouts and spinach that tasted like old dishrags. Individual wooden salad bowls, twelve inches in diameter and rancid with age, were heaped with anemic lettuce and wedges of synthetic tomato. But the speciality of the house was the dessert buffet with twenty-seven cream pies from instant vanilla pudding.

Yet, such was the magic of the occasion that neither Qwilleran nor Rosemary thought to complain about the food.

While they were lingering over cups of what the Rattlesnake Inn called coffee, Rosemary came to the point. "I want to talk to you about William," she said. "We've become good friends. A young man needs an older woman for a confidante—not his mother. Don't you agree?"

Qwilleran nodded.

"William has some good qualities. He lacks direction, but I have always been confident that he will find himself eventually. I know he thinks highly of you, and that's why I'm telling you this . . . I'm worried about him. I'm alarmed at his absence."

Qwilleran stroked his mustache. "What's the reason for your alarm?"

"He came home about eleven o'clock last night, after going to see his mother, and he stopped in my apartment and told me a few things."

"What kind of things?"

"Well, he's a very inquisitive person . . ."

"That I know."

"And he's been questioning some of the recent incidents at Maus Haus. He thinks there is more to them than meets the eye."

"Did he mention anything specifically?"

"He told me he thought he 'had something' on Dan Graham and he was going to investigate. He fancies himself a detective, you know, and he reads all those crime stories. I told him not to meddle."

"You have no idea what sort of malfeasance he suspected?"

"No, he just said he was going to visit Dan last night and sponge a nightcap; he thought he might come up with some evidence."

"Did he go?"

"As far as I know. And this morning . . ."

"No William," said Qwilleran. "I went looking for him, and his bed hadn't been slept in, I'm sure of that."

"And yet his car is in the carport . . . I don't know . . . No one else seems to be concerned. Mr. Maus says he's impetuous. Mrs. Marron says he's unreliable. What do you think, Qwill?"

"If he isn't there when we get home tomorrow night, we'll make some inquiries. Do you know how to get in touch with his mother?"

"She's in the phone book, I suppose. William also has a fiancée—or whatever."

"Do you think he might have gone off somewhere with her? Do we know who she is or where to reach her?"

Rosemary shook her head, and they both fell silent. After a while Qwilleran said, "I've been doing a little worrying myself. About Joy Graham. Was she interested in that food buyer? Would she go to Miami to be with him?"

"Mr. Hamilton? I don't think so. She has an exhibition coming up, and she's terribly dedicated to her art."

"Dan said he got a postcard, and she's on her way to Miami; she wants her summer clothes shipped down there. She happened to tell me she hates Florida, so I don't know what to believe. How do you size up her husband, Rosemary?"

"I'm sorry, but I've never liked that man, and I'm sure the others feel the same way. Haven't you noticed the chill that falls on the conversation whenever Dan opens his mouth?"

"You know about the nasty situation at the Golden Lamb Chop," Qwilleran said. "Did that start after the Grahams arrived at Maus Haus?"

"I believe it did."

"Do you suppose Dan could be responsible? He's the jealous type."

"I really don't think there's anything going on between Joy and Max. They're too friendly in public. If they were having an affair, they'd be carefully ignoring each other at the dinner table. Besides, I think Max is too fastidious to have affairs. He never even shakes hands with anyone, male or female." She stopped to giggle. "William says Max is the kind who dries his toothbrush with a hair blower."

Qwilleran pulled on his pipe, and Rosemary sipped the stuff

in her coffee cup. After a while she said, "Did it ever occur to you that Mr. Maus is a lonely and unhappy man?"

"I don't know why he should be," said Qwilleran. "He has his French knives and his eight-burner stove."

"You're not being serious," she chided. "His wife is dead, you know, and his heart isn't in the law business; he should be running a fine restaurant. On Tuesday night, after I'd had dinner at my son's house, I came home after midnight and saw a light in the kitchen, so I went in to investigate. There was Mr. Maus sitting at the table with his head in his hands. He was holding a piece of raw meat on his eye."

"Filet mignon, of course."

"All right. I won't tell you the rest of it."

"Please. I'm sorry."

"Well, he told me he'd been sitting on the bench down by the river and tripped on the boardwalk when he started to leave. Don't you think that's rather sad—sitting down by the river all alone?"

"He had a different explanation for me," Qwilleran said. "Would you like to dance? I'm a sad, lonely, unhappy man, too."

They danced slowly and thoughtfully, and Qwilleran was thinking of suggesting a walk in the moonlight when he was suddenly overcome by complete exhaustion. His shoulders sagged; his face felt drawn. He had been up since dawn, tramping around the farmers' market, and then there had been the long drive, followed by boating (he hadn't rowed a boat for fifteen years) and then dancing and a large meal . . .

"Are you tired?" Rosemary asked. "You've had a long day. Why don't we go upstairs?"

Qwilleran agreed gratefully.

"Would you like me to massage your neck and shoulders?" she asked. "It will relax you, and you'll sleep beautifully. But first a hot bath, so you won't have sore muscles after all that rowing."

She drew the bath for him, coloring the water lettuce green with mineral salts, and after he had soaked the prescribed twenty minutes, she produced a bottle of lotion that smelled faintly of cucumber. The soothing massage, the aromatic lotion, and Rosemary's murmured phrases that he only half heard made him drowsy. He felt—he wondered—he wanted to say—

but he was so relaxed . . . so sleepy . . . perhaps tomorrow . . .

It was noon when Qwilleran awoke on Sunday and learned
that Rosemary had been up since seven and had hiked around
the lake. They lunched hurriedly and reported to the ballroom
for the cake-judging, only to discover that the plans had been
changed. The judging had taken place before noon to accommodate the television crews. However, Qwilleran was towed around
the ballroom by a public relations person to meet the beaming
winners.

He congratulated the grandmotherly creator of the inside-out
marble mocha whipped cream cake, the vivacious young matron
with her brazil nut caramel angel cake, the delicate young man
who was so proud of his sour cream chocolate velvet icebox cake,
and finally the winner in the teenage class. She was a tiny girl
with long straight hair and a wistful smile, and she had con-
cocted a psychedelic cake. Qwilleran stared at the conglomeration of chocolate, nuts, marshmallows, strawberries, and coconut
—the banana split cake of twenty-five years ago. He looked at
the girl and saw Joy.

"Let's get out of here," he whispered to Rosemary. "I'm seeing ghosts."

They drove home in the late evening—both of them relaxed
and content to talk or not to talk as the mood prevailed—and it
was midnight when they walked into the Great Hall at Maus
Haus.

"When can I take you out to dinner again?" he asked Rosemary. "How about Tuesday evening?"

"I'd love to," she said, "but I have to attend a recital. One of
my grandsons is playing the violin."

"You have a *grandson?*"

"I have three grandchildren."

"I can't believe you're a grandmother! This violinist must be
an infant prodigy."

"He's twelve," said Rosemary as they started to climb the
stairs. "He's the youngest. The other two are in college."

Qwilleran gazed at the grandmother-of-three with admiration.
"You'd better get me some of that wheat germ," he said. She
smiled sweetly and triumphantly, and Qwilleran dropped the
suitcases and kissed her.

At that moment they heard an outcry. Mrs. Marron came running from the kitchen corridor. She burst into tears.

Rosemary ran downstairs and put an arm around the housekeeper. "What is it, Mrs. Marron? What's wrong?"

"Something—something terrible," the woman wailed. "I don't know how to tell you."

Qwilleran hurried down the stairs. "Is it William? What's happened?"

Mrs. Marron gave him a terrified glance and launched another torrent of tears. "It's the cats!" she wailed. "They took sick."

"*What!*" Qwilleran started to bolt up the stairs three at a time but suddenly stopped. "Where are they?"

Mrs. Marron groaned. "They were—they were taken away."

"Where?" he demanded. "To the vet? Which one? To the hospital?"

She shook her head and covered her face with her hands. "I called . . . I called the . . . Sanitation Department. They're dead!"

"*Dead!* They can't be! *Both* of them? They were perfectly all right. What happened?"

The housekeeper was too shaken to answer. She could only moan.

"Were they poisoned? They must have been poisoned! Who went near them?" He took Mrs. Marron by the shoulders and shook her. "Who got into my apartment? What did you feed them?"

She moved her head miserably from side to side.

"By God!" Qwilleran said, "If it was poison, I'll kill the one who did it!"

TWELVE

QWILLERAN PACED THE floor of his apartment. Rosemary had offered to sit with him, but he had sent her away.

"My God! The Sanitation Department!" he said aloud, slapping his forehead with the palm of his hand. "Not even a chance to—I could have—at least I could have buried them with some kind of dignity." He stopped, aware that he was talking to the four walls. He was accustomed to an audience. They had been such attentive listeners, such satisfactory companions, always ready to supply encouragement, entertainment, or solace, depending on his mood, which they had been able to sense unerringly. And now they were gone. He could not come to terms with the idea.

"The Sanitation Department!" he said again with a groan. Now he remembered: Koko had not wanted him to take the weekend trip. Perhaps the cat had an intimation of danger. The thought made Qwilleran's grief all the more painful. His hands were clenched, his forehead damp. He was ready to destroy the beast who had destroyed those two innocent creatures. But where could he pin the blame? And how could he prove anything? Without the two small bodies he could never prove poison. But someone must have entered his apartment during his absence. Who? The only tenants in the house over the weekend, besides Mrs. Marron, were Max Sorrel, Charlotte Roop, Hixie, and Dan Graham. And perhaps William, if he had returned.

Qwilleran picked up the cats' empty food plate and sniffed it. He took a sip from their water dish and spit it out. He smelled nothing unusual, tasted nothing suspicious. But he heard footsteps coming up the stairs. It would be Maus, he decided, returning from his weekend in Miami.

Qwilleran threw open his door and stepped into the hall to confront his landlord. It was not Maus; it was Max Sorrel.

"Man, what's wrong with you?" Sorrel said. "You look like you've got the d.t.'s."

"Did you hear what happened to my cats?" Qwilleran bellowed. "I went away overnight, and they took sick and died. At least, that's the story I got."

"Damn shame! I know how you felt about those little monkeys."

"I'll tell you one thing! I'm not satisfied with the explanation. I think they were poisoned! And whoever did it is going to regret it!"

Sorrel shook his head. "I don't know. I think there's a jinx on this house. First the housekeeper and then me and then—"

"What do you mean? What about the housekeeper?" Qwilleran demanded.

"Tragic! Really tragic! Her grandson came to visit—little kid *this high*—and he fell in the river. Loose board in the boardwalk, they think . . . Look, Qwilleran, you need a slug of whiskey. Come on in and have a shot."

"No, thanks," said Qwilleran wearily. "I've got to work it out in my own way."

He returned to Number Six and gazed at the emptiness. He wanted to move out. He would leave tomorrow. Go to a hotel. He made note of the things he would no longer need: the harness and leash hanging on the back of a chair; the blue cushion; the brush he had bought and forgotten to use; the cats' commode in the bathroom with the gravel neatly scratched into one corner. They had been so meticulous about their housekeeping. Qwilleran's eyes grew moist.

Knowing he would be unable to sleep, he sat down at his typewriter to turn out a column for the paper—a requiem for two lost friends. Putting it down on paper would relive the pain, he knew. Now would be the time to reveal to the public Koko's remarkable capabilities. He had solved three mysteries—homicide cases. He was probably the only cat in the country who owned a press card signed by the chief of police. Qwilleran rested his hands on the typewriter keys and wondered how to start, and as his mind swam in an ocean of words—none of them adequate—his eyes fell on the sheet of paper in the machine. There were two letters typed there: pb.

The newsman felt a chill in the roots of his mustache: *poisoned beef!*

Just then he heard a distant cry. He listened sharply. It sounded like a child's cry. He thought of the drowned boy and shuddered. The cry came again, louder, and in the darkness outside the window there was a pale form hovering. Qwilleran rubbed his eyes and stared in disbelief. There was a scratching at the window.

"Koko!" the man yelled, yanking open the casement.

The cat hopped down onto the desk, followed by Yum Yum, both of them blinking at the lamplight. They made no sign of greeting but jumped to the floor and trotted to the kitchen, looking for their dinner plate. Avidly they lapped up water from their bowl.

"You're starved!" Qwilleran said. "How long have you been out there? . . . Sanitation Department! What's wrong with that woman? She was hallucinating!" He hurried to open a can of red salmon and watched them as they gobbled it. There was no observation of feline protocol this time, no nonsense about males before females; Yum Yum fought for her share.

Now Qwilleran dropped into his armchair, feeling an overwhelming fatigue. The cats finished eating, washed their faces, and then climbed into his lap together—something they had never done before. Their feet and tails were cold. They crawled up Qwilleran's chest and lay on their bellies, side by side, looking into his face. Their eyes were large and anxious.

He hugged them both. He hugged Yum Yum tightly because he remembered how—in his first frenzied reaction to the bad news—his concern had been chiefly for Koko. He reproached himself now. He cherished them both equally, and if he valued Koko for his special talents, he also valued Yum Yum for her winning ways and the heartbreaking way she looked at him with slightly crossed eyes. In apology he hugged her more tightly.

To Koko he said, "And I don't care if you never solve another case."

There was a definite odor about the cats. He sniffed their fur. It smelled earthy.

After a while they warmed their extremities and felt contented enough to purr, and eventually they dozed, still huddled on Qwilleran's chest. He fell asleep himself and woke at daybreak, his shoulders stiff and his neck virtually paralyzed. The cats had moved to more comfortable berths elsewhere.

At first he had difficulty convincing himself that the panic of the night before had not been a nightmare, but as he took a hot shower he remembered the pleasures of the weekend as well as the pain he had felt upon arriving home. On his way down to breakfast he slipped a note under Rosemary's door: "False alarm! Cats are home. Just wandered away. Mrs. M. is crazy."

In the kitchen he found only Hixie, scrambling eggs and toasting split pecan rolls.

"Have you heard the news?" she asked with glee.

"Mickey Maus is in Cuba. His plane was hijacked. And Mrs. Marron has quit, so we're all on our own this morning."

"She's quit her job?"

"She left a note on the kitchen table saying she couldn't stay after what happened this weekend. What happened? Did she get raped or something?"

"I don't know exactly what happened or how," Qwilleran said, "but she told a fib. I don't know why, but she told me the cats got sick and died. Actually they'd climbed out the window, and they came home after midnight."

"She was acting funny all day yesterday," Hixie said. "Why would she say they were dead?"

"Do you know how to get in touch with her? I'd like to tell her to come back."

"She has a married daughter somewhere in town . . . Oh, brother! This was the weekend that shouldn't! Yesterday the hot water heater conked out; Mickey Maus was out of town; a delegation from the tennis club came over with a complaint; William never showed up; Max was working; Charlotte had the pip; so little me had to cope with everything, as if I didn't have enough troubles of my own. Want some scrambled eggs?"

After breakfast Qwilleran telephoned Mrs. Marron's daughter. "Tell her everything is all right. Tell her the cats have come back. Ask her if she'll come to the phone and speak to Mr. Qwilleran."

After some delay, Mrs. Marron came on the line, whimpering.

"Don't worry about anything," Qwilleran reassured her. "There's no harm done, except that you gave me some anxious moments. The cats apparently got out on the roof. Did you open the window when you cleaned my room Saturday?"

"Just for a minute, when I shook the dustmop. They were asleep on that blue cushion. I looked to see."

"Perhaps you didn't latch the window completely; Koko is expert at opening latches if they're halfway loose. But why did you invent that story about the Sanitation Department?"

Mrs. Marron was silent, except for moist sniffing.

"I'm not angry, Mrs. Marron. I just want to know why."

"I knew they had gone. When I went in to feed them on Sunday morning, I couldn't find them. I thought—I thought they'd been snatched. You know what Mr. Graham always says—"

"But why did you tell me they were dead?"

"I thought—I thought it would be better for you to—think they were dead than not to know." She started to sob. "My little Nicky, my grandson, he was missing for two weeks before they found him. It's terrible not to know."

Gently Qwilleran said, "You must come back, Mrs. Marron. We all need you. Will you come back?"

"Do you mean it?"

"Yes, I mean it sincerely. Hurry back before Mr. Maus returns, and we won't say a word about the incident."

Before leaving for the office, Qwilleran groomed the cats' fur with the new brush. Koko took a fiendish delight in the procedure—arching his back, craning his neck, gargling throaty comments of appreciation. Then he flopped down on his side and made swimming motions.

"You've got a pretty good sidestroke," Qwilleran said. "We may get you on the Olympic team."

Yum Yum, however, had to be chased around the apartment

for five minutes before she would submit to the brushing process, which she obviously adored.

"Typical female," Qwilleran muttered, breathing heavily after
the chase.

Their fur still smelled strongly of something. Was it clay? Had
they been in the Grahams' clay room? They could have gone out
the window, around the ledge, and through another window.
Then Mrs. Marron, coming in to feed them, had latched the
casement, locking them out. Had they climbed onto the ledge to
look for pigeons? Or did Koko have a reason for wanting to
snoop in the pottery? Qwilleran felt an uneasiness in the roots of
his mustache.

He opened the window to inspect the ledge. He moved the
desk and gave a jump, hoisting himself across the high sill. Leaning far out, teetering across the sill, he could see the entire
length of the ledge as it passed under the high windows of the
kiln room and the large windows of a room beyond, probably
the Grahams' loft apartment. But when he tried to wriggle back
into the apartment, the window seemed to have shrunk. Inside
the room his legs kicked ineffectually, while the bulk of his
weight was outside.

Koko, fascinated by the spectacle of half a man where there
should have been a whole one, leaped to the desk and howled.

"Don't yell at me! Call for help!" Quilleran shouted over his
shoulder, but Koko only came closer and howled in the vicinity
of Qwilleran's hip pocket.

"What are you doing up there?" came a woman's voice from
below. Hixie was on her way to the garage.

"I'm stuck, dammit! Come up and give me a toehold."

He continued to teeter on the fulcrum of the sill while Hixie
ran indoors, ran upstairs to Number Six, ran downstairs to get
the key from the kitchen, and ran upstairs again. After a few
minutes of pulling, pushing, bracing, squeezing, and grunting—
with Hixie squealing and the cats yowling—Qwilleran was dislodged. He thanked her gruffly.

"Would you like to go to a meeting with me tomorrow night?"
she asked. "It's the dinner meeting of the Friendly Fatties. . . .
Nothing personal, of course," she added.

Qwilleran mumbled that he might consider it.

"So this is the famous Siamese pussycat," she said on her way out. *"Bon jour,* Koko."

"Yaeioux," said Koko, replying in French.

Qwilleran went to his office to write a routine piece about the cake-baking contest for the second edition and to get a confirmation on his photo requisition. The assignment was on the board for five o'clock, earmarked for Bunsen, and Qwilleran telephoned Dan Graham to alert him.

"Swell! That's swell!" said Dan. "Didn't think you'd be able to swing it. That's a real break. Don't mind telling you I appreciate it. I'd like to do something for you. How about a bottle? Do you like bourbon? What does your photographer drink?"

"Forget the payola," Qwilleran said. "The story may never get in the paper. All we can do is write it and shoot the pictures and pray a lot." And then he added, "Just remembered, I have some friends on the Miami papers, including an art critic who might like to meet Joy while she's there. Could you give me her address?"

"In Miami? I don't know. She didn't know where she'd be holing up."

"How are you mailing her summer clothes, then?"

"To General Delivery," said Dan.

Qwilleran waited in the office for the first edition. He wanted to see how they were handling his new column. *Prandial Musings* appeared in thumb position on the op-ed page—a good spot!—with a photograph of the mustached author looking grimly pleased.

"Who thought of the name for my column?" he grumbled to Arch Riker. "It sounds like gastric burbulance. Ninety percent of our readers won't know what it means."

"Make that ninety-eight percent," said Arch.

"It sounds as if the byline should be Addison and Steele."

"The boss wanted something dignified," the feature editor explained. "Would you rather call it *Swill with Qwill?* That title did cross my mind . . . How was your weekend?"

"Not bad. Not bad at all. The cats gave me a helluva scare when I got home, but it turned out all right."

"Any news from Joy?"

Qwilleran related Dan's story about the alleged postcard and

Joy's alleged plans to go to Miami. "And we've had another disappearance," he said. "Now the houseboy has vanished."

He went to his desk and telephoned the Penniman Art School. William, who should have been in freehand drawing that hour, was absent, according to the registrar's office. The newsman then looked up Vitello in the phone book and called the only one listed; it was a tealeaf reading salon and the proprietor had never heard of William. Blowing into his mustache, as he did when his course was not clear, Qwilleran ambled out of the office. He was passing the receptionist's desk when a girl who was waiting there touched his sleeve.

"Are you Mr. Qwilleran?" she asked. "I recognized you from your picture. I'm a friend of William Vitello. May I talk to you?" She was a serious young girl, wearing serious glasses and unflattering clothes. The ragbag look, Qwilleran thought. She's an art student, he decided.

"Sure," he said. "Let's sit down over here." He led the way into one of the cubicles where reporters patiently listened to the irate readers, petitioners, publicity-seekers, and certifiable cranks who daily swarmed into the *Fluxion* editorial offices. "Have you seen William lately?" he asked the girl.

"No. That's what I wanted to talk about," she said. "We had a date Saturday night, but he never showed up. Never even called. Sunday I phoned Maus Haus, and he wasn't there. Some woman answered the phone, but she wasn't very coherent. Today he's not in school."

"Did you get in touch with his mother?"

"She hasn't heard from him since he took her a birthday present Friday night. I don't know what I should do. I thought of you because William talked about you a lot. What do you think I should do?"

"William is impetuous. He might have decided to take a trip somewhere."

"He wouldn't go without telling me, Mr. Qwilleran. We're very close. We even have a joint bank account."

The newsman propped one elbow on the arm of the chair and combed his mustache with his fingertips. "Did he ever discuss the situation at Maus Haus?"

"Oh, he's always talking about that weird place. He says it's full of characters."

"Did he ever mention Dan Graham?"

The girl nodded, giving Qwilleran a glance from the corner of her eye.

"Anything you want to tell me is confidential," he assured her.

"Well, I really didn't take him seriously. He said he was spying on Mr. Graham. He said he was going to dig up some dirt. I thought he was just kidding, or showing off. Billy likes to read spy stories, and he gets ideas."

"Do you know what kind of irregularity he suspected? Was it a morals situation?"

"You mean—like sex?" The girl bit her thumbnail as she considered that possibility. "Well, maybe. But the main story had something to do with the way Mr. Graham was running the pottery. Something fishy was going on in the pottery, Billy said."

"When did he last mention this?"

"Friday night. He phoned me after he had dinner with you."

"Did he mention any specific detail about the pottery operation? Think hard."

The girl frowned. "Only that . . . he said he thought Mr. Graham was going to blow a whole load of pots."

"Destroy them?"

"Billy said he was firing the kiln wrong and the whole load would blow. He couldn't understand it, because Mr. Graham is supposed to be a good fireman . . . I'm not much help, am I?"

"I'll be able to answer that later," Qwilleran told her. "Wait another forty-eight hours, and if William doesn't turn up, you'd better notify Missing Persons, or have his mother do it. And another thing: You might check your joint bank account for sizable withdrawals."

"Yes, I'll do that, Mr. Qwilleran. Thank you so much, Mr. Qwilleran." Her wide eyes were magnified through the lenses of her glasses. "Only . . . all we've got in the bank is eighteen dollars."

THIRTEEN

QWILLERAN RETURNED to Maus Haus on the River Road bus, pondering the pieces of the puzzle: two missing persons, a drowned child, a slandered restaurateur, a lost cat, a black eye, a scream in the night. Too many pieces were missing.

Up in Number Six the cats were snoozing on the blue cushion. They had been busy, however, and several pictures were tilted. Qwilleran automatically straightened them, a chore to which he had become accustomed. The cats had to have their fun, he rationalized. Cooped up in a one-room apartment, they had to use ingenuity to amuse themselves, and Koko found a peculiar satisfaction in scraping his jaw on the sharp corners of a picture frame. Qwilleran straightened two engravings of bridges over the Seine, a Cape Cod watercolor, and a small oil painting of a beach scene on the Riviera. In the far corner an Art Nouveau print had been tilted so violently that it was hanging sideways. As he rectified the situation, he noticed a patch on the wall.

It was a metal patch, painted to match the stucco walls. He touched it, and it moved from side to side, pivoting on a tiny screw. Small arcs scratched in the wall paint indicated that the patch had been swung aside before, perhaps recently. Qwilleran swung it all the way around and discovered what it was concealing: a deep hole in the wall.

Leaning across the bookcase, he peered through the opening and looked down into the two-story kiln room behind his own apartment. The lights were turned on, and Qwilleran could see a central table with a collection of vases in brilliant blues, greens, and reds. Shifting his position to the left, he could see two of the kilns. Shifting to the right, he saw Dan Graham sitting at a small side table, copying from a loose-leaf notebook into a large ledger.

Qwilleran closed the peephole and replaced the picture, asking himself questions: What was its purpose? Did William know about it? Mrs. Marron said he had washed the walls recently. Had William been spying on Dan from this vantage point?

The telephone rang, and Odd Bunsen was on the line. "Say, what's the assignment you've got on the board for five o'clock? It sounds like a sizable job. When do I get to eat?"

"You can have dinner here," Qwilleran said, "and shoot the pictures afterward. The food here is great!"

"The requisition says two-five-five-five River Road. What is that place, anyway?"

"It's an old pottery, now a gourmet boarding house."

"Sure, I know the place. There were a couple of murders there. We keep running stories on them. Any special equipment I should bring?"

"Bring everything," Qwilleran advised. He lowered his voice with a glance in the direction of the peephole. "I want you to put on a good show. Bring lots of lights. I'll explain when you get here."

Qwilleran went downstairs to tell Mrs. Marron there would be an extra guest for dinner. She was in the Great Hall, nervously setting the dinner table, which had been moved under the balcony to make room for the pottery exhibit.

"I don't know what to do," she was whimpering. "They said they'd do a demonstration dinner, but I don't know how they want it set up. Nobody told me. Nobody's here."

"What's a demonstration dinner?" Qwilleran asked.

"Everybody cooks something at the table. Mr. Sorrel, he's making the steak. Mrs. Whiting, she's making the soup. Miss Roop, she's—"

"Have you seen William?"

"No, sir, and he was supposed to clean the stove—"

"Any news from Mr. Maus?"

"No, sir. Nobody knows when he'll be back . . . You're not going to tell him, are you? You said you wouldn't tell him."

"We're going to forget the whole matter," Qwilleran assured her. "Stop worrying about it, Mrs. Marron."

Tears came to her dull eyes, and she rubbed them away with the back of her hand. "Everybody is so good to me here. I try not to make mistakes, but I can't get little Nicky off my mind, and I don't sleep nights."

"We all understand what you've been through, but you must pull yourself together."

"Yes, sir." The housekeeper stopped her nervous puttering and turned to face him. "Mr. Qwilleran," she said hesitantly, "I heard something else in the night."

"What do you mean?"

"Saturday night, when I couldn't sleep, I was just lying there, worrying, and I heard a noise."

"What kind of noise?"

"Outside my window. Somebody coming down the fire escape."

"The one at the back of the house?"

"Yes, sir. My room is on the river side."

"Did you see anything?"

"No, sir. I got up and peeked out the window, but it was so dark. All I could see was somebody crossing the grass."

"Hmmm," Qwilleran mused. "Did you recognize the person?"

"No, sir. But I think it was a man. He was carrying a heavy load of something."

"What kind of load?"

"Like a big sack."

"How big?"

"This big!" The housekeeper spread her arms wide. "He was carrying it down to the river. When he got beyond the bushes, I couldn't see him anymore. But I *heard* it."

"What did you hear?"

"A big splash."

"And what happened then?"

"He came back."

"Did you get a look at his face then?"

"No, sir. There wasn't any light at the back of the building—

just the bright lights across the river. But I could see him moving across the grass, and then I heard him going up the fire escape again."

"Is that the one that leads to the Grahams' loft?"

"Yes, sir."

"What time did this happen?"

"It was very late. Maybe four o'clock." The housekeeper looked at him hopefully, waiting for his approval.

Qwilleran studied her face briefly. "If it was Mr. Graham, there was probably some logical explanation. Think nothing of it."

"Yes, sir."

He went upstairs wondering: Did she really see Dan Graham dropping a sack in the river? She made up a story once before, and she could do it again. Perhaps she thinks I'm the kind that drools over mysteries, and she's trying to please me. And why all that yes-sir, no-sir business all of a sudden?

In his apartment Qwilleran's eye went first to the Art Nouveau print over the bookcase, and it gave him an idea. A few months before, he had interviewed a commercial potter who specialized in contemporary figurines, and now he telephoned him.

"This may sound like a crazy question," he told the potter, "but I'm trying my hand at writing a novel—kind of a Gothic thriller about skulduggery in a pottery. Would it be too far-fetched to have a peephole in a wall overlooking the kiln room?"

"So the firing operation could be observed?"

"Yes. Something like that."

"Not a bad idea at all. I once suspected an employee of sabotaging my work, and I had to set up an expensive surveillance system. A simple peephole might have saved me a lot of money. Why didn't I think of that? All potters are professional voyeurs, you know. We're always looking through the spyholes in the kilns, and I can't pass a knothole in a board fence without taking a peek."

Odd Bunsen arrived at Maus Haus at five o'clock, and Qwilleran invited him to Number Six for a drink.

"Hey, you're getting taller," the photographer said. "It couldn't be thinner."

"I've lost seven pounds," Qwilleran boasted, unaware that three of them had been contributed in the beginning by Koko.

"Where are those crazy cats? Hiding?"

"Asleep on the shelves, behind the books."

Bunsen flopped in the big lounge chair, propped his feet on the ottoman, lit a cigar, and accepted a glass of something ninety-proof. "I wish the boss could see me now. Do you realize the *Fluxion* is paying me for this?"

"The work will come later." Qwilleran went to the peephole and checked the metal patch.

"What kind of hanky-panky did you have in mind?"

"Keep your voice down," Qwilleran advised. "If possible."

"Are you telling me I'm a loudmouth?"

"To put it tactfully . . . yes."

"What's the assignment all about? Don't keep me in suspense."

The newsman sat down and lit his pipe. "Ostensibly you'll be taking pictures for a layout on Dan Graham, who runs the pottery."

"But without any film in the camera?"

"We might use one or two pictures, but I want you to keep the camera clicking all over the place. I'd also like an excuse to get Koko into the pottery, but I don't want to suggest it myself." He groomed his mustache with his pipe stem.

Bunsen recognized the gesture. "Not another crime! Not again!"

"Lower your voice," Quilleran said with a frown. "While you're preparing to shoot pictures, I want to browse around the premises, so take a lot of time doing it."

"You got the right man," said Bunsen. "I can set up a tripod slower than any other photographer in the business."

Later, at the dinner table, everyone liked the *Fluxion* photographer. Bunsen had a way of taking over a social occasion, bursting on the scene with his loud voice and jovial manner and stale jokes, jollying the women, kidding the men. Rosemary smiled at him, Hixie giggled, and even Charlotte Roop was fascinated when he called her a doll-baby. Max Sorrel invited Bunsen to bring his wife to dinner at the Golden Lamb Chop some evening. Dan Graham had not yet arrived.

For the first course Rosemary stood at the head of the table and demonstrated a sixty-second cold soup involving yogurt, cucumbers, dill, and raisins.

"Best soup I ever tasted!" Bunsen announced.

Dan Graham, arriving at the table late, was greeted coolly by the Maus Haus regulars, but the photographer jumped up and pumped his hand, and the potter glowed with suppressed excitement. He had had a haircut, and his shabby clothes were neater than usual.

Sorrel sautéed steak *au poivre*, which was served with Mrs. Marron's potato puffs and asparagus garnished with pimiento strips.

Then Charlotte Roop demonstrated the tossing of a salad. "Dry the greens carefully on a linen towel," she said. "Be careful not to bruise the leaves. Tear them apart tenderly . . . And now the dressing. I add a little Dijon mustard and thyme. Toss all together. Gently! Gently! Forty times. Less dressing and more tossing—that's the secret."

"Best salad I ever tasted in my whole life!" Bunsen proclaimed.

"A salad has to be made with *love*," Miss Roop explained to him, beaming and nodding at his compliments.

For dessert Hixie prepared cherries jubilee. "Nothing to it," she said. "Dump the cherries in the chafing dish. Throw in a blob of butter and slosh it around. Then a slurp of cognac. Oops! I slurped too much. And then . . . you light it with a match. *Voilà!*"

The blue flame leaped from the pan, and the company watched the ritual in hypnotized silence. Even Odd Bunsen was speechless.

As the flame started to burn out, Qwilleran thought he heard a crackling sound. He glanced up at Hixie and saw her lofty bouffant hairdo unaccountably shriveling. Jumping up, he tore off his jacket and threw it over her head. The women shrieked. Chairs were knocked over as Sorrel and Bunsen rushed to help.

It was a stunned and wide-eyed Hixie who emerged from under the jacket, her hands exploring what was left of her hair. "It feels like straw," she said. "I guess I sprayed too much lacquer on it."

"Come on, Bunsen," Qwilleran said. "You and I have got to go to work. Dan, are you ready?"

"Wait a minute," said the potter, walking to the head of the table. "I haven't done anything tonight—I can't cook—so I'll sing you a song."

The diners sat down and listened uncomfortably as Dan sang about the charms of Loch Lomond in a wavering tenor voice. Qwilleran watched the pathetic Adam's apple bobbing up and down and felt almost guilty about the ruse he was planning.

The song ended and the listeners applauded politely, all except Bunsen, who hopped on a chair and shouted "Bravo!" To Qwilleran he muttered: "How'm I doing?"

As the diners wandered away from the table, chattering about Hixie's narrow escape, Qwilleran helped the photographer carry his equipment in from the car.

"You fellows certainly use a lot of gear," said the potter.

"Only for big assignments like this," Bunsen said, bustling about with exaggerated industry.

"Here's what we had in mind," Qwilleran explained to Dan. "We want a series of pictures showing how you make a pot, and then a few shots of you with some of your finished work."

"Wait a minute," the photographer interrupted. "It'll never get in the paper. Who wants to look at a homely old geezer?" He gave Dan a friendly dig in the ribs. "What we need is a gorgeous blonde to jazz it up. Are you hiding any dames upstairs?"

"I know what you mean," the potter said. "You fellows always like cheesecake. But my old lady's out of town."

"How about pets? Got any cats? Dogs? Parakeets? Boa constrictors? Best way to get your picture in the paper is to pose with a boa constrictor."

"We used to have a cat," Dan said apologetically.

"Why don't we borrow one of Qwill's spoiled brats?" the photographer said with a sudden enthusiasm. "We'll put him in a big jug with his head sticking out—and Dan in the background. Then you'll be sure of making the front page."

FOURTEEN

KOKO, WEARING HIS blue harness and leading Qwilleran on the twelve-foot leash, entered the pottery with the confidence of one who had been there before. There was no hesitation on the threshold, no cautious sniffling, and none of that usual stalking with underslung belly.

Qwilleran said, "Let's start by taking some shots of Dan at the wheel."

"To be honest with you fellows, I specialize in slab-built pots," Dan said. "But if that's what you want—" He scooped up a handful of clay from a barrel and sat down at the power wheel.

"Leave the cat out of this picture," Qwilleran instructed the photographer. "Just get a series of candids as the pot takes shape."

"It won't be too good," the potter said. "I've got a bad thumb." The clay started to spin, rising under his wet hands, then falling, building up to a core, lowering into a squat mound, gradually hollowed by the potter's left thumb, and eventually shaped into a bowl.

All the while, Bunsen was clicking the camera, bouncing around from one angle to another, and barking terse instructions: "Bend over . . . Glance up . . . Raise your chin . . . Don't look at the camera." And all the while, Koko was exploring the studio, nosing a clutter of mortars and pestles, crocks, sieves, scoops, ladles, and funnels. Fascinated by things mechanical, he was especially interested in the scales.

"The big story," Dan insisted, "is about my glazes. I've come up with something that's kind of cool, if you know what I mean."

"First, let's look at the clay room," Qwilleran insisted. "There may be some possibilities there for action shots."

Dan hung back. "There's nothing in that room but a lot of equipment we don't use anymore. It's all fifty, sixty years old."

"I'd like to have a look," Bunsen said. "You never know where you'll find a great picture, and I've got lots of film."

It was cold and damp in the dimly lighted clay room. Qwilleran asked intelligent questions about the blunger, pug mill, and filter press, meanwhile keeping an eye on Koko and a firm hand on the leash. The cat was attracted to a trapdoor in the floor.

"What's down there?" Qwilleran asked.

"Nothing. Just a ladder to the basement," the potter said.

The newsman thought otherwise. Joy had called it the slip tank. He leaned over and pulled up on the iron ring, swinging open the door and peering down into blackness.

A strange sound came from Koko, teetering on the edge of the square hole. It started as a growl and ended in a falsetto shriek.

"Careful!" the potter warned. "There are rats down there."

The newsman pulled Koko back and let the trapdoor fall into place with a crash that shook the floor.

"Smells pretty potent in here," Bunsen observed.

"That's the clay ripening," Dan explained. "You get used to it. Why don't we go to the kiln room? It's more comfortable, and there's not so much stink."

The high-ceilinged kiln room with its mammoth ovens and flues was pleasantly warm and clean, having neither the mud of the clay room nor the dust of the studio. On a table in the center stood a collection of square-cut vases and pots with the radiantly colorful glazes Qwilleran had glimpsed through the peephole. From a distance he had been attracted to their brilliant blues, reds, and greens; at close hand he saw that they were much more than that. There seemed to be movement in the depths of the glaze. The surfaces looked wet—and alive. The two newsmen were silent and curious as they walked around the ceramics and studied the baffling effect.

"How do you fellows like it?" asked Dan, aglow with pride. "I call it my Living Glaze."

"Sort of makes my hair stand on end," Bunsen said. "No kidding."

"Amazing!" said Qwilleran. "How do you do it?"

"Potter's secret," Dan said smugly. "All potters have their secrets. I had to work out a formula and then experiment with the fire. Cobalt oxide makes blue. Chromium oxide makes green, except when it comes out pink. You have to know your onions, if you know what I mean."

"Crazy!" said Bunsen.

"You can change colors by adding wood ash—even tobacco ash. We have a lot of tricks. Use salt, and you get orange-peel texture. I'm just giving you some interesting facts you can use in your article, if you want to make notes."

"Did Joy know you'd come up with this Living Glaze?" Qwilleran asked.

"Oh, she knew, all right!" The potter chuckled. "And it wouldn't surprise me if the old gal's nose was out of joint. Probably why she made herself scarce. She's got a pretty good opinion of herself, and she couldn't stand to see someone steal the show." He smiled and shook his head sadly.

"I like the red pots best," Qwilleran said. "Really unusual. I'm partial to red . . . So is Koko, I guess." The cat had jumped to the tabletop with the weightlessness of a feather and was gently nosing a glowing red pot.

"Red's hardest to get. You never know how it'll turn out," Dan said. "It has to get just so much oxygen, or it fades out. That's why you don't see much red pottery—honest-to-gosh red, I mean. Would you fellows like to peek in the kiln?" Dan uncovered the spyhole in one of the kilns, and the newsmen peered into the blazing red inferno. "You get so you can tell the temperature by the color of the fire," the potter said. "Yellow-hot is hotter than red-hot."

"How long does it take to fire a mess of pots?"

"Two days on the average. One day heating up, one day cooling down. Know why a dish cracks in your kitchen oven? Because your stove heats up too fast. Betcha didn't know that."

"Well, let's shoot some pictures," Bunsen said. "Dan, we'll get you standing behind the table with the crockery in the foreground. Too bad these pictures aren't in color . . . Now, we'll put Old Nosy into one of the biggest pots. You'll have to take his harness off, Qwill . . . Where's Old Nosy?"

Koko had wandered off and found a loose-leaf notebook on one of the other tables, and he was sharpening his claws on the cover.

"Hey, don't do that!" Qwilleran shouted, and then he explained: "Koko uses a big dictionary as a scratching pad—it's one of our family jokes—and he thinks that's what all books are for."

The photographer said, "You slip him in the pot, Qwill, hind feet first. Then step back out of the way and hope he stays put. Dan, you hang on to the pot so he doesn't kick it over. Old Nosy's got a kick like a mule. If he tries to jump out shove him back down. I'll shoot fast. And don't look at the camera."

Qwilleran did his part, jamming the squirming cat down into the square vase, and then he stepped away. He missed the rest of the performance; he was curious about the notebook Koko had been scratching. The cover was labeled *Glazes*. With a casual finger Qwilleran flipped open the cover and glanced at a few words written in a familiar scrawl:

Wuu uuu . . . .
Quuuuz . . . .
Cwu uuy 4

He riffled the pages quickly. Even without his glasses he recognized Joy's cryptic writing from cover to cover.

"Okay," said Bunsen. "That should do it. Old Nosy's turning into a pretty good model. What do you want next, Qwill?"

"How about some pictures of Dan in his living quarters?"

"Great!" said the photographer.

Dan protested. "No, you fellows wouldn't want to take any pictures up there."

"Sure we do. Readers like to know how artists live."

"It's a rat's nest, if you know what I mean," the potter said, still balking. "My wife isn't much of a housekeeper."

"What are you scared of?" the photographer said. "Have you got a broad up there? Or is that where you hid the body?"

Qwilleran kicked him under the table and said to Dan, "We just want to give the story a little human interest, so it won't look like a commercial plug. You know how editors are. They'll give the story more space if there's a human interest angle."

"Well, you fellows know how it's done," Dan said reluctantly. "Come on upstairs."

The Grahams' loft was one large cave, with Indian rugs on the wall, lengths of Indian fabric sagging across the ceiling, and a floor carpeted from wall to wall with old newspapers, books, magazines, half-finished sewing, and dropped articles of clothing. Crowded in that one room, without arrangement or organization, were beds, barrels, tables, kitchen sink, chairs, packing boxes covered with paisley shawls, and mop pails full of pussywillows. Two pieces of luggage were open on one of the beds.

"Taking a trip?" asked Qwilleran in his best innocent manner.

"No, just packing some of my wife's clothes to ship down south." He closed the suitcases and set them on the floor. "Sit down. Would you fellows like a beer or a shot? Us potters have to drink a lot because of the dust." He winked broadly.

"I'll take a beer," Bunsen said. "I've swallowed a little dust myself."

Qwilleran, who had carried Koko up the stairs, now placed him on the floor, and the cat hardly knew which way to turn. He stepped gingerly across a slippery stack of art magazines and sniffed a pile of clothing in odd shades of eggplant and Concord grape. They were obviously Joy's garments; they had the familiar look of old curtain remnants that had been given a homemade dye job.

The newsman plied Dan with questions: Is it true they used to glaze pottery with pulverized jewels? What's the temperature inside the kiln? Where does the clay come from? What's the hardest shape to make?

"A teapot," Dan replied. "Handles can crack in the kiln. Or the spout drips. Or the lid doesn't fit. Sometimes the whole thing looks like hell, although the ugliest ones sometimes do the best pouring."

Bunsen took a few more pictures of Dan gazing out the window at the lights across the river, Dan reading an art magazine,

Dan drinking a can of beer to counteract the dust, Dan scratching his head and looking thoughtful. The photographer had never shot a series so complete, or so ridiculous.

"You've got good bones in your face," he commented. "You could be a professional model. You could do TV commercials."

"You think so?" Dan asked. He had loosened up and was relishing the attention.

By the time the shooting session was over, Qwilleran and Koko had examined every inch of the room. There was a phone number written on a pad near the telephone, which the newsman memorized. Koko found a woman's silver-backed hairbrush, which he knocked to the floor while trying to bite the bristles. The cat also showed interest in a large ceramic jardiniere containing papers and small notebooks and a packet of dusty envelopes tied with faded ribbon. Qwilleran managed to transfer the envelopes to his inside jacket pocket. A familiar prickling sensation on his upper lip had convinced him it was the right thing to do.

The newsmen finally said good night to Dan, promised him some copies of the pictures, and trooped back to Qwilleran's apartment, dragging a reluctant cat on the leash.

"Okay, let's have it," Bunsen demanded. "What's this playacting all about?"

"Wish I knew," Qwilleran admitted. "As soon as I find out, I'll buy you a porterhouse on my expense account and fill you in on the sordid details."

"How are you going to explain to that poor guy when the *Fluxion* runs a half-column head shot and twenty words of copy?"

Qwilleran shrugged and changed the subject. "How's Janie?"

"Fine, considering everything. We're expecting another in August."

"How many have you got now?"

"Five . . . no, six."

Qwilleran poured a stiff drink for Bunsen and opened a can of crabmeat for Koko and Yum Yum. Then he dialed the number he had found on the Graham's telephone pad. It proved to be an overseas airline.

He also thought about Joy's silver-backed hairbrush; he had given it to her for Christmas many years before. Wouldn't she have taken it if she intended to leave town? A hairbrush was as important as a toothbrush to that girl. She used to brush her long hair by the hour.

"Say," Qwilleran said to Bunsen, "do you still hang around with that scuba diver you brought to the Press Club last winter?"

"I see him once in a while. I'm doing his wedding pictures in June."

"Would you ask him to do us a favor?"

"No sweat. He loves the *Fluxion* after that layout we gave him in the magazine section. What did you have in mind?"

"I'd like him to go down under the wharf behind this building. Just to see what he can find. And the sooner the better."

"What are you looking for?"

"I don't know, but a large unidentified object was dumped into the river in the middle of the night, and I'd like to know what it was."

"It could be halfway to Goose Island by now."

"Not necessarily. The body of the sculptor who drowned here was found lodged against the piling under the boardwalk." Qwilleran patted his mustache smugly. "I have an idea something might be trapped down there right now."

After the photographer left, the newsman sat at the desk and opened the pack of letters he had filched from the jardiniere. They were all addressed to Helen Maude Hake and had been mailed at various times from Paris, Brussels, Sydney, and Philadelphia: *I miss the thrill of you, the lure of you, you beautiful witch . . . Your warm and tender love haunts my nights . . . Home soon, beloved . . . Be true to Popsie or Popsie will spank.* All the letters were signed *Popsie.*

Qwilleran snorted into his mustache and dropped the letters in a desk drawer. He lighted his pipe and stretched out in his lounge chair, and Yum Yum cuddled on his lap—until Koko scolded her. Then she promptly deserted the man and went to lick Koko's nose and ears.

Suddenly Qwilleran felt lonely. Koko had his Yum Yum. Bunsen had his Janie. Riker had his Rosie.

He telephoned Rosemary Whiting. "I hope it's not too late. I need some moral support . . . You know those vitamins you gave me for the cats? I've never popped a pill down a cat's gullet."

Within a few minutes she knocked on the door of Number Six, wearing a red silk tunic and harem pants, with her licorice-black hair tied back in a young-looking ponytail. Qwilleran answered her knock just as Charlotte Roop climbed the stairs with a glass of steaming milk on a little tray. Miss Roop said good evening, but her greeting was cool.

The cats were waiting, and they knew something was up. They were bracing themselves.

Qwilleran said, "Let's take Koko first. He's the more sensible of the two."

"Hello, Koko," Rosemary said. "You're a beautiful cat. Here's a candy. Open up! There!" She had merely put a hand around the back of Koko's head, forced his mouth open, and dropped a pill into the yawning pink cavern. "It's really simple when you know how."

"I hate to think what will happen if Koko gets any healthier," Qwilleran said.

Just then Koko lowered his head, opened his mouth, deposited the pellet at Qwilleran's feet. It was slightly damp but otherwise as good as new.

"Well! We'll try it again. It always works," said Rosemary, undismayed. "We'll just push it down a little farther. Qwill, you watch how I do it. Press his jaw open at the hinge; pull his head back until you can see clear down his throat; and then—*plop!* Now we stroke his throat so that he is forced to gulp."

"It looks easy," Qwilleran said, "but I think Koko is cooperating because you are a lovely lady . . . Oops!" Koko coughed, and up came the pill, shooting across the room and disappearing in the shaggy pelt of the bear rug. "Don't worry about it, Rosemary. I have a confession to make. I really lured you over here because I wanted someone to talk with."

He told her about the love letters he'd found in the jardiniere, the uncanny brilliance of Dan's exhibition pottery, and the trapdoor in the clay room. "Dan told us there were rats down there."

"Rats!" Rosemary shook her head. "Mr. Maus is very particular. He has the exterminators check the building regularly."

He told her about the visit from William's girl friend and about the peephole in the wall, overlooking the kiln room.

"But can't it be seen from the other side?"

"It's camouflaged by the mural in the kiln room. I looked for it while we were in there taking pictures."

Rosemary asked if she could read the love letters. "Believe it or not," she said, "I've never in my life received a love letter." She moved to the bed, turned on the lamp, and curled up among the pillows. As she read, her eyes grew moist. "The letters are so lovely."

On a sudden impulse Qwilleran pitched the cats into the bathroom, threw their blue cushion in after them, and slammed the door. They howled for a while and then gave up.

It was midnight when Rosemary left and the indignant animals were released from their prison. Koko stalked about the apartment, complaining irritably.

"Live and let live," Qwilleran reminded him. He was moving around the apartment himself, aimlessly, fired with ambition but devoid of direction. He sat down at the typewriter, thinking he could write a better love letter than that ridiculous Popsie. The typewriter still bore Koko's message from the night before: pb.

"Pb!" Qwilleran said aloud. *"Pb!"* He remembered the crocks in the pottery, with their cryptic labels. He jumped up and went to the dictionary as his mustache sent him frantic signals.

"Pb: Latin *Plumbum*," he read aloud. "Chemical symbol for *lead!*"

FIFTEEN

THE SECOND APPEARANCE of Qwilleran's *Prandial Musings*—in the Tuesday edition of the *Daily Fluxion*—dealt with the culinary virtuosity of Robert Maus, member of the important downtown law firm of Teahandle, Hansblow, Burris, Maus and Castle. The column was wittily written, and Qwilleran accepted congratulations from copyboys and editors alike when he went to the office to open his mail.

"How do you get these plum assignments?" he was asked at the Press Club that noon. "How much weight do you expect to gain on your new beat? . . . Do you mean to say that the *Flux* is footing the bill? The comptroller must have flipped."

He spent a day at the office, writing a column on the whimsical theories of Max Sorrel: "If you want to test a guy's sincerity," Max had said, "serve him a bad cup of coffee. If he praises it, he's not to be trusted."

In the middle of every paragraph he was interrupted, however, by phone calls: from the electric company, objecting to Maus's hotly argued preference for gas cooking; from the aluminum industry, protesting the gourmet's antipathy to foil jackets on baked potatoes; from purveyors of ketchup, processed cheese, and frozen fish, all of which made Robert Maus shudder.

One interruption was a blustering phone call from old Teahandle, senior partner of the law firm. "Did Robert Maus authorize that article in today's paper?" he demanded.

"He didn't read the finished copy," said Qwilleran, "but he allowed me to interview him."

"Humph! Are you aware that one of our major clients is a manufacturer of electric ranges?"

"Even so, Maus is entitled to his opinion, don't you think?"

"But you didn't have to *print* it!" the partner snapped. "I shall discuss this with Mr. Maus when he returns to the city."

Between answering complaints and accepting compliments, Qwilleran made some phone calls of his own. Koko had left the letter Z in the typewriter that morning, and it inspired the newsman to call Zoe Lambreth, a painter he had known briefly but well when he first came to the city. He read Zoe a list of artists' names he had copied from an old newspaper account of the scandal at the pottery.

"Are any of these people still around?" he asked.

"Some of them have died," Zoe said in the melodic voice that always captivated him. "Herb Stock has retired to California. Inga Berry is head of the pottery department at Penniman School. Bill Bacon is president of the Turp and Chisel Club."

"Inga Berry, you say? I'd like to interview her."

"I hope you're not raking up that old scandal," the painter said. "Inga refuses to talk about it. All the 'slovenly Bohemians' mentioned in the newspapers eventually became important members of the art community, and yet they're still hounded by reporters. I don't understand newspapers."

Next, Qwilleran telephoned Inga Berry, plotting his course carefully. She answered in a hearty voice, but as soon as he identified himself as a feature writer for the *Daily Fluxion,* her manner stiffened. "What do you want?"

He talked fast and summoned all his vocal and verbal charm. "Is it true, Miss Berry, that pottery is considered the most enduring of the crafts?"

"Well . . . yes," she said, taken by surprise. "Wood crumbles, and metal corrodes, but examples of pottery have survived for thousands of years."

"I understand that pottery is due for a renaissance—that it might eclipse painting and sculpture as an art form within ten years."

"Well, I don't know . . . Well, perhaps yes!" The instructor said as she considered the flattering prospect. "But don't quote me. You'll have all the painters and sculptors yelling for my blood."

"I'd like to discuss the subject with you, Miss Berry. I have a young friend—one of your students—who paints a glowing picture of your contribution to the art of ceramics."

"Oh, he does, does he? Or is it a she?" Miss Berry was warming up.

"Do you know William Vitello?"

"He's not in my classes, but I'm aware of him." She chuckled. "He's hard to overlook."

"Have you seen him in the last couple of days?"

"I don't believe so. We haven't had any major catastrophes at the studio, so he must be absent."

"By the way, Miss Berry, is it usual to use lead in the composition of glazes?"

"Oh, yes, it's quite usual. Lead causes the pigment to adhere to the clay."

"Isn't it poisonous?"

"We take precautions, of course. Would you like to visit our studio, Mr.—Mr. . . ."

"Qwilleran, spelled with a *Q-w*. That's very kind of you, Miss Berry. I have a great curiosity about potting. Is it true that clay begins to smell bad when it ripens?"

"Yes, indeed! The longer you keep it, the more it gains in elasticity. Actually it's decomposing."

During this conversation the receptionist in the feature department was signaling to Qwilleran; two incoming phone calls were waiting. He shook his head and waved them away.

He told the potter, "I've taken an apartment at the old pottery on River Road. It's a fascinating place. Are you familiar with it?"

There was a chilling pause on the other end of the line. "You're not going to bring up the subject of Mortimer Mellon, are you?"

"Who is he?" Qwilleran asked with an outrageous display of naiveté.

"Never mind. Forget I mentioned him."

"I was going to tell you," he said in his most engaging voice, "that my apartment has a secret window overlooking the kiln room, and my curiosity is aroused. What might its purpose be?"

There was another pause. "Which studio do you have?"

"Number Six."

"That used to be Mr. Penniman's."

"I didn't know he was an artist," Qwilleran said. "I thought he was a newspaper publisher and financier."

"He was a patron of the arts, and his studio served as a—as a—"

"Pied-á-terre?" the newsman supplied.

"You see," Miss Berry added cautiously, "I used to work in the Penniman pottery in the early days."

He expressed surprise and then inquired if she planned to attend the opening of the Graham exhibition.

"I hadn't intended to, but . . ."

"Why don't you come, Miss Berry? I'll personally keep your champagne glass filled."

"Maybe I shall. I never waste time on social openings, but you sound like an interesting young man. Your enthusiasm is refreshing."

"How will I recognize you, Miss Berry?"

"Oh, you'll know me. I have gray hair and bangs and a bit of a limp. Arthritis, you know. And of course I have clay under my fingernails."

Pleased with his own persuasiveness, Qwilleran hung up and finished the Max Sorrel column in high spirit. He handed in his copy to Riker and was leaving the office with spring in his step, when his phone rang again.

A man's voice said, "You write that column on restaurants, yeah?"

"Yes, I write the gourmet column."

"Just wanna give you some advice, yeah? Lay off the Golden Lamb Chop, yeah?"

"For what reason?"

"We don't want nothin' in the paper about the Golden Lamb Chop, y'understand?"

"Are you connected with the restaurant—*sir?*"

"I'm just tellin' you. Lay off or you're liable to lose a lot of advertisin' in the paper, yeah?" There was a click on the line.

Qwilleran reported the call to Riker. "He sounded like one of the bad guys in an old gangster movie. But now they don't threaten to bump you off; they threaten to withdraw their advertising. Did you know there's an underground movement afoot to ruin Sorrel's restaurant?"

"Ho-hum, I'll check it out with the boss," Riker said with a bored sigh. "We have your cheese column for tomorrow, and then the farmers' market piece, but we can't run what you wrote about the Petrified Bagel. 'Embalmed shrimp! Delicious toothpicks!' Are you out of your mind? What else have you lined up?"

"The Friendly Fatties. I'm going there tonight."

"Any word from Joy?"

"No word. But I'm building up a case. If I can get just one break . . ."

Qwilleran met Hixie Rice at the Duxbury Memorial Center. She was looking oddly unglamorous, despite a frizzy wig and a snugly fitted orange-and-white polkadot ensemble.

"Do I look dumb?" she asked. "I just lost my eyelashes. I'm a loser, that's all. Everywhere except on the bathroom scales. *C'est la vie!*"

The dinner meeting of the Friendly Fatties—all sixteen tons of them—was held in a public meeting room at the center, which was noted for the mediocrity of its cuisine.

There was a brief sermon on Thinking Thin. The week's champion losers were announced, and a few backsliders—Hixie among them—confessed their sins. Then cabbage juice cocktails were served, followed by a light repast.

"Ah! Another thin soup!" Hixie exclaimed in feigned rapture. "This week they actually dragged a bouillon cube through the hot water. And the melba toast! Best I've tasted since I was a girl in Pigeon, Michigan, and ate the shingles off the barn roof . . . Do you think this is really hamburger?" she asked Qwilleran when the main course arrived. "I think it's grape seeds stuck together with epoxy glue. Don't you love the Brussels sprouts? They taste like—mmmmmm—wet papier-mâché. But wait till you try the dessert! They make it out of air, water, coal tar, disodium phosphate, vegetable gum, and artificial flavoring. *Et voilà!* Prune whip!"

On the way home Hixie said, "Honestly, life is unfair. Why wasn't I born with a divine figure instead of a brilliant intellect and a ravishingly beautiful face? I can't get a man because I'm fat, and I stay fat because I can't get a man."

"What you need is a hobby," Qwilleran advised. "Some new consuming interest."

"I've got a hobby: consuming food," she said in her usual glib way, but as they walked up the stairs at Maus Haus, the happy-go-lucky fat girl burst into tears, covering her face with her hands.

"Hixie! What's the matter?" Qwilleran asked.

She shook her head and gave vent to a torrent of sobs.

He grasped her arm firmly and steered her up the stairs. "Come up to Number Six, and I'll fix you a drink."

His kind voice only made the tears gush more freely, and blindly she went along with him. Koko was alarmed at her entrance; he had never seen or heard anyone cry.

Qwilleran situated her in the big armchair, gave her a box of tissues, lit a cigarette for her, and poured two ounces of scotch over ice. "Now what's the reason for the sudden cloudburst?"

"Oh, Qwill," she said, "I'm so miserable."

He waited patiently.

"I'm not looking for a millionaire or a movie star. All I want is an ordinary, run-of-the-mill type of husband with a few brains or a little talent, not necessarily both. But do you think I ever meet that kind?" She enumerated a discouraging tally of her near-hits and total misses.

He had heard this tale of woe before. Young women often confided in him. "How old are you, Hixie?"

"Twenty-four."

"You've got lots of time."

She shook her head. "I don't think I'll ever appeal to the right kind of man. I don't want to be a swinger, but I attract men who want a swinger and nothing else. Me, I want a wedding ring, a new name, babies—all that corny stuff."

Qwilleran looked at her dress—too short, too tight, too bright —and wondered how to phrase some advice. Perhaps Rosemary could take her in hand.

"May I have another drink?" she asked. "Why is your cat staring at me?"

"He's concerned. He knows when someone's unhappy."

"I don't usually come apart like this, but I've just lived

through a traumatic experience. I haven't slept for five nights. Do you mind if I tell you all the nasty details? You're so understanding."

Qwilleran nodded.

"I've just ended an affair with a married man." She paused to observe Qwilleran's reaction, but he was lighting his pipe. She went on: "We couldn't come to terms. He wanted me to go away with him, but I refused to go without making it legal. I want a marriage license. Am I a nut?"

"You're surprisingly conventional."

"But it's the same old story. He's reluctant to get a divorce. He keeps putting it off . . . Mmmm, this is good scotch. Why don't you drink, Qwill?"

"Too young."

Hixie wasn't really listening. She was intent on her own problem. "Our plans were all made. We were going to live in Paris. I was even studying French, and Dan announced—" She caught her tongue, threw Qwilleran a panicky glance.

He kept an expressionless face.

"Well, now you know," she said, throwing up her hands. "I didn't mean to let it slip. For God's sake, don't—"

"Don't worry. I'm not a—"

"I'd hate for Robert to find out. He'd have a fit. You know how he is. So proper!" She stopped and groaned with chagrin. "And Joy is a friend of yours! Ooh! I really put my foot in it this time. Promise me— Your drinks are so— Haven't slept for five— I'm so tired."

"The scotch will make you sleep well," Qwilleran said. "Shall I walk you home?"

She was a little unsteady on her feet, and he escorted her around the balcony to her own apartment just in time to say good evening to a tight-lipped Charlotte Roop, who was coming home from work.

When he returned to his own place, he found Koko busy tilting pictures.

"Stop that!" Qwilleran barked. He walked to the Art Nouveau print and took it off the hook, slid the metal plate aside, and peered through the aperture. He saw Dan toss a bundle of rags into one of the small kilns. He saw Dan look through the spyhole

of a larger kiln and make a notation in a ledger. He saw Dan set
an alarm clock and lie down on a cot.

Qwilleran slowly turned away from the peephole. He had recognized the rags.

SIXTEEN

Qwilleran skipped breakfast Wednesday morning. He made a cup of instant coffee in his apartment and got an early start on the column about the Friendly Fatties. Koko was sitting on the desk, trying to help, rubbing his jaw on the button that changed margins, getting his tail caught in the cylinder when Qwilleran triple-spaced.

"At the Friendly Fatties' weekly dinner," the man was typing, "the Fun is more fun than the Food."

There was a knock at his door, and he found Robert Maus standing there, his round-shouldered posture looking less like a gracious bow and more like a haggard droop.

"May I violate the privacy of your sanctum sanctorum?" asked the attorney. "I have a matter of some moment, as it were, to discuss with you."

"Sure. Come in. I hear you've had an unscheduled trip out of the country. You look weary."

"Weary I am, but not, I must admit, as a result of the unexpected detour in my itinerary. The fact of the matter is . . . that I returned to find a situation resembling mild . . . chaos."

"Will you have a chair?"

"Thank you. Thank you indeed."

The cats were regarding the visitor solemnly from the dining table, where they sat at attention, shoulder to shoulder and motionless.

"It is safe to assume," said the attorney, "that these are the two celebrated feline gastronomes."

"Yes, the big one is Koko, and the other is Yum Yum. When did you get back?"

"Late last evening, only to be confronted by a series of complications, which I will endeavor to enumerate, if I may. Whereas, three hundred persons have been invited to the opening of the pottery exhibition, and we are without a houseboy. Whereas, Mrs. Marron is suffering from allergic rhinitis. Whereas, the tennis club, our immediate neighbor to the west, has made a formal complaint about the issue of smoke from our chimneys. Whereas, the senior partner of Teahandle, Hansblow, Burris, Maus and Castle informs me that a major client has severed connections with our firm as a result of your column in yesterday's press."

"I'm sorry if—"

"The blame does not lie with you. However . . . permit me one more whereas. The esteemed Miss Roop has tendered a bill of complaint alleging scandalous conduct on the premises . . . One moment, I beg of you," Maus said when Qwilleran tried to interrupt. "It is well known to us all that the lady in question is a —you might say—bluenose. But it behooves us to humor the plaintiff for reasons best known to—"

"Never mind the preamble," Qwilleran said. "What's she objecting to?"

Maus cleared his throat and began: "To wit, one female tenant observed entering Number Six at a late hour *en négligé*. To wit, a second female tenant observed *leaving* Number Six at a late hour in a flagrant state of inebriation."

Qwilleran blew into his mustache. "I hope you don't think I'm going to dignify that gossip with an explanation."

"Explanations are neither requested nor expected—far from it," said Maus. "Let me, however, state my position. The firm with which I have the honor to be associated is of an extremely conservative bent. In the year of our Lord one thousand nine hundred and thirteen, a member of the firm was ousted from that august body—then known as Teahandle, Teahandle and Whitbread—for the simple misdemeanor of drinking three cups of punch at a garden party. I find it imperative, therefore, to avoid any suggestion of impropriety in this house. Any hint of unconventional conduct, if it reached the ears of my colleagues, would embarrass the firm, to state it mildly, and would, in all probability, relieve me of my partnership. The mere fact that I am the proprietor of what is unfortunately called a boarding house . . . places me on the brink of . . . disgrace."

"It's my guess," said Qwilleran, "that there's more unconventional conduct in Maus Haus than you realize."

"Spare me the details at the moment. When the exigencies of this day have abated, I shall—"

The telephone rang.

"Excuse me," said Qwilleran. He went to the desk and picked up the receiver. "Yes . . . Yes, what can I do for you? . . . Overdrawn! What do you mean?" He opened a desk drawer and brought out his checkbook, tucking the receiver between shoulder and ear while he found his current balance. "Seventeen-fifty! That's the wrong figure. I wrote a check for *seven*-fifty! Seven hundred and fifty dollars . . . I can't believe it. What's the endorsement? . . . I see . . . Are both signatures quite legible? . . . To be authentic, the last name in the first endorsement should look like *G-w-w-w* . . . Well, then, it's a forgery. And somebody has tampered with the amount of the check . . . Thanks for calling me. I can track it down at this end . . . No, I don't think there'll be any problem. I'll get back to you."

Qwilleran turned to his visitor, but the attorney had slipped out, closing the door. The newsman sat down and studied his next move with circumspection.

At four o'clock that afternoon the Great Hall was flooded with diffused light from the skylight three stories overhead. It fell on the jewellike objects exhibited on pedestals in the center of the floor. In this dramatic light the Living Glaze was brilliant, magnetic, even hypnotic. Elsewhere in the hall were the graceful shapes of Joy's thrown pots, bowls, vases, jars, and pitchers in subtle speckled grays and gray-greens, rough and smooth at the same time, like half-melted ice. Also on display were the brutal, primitive shapes of Dan's earlier slab pots in blackish browns and slate blues, decorated with globs of clay like burnt biscuits.

Under the balconies on both sides of the hall were long tables loaded with ice buckets, rented champagne glasses, and trays of hors d'oeuvres. The waiters were hurriedly enlisted students from the art school, awkward in white coats with sleeves too long or too short.

Qwilleran wandered through the hall and recognized the usual vernissage crowd: museum curators looking scholarly and aloof; gallery directors reserving their opinions; collectors gossiping among themselves; art teachers explaining the pots to one another; miscellaneous artists and craftsmen enjoying the free champagne; Jack Smith, the *Fluxion* art critic, looking like an undertaker with chronic gastritis; and one little old lady reporter from the *Morning Rampage* writing down what everyone was wearing.

And then there was Dan Graham, looking as seedy as ever, making a great show of modesty but bursting with vanity, his eyes eagerly fishing for compliments and his brow furrowing with concern whenever anyone asked him about Mrs. Graham.

"Helluva shame," he would say. "She's been working like a dog, and the little old gal was ready to crack up, so I sent her to Florida for some R-and-R. I don't want her to get sick. I don't want to lose her."

Qwilleran said to Graham, "The pottery racket must be booming, if you can afford a bash like this."

Dan gave a twisted smile. "Just got a swell commission from a restaurant in L.A., with a sizable advance, so I went out on a limb for the bubble-water. Maus kicked in the snick-snacks." He jerked his head at the refreshment table, where Mrs. Marron, red-nosed and sniffling, was replenishing the supply of crab puffs, ham fritters, cheese croquettes, cucumber sandwiches, stuffed mushrooms, tiny sausage rolls, and miniature shrimp quiches.

Then Qwilleran sought out Jack Smith. "What do you think of Dan's Living Glaze?"

"I hardly know what to say. He's done the impossible," said the critic, with an expression like cold marble. "How does he get that effect? How does he get that superb red? I saw some of his pots in a group show last winter, and I said they had the character and vitality of sewer crocks. He didn't like that, but it was true. He's come a long way since then. The merit, of course, is all in the glaze. In form they're appallingly pedestrian. Those slab pots! Made with a rolling pin . . . If only they had put *his* glaze on *her* pots: I'm going to suggest that in my review."

A young girl in owlish glasses was staring at Qwilleran, and he walked in her direction.

"Was it all right for me to come here, Mr. Qwilleran?" she asked shyly. "You told me to wait forty-eight hours."

"Any word from William?"

She shook her head sadly.

"Did you check the bank account?"

"It hasn't been touched, except that the bank added twenty-six cents interest."

"Then you'd better notify the police. And try not to worry. Here, let me get you something to eat or drink."

"No, thanks. I don't feel like it. I think I'll go home."

Qwilleran escorted her to the door and told her where to catch the River Road bus.

Returning, and wandering among the crowd, he was surprised to see the Penniman brothers. Tweedledum and Tweedle-dee, as they were called by irreverent citizens, seldom attended anything below the status-level of a French Post-Impressionist show.

While the other guests accorded them the deference that their wealth and name warranted, the brothers stood quietly listening, neither smoking nor drinking, and wearing the baffled expression that was their normal look at art functions. They represented the money, not the brains, behind the *Morning Rampage*, Qwilleran had been told.

He edged into the circle surrounding them and deftly maneuvered them away from the fund-raisers, job-seekers, and apple-polishers by a method known only to veteran reporters. "How do you like the show?" he asked.

Basil Penniman, the one with a cast in his left eye, looked at his brother Bayley.

"Interesting," said Bayley, at length.

"Have you ever seen a glaze like that?"

It was Bayley's turn to toss the conversational ball to Basil, whom he regarded inquiringly.

"Very interesting," said Basil.

"This is not for publication, is it?" asked Bayley, suddenly on guard.

"No, art isn't my beat anymore," said Qwilleran. "I just happen to live here. Wasn't it your father who built the place?"

The brothers nodded cautiously.

"This old building must have some fascinating secrets to tell," Qwilleran ventured. There was no reply, but he observed a faint stirring of reaction. "Before Mrs. Graham left town, she lent me some documents dealing with the early days of the pottery. I haven't read them yet, but I imagine they might make good story material. Our readers enjoy anything of a historical nature, especially if there's human interest involved."

Basil looked at Bayley in alarm.

Bayley turned pink. "You can't print anything without permission."

"Mrs. Graham promised the papers to us," said Basil.

"They're family property," said Bayley.

"They belong in the family," his brother echoed.

"We can take legal action to get them."

"Say, what's in those papers?" Qwilleran asked in a bantering tone. "It must be pretty hot stuff! Maybe it's a better story than I thought."

"You print that," said Bayley, his flush deepening to crimson, "and we'll—we'll—"

"Sue," Basil contributed hesitantly.

"We'll sue the *Fluxion*. That's yellow journalism, that's what it is!" Bayley was now quite purple.

Basil touched his brother's arm. "Be careful. You know what the doctor told you."

"Sorry if I alarmed you," Qwilleran said. "It was all in jest."

"Come," said Basil to Bayley, and they left the hall quickly.

Qwilleran was preening his mustache with wicked satisfaction when he spotted a tall, gaunt, gray-haired woman moving across the hall with halting step. "Inga Berry!" he exclaimed. "I'm Jim Qwilleran."

"Why, I was expecting a much younger man," she said. "Your voice on the phone had so much enthusiasm and—innocence, if you'll pardon the expression."

"Thank you, I think," he replied. "May I get you some champagne?"

"Why not? We'll take a quick look at the dirty old pots and then sit down somewhere and have a nice chat . . . Oh, my! *Oh, my!*" She had caught sight of the Living Glaze. She walked as quickly as she could toward the radiant display, leaning on her furled umbrella. "This is—this is better than I expected!"

"Do you approve?"

"They make me feel like going home and smashing all my own work." She drank her champagne rather fast. "One criticism: It's a shame to waste this magnificent glaze on rolled clay."

"That's what our critic said."

"He's right—for once in his life. You can tell him I said so." She stopped and stared across the hall. "Is that Charlotte Roop? Haven't seen her for forty years. Everybody ages but me."

"How about another glass of champagne?"

Miss Berry looked around critically. "Is that all they've got?"

"I have some scotch and bourbon in Number Six, if you'd care to come up," Qwilleran suggested.

"Hot dog!"

"I know you potters have to drink because of the dust."

"You scalawag!" She poked him with the umbrella. "Where did you hear that? You know too much."

She ascended the stairs slowly, favoring one knee, and when the door of Number Six was thrown open, she entered as if in a dream. "My, this brings back memories. Oh, the parties we used to give here! We were devils! . . . Hello, cats . . . Now where's this secret window you told me about?"

Qwilleran uncovered the peephole, and Miss Berry squinted through it.

"Yes," she nodded. "Penniman probably had this window cut for surveillance."

"What would he be spying on?"

"It's a long story." She sat down, groaning a little. "Arthritis," she explained. "Thank God it's in my nether joints. If it happened to my hands, I'd cut my throat. A potter's hands are his fortune. His finest tool is his thumb . . . Thank you. You're a gentleman and a scholar." She accepted a glass of bourbon. "My, this was a busy place in the old days. The pottery was humming. We had easel painters in the studios, and one weaver, and a metalsmith. Penniman had a favorite—a beautiful girl but a mediocre potter. Then along came a young sculptor, and he and the girl fell in love. He was as handsome as the dickens. They tried to keep their affair a secret, but Papa Penniman found out, and soon after that . . . well, they found the young man's body in the river . . . I'm telling you this because you're not like those other reporters. It's all ancient history now. You must be a new boy in town."

Qwilleran nodded. "Do you think his drowning was an accident, or suicide, or murder?"

Miss Berry hesitated. "The official verdict was suicide, but some of us—you won't write anything about this, will you?—some of us had our suspicions. When the reporters started hounding us, we all played dumb. We knew which side our bread was buttered on!"

"You suspected . . . Popsie?"

Miss Berry looked startled. "*Popsie!* How did you—? Well, never mind. The poor girl jumped in the river soon after. She was pregnant."

"You should have done something about it."

The potter shrugged. "What could we do? Old Mr. Penniman was a wealthy man. His money did a lot of good for the city. And we had no proof . . . He's dead now. Charlotte Roop—that woman I saw downstairs—was his secretary at the time of the drownings. She used to come to our parties, but she was a fifth wheel. We were a wild bunch. The kids today think they've invented free love, but they should have been around when *we* were young! My, it's nice to be seventy-five and done with all that nonsense . . . Hello, cats," she said again.

The cats were staring at her from their blue cushion—Koko as if he understood every word, and Yum Yum as if she had never seen a human before.

Qwilleran asked, "Why did Charlotte Roop hang around, if she didn't fit in?" He was casually lighting his pipe.

"Well, the gossips said she had a crush on her boss, and she was jealous of his beautiful paramour." Miss Berry lowered her voice. "We always thought it was Charlotte who tattled to Penniman about the affair that was going on behind his back."

"What gave you that impression?"

"Just putting two and two together. After the tragedy, Charlotte had a nervous collapse and quit her job. I lost track of her then. And if somebody didn't tip him off, why would Penniman have cut that peephole in the wall?" She leaned forward and jabbed a finger toward the newsman. "It was *just before the tragedy* that Penniman commissioned Herb Stock to paint that Egyptian-style mural in the kiln room. Now I can guess why!" Miss Berry sipped her drink and mused about the past. "Penniman was very generous with commissions, but you didn't dare cross him! You couldn't print any of this in your paper, of course."

"Not unless we wanted to start a newspaper war," Qwilleran said. It always amazed him how carelessly people spoke their minds to the press, and how surprised and indignant they were when they found themselves quoted in print.

The telephone rang.

Qwilleran picked up the receiver and said, "Hello? . . . Yes, did Odd Bunsen tell you what we want? . . . You did? Quick work! What did you find? . . . Wine bottles! Anything else? . . . What *kind* of broken crockery? . . . All of it? Wow! . . . Would you say the broken stuff was once a part of round or square pieces? . . . I see. You've been a great help. How much do I owe you? . . . Well, that's kind of you. Hope it wasn't too cold down there . . . Let me know if I can do anything for you."

Qwilleran offered to take Miss Berry to dinner, but she said she had other plans. As he accompanied her to the door he asked casually, "By the way, what happens if you heat up a kiln too fast?"

"You lost a month's work! The pots explode! It's the most heartbreaking fireworks you ever heard—pop! pop! pop!—one after the other, and it's too late to do anything about it."

Qwilleran was glad Miss Berry had other plans. He wanted to dine alone, to think. First he telephoned Dan Graham's loft and invited the potter in for a drink after dinner. To celebrate, he said. Then he went to Joe Pike's Seafood Hut.

It was a frustrating situation. Qwilleran had all kinds of curious notions that a crime had been committed but no proof—except the forged endorsement on an altered check. Added to the baffling evidence now was the frogman's report. According to his description of the "crockery" found in the river, Dan had dumped a load of broken pots. They were round pots! Joy's work, not his own. And the bright blues and greens described by the diver were the Living Glaze. Even in the muddy water, the diver said, the fragments glowed.

As Qwilleran sipped the green turtle soup, he feared that the situation was hopeless. With the baked clams he began to take heart. Halfway through the red snapper he hit upon an idea, and the salad brought him to a decision. He would take the bold step—a confrontation with Dan—and hope to expose the potter's hand. The manner of approach was the crucial factor. He was sure he could handle it.

Dan arrived at Number Six about nine o'clock, glowing with the day's success. Patting his stomach, he said, "You missed a good supper downstairs. Pork chops and some kind of mashed potatoes. I don't go for the fancy grub that Maus cooks, but the housekeeper can put on an honest-to-gosh feed when she wants to. I'm a meat-and-potatoes man myself. How about you?"

"I can eat anything," Qwilleran said over his shoulder as he rattled ice cubes. "What do you like with your bourbon?"

"Just a little ginger ale." Dan made himself at home in the big chair. "My first wife was a humdinger of a cook."

"You were married before you met Joy?"

"Yep. It didn't work out. But she sure could cook! That woman could make chicken taste like *roast beef!*"

Qwilleran served Dan his drink, poured ginger ale for himself, and made a cordial toast to the success of the potter's exhibition. Then he looked around for the cats; he always noted their reaction to visitors, and often he was influenced by their attitudes. The cats had retired behind the books on the bookshelf. He could see three inches of tail curling around a volume of English history, but it was not a tail in repose. The tip lifted in regular rhythm, tapping the shelf lightly. It meant Koko was listening. Qwilleran knew the tail belonged to Koko; Yum Yum's tail had a kink in the tip.

After Dan had quoted with relish all the compliments he had received at the champagne party, Qwilleran made a wry face and said, "I don't know whether to believe you or not."

"Whatcha say?"

"Sometimes I think you're the world's champion liar." Qwilleran used his most genial tone. "I think you're pulling my leg half the time."

"What do you mean?" Dan clearly did not know whether to grin or scowl.

"Just for example, you told me you threw the switch when Joy's hair caught in the wheel, and you saved her life. But *you* know and *I* know she never uses the electric wheel. I think you just wanted to play the big hero. Come on, now. Confess!" Qwilleran's eyes were gently mocking.

"No, you've got me all wrong! Cripes! The kickwheel was on the blink that night, and she was rushing to finish some pots for the next firing, so she used the power wheel. There's no law against that, is there?"

"And then you told Bunsen and me there were rats in the basement; we all know that Maus had the exterminator in last month. What is this guff you're handing me?"

"Well, I'll tell you," Dan said, relaxing as he came to the conclusion that the newsman was ribbing him. "You fellows were off the track. You were trying too hard to squeeze a story out of that broken-down clay room. The real story was the Living Glaze. Am I right? No use wasting your time on stuff that isn't interesting. I know how valuable your time is. I just wanted to get you into the kiln room, that's all. Can't a guy use a little psychology, if you know what I mean?"

Qwilleran concentrated on lighting his pipe, as if it were his primary concern. "All right"—puff, puff—"I'll buy that"—puff, puff—"but how about that cock-and-bull story that Joy is in Miami for"—puff, puff—"rest and relaxation? She hates Florida."

"I know she's always saying that, but dammit, that's where she went. This guy Hamilton is down there. I think she traipsed off to see him. They had a little thing going, you know. Joy's no saint, if you know what I mean."

"Then why didn't you ship her clothes"—puff, puff—"the way she asked? How come you burned them?" Qwilleran examined his pipe critically. "There's something wrong with this tobacco." To himself he said, Watch it, Qwill. You're on thin ice.

"So help me, they were some rags she didn't want," Dan said. "You can burn cloth in a kiln to give the pots a special hazy effect. You can pull all kinds of tricks by controlling the burning gases . . . How did you know, anyway?" Dan's eyes grew steely for a moment.

"You know how reporters are, Dan. We're always snooping around. Occupational disease," the newsman explained amiably. "Have some cheese? It's good Roquefort."

"No, I'm stuffed. Man, you nag just like my wife. You're like a dog with a bone."

"Don't let it burn you. I'm playing games, that's all. Shall I refill your glass?" Qwilleran poured Dan another drink. "Okay, try this on for size: You said you weren't taking a trip, but according to the grapevine you're heading for Paris."

"Well, I'll be jiggered! You're a nosy bugger." Dan scratched his cheek. "I suppose that nutty Hixie's been blabbing. I had to tell her *something* to get her off my neck. That kid's man-hungry, I'm telling you."

"But are you really planning to leave? I have a friend who might take over the pottery if you're giving it up."

"Just between you and me and the gatepost," the potter said, lowering his voice, "I can't warm up to this neck of the woods. I'd go back to California if I could break my contract with Maus, but I don't want to spill the beans till I know for sure."

"Is that why you broke all those pots and dumped them in the river?"

Dan's mouth fell open. "What?"

"All those blue and green pots. You can see them down there, shining right through the mud. Must be the Living Glaze."

"Oh, those!" Dan took a long swallow of bourbon and ginger ale. "Those were rejects. When I got the notion for the new glaze, I tried it out on some bisque that had sagged in the kiln. Those pots were early experiments. No point in keeping them."

"Why'd you dump them in the river?"

"Are you kidding? To save a little dough, man. The city charges by the bushel for collecting rubbish, and Maus—that old pinch-penny—makes me pay for my own trash removal."

"But why in the middle of the night?"

Dan shrugged. "Day or night, I don't know the difference. Before a show you work twenty-four hours a day. When you're firing, you check the kiln every couple of hours around the clock . . . Say, what are you? Some kind of policeman?"

"Old habit of mine," Qwilleran said; the ice was getting thinner. "When I see something that doesn't add up, I have to check it out . . . such as . . . when I write a check for seven hundred and fifty dollars and somebody ups it a thousand dollars." He regarded the potter calmly but steadily.

"What do you mean?"

"That check I gave Joy, so she could take a vacation. *You* cashed it. You should know what I mean." Qwilleran loosened his tie.

"Sure, I cashed it," Dan said, "but it was made out for seven-*teen*-fifty. Joy left in a hurry, I guess, and forgot to take it with her. She'd forget her head if it wasn't fastened on. She called me from Miami and said she'd left a check for seventeen hundred and fifty dollars in the loft, and I should endorse it for her and wire her half of the money. She told me to use the rest for a big swing-ding for the opening."

"This afternoon you told me the champagne party was financed by the Los Angeles deal."

Dan looked apologetic. "Didn't want you to know she'd handed me half of your dough. Didn't want to rile you up . . . Are you sure you didn't make out that check for seventeen fifty? How could anybody add a thousand bucks to a check?"

"Easy," Qwilleran said. "Put a one in front of the numeral and add *teen* to the end of the word *seven*."

"Well, that's what she did, then, because it sure as hell wasn't me. I told you she's no saint. If you'd been married to her for fifteen years, you'd find out." Dan shifted impatiently in his chair. "Jeez! You're an ornery cuss. If I wasn't so good-natured, I'd punch you in the kisser. But just to prove there's no hard feelings, I'm going to give you a present." He pushed himself out of the deep chair. "I'll be right back, and if you want to sweeten my drink while I'm gone, that's okay with me."

That was when Qwilleran felt a tremor of uncertainty. That check he had given Joy—he had written it without his glasses and in a state of emotion. Perhaps he had made a mistake himself. He paced the floor, waiting for Dan's return.

"Koko, what are you hiding for?" he mumbled in the direction of the bookcase. "Get out here and give me some moral support!"

There was no reply, but the length of the brown tail that was visible slapped the shelf vehemently.

Shortly Dan returned with two pieces of pottery: a large square urn with a footed base and a small rectangular planter. The large piece was in the rare red glaze.

"Here!" he said, shoving them across the desk. "I appreciate what you're doing for me at the paper. You said you like red, so the big one's for you. Give the blue one to the photographer. He was a good egg. See that he gets me some copies of the pictures, will you? . . . Well, here—take 'em—don't be bashful."

Qwilleran shook his head. "We can't accept those. They're too valuable." The red pots in the exhibition, he remembered, had been priced in four figures.

"Don't be a stuffed shirt," Dan said. "Take the damn things. I sold all the rest of the Living Glaze. People gobbled them up! I've got a stack of checks that would make you cross-eyed. Don't worry; I'll make up that thousand bucks. Just see that I get some good space in the paper."

Dan left the apartment, and Qwilleran felt his face growing hot. The confrontation had settled none of his doubts. Either he was on the wrong track entirely, or Dan was a fast-talking con man. The potter's seedy appearance was deceiving; he was slick —too slick.

There was a grunt from the bookshelves, and a cat backed into view—first the sleek brown tail, then the dark fawn haunches, the lighter body, and the brown head. Koko gave an electric shudder that combed, brushed, and smoothed his fur in one efficient operation.

"I thought I had everything figured out," Qwilleran said to him, "but now I'm not so sure."

Koko made no comment but jumped from the bookcase to the desk chair and then to the desktop. He paused, warily, before beginning to stalk the red urn. With his body low and his tail stiffened, he approached it with breathless stealth, as if it were a living thing. Cautiously he passed his nose over its surface, his whiskers angling sharply upward. His nose wrinkled, and he bared his teeth. He sniffed again, and a growl came from his throat, starting like a distant moan and ending in a hair-raising screech.

"Both of us can't be wrong," Qwilleran said. "That man is lying about everything, and Joy is dead."

SEVENTEEN

JOY HAD HATED and feared the river, and now Qwilleran was repelled by the black water beyond the window. Even Koko had shrunk from it when they explored the boardwalk. Two artists had drowned there long ago, more recently a small child, and now perhaps Joy, perhaps William. A fog was settling on the river. Boats hooted, and the foghorn at Plum Point was moaning a dirge.

Qwilleran dialed the press room at police headquarters, and while he waited for the *Fluxion* night man to come on the line, he summed up his deductions. The Living Glaze was Joy's creation; he had seen Dan copying formulas from her loose-leaf notebook into a ledger. That being true, everything else fell into place: Dan's refusal to let her show her work prior to the exhibition; the broken ceramics in the river in shapes typical of Joy's handiwork; the consensus among exhibition visitors that the glaze was too good for the clay forms beneath. Yet Dan was brazenly taking credit for the Living Glaze. Would he dare take credit if he knew Joy was alive?

Lodge Kendall barked into the press room phone.

"Sorry to bother you again, Lodge," said Qwilleran. "Remember what I asked you about last week? I'm still interested in anything they find in the river. Where do bodies usually wash up? . . . How far is that? . . . How long does it take before they drift down to the island? It wouldn't hurt to alert the police, although I have no definite proof at this time. How about bringing Lieutenant Hames to the Press Club tomorrow? . . . Fine! See what you can do. Better still, bring him to the Golden Lamb Chop, and I'll buy . . . Yes, I *am* desperate!"

Koko was still crouched on the desktop, watching the red thing suspiciously. The small blue planter had the same fantastic glaze, yet Koko ignored it.

Cats can't distinguish colors, Qwilleran remembered. Joy had told him so. There was something else about the red urn that bothered the small animal. On the other hand, the red library book also had offended Koko; twice he had pushed it from the bookshelf to the floor.

Qwilleran found the red volume where he had wedged it between two larger books for security. It was quite a definitive book on ceramics, and Qwilleran settled down in his chair to browse through chapters on wedging clay, using the wheel, pulling a lip, beveling a foot, formulating a glaze, packing a kiln, firing a load. It ended with a chatty chapter on the history and legend of the ceramic art.

Halfway through the last chapter Qwilleran felt nauseated. Then the blood rushed to his face, and he gripped the arms of the chair. In anger he jumped up, strode across the room, and swung the book at the red pottery urn, sweeping it off the desk. The cats fled in alarm as the urn shattered on the ceramic floor tiles.

Still gripping the book, Qwilleran lunged out of the apartment and around the balcony to Number One. Robert Maus came to the door, tying the belt of a flannel robe.

"Got to talk to you!" Qwilleran said abruptly.

"Certainly. Certainly. Please come in. I presume you have heard the midnight newscast: a bomb scare at the Golden Lamb Chop . . . My dear fellow, are you ill? You are shaking!"

"You've got a madman in the house!" Qwilleran blurted.

"Sit down. Sit down. Calm yourself. Would you accept a glass of sherry?"

Qwilleran shook his head impatiently.

"Some black coffee?"

"Dan has murdered his wife! I know it, I know it!"

"I beg your pardon?"

"And probably William, too. And I think Joy's cat was the first victim. I think the cat was an experiment."

"One moment, I beg of you," said Maus. "What is this incoherent outburst? Will you repeat it? Slowly, please. And kindly sit down."

Qwilleran sat down as if his knees had collapsed. "I'll take that black coffee."

"It will require only a moment to filter a fresh cup."

The attorney stepped into his kitchenette, and Qwilleran gathered his thoughts. He was in better control when Maus returned with the coffee. He repeated his suspicions: "First, the Grahams' cat disappeared; then Joy disappeared; then William. I say he has murdered them all. We've got to do something!"

"This is a preposterous accusation! Where is your proof, if I may ask?"

"There's no tangible proof, but I *know!*" Qwilleran touched his mustache nervously; he thought it better not to mention Koko's behavior. "In fact," he said, "I'm going to see a homicide detective tomorrow."

Maus raised a hand. "One moment! Let us consider the consequences before you speak to the authorities."

"Consequences? You mean adverse publicity? I'm sorry, Maus, but publicity is inevitable now."

"But pray what brings you to the . . . monstrous conclusion that Graham has . . . has—"

"Everything points to it. For years Joy has been outshining her husband. Now she formulates a spectacular glaze that will allow her to eclipse him completely. The man has a sizable ego. He desperately wants attention and acclaim. The solution is simple: Why not get rid of his wife, apply her glaze to his own pottery, and take the credit? The marriage is falling apart anyway. So why not? . . . I tell you it's true! And once Joy was out of the way, Dan took the precaution of destroying all her pottery that carried the new glaze. We found the stuff—"

"You must pardon me if I say," the attorney interrupted, "that this . . . this wild scenario sounds like a figment of an overwrought imagination."

Qwilleran ignored the remark. "Meanwhile, Dan discovers

that William suspects him, and so the houseboy must be silenced. You have to admit that William has been conspicuously absent."

The attorney stared in disbelief.

"Furthermore," the newsman went on. "Dan is preparing to leave the country. We've got to act fast!"

"One question, if you please. Can you produce the prime evidence?"

"The bodies? No one will ever find them. At first I thought he'd dumped them in the river. Then I found a sickening fact in a book—in *this* book." Qwilleran shook the red volume at his incredulous listener. "In ancient China they used to throw the bodies of unwanted babies into the pottery kilns."

Maus made no move. He looked stunned.

"Those kilns downstairs can heat up to twenty-three hundred degrees! I repeat: The bodies will never be found."

"Ghastly!" the attorney said in a whisper.

"You remember, Maus, that the tennis club complained about the smoke last weekend. And William knew something was wrong. Ordinarily pots take twenty-four hours for firing and twenty-four for cooling. If you speed it up, they explode! William told me Dan was firing too fast. The pottery door was locked, but William knew about the tiny window in Number Six, overlooking the kiln room . . . Do you know about the peephole?"

Maus nodded.

"And there's another story in this book," Qwilleran said. "It happened centuries ago in China. A barnyard animal wandered into a kiln while it was being loaded. The animal was cremated, and the clay pots emerged in a glorious shade of *red!*"

The attorney looked acutely uncomfortable.

"Joy's cat was probably the first experiment," Qwilleran added.

Maus said, "I feel unwell. Let us discuss this in the morning. I must think."

That night Qwilleran found it impossible to sleep. He was up, he was down, he tried to read, he walked back and forth in the apartment. Koko was also awake and alert, watching the man with concern. For one brief moment Qwilleran considered a knockout shot of whiskey, but he caught Koko's eye and desisted. Eventually he remembered some cough syrup in the medicine cabinet. It contained a strong sedative. He took a double dose.

Soon he was sleeping too deeply to dream. The foghorn continued to moan, and the boats hooted their continual warnings, but he heard nothing.

Suddenly he catapulted out of the depths of his drugged sleep and found himself sitting up in the dark. In his groggy state he thought there had been an explosion. He shook his head, remembered where he was. A kiln! That's what it was, he told himself. A kiln had exploded. He switched on the bed lamp.

There had been no explosion—only the fall of a body, the crash of a chair, the crack of a head hitting the ceramic tile floor, the shattering of a window. On the floor, his head bloodied, lay Dan Graham, his legs sprawled across a tangle of gray yarn. The room was crisscrossed with yards and yards of gray strands, like a giant spiderweb.

On the bookcase sat Koko, his ears back and his slanted eyes shining red in the lamplight.

"And that's how it happened," Qwilleran explained to Rosemary when she dropped in at Number Six before dinner on Thursday. He was wearing his new suit for the first time, planning to take Rosemary to the Golden Lamb Chop, and the scale indicated he was ten pounds lighter. He also felt ten years younger.

"Koko had booby-trapped the apartment with your ball of yarn," he said, "and Dan tripped over it in the dark."

"How do you know Koko spun the web?" Rosemary asked. "More likely it was Yum Yum."

"I bow to your feminine intuition. Forgive my chauvinism."

"What was Dan going to attack you with? One newscaster called it a blunt weapon. The newspaper said it was a wooden club."

"You'd never believe it, but it was a rolling pin! A heavy wooden one that potters use to roll clay for slabpots. When Dan stumbled into the booby trap, the rolling pin flew out of his grasp and broke a window."

Rosemary shook her head in wonder. "He wasn't a brainy man, but he was crafty, and I'm surprised he thought he could get away with it."

"He was all ready to leave the country. The Renault was packed and ready to leave for an early morning flight. He wasn't even going to hang around to read the reviews of his show."

The cats had just finished eating a beef and oyster pâté sent up by Robert Maus, and now they were sitting on the desk, washing faces and paws in an aura of absolute contentment. Qwilleran regarded them with pride and gratitude. He remembered the *pb* on the page in the typewriter.

"I was wrong about one detail," he went on. "They found William's body. If Dan had committed only one murder, he could have risen to fame with Joy's glazes. But when he spiked William's drink with lead oxide, he was in trouble. He couldn't dispose of William's body in the kiln; it was full of pots in the cooling stage. So he stored it in the slip tank in the basement of the clay room."

There was a knock on the door, and Qwilleran opened it to admit Hixie.

"Did I hear the rattle of ice cubes?" she asked.

"Come in. We'll open the bottle of champagne the Press Club sent to Koko. And Yum Yum," Qwill added, with an apologetic glance at Rosemary.

Hixie said, "I wonder how Teahandle, Hansblow, Et Cetera, Et Cetera reacted to the publicity? Television and everything! I'll bet Mickey Maus is in the soup."

"It's a blessing in disguise," said Rosemary. "Now he'll retire from law and do what he has always wanted to do—open a restaurant."

There was another knock at the door—a positive, urgent, angry knock. Charlotte Roop was standing there with tense lips and clenched fists. She marched into the apartment with an aggressive step and announced, "Mr. Qwilleran, I would like a drink. A strong drink! A glass of *sherry!*"

"Why . . . certainly, Miss Roop. I think we have sherry. Or would you like champagne?"

"I need something to quiet my nerves." She put a trembling hand to her flushed throat. "I have just resigned from the Heavenly Hash House chain. I resigned in moral indignation!"

"But you liked your job so much!' Rosemary protested.

"What happened?" Qwilleran asked.

"The three owners," Charlotte began, her voice beginning to

quaver, "the men I respected so highly have been engaged in the most disreputable maneuver I have ever encountered in the business world. I overheard a conversation—quite by accident, of course—in the conference room . . . Is this champagne? Thank you, Mr. Qwilleran." She took a cautious sip.

"Well, go on," said Hixie. "What have they been doing? Watering the soup?"

Charlotte looked flustered. "How can I tell you? It pains me to mention it . . . *They* are the ones who have been trying to ruin Mr. Sorrel's restaurant!"

"But they're not in the same league," Qwilleran protested. "The Hash Houses don't compete with the Golden Lamb Chop."

"The Golden Lamb Chop," Charlotte explained, "occupies a very valuable corner, with exposure to three major highways. The Hash House syndicate, through brokers, has been trying to buy it, but Mr. Sorrel would not sell. So they resorted to unscrupulous tactics. I am horrified!"

"Would you testify in court?" Qwilleran asked.

"Yes indeed! I would testify even if their gangster friends threatened to—threatened to—"

"Waste you," Hixie said. "A five-letter word meaning 'to bump off.' "

"If Mr. Maus opens a restaurant, you can manage it for him," Rosemary said.

The voices of the three women rambled on, and Qwilleran listened with bemused inattention. He liked the gentle-voiced Rosemary; he felt comfortable with her, and comfort was beginning to be of utmost importance. His emotional but brief reunion with Joy had been a misstep in the march of time, and now her memory was relegated to the past, where it belonged. He doubted, however, that he would ever again say that his favorite color was red.

There was a click on the desk, and he looked up to see Koko walking across the typewriter keyboard.

"Look!" Hixie squealed. "He's typing!"

Qwilleran walked over and looked at the sheet of paper. He put on his glasses and looked again. "He's ordering a bite to eat," the newsman said. "Since we moved to Maus Haus, he has learned to like caviar."

Koko had stepped on the *K* with his right paw, on *V* with his left, and then on the *R*.

The Cat Who Played Brahms

ONE

FOR JIM QWILLERAN, veteran journalist, it was one of the most appalling moments of his career. Years before, as a war correspondent, he had been strafed on the beaches; as a crime reporter he had been a target of the Mob. Now he was writing restaurant reviews for a midwestern newspaper, the *Daily Fluxion*, and he was not prepared for the shocking situation at the Press Club.

The day had started well enough. He had eaten a good breakfast at his boarding house: a wedge of honeydew melon, an omelette *fines herbes* with sautéed chicken livers, cheese popovers, and three cups of coffee. He planned to lunch with his old friend Arch Riker at the Press Club, their favorite haunt.

At twelve noon Qwilleran bounded up the steps of the grimy limestone fortress that had once been the county jail but now dispensed food and drink to the working press. As he approached the ancient nail-studded portal, he sensed that something was wrong. He smelled fresh varnish! His sharp ear detected that the massive door no longer creaked on its hinges! He stepped into the lobby and gasped. The murky, smoky ambience that he loved so well was now all freshness and sparkle.

Qwilleran was aware that the Press Club had been closed for two weeks for something called annual housekeeping, but no one had hinted at this metamorphosis. It had happened while he had been out-of-town on assignment.

His luxuriant pepper-and-salt moustache was rampant with rage, and he pounded it into submission with his fist. Instead of the old paneled walls, black with numberless coats of cheap varnish, the lobby was wallpapered with something resembling his grandmother's tablecloths. Instead of the scarred plank floor rippled with a century of wear, there was wall-to-wall carpet over thick rug padding. Instead of fluorescent tubes glaring on the domed ceiling, there was a chandelier of polished brass. Even the familiar mustiness was missing, replaced by a chemical smell of newness.

Gulping down his shock and dismay, the newsman dashed into the bar, where he always lunched in a far dark corner. There he found more of the same: creamy walls, soft lighting, hanging baskets of plastic plants, and mirrors. *Mirrors!* Qwilleran shuddered.

Arch Riker, his editor at the *Daily Fluxion,* was sitting at the usual table with his usual glass of Scotch, but the scarred wooden table had been sanded and varnished, and there were white paper placemats with scalloped edges. The waitress was there promptly with Qwilleran's usual glass of tomato juice, but she was not wearing her usual skimpy white uniform with frilly handkerchief in the breast pocket. All the waitresses were now dressed as French maids in chic black outfits with white aprons and ruffled caps.

"Arch! What happened?" Qwilleran demanded. "I don't believe what I'm seeing!" He lowered his substantial bulk into a chair and groaned.

"Well, the club has lots of women members now," Riker explained calmly, "and they got themselves appointed to the housekeeping committee so they could clean the place up. It's called reversible renovation. Next year's housekeeping committee can rip out the wallpaper and carpet and go back to the original filth and decrepitude. . . ."

"You sound as if you like it. Traitor!"

"We have to swing with the times," Riker said with the bored equanimity of an editor who has seen it all. "Look at the menu and decide what you want to eat. I've got a meeting at one-thirty. I'm going to order the lamb curry."

"I've lost my appetite," Qwilleran said, his disgruntled expression accentuated by the downcurve of his moustache. He waved an arm at the surrounding scene. "The place has lost all its character. It even smells phony." He raised his nose and sniffed. "Synthetic! Probably carcinogenic!"

"You're getting to have a nose like a bloodhound, Qwill. No one else has complained about the smell."

"And another thing," Qwilleran said with belligerence. "I don't like what's happening at the *Fluxion* either."

"What do you mean?"

"First they assigned all those women to the copy desk in the City Room and switched all those men to the Women's Department. Then they gave us unisex restrooms. Then they moved in all those new desks in green and orange and blue. It looks like a circus! Then they took away my typewriter and gave me a video display terminal that gives me a headache."

Riker said in his soothing tone: "You never forgot those old movies, Qwill. You still want reporters to type with their hats on and poke the keys with two fingers."

Qwilleran slumped in his chair. "Look here, Arch. I've been trying to make up my mind about something, and now I've made a decision. I've got three weeks of vacation coming and two weeks of comp time. I want to add some leave-of-absence and go away for three months."

"You've gotta be kidding."

"I'm tired of writing flattering hogwash about restaurants that advertise in the *Fluxion*. I want to go up north and get away from city hype and city pollution and city noise and city crime."

"Are you all right, Qwill?" Riker asked with alarm. "You're not sick or something, are you?"

"Is it abnormal to want to breathe a little fresh air?"

"It'll kill you! You're a city boy, Qwill. So am I. We were both brought up on carbon monoxide and smoke and all that dirt that blows around Chicago. I'm your oldest friend, and I say: *Don't do it!* You're just getting on your feet financially, and . . ." (he lowered his voice) "Percy is thinking about a great new assignment for you."

Qwilleran grunted. He knew all about the managing editor's great new assignments. Four of them had come his way in the last few years, and every one of them was an insult to a former war correspondent and prize-winning crime reporter. "What is it this time?" he mumbled. "Obituaries? Household hints?"

Riker smiled smugly before saying in a whisper: "Investigative reporting! You can call your own shots. Expose political graft, corporate fraud, environmental violations, government spending, anything you dig up."

Qwilleran touched his moustache gingerly and stared across the table at his editor. Investigative reporting was something he had wanted to do long before it became the media rage. Yet his sensitive upper lip—the source of his best hunches—was sending him signals. "Maybe next fall. Right now I want to spend the summer where people don't lock their doors or take the car keys out of the ignition."

"The job may not be open next fall. We've found out the *Morning Rampage* is hunting for an investigative reporter, and Percy wants to beat them to the gun. You know how he is. You're taking a big gamble if you're not here to grab it when it's offered to you."

The waitress returned to serve Riker another Scotch and take their lunch order. "You're looking thin," she said to Qwilleran. "What'll you have? Half-pound burger with fries, double malt, and apple pie?"

He threw her a grouchy look. "I'm not hungry."

"Order a TLT," she suggested. "You can eat the lettuce and tomato and take the turkey home to Koko. I'll bring you a doggie bag."

Qwilleran's Siamese cat was a celebrity at the Press Club. Koko's portrait hung in the lobby along with Pulitzer Prize winners, and he was probably the only cat in the history of journalism who had his own press card signed by the chief of police. Although Qwilleran's suspicious nature and inquisitive mind had brought a few criminals to justice, it was commonly understood at the Press Club that the brains behind his success belonged to a feline of outstanding intelligence and sensory perception. Koko always seemed to sniff or scratch in the right place at the right time.

The two newsmen applied themselves to the lamb curry and the turkey sandwich in silence, indicating deep thought. Finally Riker asked: "Where would you go if you took the summer off?"

"I'd take a little place on the lake, about four hundred miles north. Near Mooseville."

"That far away? What would you do with the cats?"

"Take them along."

"You don't have a car. And there are no taxis in the north woods."

"I could put a down payment on a car—a used car, of course."

"Of course," said Riker, knowing his friend's reputation for thriftiness. "And I suppose the feline genius will get a driver's license."

"Koko? I wouldn't be surprised. He's getting interested in pushbuttons, knobs, dials, levers—anything mechanical."

"But what would you *do*, Qwill, in a place like Mooseville? You don't fish. You don't sail. The lake up there is too cold for swimming. It's frozen ice in winter and melted ice in summer."

"Don't worry, Arch. I've got plans. I've got a great idea for a book. I'd like to try writing a novel—with lots of sex and violence. All the good stuff."

Riker could only stare and search his mind for more objections. "It would cost you a bundle. Do you realize the rent they're getting for summer cottages?"

"Actually," Qwilleran said with a note of triumph, "it won't cost me a cent. I've got an old aunt up there, and she has a cabin I can use."

"You never told me about any old aunt."

"She's not really a relative. She was a friend of my mother's, and I called her Aunt Fanny when I was a kid. We lost touch, but she saw my byline in the *Fluxion* and wrote to me. We've been corresponding ever since. . . . Speaking of bylines, my name was spelled wrong in yesterday's paper."

"I know, I know," Riker said. "We have a new copy editor, and no one told her about that ridiculous *W*. We caught it in the second edition."

The waitress brought the coffee—a brew as black as the sooty varnish concealed by the new wallpaper—and Riker studied his cup in search of clues to Qwilleran's aberrant behavior. "How about your friend? The one who eats health foods. What does she think about your sudden insanity?"

"Rosemary? She's in favor of fresh air, exercise, all that jazz."

"You haven't been smoking your pipe lately. Is that her idea?"

"Are you implying I never have any ideas of my own? What happened, I realized how much trouble it is to buy tobacco, fill a pipe, tamp it, light it, relight it two or three times, knock out the ashes, empty the ashtray, clean the pipe . . ."

"You're getting old," Riker said.

After lunch the restaurant reviewer went back to his olive-green desk with matching telephone and VDT, and the feature editor attended the meeting of assistant editors, sub-editors, group editors, divisional editors, managing editors, and executive editors.

Qwilleran was pleased that his announcement had jarred Riker's professional cool. Admittedly the editor's questions had dented his resolve. How would he react to three months of the simple life after a lifetime of urban chaos? It was true he planned to do some writing during the summer, but how many hours a day can one sit at a typewriter? There would be no lunches at the Press Club, no telephone calls, no evenings with friends, no gourmet dinners, no big league ballgames, no Rosemary.

Nevertheless, he needed a change. He was disenchanted with the *Fluxion,* and the offer of a lakeside hideaway for the entire season appealed to his thrifty nature.

On the other hand, Aunt Fanny had mentioned nothing about comforts and conveniences. Qwilleran liked an extra-long bed, deep lounge chairs, good reading lamps, a decent refrigerator, plenty of hot water, and trouble-free plumbing. He would undoubtedly miss the amenities of Maus Haus, the glamorous boarding house where he occupied a luxury apartment. He would miss the Robert Maus standard of elegant dining and the camaraderie of the other tenants, especially Rosemary.

The green telephone on his desk buzzed, and he answered it absent-mindedly.

"Qwill, have you heard the news?" It was Rosemary's velvet voice, but it had the high pitch of alarm.

"What's happened?" There had been two homicides at Maus Haus in the last year, but the murderer was now behind bars, and the residents had settled down to pleasurable living and a sense of security.

"Robert is selling the building," Rosemary said plaintively, "and we've all got to move out."

"Why is he selling? Everything was going so well."

"Someone made him a wonderful offer for the property. You know he's always wanted to give up his law practice and open a fine restaurant. He says this is his chance. It's prime real estate, and a developer wants to build a high-rise apartment house."

"That's really bad news," Qwilleran agreed. "Robert has spoiled us all with his Châteaubriand and his lobster thermidor and his artichoke hearts Florentine. Why don't you come over to Number Six when you get home? We'll talk about it."

"I'll bring a bottle. Chill the glasses," Rosemary said. "We just got a shipment of pomegranate juice." She was part-owner of a specialty food store called Helthy-Welthy, a coy spelling that Qwilleran found obnoxious.

He replaced the receiver thoughtfully. The bad news had been a message from the fates, telling him to go north. He left the office early that afternoon with a small bag of turkey from the Press Club and a tape measure from the Blue Dragon antique shop.

The River Road bus dropped him at a used car lot, and he went directly to a row of small fuel-efficient automobiles. Methodically he moved from one vehicle to the next, opening the door and measuring the floor space behind the driver's seat.

A salesman who had been watching the performance sauntered into the picture. "Interested in a compact?"

"It all depends," Qwilleran mumbled with his head buried in the back seat. He made a mental note: *twelve by fifteen.*

"Looking for any particular model?"

"No." The drive-shaft seemed to be the problem. *Thirteen by fifteen.*

"You want automatic or stick?"

"Doesn't matter," Qwilleran said as he busied himself with the tape measure again. *Thirteen by sixteen.* After years of driving company cars from newspaper garages, he could drive anything; his selectivity had been numbed.

The salesman was studying the heavy drooping moustache and the mournful eyes. "I know you," he finally said. "Your picture's in the *Fluxion* all the time. You write about restaurants. My cousin has a pizza place in Happy View Woods."

Qwilleran grunted from the innards of a four-door.

"I'd like to show you a job that just came in. We haven't even cleaned it up yet. Last year's model—only two thousand miles. Came from an estate."

Qwilleran followed him into the garage. There stood a green two-door, not yet sprayed with New Car Scent. He ducked into the back seat with his tape measure. Then he moved the driver's seat back to accommodate his long legs and measured again. *Fourteen by sixteen.* "Perfect," he said, "although I might have to cut off the handles. How much?"

"Come in the office and we'll work out a deal," the salesman said.

The newsman drove the green car around the block and noted that it lurched, bounced, chugged, and rattled less than any company car he had ever driven. And the price was right. He made a down payment, signed some papers, and drove home to Maus Haus.

As he expected, there was a letter in his mailbox from Robert Maus, written on the man's legal stationery. It explained with the utmost compunction that the property heretofore known as Maus Haus had been purveyed, after due deliberation, to a syndicate of out-of-town investors who would be pursuing extensive plans requiring, it was regretted, the eviction of present tenants at a date not later than September 1.

Qwilleran, who had torn the envelope open on the spot, shrugged and climbed the stairs to his apartment on the balcony. As he unlocked the door to Number Six he was accompanied by a delicate essence of turkey that should have brought two hungry Siamese to meet him, prancing in leggy circles and figure eights, crowing and wailing in a discordant duet of anticipation. Instead, the two ingrates sat motionless on the white bearskin rug in a conspiracy of silence. Qwilleran knew why. They sensed an upheaval in the status quo. Although Koko and his accomplice Yum Yum were experts at devising surprises of their own, they resented changes originated by others. At Maus Haus they were perfectly satisfied with the wide sunny windowsill, the continuous entertainment provided by neighborhood pigeons, and the luxury of a bearskin rug.

"Okay, you guys," Qwilleran said. "I know you don't like to move, but wait till you see where we're going! I wish we could take the rug but it doesn't belong to us."

Koko, whose full name was Kao K'o-Kung, had the dignity of

an Oriental potentate. He sat regally tall with disapproval in every whisker. Both he and Yum Yum were aware of how magnificent they looked on the fluffy white rug. They had the classic Siamese coloring and conformation: blue eyes in a dark brown mask, pale fawn-colored fur of a quality that made mink look second-rate, elegantly long brown legs, and a graceful whip of a tail.

The man chopped the turkey for them. "C'mon and get it! They sliced it off an actual turkey this time." The two Siamese maintained their frigid reserve.

A moment later Qwilleran raised his nose. He identified a familiar perfume, and soon Rosemary knocked on the door. He greeted her with a kiss that was more than a perfunctory social peck. The Siamese sat in stony immobility.

Pomegranate juice was poured over ice with a dash of club soda, and a toast was drunk to the condemned building in memory of everything that had happened there.

"It was a way of life we'll never forget," Qwilleran said.

"It was a dream," Rosemary added.

"And occasionally a nightmare."

"I suppose you'll accept your aunt's offer now. Will the *Fluxion* let you go?"

"Oh sure. They may not let me come back, but they'll let me go. Have you made any plans?"

"I may return to Canada," Rosemary said. "Max wants to open a natural food restaurant in Toronto, and if I can sell my interest in Helthy-Welthy I might go into partnership with him."

Qwilleran huffed into his moustache. Max Sorrel! That womanizer! He said: "I was hoping you'd come up north and spend some time with me."

"I'd love it if I don't get involved in Toronto. How will you get up there?"

"I bought a car today. The cats and I will drive up to Pickax City to say hello to Aunt Fanny and then go on up to the lake. I haven't seen her for forty years. Judging from her correspondence she's a character. Her letters are cross-written."

Rosemary looked puzzled.

"My mother used to do cross-writing. She'd handwrite a page in the usual way, then turn the paper sideways and write across the original lines."

"What for? To save paper?"

"Who knows? Maybe to preserve privacy. It isn't easy to read. . . . She's not my real aunt," he went on. "Fanny and my mother were doughnut girls in World War I. Then Fanny had a career of some kind—never married. When she retired she went back to Pickax City."

"I never heard of the place."

"It used to be mining country. Her family made their fortune in the mines."

"Will you write to me, Qwill dearest?"

"I'll write—often. I'll miss you, Rosemary."

"Tell me all about Aunt Fanny after you meet her."

"She calls herself Francesca now. She doesn't like to be called Aunt Fanny. She says it makes her feel like an old woman."

"How old is she?"

"She'll be ninety next month."

TWO

QWILLERAN PACKED THE green car for the trek north: two suitcases, his typewriter, the thirteen-pound dictionary, five hundred sheets of typing paper, and two boxes of books. Because Koko refused to eat any commercial product intended for cats, there were twenty-four cans of boned chicken, red salmon, corned beef, solid pack white tuna, cocktail shrimp, and Alaska crabmeat. On the back seat was the blue cushion favored by the Siamese, and on the floor was an oval roasting pan with the handles sawed off in order to fit between the drive-shaft and the rocker-panel. It contained an inch-thick layer of kitty gravel. This was the cats' commode. After their previous commode of hand-painted tole had rusted out, Robert Maus had donated the roasting pan from his well-stocked kitchen.

The furniture in Qwilleran's apartment belonged to an earlier tenant, and his few personal possessions—such as the antique scale and a cast-iron coat of arms—were now stored for the summer in Arch Riker's basement. Thus unencumbered, the newsman started for the north country with a light heart.

His passengers in the back seat reacted otherwise. The little female howled in strident tones whenever the car turned a corner, rounded a curve, crossed a bridge, passed under a viaduct, encountered a truck, or exceeded fifty miles an hour. Koko scolded her and bit her hind leg, adding snarls and hisses to the orchestrated uproar. Qwilleran drove with clenched jaw, enduring the stares and glares of motorists who passed him, their fretful horn-honking and hostile tailgating.

The route passed through a string of suburbs and then the winding roads of horse country. Beyond that came cooler temperatures, taller pine trees, deer-crossing signs, and more pickup trucks. Pickax City was still a hundred miles ahead when Qwilleran's jangled nerves convinced him to stop for the night. The travelers checked into a tourist camp, where rickety cabins of pre-motel vintage were isolated in a wooded area. All three of them were in a state of exhaustion, and Koko and Yum Yum immediately fell asleep in the exact center of the bed.

The next day's journey was marked by fewer protests from the back seat. The temperature dropped still further, and deer-crossings became elk-crossings. The highway gradually ascended into hilly country and then plunged into a valley to become the main thoroughfare of Pickax City. Here majestic old houses reflecting the wealth of the mining and lumbering pioneers lined both sides of Main Street, which divided in the center of town and circled a little park. Facing the park were several impressive buildings: a nineteenth century courthouse, a library with the columns of a Greek temple, two churches, and a stately residence with a polished brass house number that was Aunt Fanny's.

It was a large square mansion of fieldstone, with a carriage house in the rear. A blue pickup truck stood in the driveway, and a gardener was working on the shrubs. He stared pointedly at Qwilleran with an expression the newsman could not identify. In the front door there was an old-fashioned mail slot framed in brass and engraved with the family name: Klingenschoen.

The little old lady who answered the doorbell was undoubtedly Aunt Fanny: a vigorous eighty-nine, tiny but taut with energy. Her white, powdery, wrinkled face wore two slashes of orange lipstick and glasses that magnified her eyes. She gazed at her visitor and, after focusing through the thick lenses, flung her arms wide in a dramatic gesture of welcome. Then from that little woman came a deep chesty growl:

"Bless my soul! How you have grown!"

"I should hope so," Qwilleran said genially. "The last time you saw me, I was seven years old. How are you, Francesca? You're looking great!"

Her exotic name was in keeping with her flamboyant garb: an orange satin tunic embroidered with peacocks and worn over slim black trousers. A scarf, also orange, was tied around her head and knotted on top in a way that added height to her four-feet-three.

"Come in, come in," she growled pleasantly. "My, how glad I am to see you! . . . Yes, you look just like your picture in the *Fluxion*. If only your dear mother could see you now, rest her soul. She would *adore* your moustache. Are you ready for a cup of coffee? I know you journalists drink a lot of coffee. We'll have it in the sun parlor."

Aunt Fanny led the way through a high-ceilinged hallway with a grand staircase, past a formal drawing room and ornate dining room, past a paneled library and a breakfast room smothered in chintz, into an airy room with French windows, wicker furniture, and ancient rubber plants.

In her chesty voice she said: "I have some *divine* cinnamon buns. Tom picked them up from the bakery this morning. You *adored* cinnamon buns when you were a little boy."

While Qwilleran relaxed on a wicker settee his hostess trotted away in little black Chinese slippers, disappearing into a distant part of the house, continuing a monologue that he could only half-hear. She returned carrying a large tray.

Qwilleran sprang to his feet. "Here, let me take that, Francesca."

"Thank you, dear," she barked. "You were always such a thoughtful little boy. Now you must put cream in your coffee. Tom picked it up from the dairy farm this morning. You don't get cream like this in the city, my dear."

Qwilleran preferred his coffee black, but he accepted cream, and as he bit into a doughy cinnamon bun his gaze wandered to the French windows. The gardener was leaning on his rake and peering into the room.

"Now you're going to stay for lunch," Aunt Fanny said from the depths of a huge wicker rocking chair that swallowed her tiny figure. "Tom will go to the butcher to pick up a steak. Do you like Porterhouse or Delmonico? We have a *marvelous* butcher. Would you like a baked potato with sour cream?"

"No! No! Thank you, Francesca, but I have two nervous animals in the car, and I want to get them up to the cabin as soon as possible. I appreciate the invitation, but I'll have to take a rain check."

"Or maybe you'd prefer pork chops," Aunt Fanny went on. "I'll make you a big salad. What kind of dressing do you like? We'll have crêpes suzette for dessert. I always made them for gentlemen callers when I was in college."

Qwilleran thought: Is she deaf? Or doesn't she bother to listen? The trick is to get her attention. "*Aunt Fanny!*" he shouted.

She looked startled at the name and the tone. "Yes, dear?"

"After we're settled," he said in a normal voice, "I'll come back and have lunch with you, or you can drive up to the lake and I'll take you to dinner. Do you have transportation, Francesca?"

"Yes, of course! Tom drives me. I lost my license a few years ago after a little accident. The chief of police was a *very* disagreeable person, but we got rid of him, and now we have a *charming* man. He named his youngest daughter after me . . ."

"*Aunt Fanny!*"

"Yes, dear?"

"Will you tell me how to reach the cabin?"

"Of course. It's very easy. Go north to the lake and turn left. Watch for the ruins of a stone chimney; that's all that's left of an old log schoolhouse. Then you'll see the letter *K* on a post. Turn into the gravel driveway and follow it through the woods. That's all my property. The wild cherries and sugarplums should be in blossom now. Mooseville is only three miles farther on. You can drive into town for restaurants and shopping. They have a *charming* postmistress, but don't get any ideas! She's married . . ."

"*Aunt Fanny!*"

"Yes, dear?"

"Do I need a key?"

"Goodness, no! I don't believe I've ever seen a key to the place. It's just a little old log cabin with two bunkrooms, but you'll be comfortable. It will be nice and quiet for writing. It was *too* quiet for my taste. I was in clubwork in New Jersey, you know, and I had *scads* of people around all the time. I'm so happy you're writing a book, dear. What is the title? Your dear mother would be so proud of you."

Qwilleran was travel-weary and eager to reach his destination. It required all his wiles to disengage himself from Aunt Fanny's overwhelming hospitality. As he left the house the gardener was doing something to the bed of tulips around the front steps. The man stared, and Qwilleran gave him a mock salute.

His passengers celebrated his return with howls of indignation, and Yum Yum's protests continued as a matter of principle even though there were no turns, bridges, viaducts, or large trucks. The highway ran through desolate country, some of it devastated by forest fires; skeletons of ravaged trees were frozen in a grotesque dance. Behind a sign advertising *Hot Pasties,* a restaurant had collapsed and was overgrown with weeds. Traffic was sparse, mostly pickup trucks whose drivers waved a greeting to the green two-door. The sites of defunct mines—the Dimsdale, the Big B, the Goodwinter—were marked by signs warning *Danger—Keep Out.* There was no Klingenschoen mine, Qwilleran noticed. He tuned in a local station on the car radio and turned it off in a hurry.

So Aunt Fanny had been a clubwoman! He could visualize her bustling about at afternoon teas, chairing committees, wearing flowered hats, being elected Madame President, presiding at conventions, organizing charity balls.

His ruminations were interrupted by a glance in the rearview mirror. He was being followed by a blue pickup truck. Qwilleran reduced his speed, and the truck slowed accordingly. The game continued for several miles until he was distracted by the appearance of a farm with several low sheds. Their rooftops as well as the farmyard itself were in constant motion—a bronze-colored mass, heaving and rippling. "Turkeys!" he said to his passengers. "You're going to live near a turkey farm, you lucky guys."

When he glanced again in the rearview mirror the blue pickup was nowhere to be seen.

Farther on he passed a large cultivated estate—well-kept lawns and flower beds behind a high ornamental fence. Set far back on the property were large buildings of an institutional nature.

The highway ascended a hill. Immediately two heads were raised in the back seat. Two noses sniffed the first hint of water, still a mile away. Irritable yowls changed to excited yips. Then the lake itself came into view, an endless stretch of placid blue water stretching to meet an incredibly blue sky.

"We're almost there!" Qwilleran told his restless passengers.

The route now followed the shoreline, sometimes close to the beach, sometimes dipping back into the woods. It passed a rustic gate guarding the private road to the Top o' the Dunes Club. Half a mile beyond was the crumbling chimney of the old schoolhouse—and the letter *K* on a post. Qwilleran turned into a gravel driveway that snaked through a forest of evergreens and oaks. Occasional sunlit clearings were filled with wild flowers, tree stumps, and fragrant flowering shrubs. He wished Rosemary were with him; she noticed everything and appreciated everything. After climbing over a succession of sandy dunes the driveway ended in a clearing with a sudden view of the lake, dotted with sailboats far out near the horizon.

There, perched on top of the highest dune and dwarfed by hundred-foot pine trees, was the picturesque cabin that would be his home for the summer. Its logs and chinking were dark with age. A screened porch overlooking the lake promised quiet hours of thought and relaxation. A massive fieldstone chimney and an ample woodpile suggested lazy evenings with a good book in front of a blazing fire.

The entrance to the cabin was through a second screened porch facing the woods and the clearing that served as parking lot. As Qwilleran approached it a squirrel ran up a tree, looked down at him, and scolded. Flurries of little yellow birds darted and twittered. On top of the woodpile a tiny brown animal sat up, cocked its head, and looked at the man inquiringly.

Qwilleran shook his head in disbelief. All these mysterious pleasures of nature, this peaceful country scene—they were his for three months.

A ship's bell in gleaming brass hung at the entrance to the porch. Its dangling rope tempted him to ring it for sheer joy. As he walked toward it, something slimy and alive dropped off a tree onto his head. And what was that hole in the screened door? Jagged edges bent inward as if someone had thrown a bowling ball through the wire mesh. He pressed the thumb latch of the door and stepped cautiously onto the porch. He saw a grass rug and weatherproof furniture and antique farm implements hanging on the back wall—and something else. There was a slight movement in a far corner. A beady eye glistened. A large bird with a menacing beak perched on the back of a chair, its rapa-

cious claws gripping the vinyl upholstery: A hawk? It must be a
hawk, Qwilleran thought. It was his first encounter with a bird of
prey, and he was glad he had left the Siamese in the car; the bird
might be injured—and vicious. Powerful force had been necessary to crash through that screen, and the piercing eyes were far
from friendly.

The implements hanging on the wall included a primitive
wooden pitchfork, and Qwilleran reached for it in slow motion.
Quietly he opened the screened door and wedged it. Cautiously
he circled behind the bird, waving the pitchfork, and the hawk
shot out through the doorway.

Qwilleran blew a sigh of relief into his moustache. Welcome to
the country, he said to himself.

Although the cabin was small, the interior gave an impression
of spaciousness. An open ceiling of knotty pine soared to almost
twenty feet at the peak, supported by trusses of peeled log. The
walls also were exposed logs, whitewashed. Above the fieldstone
fireplace there was a moosehead with a great spread of antlers,
flanked by a pickax and a lumberjack's crosscut saw with two-
inch teeth.

Qwilleran's keen sense of smell picked up a strange odor.
Dead animal? Bad plumbing? Forgotten garbage? He opened
doors and windows and checked the premises. Everything was
shipshape, and soon the cross-ventilation brought in the freshness of the lake and the perfume of wild cherry blossoms. Next
he examined the window screens to be sure they were secure.
Koko and Yum Yum were apartment cats, never allowed to roam
outdoors, and he was taking no chances. He looked for trap
doors, loose boards, and other secret exits.

Only then did he bring the Siamese into the cabin. They advanced warily, their bellies and tails low, their whiskers back,
their ears monitoring noises inaudible to humans. But by the
time the luggage was brought in from the car, Yum Yum was
somewhere overhead leaping happily from beam to beam while
Koko sat imperiously on the moose head, surveying his new domain with approval. The moose—with his long snout, flared nostrils, and underslung mouth—bore this indignity with sour resignation.

Qwilleran's approval of the cabin was equally enthusiastic. He
noted the latest type of telephone on the bar, a microwave oven,

a whirlpool bath, and several shelves of books. The latest issues of status magazines were on the coffee table, and someone had left a Brahms concerto in the cassette slot of the stereo. There was no television, but that was unimportant; Qwilleran was addicted to the print media.

He opened a can of boned chicken for his companions and then drove into Mooseville for his own dinner. Mooseville was a resort village stretched out along the lakeshore. On one side of Main Street were piers and boats and the Northern Lights Hotel. Across the street were commercial establishments housed largely in buildings of log construction. Even the church was built of logs.

At the hotel Qwilleran had mediocre pork chops, a soggy baked potato, and overcooked green beans served by a friendly blonde waitress who said her name was Darlene. She recognized him from his picture in the *Daily Fluxion* and insisted on serving second helpings of everything. At the office he had frequently questioned the wisdom of publishing the restaurant-reviewer's photograph, but it was *Fluxion* policy to print headshots of columnists, and at the *Fluxion,* policy was policy.

It was not only Qwilleran's moustache that made him conspicuous at the Northern Lights Hotel. In the roomful of plaid shirts, jeans, and windbreakers his tweed sports coat and knit tie were jarringly out-of-key. Immediately after the gelatinous blueberry pie he went to the General Store and bought jeans, sports shirts, deck shoes . . . *and* a visored cap. Every man in Mooseville wore one. There were baseball caps, nautical caps, hunting caps, beer caps, and caps with emblems advertising tractors, fertilizer, and feed. Qwilleran chose hunter orange, hoping it would prove an effective disguise.

The drug store carried both the *Daily Fluxion* and its competitor, the *Morning Rampage,* as well as the local paper. He bought a *Fluxion* and a *Pickax Picayune* and headed back to the cabin.

On the way he was stopped by a police roadblock, but a polite trooper said: "Go right ahead, Mr. Qwilleran. Are you going to write about the Mooseville restaurants?"

"No, I'm on vacation. What's happening here, officer?"

"Just routine war games," the trooper joked. "We have to keep in practice. Enjoy your vacation, Mr. Qwilleran."

It was June. The days were long in the city and even longer in the north country. Qwilleran was weary and kept looking at his watch and checking the sun, which was reluctant to set. He slipped down the side of the dune to inspect the shore and the temperature of the water. It was icy, as Riker had warned. The lake was calm, making the softest splash when it lapped the beach, and the only sound was the humming of mosquitoes. By the time Qwilleran scrambled frantically up the hill he was chased by a winged horde. They quickly found the hole in the screen and funneled into the porch.

He dashed into the cabin, slammed the door, and made a hurried phone call to Pickax.

"Good evening," said a pleasant voice.

"Francesca, just want you to know we arrived safely." Qwilleran talked fast hoping to get his message across before her attention wandered. "The cabin is terrific, but we have a problem. A hawk crashed through the screen and left a big hole. I shooed him off the porch, but he had messed up the rug and furniture."

Aunt Fanny took the news calmly. "Now don't you worry about it, dear," she growled sweetly. "Tom will be there tomorrow to fix the screen and clean the porch. No problem at all. He enjoys doing it. Tom is a jewel. I don't know what I'd do without him. How are the mosquitoes? I'll have Tom get you some insect spray. You'll need it for spiders and hornets, too. Let me know if the ants invade the cabin; they're very possessive. Don't kill any ladybugs, dear. It's bad luck, you know. Would you like a few more cassettes for the stereo? I have some *marvelous* Chicago jazz. Do you like opera? Sorry there's no television, but I think it's a waste of time in the summer, and you won't miss it while you're busy writing your book."

After the conversation with Madame President, Qwilleran tried the cassette player. He punched two buttons and got the Double Concerto with excellent fidelity. He had once dated a girl who listened to nothing but Brahms, and he would never forget good old Opus 102.

The sun finally slipped into the lake, flooding the water and sky with pink and orange, and he was ready for sleep. The Siamese were abnormally quiet. Usually they indulged in a final romp before lights-out. But where were they now? Not on the moose head or the beams overhead. Not on their blue cushion that he had placed on top of the refrigerator. Not on the pair of white linen sofas that angled around the fireplace. Not on the beds in either of the bunkrooms.

Qwilleran called to them. There was no answer. They were too busy watching. Crouched on a windowsill in the south bunkroom they stared out at something in the dusk. The property had been left in a wild state, and the view offered nothing but the sand dune, underbrush, and evergreens. A few yards from the cabin there was a depression in the sand, however—roughly rectangular. It looked like a sunken grave. The Siamese had noticed it immediately; they always detected anything unusual.

"Jump down," Qwilleran said to them. "I've got to close the window for the night."

He chose the north bunkroom for himself because it overlooked the lake, but—tired though he was—he could not sleep. He thought about the grave. What could be buried there? Should he report it to Aunt Fanny? Or should he just start digging. There was a toolshed on the property, and there would be shovels.

He tossed for hours. It was so dark! There were no street lights, no neon signs, no habitations, no moon, no glow from any nearby civilization—just total blackness. And it was so quiet! No rustling of trees, no howling of wind, no crashing of waves, no hum of traffic on the distant highway—just total silence. Qwilleran lay still and listened to his heart beating.

Then through his pillow he heard an irregular *thud-thud-thud.* He sat up and listened carefully. The thudding had stopped, but he could hear voices—a man's voice and a woman's laughter. He looked out the window into the blackness and saw two flashlights bobbing on the beach at the foot of the dune, bound in an easterly direction. He lay down again, and with his ear to the pillow he heard *thud-thud-thud.* It had to be footsteps on the packed sand. The sound gradually faded away.

It was well after midnight. He wondered about the prowlers on the beach. He wondered about the grave. And then there was a crackling in the underbrush—someone climbing a tree—footsteps on the roof, clomping toward the chimney.

Qwilleran leaped out of his bunk, bellowing some curse he had learned in North Africa. He turned on lights. He shouted at the cats, who flew around the cabin in a frenzy. He punched buttons on the cassette player. Brahms again! He banged pots and pans in the kitchen. . . . The footsteps hurried back across the roof; there was scrambling in the underbrush, and then all was quiet.

Qwilleran sat up reading for the rest of the night until the sun rose and the birds began their dawn chirruping, tweeting, cawing, and skreeking.

THREE

❦

Mooseville, Tuesday

DEAR ARCH,

If I get any mail that looks personal, please forward it c/o General Delivery. Will appreciate. We arrived yesterday, and I'm a wreck. The cats yelled for four hundred miles and drove me crazy. What's more, I bought a car to fit their sandbox, and they didn't use it once! They waited till we got to where we were going. Siamese! Who can figure them out?

This is beautiful country, but I didn't sleep a wink last night. I'm suffering from culture shock.

Fortunately Mooseville gets the outstate edition of the *Fluxion*. The *Pickax Picayune* is just a chicken-dinner newspaper.

Qwill

Looking haggard, but buoyed by the excitement of a new environment, Qwilleran drove into Mooseville for breakfast. On the way he was stopped by another roadblock. This time a friendly character in a moose costume handed him a *Welcome to Mooseville* brochure and urged him to visit the tourist information booth on Main Street.

At the bank Qwilleran opened a checking account. Although
the log building was imitation antique, he could detect the characteristic aroma of fresh money. The teller was a sunburned
blonde named Jennifer, almost unbearably friendly, who remarked that the weather was super and she hoped he was going
fishing or sailing.

At the post office he was greeted by a young woman with long
golden hair and a dazzling smile. "Isn't this gorgeous weather?"
she said. "I wonder how long it will last. They say there's a storm
brewing. What can I do for you? I'm Lori, the postmistress."

"My name is Jim Qwilleran," he told her, "and I'll be staying
at the Klingenschoen cabin for three months. My mail will come
addressed to General Delivery."

"Yes, I know," she said. "Ms. Klingenschoen informed us. You
can have rural delivery if you want to put up a mailbox."

Precisely at that moment Qwilleran's nostrils were assaulted by
the foulest odor he had ever encountered. He looked startled,
mumbled "no thanks," and bolted from the building, feeling
sick. Other postal patrons who had been licking stamps or un-
locking numbered mailboxes made their exit quietly but swiftly.
Qwilleran stood on the sidewalk gulping fresh air; the others
walked away without comment or any visible reaction to the experience. There was no explanation that he could imagine. In
fact, there were many unexplained occurrences in this north
country.

For example, everywhere he went he seemed to be haunted by
a blue pickup truck. There was one parked in front of the post
office, its truck-bed empty except for a rolled tarpaulin. There
was another in front of the bank, hauling shovels and a wheel-
barrow. On the highway the driver of a blue truck had tooted his
horn and waved. And the truck that had followed him on the
Pickax Road the night before was blue.

Tugging the visor of his orange cap down over his eyes he
approached a log cabin with a freshly painted sign: *Information
Center—Tourist Development Association.* The interior had the pun-
gent odor of new wood.

Behind a desk piled with travel folders sat a pale young man
with a very black beard and a healthy head of black hair. Qwilleran realized that his own graying hair and pepper-and-salt

moustache had once been equally black. He asked: "Is this where tourists come to be developed?"

The young man shrugged apologetically. "I told them it should be *tourism*. But who was I to advise the Chamber of Commerce? I was only a history teacher looking for a summer job. Isn't this great weather? What can I do for you? My name is Roger. You don't need to tell me who you are. I read the paper."

"The *Daily Fluxion* seems to have a big circulation up here," Qwilleran said. "The *Fluxion* was almost sold out at the drug store yesterday, but they still had a big stack of the *Morning Rampage*."

"Right," said Roger. "We're boycotting the *Rampage*. Their travel editor did a write-up on Mooseville and called it Mosquitoville."

"You have to admit they're plentiful. And large."

Roger glanced aside guiltily and said in a lowered voice: "If you think the mosquitoes are bad, wait till you meet the deer flies. This is off-the-record, of course. We don't talk about deer flies. It's not exactly good for tourism. Are you here to write about our restaurants?"

"No, I'm on vacation. I'll be around for three months. Is there a barber in town?"

"Bob's Chop Shop at the Cannery Mall. Men's and women's hair styling." Roger handed Qwilleran another copy of the Mooseville brochure. "Are you a fisherman?"

"I can think of things I'd rather do."

"Deep-sea fishing is a great experience. You'd enjoy it. You can charter a boat at the municipal pier and go out for a day or half a day. They supply the gear, take you where the fish are biting, even tell you how to hold the rod. And they guarantee you'll come back with a few big ones."

"Anything else to do around here?"

"There's the museum; it's big on shipwreck history. The flower gardens at the state prison are spectacular, and the prison gift shop has some good leather items. You can see bears scrounging at the village dump, or you can hunt for agates on the beach."

Qwilleran was studying the brochure. "What's this about a historic cemetery?"

"It's not much," Roger admitted. "It's a nineteenth century

burial ground, abandoned for the last fifty years. Sort of vandal-
ized. If I were you, I'd take a fishing trip."

"What are these pasties everyone advertises?"

"It's like a turnover filled with meat and potatoes and turnips.
Pasties are traditional up here. The miners used to carry pasties
in their lunch buckets."

"Where's a good place to try one?"

"Hats-off or hats-on?"

"What?"

"What I mean—we have some restaurants with a little class,
like the hotel dining room, and we have the other kind—casual
—where the guys eat with their hats on. For a good hats-off place
you could try a little bistro at the Cannery Mall, called the Nasty
Pasty. A bit of perverse humor, I guess. The tourists like it."

Qwilleran said he would prefer real north country atmosphere.

"Right. So here's what you want to do: Drive west along the
shore for about a mile. You'll see a big electric sign that says
FOO. The *D* dropped off about three years ago. It's a dump, but
they're famous for pasties, and it's strictly hats-on."

"One more question." Qwilleran touched his moustache tenta-
tively, as he did when a situation was bothering him. "How come
there are so many blue pickup trucks in this neck of the woods?"

"I don't know. I never really noticed." Roger jumped up and
went to the side window overlooking the parking lot of the Shipwreck Tavern. "You're right. There are two blue pickups in the
lot. . . . But there's also a red one, and a dirty green, and a sort
of yellow."

"And here comes another blue one," Qwilleran persisted. It
was the truck with the shovels. The agile little man who jumped
out of the driver's seat wore overalls and a visored cap and a
faceful of untrimmed gray whiskers.

"That's old Sam the gravedigger. He's got a lot of bounce,
hasn't he? He's over eighty and puts away a pint of whiskey
every day—except Sunday."

"You mean you still dig graves by hand?"

"Right. Sam's been digging graves and other things all his life.
Keeps him young. . . . Look at that sky. We're in for a storm."

"Thanks for the information," Qwilleran said. "I think I'll go and try the pasties." He glanced at his wrist. "What time is it? I left my watch at the cabin."

"That's normal. When guys come up here, the first thing they do—they forget to wear their watches. Then they stop shaving. Then they start eating with their hats on."

Qwilleran drove west until he saw an electric sign flashing its message futilely in the sunshine: *FOO . . . FOO . . . FOO.* The parking lot was filled with pickups and vans. No blue. He thought: Why am I getting paranoid about blue pickups? The answer was a familiar uneasiness on his upper lip.

The restaurant was a two-story building in need of paint and shingles and nails. A ventilator expelled fumes of fried fish and smoking hamburgers. Inside, the tables were filled, and red, green, blue, and yellow caps could be seen dimly through the haze of cigarette smoke. Country music on the radio could not compete with the hubbub of loud talk and laughter.

Qwilleran took a stool at the counter not far from a customer with a sheriff's department patch on his sleeve and a stiff-brimmed hat on his head.

The cook shuffled out of the kitchen and said to the deputy: "We're in for a big one."

The brimmed hat nodded.

"Another roadblock last night?"

Two nods.

"Find anything?"

The hat waggled from side to side.

"We all know where the buggers go."

Another nod.

"But no evidence."

The hat registered negative.

The waitress was standing in front of Qwilleran, waiting wordlessly for his order.

"A couple of pasties," he said.

"To go?"

"No. To eat here."

"Two?"

Qwilleran found himself nodding an affirmative.

"You want I should hold one back and keep it hot till you eat the first one?"

"No, thanks. That won't be necessary."

The conversation at the tables concerned fishing exclusively, with much speculation about an approaching storm. The movement of the lake, the color of the sky, the behavior of the seagulls, the formation of the clouds, the feel of the wind—all these factors convinced veteran fishermen that a storm was coming, despite predictions on the local radio station.

When Qwilleran's two pasties arrived they completely filled two large oval platters. Each of the crusty turnovers was a foot wide and three inches thick. He surveyed the feast. "I need a fork," he said.

"Just pick 'em up," the waitress said and disappeared into the kitchen.

Roger was right. The pasties were filled with meat and potatoes and plenty of turnip, which ranked with parsnip at the bottom of Qwilleran's list of edibles. He chomped halfway through the first pasty, lubricating each dry mouthful with gulps of weak coffee, then asked to have the remaining artifacts wrapped to take home. He paid his check glumly, receiving his change in dollar bills that smelled of cigar smoke.

The cashier, a heavy woman in snugly fitting pants and a Mooseville T-shirt, leered at his orange cap and said: "All ready for Halloween, Clyde?"

Glancing at her blimplike figure he thought of an apt retort but curbed his impulse.

He returned home with one and a half pasties in soggy waxed paper and discovered some new developments. The damaged screen in the porch door had been replaced, and the hawk-spotted furnishings had been cleaned. There was a can of insect spray in the kitchen. Additional cassettes were stacked on the stereo cabinet. And his watch was missing. He clearly remembered placing it on a bathroom shelf before showering. Now it was gone. It was an expensive timepiece, presented to him by the Antique Dealers' Association at a testimonial dinner.

With mystification and annoyance muddling his head he sat down to think. Koko rubbed against his ankles, and Yum Yum jumped upon his knee. He stroked her fur absently as he reviewed the last twenty-four hours.

First there was the sunken grave; the cats were still mesmerized and kept returning to their vantage point in the guest-room window. Next there were the footsteps on the roof; the intruder was heading for the chimney when frightened away by light and noise. This morning there had been the incredible odor at the post office. And why did Roger discourage him from visiting the old cemetery? The Chamber of Commerce brochure recommended it to history buffs, photographers, and artists interested in making rubbings of nineteenth century tombstones.

And now his watch had been stolen. He had another he could use, but the missing watch was gold and had pleasant associations. Would Aunt Fanny's trusted employee attempt a theft so easily traceable? Perhaps he had a light-fingered helper; after all, a lot of work had been accomplished in a very short time.

Qwilleran's reverie was interrupted by the sound of a vehicle moving slowly up the driveway, tires crunching on gravel. It had the purring motor of an expensive car.

The cats were alerted. Koko marched to the south porch to inspect the new arrival. Yum Yum hid under one of the sofas.

The man who stepped out of the car was an alarming sight in this northern wilderness. He wore a business suit, obviously tailor-made, and a white shirt with a proper striped tie. There was a hint of cologne, a conservative scent. His long thin face was somber.

"I presume you are Miss Klingenschoen's nephew," he said when Qwilleran advanced. "I'm her attorney . . ."

"Is anything wrong?" Qwilleran cut in quickly, alarmed by the funereal tone.

"No, no, no, no. I had business in the vicinity and merely stopped to introduce myself. I'm Alexander Goodwinter."

"Come in, come in. My name is Qwilleran. Jim Qwilleran."

"So I am aware. Spelled with a *W*," the attorney said. "I read the *Daily Fluxion*. We all read the *Fluxion* up here, chiefly to convince ourselves that we're fortunate to live four hundred miles away. When we refer to the metropolitan area as Down Below, we are thinking not only of geography." He seemed entirely at ease in the cabin, seating himself on Yum Yum's sofa and crossing his knees comfortably. "I believe a storm is imminent. They can be quite violent up here."

The newsman had learned that any conversation in the north country opened with comments on the weather, almost as a matter of etiquette. "Yes," he said with a declamatory flourish, "the texture of the lake and the lambency of the wind are rather ominous." When the attorney gave him a wary look, Qwilleran quickly added: "I'd offer you a drink, but I haven't had a chance to stock up. We arrived only yesterday."

"So Fanny informed me. We are pleased to have one of her relatives nearby. She is so very much alone—the last of the Klingenschoens."

"We're not . . . really . . . relatives," Qwilleran said with a slight lapse of concentration. He could see Yum Yum's nose emerging stealthily under the skirt of the sofa, not far from the attorney's foot. "She and my mother were friends, and I was encouraged to call her Aunt Fanny. Now she disclaims the title."

"Fanny is her legal name," Goodwinter said. "She was Fanny when she left Pickax to attend Vassar or Wellesley or whatever, and she was Francesca when she returned forty years later." He chuckled. "I find the name Francesca Klingenschoen a charming incongruity. Our firm has handled her family's legal affairs for three generations. Now my sister and I are the sole partners, and Fanny retains Penelope to handle her tax-work and lawsuits and real estate transactions. We have been urging her to sell this place. Anyone who owns shore property has a gold mine, you may be aware. Fanny should liquidate some of her holdings to expedite—ah—future arrangements. She is, after all, nearing ninety. No doubt you will be seeing her during the summer?"

"Yes, she promised to come up for lunch, and I have a rain check on a steak dinner in Pickax."

"Ah, yes, we all know Fanny's steak dinners," Goodwinter said with a humorous grimace. "She promises steak, but when the time comes she serves scrambled eggs. One forgives her eccentricities because of her—ah—*energetic* involvement in the community. It was Fanny who virtually blackmailed the city fathers of Pickax into installing new sewers, repairing the sidewalks, and solving the parking problem. A very—ah—*determined* woman."

Yum Yum's entire head was now visible, and one paw was coming into view.

The attorney went on: "My sister and I are hoping you will break bread with us before long. She reads your column religiously and quotes you as if you were Shakespeare."

"I appreciate the invitation," Qwilleran said, "but it remains to be seen how sociable I will be this summer. I'm doing some writing." He waved his hand toward the dining table across the room, littered with books, typewriter, paper, pens, and pencils. As he did so, he noticed Yum Yum's paw reaching slowly and cautiously toward the attorney's shoelace.

"I applaud your intentions," Goodwinter said. "The muse must be served. But please remember: the latch-string is out at the Goodwinter residence." After a small cough he added: "Did you find Fanny looking—ah—*well* when you visited her?"

"Remarkably well! Very active and spirited for a woman of her age. Only one problem: It's hard to get her attention."

"Her hearing is excellent, according to her doctor. But she seems preoccupied most of the time—in a world of her own, so to speak." The attorney coughed again. "To be perfectly frank— and I speak to you in confidence—we have been wondering if Fanny is—ah—drinking a little."

"Some doctors recommend a daily nip for the elderly."

"Ah, well . . . the truth of the matter is . . . the druggist informs me she has been buying a considerable amount of liquor lately. A bottle of good sherry used to take care of her needs for two months, I am told, but the houseman who does her shopping has been picking up hard liquor two or three times a week."

"He's probably drinking it himself," Qwilleran said.

"We doubt that. Tom has been under close observation since coming to Pickax to work for Fanny, and all reports are good. He's a simple soul but dependable—a competent handyman and careful driver. The local bar owners assure me that Tom never drinks more than one or two beers."

"What kind of liquor is he buying?"

"Rye, gin, Scotch. No particular label. And only a pint at a time. You might keep this confidential matter in mind when you see Fanny. We all consider her a community treasure and feel a sense of responsibility. Incidentally, if she asks your advice, you might suggest selling the large house in Pickax and moving into smaller quarters. She has had a few fainting spells recently—or so she describes them. You can see why we are all concerned about this gallant little lady. We don't want anything to happen to her."

When the attorney had said goodbye and had tied his shoelace and had driven away, Koko and Yum Yum gave Qwilleran the hungry eye. He scooped the filling from half a pasty, mashed it into a gray paste, warmed it slightly, and spread it on what looked like a handmade raku plate. The Siamese approached the food in slow motion, sniffed it incredulously, walked around it in an effort to discover its purpose, withdrew in disdain, and looked at Qwilleran in silent rebuke, shaking their front paws in a gesture of loathing.

"So much for pasties," he said as he opened a can of red salmon.

An evening chill was descending and he tried to light a fire. There were twigs and old newspapers in a copper coal scuttle, split logs in the wood basket, and long matches in a brass holder, but the paper was damp and the matches only glowed feebly before expiring. He made three attempts and then gave up.

After the nerve-wracking drive from Down Below and two sleepless nights, he was weary. He was also disoriented by the sudden change from concrete sidewalks to sand dunes, and by odd situations he did not understand.

He went to the row of windows overlooking the lake—a hundred miles of water with Canada on the opposite shore. It shaded from silver to turquoise to deep blue. How Rosemary would enjoy this view! As he tried to imagine it through her eyes he heard an eerie whistling in the tops of the tallest pines. There was no breeze—only the soft shrill hissing. At the same time, the Siamese—who should have been drowsy after their feast of salmon—began prowling restlessly. Yum Yum emitted ear-splitting howls for no apparent reason, and Koko butted his head belligerently against the legs of tables and chairs.

Within minutes the lake changed to steel gray dotted with whitecaps. Then a high wind rushed in without warning. The whitecaps became breakers crashing in maelstroms of foam. When the tall pines started to sway, the maples and birches were already bending like beach grass. Suddenly rain hit the windows with the staccato racket of machine gun fire. The gale howled; the surf pounded the shore; tree limbs snapped off and plunged to the ground.

For the first time since his arrival Qwilleran felt really comfortable. He relaxed. The peace and quiet had been insufferable; he was used to noise and turmoil. It would be a good night to sleep.

First he had an urge to write to Rosemary. He put a sheet of paper in the typewriter and immediately ripped it out. It would be more appropriate to write with the gold pen she had given him for his birthday.

Rummaging among the jumble on his writing table he found yellow pencils, thick black *Fluxion* pencils, cheap ballpoints, and an old red jumbo fountain pen that had belonged to his mother. The sleek gold pen from Rosemary was missing.

FOUR

QWILLERAN SLEPT WELL, lulled by the savage tumult outdoors. He was awakened shortly after dawn by the opening chords of the Brahms Double Concerto. The cassette was still in the player, and Koko was sitting alongside it, looking pleased with himself. He had placed one paw on the "power" button, activating a little red light, and another on "play."

The storm was over, although the trees could be heard dripping on the roof. The wind had subsided, and the lake had flattened to a sheet of silver. Everywhere there was the good wet smell of the woods after a heavy rain. The birds were rejoicing.

Even before he rolled out of bed Qwilleran's thoughts went to the stolen pen and the stolen watch. Should he report the theft to Aunt Fanny? Should he confront Tom? In this strange new environment he felt it was a case of foreign diplomacy, requiring circumspection and a certain finesse.

Koko was the first to hear the truck approaching. His ears snapped to attention and his body became taut. Then Qwilleran heard the droning of a motor coming up the hilly, winding drive. He pulled on some clothes hastily while Koko raced to the door and demanded access to the porch, his official checkpoint for arriving visitors. Qwilleran's tingling moustache told him it would be a blue truck, and the message was correct. A stocky little old man was taking a shovel from the truckbed.

"Hey, what's going on here?" Qwilleran demanded. He recognized the gravedigger from the parking lot of the Shipwreck Tavern.

"Gotta dig you up," said Old Sam, heading for the grave on the east side of the cabin.

"What for?" Qwilleran slammed the porch door and raced after him.

"Big George be comin' soon."

"Who told you to come here?"

"Big George." Old Sam was digging furiously. "Sand be heavy after the storm."

Qwilleran spluttered in a search for words. "What—who—look here! You can't dig up this property unless you have authorization."

"Ask Big George. He be the boss." Sand was flying out of the shallow hole, which was becoming more precisely rectangular. Soon the shovel hit a concrete slab. "There she be!" After a few more swings with the shovel Old Sam climbed out of the hole, just as a large dirty tank truck lumbered into the clearing that served as a parking lot.

Qwilleran strode to the clearing and confronted the driver. "Are you Big George?"

"No, I'm Dave," said the man mildly, as he unreeled a large hose. "Big George is the truck. The lady in Pickax—she called last night. Told us to get out here on the double. Are you choked up?"

"Am I *what?*"

"When she calls, we jump. No foolin' around with that lady. Should've pumped you out last summer, I guess."

"Pumped what?"

"The septic tank. We had to get Old Sam outa bed this morning, hangover and all. He digs; we pump. No room for the backhoe in here. Too heavily wooded. You new here? Sam'll come and fill you in later. He doesn't fill all the way; makes it easier next time. Unless you want him to. Then he'll level it off."

Old Sam had driven away, but now a black van appeared in the clearing, driven by a slender young man in a red, white, and blue T-shirt and tall silk opera hat.

Qwilleran stared at him. "And who are you?"

"Little Henry. You having trouble? The old lady in Pickax said you'd catch on fire any minute. Man, she's a tough baby. Won't take no excuses." He removed his topper and admired it. "This is my trademark. You see my ads in the *Picayune?*"

"What do you advertise?"

"I'm the only chimney sweep in Moose County. You should be checked every year. . . . Is that your phone ringing?"

Qwilleran rushed back into the cabin. The telephone, which stood on the bar dividing kitchen from dining area, had stopped ringing. Koko had nudged the receiver off the cradle and was sniffing the mouthpiece.

Qwilleran grabbed it. "Hello, hello! *Get down!* Hello?" Koko was fighting for possession of the instrument. *"Get down, dammit!* Hello?"

"Is everything all right, dear?" the deep voice said after a moment's hesitation. "Did the storm do any damage? Don't worry about it; Tom will clean up the yard. You stick to your typewriter. You've got that wonderful book to finish. I know it will be a best-seller. Did you see Big George and Little Henry? I don't want anything to go wrong with the plumbing or the chimney while you're concentrating on your writing. I told them to get out there immediately or I'd have their licenses revoked. You have to be firm with these country people or they go fishing and forget about you. Are you getting enough to eat? I've bought some of those *divine* cinnamon buns to keep in your freezer. Tom will drive me up this morning, and we'll have a pleasant lunch on the porch. I'll bring a picnic basket. Get back to your writing, dear."

Qwilleran turned to Koko. "Madame President is coming. Try to act like a normal cat. Don't answer the phone. Don't play the music. Stay away from the microwave."

When Big George and Little Henry had finished their work, Qwilleran put on his orange cap and drove to Mooseville to mail his letter to Rosemary and to buy supplies. His shopping list was geared to his culinary skills: instant coffee, canned soup, frozen stew. For guests he laid in a supply of liquor and mixes.

In the canned soup section of the supermarket he noticed a black-bearded young man in a yellow cap with a spark-plug emblem. They stared at each other.

"Hi, Mr. Qwilleran."

"Forget the mister. Call me Qwill. Aren't you Roger from the tourist bureau? Roger, George, Sam, Henry, Tom, Dave . . . I've met so many people without surnames, it's like biblical times."

"Mine's a tough one: MacGillivray."

"What! My mother was a Mackintosh!"

"No kidding! Same clan!"

"Your ancestor fought like a lion for Prince Charlie."

"Right! At Culloden in 1746."

"April sixteenth."

Their voices had been rising higher with surprise and pleasure, to the mystification of the other customers. The two men pumped hands and slapped backs.

"I hope that's Scotch broth you're buying," Roger said.

"Why don't we have dinner some night?" Qwilleran suggested. "Preferably not at the FOO."

"How about tonight? My wife's out-of-town."

"How about the hotel dining room? Hats-off."

Qwilleran returned to the cabin to shower and shave in preparation for the visit of Aunt Fanny and the remarkable Tom—gardener, chauffeur, handyman, errand boy, and petty thief, perhaps. Shortly before noon a long black limousine inched its way around the curves of the drive and emerged triumphantly in the clearing. The driver, dressed in work clothes and a blue visored cap, jumped out and ran around to open the passenger's door.

Out came Indian moccasins with beadwork, then a fringed suede skirt, then a leather jacket with more fringe and beadwork, then Aunt Fanny's powdered face topped with an Indian red turban. Qwilleran noticed that she had well-shaped legs for an octogenarian soon to be a nonagenarian.

"Francesca! Good to see you again!" he exclaimed. "You're looking very . . . very . . . sexy."

"Bless you, my dear," she said in her surprising baritone voice. "Little old ladies are usually called chipper or spry, and I intend to shoot the next fool who does." She reached into her fringed suede handbag and withdrew a small pistol with a gold handle, which she waved with abandon.

"Careful!" Qwilleran gasped.

"Dear me! The storm did a lot of damage. That jack pine is almost bare. We'll have to remove it. . . . Tom, come here to meet the famous Mr. Qwilleran."

The man-of-all-work stepped forward obediently, removing the blue cap that advertised a brand of fertilizer. His age was hard to guess. An old twenty or a young forty? His round scrubbed face and pale blue eyes wore an expression of serene wonder.

"This is Tom," Aunt Fanny said. "Tom, it's all right to shake hands with Mr. Qwilleran; he's a member of the family."

Qwilleran gripped a hand that was strong but unaccustomed to social gestures. "How do you do, Tom. I've heard a lot of good things about you." Thinking of the missing watch and pen he looked inquiringly into the man's eyes, but their open innocent gaze was disarming. "You did a fine job with the porch yesterday, Tom. How did you do so much work in such a short time? Did you have a helper?"

"No," Tom said slowly. "No helper. I like to work. I like to work hard." He spoke in a gentle, musical voice.

Aunt Fanny slipped something into his hand. "Go into Mooseville, Tom, and buy yourself a big pasty and a beer, and come back in two hours. Bring the picnic basket from the car before you leave."

"Tom, do you know what time it is?" Qwilleran asked. "I've lost my watch."

The handyman searched the sky for the sun, hiding in the tall pines. "It's almost twelve o'clock," he said softly.

He drove away in the limousine, and Aunt Fanny said: "I've brought some egg salad sandwiches and a thermos of coffee with that *marvelous* cream. We'll sit on the porch and enjoy the lake. The temperature is perfect. Now where are those intelligent cats I've heard so much about? And where do you do your writing? I must confess, I'm awed by your talent, dear."

As a newsman Qwilleran was expert at interviewing difficult subjects, but he was defeated by Aunt Fanny. She chattered nonstop about shipwrecks on the lake, bears in the woods, dead fish on the beach, caterpillars in the trees. Questions were ignored or evaded. Madame President was in charge of the conversation.

In desperation Qwilleran finally shouted: *"Aunt Fanny!"* After her startled pause he continued: "What do you know about Tom? Where did you find him? How long has he worked for you? Is he trustworthy? He has access to this cabin when I'm not here. You can't blame me for wanting to know."

"You poor dear," she said. "You have always lived in cities. Life is different in the country. We trust each other. Neighbors walk into your house without knocking. If you're not there and they want to borrow an egg, they help themselves. It's a friendly way of living. Don't worry about Tom. He's a fine young man. He does everything I tell him to do and nothing more."

A bell rang—the clear golden tone of the ship's bell outside the south porch.

"That's Tom," she said. "He's right on time. Isn't he a marvel? You go and talk to him while I powder my nose. This has been such a pleasant visit, my dear."

Qwilleran went into the yard. "Hello, Tom. You're right on time, even without a watch."

"Yes, I don't need a watch," he said quietly, his face beaming with pride. He stroked the brass bell. "This is a nice bell. I polished it yesterday. I like to clean things. I keep the truck and the car very clean."

Qwilleran was fascinated by the singsong inflection of his voice.

"I saw your truck in Pickax. It's blue, isn't it?"

"Yes. I like blue. It's like the sky and the lake. Very pretty. This is a nice cabin. I'll come and clean it for you."

"That's a kind offer, Tom, but don't come unless I call you. I'm writing a book, and I don't like people around when I'm writing."

"I wish I could write. I'd like to write a book. That would be nice."

"Everyone has his own talents," Qwilleran said, "and you have many skills. You should be proud of yourself."

Tom's face glowed with pleasure. "Yes, I can fix anything."

Aunt Fanny appeared, goodbyes were said, and the limousine moved carefully down the drive.

The Siamese, who had been invisible for the last two hours, materialized from nowhere. "You two weren't very sociable," Qwilleran said. "What did you think of Aunt Fanny?"

"YOW!" said Koko, shaking himself vigorously.

Qwilleran remembered offering Aunt Fanny a drink before lunch—a whiskey sour, or a gin and tonic, or a Scotch and soda, or dry sherry. She had declined them all.

Now he had four hours to kill before dining with Roger, and he had no incentive to start page one of chapter one of the book he was supposed to be writing. He might watch the bears at the village dump or visit the prison flower gardens or study shipwreck history at the museum, but it was the abandoned cemetery that tugged at his imagination, even though Roger had advised against it—or perhaps *because* Roger had advised against it.

The Chamber of Commerce brochure gave directions: Go east to Pickax Road and turn south for five miles; enter the cemetery on a dirt road (unmarked) through a cobblestone gate.

The route passed the landscaped grounds that were evidently the prison compound. It passed the turkey farm, and Qwilleran slowed to watch the sea of bronze-feathered backs rippling in the farmyard. Ahead of him a truck was turning out of a side road and heading toward him, one of those ubiquitous blue pickups. As it passed he waved to the driver, but the greeting was not returned. When he reached the cobblestone gate he realized the truck had come from the cemetery.

The access to the graveyard was merely a trail, rutted and muddy after the storm. It meandered through the woods with a clearing here and there, just big enough for a car to pull off and park; there was evidence of picnicking and beer-drinking. Eventually the trail branched in several directions through a meadow dotted with gravestones. Qwilleran followed the set of ruts that appeared to have been recently used.

Where the tire marks stopped he got out of the car and explored the burial ground. It was choked with tall grasses and vines, and he had to tear them away to read the inscriptions on the smaller stones: 1877–1879, 1841–1862, 1856–1859. So many infants were buried there! So many women had died in their twenties! The larger family monuments bore names like Schmidt, Campbell, Trevelyan, Watson.

Trampled grasses suggested a slight path leading behind the Campbell stone, and when he followed it he found signs of recent digging. Dried weeds had been thrown across freshly turned soil, barely concealing the brown plastic lid of a garbage pail. The pail itself, about a twelve-gallon size, was buried in the ground. Qwilleran removed the cover cautiously. The pail was empty.

He returned the hiding place to its previous condition and drove home, wondering who would bury a garbage pail in a cemetery—and why. The only clue was a tremor on his upper lip.

Before going to dinner in Mooseville he prepared a dish of tuna for the Siamese. "Koko, you're not earning your keep," he said. "Strange things are happening, and you haven't come up with a single clue." Koko squeezed his blue eyes languidly. Perhaps the cat's sleuthing days were over. Perhaps he would become nothing but a fussy consumer of expensive food.

At that moment Koko's ears pricked up, and he bounded to the checkpoint. The distant rumble of an approaching vehicle became gradually louder until it sounded like a Russian tank. A red pickup truck was followed by a yellow tractor with a complicated superstructure.

The driver of the truck jumped out and said to Qwilleran: "You got a jack pine that's ready to fall on the house? We got this emergency call from Pickax. Something about the power lines. We're supposed to take the tree down and cut it up."

The tractor extended its skybox; the chain saws whined; three men in visored caps shouted; Yum Yum hid under the sofa; and Qwilleran escaped to Mooseville half an hour before the appointed time for dinner.

The Northern Lights Hotel was a relic from the 1860s when the village was a booming port for shipping lumber and ore. It was the kind of frame building that should have burned down a century ago but was miraculously preserved. In style it was a shoebox with windows, but a porch had been added at the rear, overlooking the wharves. Qwilleran sat in one of its rustic chairs and indulged in his favorite pastime: eavesdropping.

Two voices nearby were in nagging disagreement. Without seeing the source Qwilleran guessed that the man was fat and red-faced and the woman was scrawny and hard-of-hearing.

"I don't think much of this town," the man said in a gasping, wheezing voice. "There's nothing to do. We could've (gasp) stayed home and sat on the patio. It would've (gasp) been cheaper."

The woman answered in a shrill voice, flat with indifference.

"You said you wanted to go fishing. I don't know why. You've always hated it."

"Your brother's been blowing off about the fishing up here for (gasp) six years. I wanted to show him he wasn't the only one (gasp) who could land a trout."

"Then why don't you sign up for a charter boat, the way the man said, and stop bitching?"

"I keep telling you—it's too expensive. Did you see how much they want (gasp) for half a day? I could buy a Caribbean cruise for (gasp) that kind of dough."

Qwilleran had checked the prices himself and thought them rather steep.

"Then let's go home," the woman insisted. "No sense hanging around."

"After driving all this way? Do you know what we've spent on gas (gasp) just to get up here?"

Roger appeared at that moment, wearing a black baseball cap.

"I see you're dressed for evening," Qwilleran said. "You didn't tell me it was formal."

"I collect 'em," Roger explained. "I've got seventeen so far. If you've got any enemies, I should warn you about that orange cap of yours; you'd make a perfect target."

They hung their caps with a dozen others on a row of pegs outside the hotel dining room, then took a side table underneath a large tragic painting of a three-masted schooner sinking in a raging sea.

"Well, we had a perfect day," Qwilleran said, opening with the obligatory weather report. "Sunny. Pleasant breeze. Ideal temperature."

"Yes, but the fog's starting to roll in. By morning you won't be able to see the end of your nose. It's no good for the trolling business."

"If you ask me, Roger, the artwork in this room isn't any good for the trolling business. Every picture on the wall is some kind of disaster at sea. It scares the hell out of me. Besides, the charter boats charge too much—that is, too much for someone like me who isn't really interested in fishing."

"You should try it once," Roger urged. "Trolling is a lot more exciting, you know, than sitting in a rowboat with a worm on a hook."

Qwilleran looked at the menu. "If the lake is full of fish, why isn't there one local product on the menu? Nothing but Nova Scotia halibut, Columbia River salmon, and Boston scrod."

"It's all sport-fishing here. The commercial fisheries down the shore net tons of fish and ship them out."

To Nova Scotia, Massachusetts, and the state of Washington, Qwilleran guessed.

Roger ordered a bourbon and water; Qwilleran, his usual tomato juice. A cranky-looking couple took a table nearby, and he noted smugly that the man was red-faced and obese and the woman wore a hearing aid.

Roger said: "Is that all you drink? I thought newsmen were hard drinkers. I studied journalism before I switched to history ed. . . . Say, you've got me counting blue pickups, and I found out you're right. My wife always says people in northern climates like blue. . . . Do you live alone?"

"Not entirely. I've adopted a couple of despotic Siamese cats. One was orphaned as the result of a murder on my beat. The female was abandoned when she was a kitten. They're both purebred, and the male is smarter than I am."

"I have a hunting dog—Brittany spaniel," Roger said. "Sharon has a Scottie. . . . Were you ever married, Qwill?"

"Once. It wasn't an overwhelming success."

"What happened?"

"She had a nervous breakdown, and I tried to pickle my troubles in alcohol. You ask a lot of questions, Roger. You should have stuck to journalism." The newsman said it with good humor. He had spent his entire career asking questions, and now he enjoyed being interrogated.

"Would you ever get married again?"

Qwilleran allowed the glimmer of a smile to twitch his moustache. "Three months ago I would have said no; now I'm not so sure." He rubbed the backs of his hands as he spoke; they were beginning to itch. The bartender at the Press Club had predicted he would get hives from drinking so much tomato juice, and perhaps Bruno was right.

The fat man at the next table seemed to be listening, so Qwilleran lowered his voice. "The police set up a roadblock Monday night. What was that all about? There was nothing in the paper or on the radio."

Roger shrugged. "Roadblocks are a social activity up here, like potluck, suppers. I think the cops do it once in a while when things get dull."

"Are you telling me there isn't enough crime in Moose County to keep them busy?"

"Not like you have in the city. The conservation guys catch a few poachers, and things get lively at the Shipwreck Tavern on Saturday nights, but the cops spend most of their time chasing accidents—single-car accidents mostly. Someone drives too fast and hits a moose, or kids get a few beers and wrap themselves around a tree. There's a lot of rescue work on the lake, too; the sheriff has two boats and a helicopter."

"No drug problem?"

"Maybe the tourists smoke a few funny cigarettes, but—no problem, really. What I worry about is shipwreck-looting. The lake is full of sunken ships. Some of them went down a hundred years ago, and their cargoes are on public record. The looters have sophisticated diving equipment—cold-water gear, electronic stuff, and all that. There's valuable cargo down there, and they're stripping the wrecks for private gain."

"Isn't that illegal?"

"Not yet. If we had an underwater preserve protected by law it would be a big boost for tourism. It could be used by marine historians, archaeologists, and sportdivers."

"What's holding you back?"

"Money! It would take tens of thousands for an archaeological survey. After that we'd have to lobby for legislation."

Qwilleran said: "It would be a tough law to enforce. You'd need more boats, more helicopters, more personnel."

"Right! And by that time there wouldn't be any sunken cargo to protect."

The men had ordered a second round of drinks, but Qwilleran stopped sipping his TJ. He rubbed his itching hands and wrists surreptitiously under the table.

Roger lowered his voice. "See those two guys sitting near the door? They're wreck-divers. Probably looters."

"How do you know?"

"Everybody knows."

When the food was served, Qwilleran rated it *E* for edible, but the conversation was enlightening. At the end of the meal he remarked to Roger: "Do you think there might be a skunk living under the post office? I went in there yesterday, and the odor drove everyone out of the building."

"Probably some hog farmer picking up his mail," Roger said. "If they come into town in their work-clothes, the whole town clears out. You wouldn't believe the way some of their kids come to school. They're not all like that, of course. One of my hunting partners raises hogs. No problem."

"Another mystery: A hawk flew through a screened door at the cabin and left a big hole. I can't figure it out."

"He was diving for a rabbit or chipmunk," Roger explained, "and he didn't put on the brakes fast enough."

"You think so?"

"Sure! I've seen a hawk carry off a cat. I was hunting once and heard something mewing up in the sky. I looked up, and there was this poor little cat."

Qwilleran thought of Yum Yum and squirmed uncomfortably. There was a moment of silence, and then he said: "A couple of nights ago I heard footsteps on the roof in the middle of the night."

"A raccoon," Roger said. "A raccoon on the roof of a cabin like yours sounds like a Japanese wrestler in space boots. I know! My in-laws have a cottage near you. One year they had a whole family of raccoons in their chimney."

"Do your in-laws give wild parties? I've heard some hysterical laughing late at night."

"That was a loon you heard. It's a crazy bird."

The fog was thickening, and the view from the dining room windows was almost obliterated. Qwilleran said he should get back to the cabin.

"I hope my wife doesn't try driving home tonight," Roger said. "She's been on a buying trip Down Below. She has a little candle and gift shop in the mall. How do you like this money clip? It came from Sharon's shop." He paid his half of the check with bills from a jumbo paper clip that looked like gold.

Qwilleran drove home at twenty miles an hour with the fog swirling in front of the windshield. The private drive up to the cabin was even more hazardous, with three trunks suddenly appearing where they were not supposed to be. As he parked the car he thought he saw two figures moving away from the cabin, down the slope toward the beach.

"Hello!" he called. "Hello there!" But they disappeared into the fog.

Indoors he first checked on the whereabouts of the Siamese. Koko was huddled on the moose head, and Yum Yum cautiously wriggled out from underneath the sofa. Nothing appeared to have been disturbed, but he detected the aroma of pipe tobacco. In the guestroom there was a slight impression in one of the bunks, where the cats took their naps, and one of his brown socks was on the floor. Yum Yum had a passion for his socks. Everything else seemed to be in order.

Then he found a note in the kitchen, scribbled on one of his own typing sheets: "Welcome to the dunes. I'm Roger's mother-in-law. See foil package in your fridge. Thought you might like some roast turkey. Come and see us."

That was all. No name. Qwilleran checked the refrigerator and found a generous supply of sliced turkey breast and chunks of dark meat. As he started chopping a portion of it for the cats' dinner, Yum Yum squealed in anticipation, and Koko pranced back and forth, warbling an aria of tenor yowls and ecstatic gutterals.

Qwilleran watched them eat, but his mind was elsewhere. He liked Roger. Under thirty, with coal-black hair, was a good age to be. But the young man had been remarkably glib on the subject of hawks, loons, raccoons, blue trucks, and police roadblocks. How many of his answers were in the interest of tourism? And if the official brochure encouraged tourists to visit the old cemetery, why did Roger try to discourage it? Did he know something about the pail? And if there was no crime in Moose County, why did Aunt Fanny make a point of carrying a gun?

FIVE

Qwilleran was wakened by Yum Yum. She sat on his chest, her blue eyes boring into his forehead, conveying a subliminal message: breakfast. The lake view from the bunkroom windows had been replaced by total whiteness. The fog had settled on the shore like a suffocating blanket. There was no breeze, no sound.

Qwilleran tried to start a blaze in the fireplace to dispel the dampness, using Wednesday's paper and some book matches from the hotel, but nothing worked. His chief concern was the condition of his hands and wrists. The itching was unbearable, and blisters were forming as large as poker chips. Furthermore he was beginning to itch here, there, and everywhere.

He dressed without shaving, fed the cats without ceremony, and—even forgetting to wear his new cap—steered the car nervously through the milky atmosphere.

There was a drug store on Main Street, and he showed his blisters to the druggist. "Got anything for this?"

"Yikes!" said the druggist. "Worse case of poison ivy I've ever seen. You'd better go and get a shot."

"Is there a doctor in town?"

"There's a walk-in clinic in the Cannery Mall. You know the mall? Two miles beyond town—an old fish cannery made into stores and whatnot. In this fog you won't be able to see it, but you'll smell it."

There was hardly a vehicle to be seen on Main Street. Qwilleran hugged the yellow line, watching the odometer, and at the two-mile mark there was no doubt he had reached the Cannery Mall. He angle-parked between two yellow lines and followed the aroma to a bank of plate glass doors opening into an arcade.

The medical clinic, smelling appropriately antiseptic, was deserted except for a plain young woman sitting at a desk. "Is there a doctor here?" he asked.

"I'm the doctor," she replied, glancing at his hands. "Where did you go to get that magnificent case of ivy poisoning?"

"I guess I picked it up in the old cemetery."

"Really? Aren't you a little old for that kind of thing?" She threw him a mischievous glance.

He was too uncomfortable to appreciate badinage. "I was looking at the old gravestones."

"A likely story. Come into the torture chamber, and I'll give you a shot." She also gave him a tube of lotion and some advice: "Keep your hands out of hot water. Avoid warm showers. And stay away from old cemeteries."

Leaving the clinic Qwilleran was in a sulky humor. He thought the doctor should have been less flip and more sympathetic. By the time he inched his car back to town through the fog, however, the medication was working, bringing not only relief but a heady euphoria, and he remembered that the doctor had attractive green eyes and the longest eyelashes he had ever seen.

At the hotel, where he stopped for coffee and eggs, four men at the next table were complaining about the weather. "The boats won't go out in this soup. Let's get a bottle of red-eye and play some cards."

At the table behind him a familiar voice said: "We're not leaving here (gasp) till we go fishing."

A shrill flat voice answered: "Why are you so stubborn? You don't even *like* to fish."

"This is different, I told you. We go out (gasp) on thirty-six-foot trollers and catch maybe twenty-pound trout."

"You said it was too expensive."

"The prices at the main dock are highway robbery, but I found a boat (gasp) that'll take us for fifteen bucks."

Qwilleran's thrifty nature sensed an opportunity, and the combination of the medication and the unnatural atmosphere gave him a feeling of reckless excitement. When the couple left the dining room he followed them. "Excuse me, sir, did I hear you say something about a troller that's less expensive?"

"Sure did! Fifteen bucks for six hours. Split three ways (gasp) that's five bucks apiece. Not bad. Two young fellahs (gasp) own the boat. You interested?"

"Is fishing any good in this weather?"

"These young fellas say it doesn't make any difference. By the way," he wheezed, "my name's Whatley—from Cleveland— wholesale hardware." He then introduced his wife, whose manner was frosty, and he volunteered to drive, since he knew the way to the dock. "The boat ties up outside of town. That's why (gasp) it's cheaper. You have to shop around to get a good buy."

The trip to the dock was another slow agonizing crawl through earthbound clouds. At one point the three giant electric letters of the FOO glowed weakly through the mist. Farther on, the Cannery Mall announced itself strongly although the building was invisible. Then there were miles of nothing. Each mile seemed like five. Whatley drove on grimly. No one talked. Qwilleran strained his eyes, peering at the road ahead, expecting to meet a pair of yellow foglights head-on or the sudden taillights of a stalled logging truck.

"How will you know when you get there?" he asked.

"Can't miss it. There's a wreck of a boat (gasp) where we turn off."

When the wreck eventually loomed up out of the mist, Whatley turned down a swampy lane bordering a canal filled with more wrecks.

"I'm sorry I came," Mrs. Whatley announced in her first statement of the day.

Where the lane ended, a rickety wharf extended into the lake, and the three landlubbers groped their way across its rotting planks. The water lapped against the pilings in a liquid whisper, and a hull could be heard creaking against the wharf.

Previously Qwilleran had seen the gleaming white fishing fleet at the municipal pier. Boats with names like *Lady Aurora*, *Queen of the Lake,* and *Northern Princess* displayed posters boasting of their ship-to-shore radios, fishing sonars, depth-finders, and automatic pilots. So he was not prepared for the *Minnie K.* It was an old gray tub, rough with scabs of peeling paint. Incrustations on the deck and railings brought to mind the visits of seagulls and the intimate parts of dead fish. The two members of the crew, who were present in a vague sort of way, were as shabby as their craft. One boy was about seventeen, Qwilleran guessed, and the other was somewhat younger. Neither had an alertness that would inspire confidence.

There were no greetings or introductions. The boys viewed the passengers with suspicion and, after collecting their money, got the boat hastily under weigh, barking at each other in meaningless syllables.

Qwilleran asked the younger boy how far out they were planning to cruise and received a grunt in reply.

Mrs. Whatley said: "This is disgusting. No wonder they call these things stink-boats."

"Whaddaya want for five bucks?" her husband said. "The *Queen Elizabeth?*"

The passengers found canvas chairs, ragged and stained, and the *Minnie K* moved slowly through the water, creating hardly a ripple. Mr. Whatley dozed from time to time, and his wife opened a paperback book and turned off her hearing aid. For about an hour the boat chugged through the total whiteness in apathy, its fishy emanations blending with exhaust fumes. Then the engine changed its tune to an even lower pitch, and the boys lazily produced the fishing gear: rods with enormous reels, copper lines, and brass spoons.

"What do I do with this thing?" Qwilleran asked. "Where's the bait?"

"The spoon's all you need," Whatley said. "Drop the line over the rail (gasp) and keep moving the rod up and down."

"And then what?"

"When you get a bite, you'll know it. Reel it in."

The *Minnie K* moved through the placid lake with reluctance. Occasionally the engine died for sheer lack of purpose and started again unwillingly. For an hour Qwilleran waved the fishing rod up and down in a trance induced by the throbbing of the engine and the sense of isolation. The troller was in a tight little world of its own, surrounded by a fog that canceled out everything else. There was no breeze, not even a splash of water against the hull—just the hollow putt-putt of the engine and the distant moan of a foghorn.

Whatley had reeled in his line and, after taking a few swigs from a flask, fell asleep in his canvas chair. His wife never looked up from her book.

Qwilleran was wondering where they were—and why he was there—when the engine stopped with an explosive cough, and the two boys, muttering syllables, jumped down into the hold. The silence became absolute, and the boat was motionless on the glassy lake. It was then that Qwilleran heard voices drifting across the water—men's voices, too far away to be distinguishable. He rested the rod on the railing and listened. The voices were coming closer, arguing, getting louder. There were shouts of anger followed by unintelligible torrents of verbal abuse, then a sharp *crack* like spitting wood . . . grunts . . . sounds of lunging . . . a heavy thump. A few seconds later Qwilleran heard a mighty splash and a light patter of spray on the water's surface.

After that, all was quiet except for a succession of ripples that crossed the surface of the lake and lapped against the *Minnie K.* The fog closed in like cotton batting, and the water turned to milk.

The crew had their heads bent over the contraption that passed for an engine. Whatley slept on, and his wife also dozed. Wonderingly Qwilleran resumed the senseless motion of the fishing rod, up and down, up and down, in exaggerated arcs. He had lost all sense of time and his watch had been left at home because of his itching wrists.

Thirty minutes passed, or an hour, and then there was a pull on the line, sending vibrations down the rod and into his arms. He shouted!

Whatley waked with a start. "Reel it in! Reel it in!"

At that magic moment, with the roots of his hair tingling, Qwilleran realized the thrill of deep-sea fishing. "Feels like a whale!"

"Not so fast! Keep it steady! Don't stop!" Whatley was gasping for breath, and so was Qwilleran. His hands were shaking. The copper line was endless.

Everyone was watching. The young skipper was leaning over the rail. "Gaff!" he yelled, and the other boy threw him a long-handled iron hook.

"Gotta be fifty pounds!" Qwilleran shouted, straining to reel in the last few yards. He could feel the final surge as the monster rose through the water. "I've got him! I've got him!"

The huge shape had barely surfaced when he lost his grip on the reel.

"Grab it!" cried Whatley, but the reel was spinning wildly. As it began to slow, the skipper pulled pliers from his pocket and cut the line.

"No good," he said. "No good."

"Whaddaya mean?" Whatley screamed at him. "That fish was thirty pounds (gasp) if it was an ounce!"

"No good," the skipper said. He swung himself up to the wheelhouse; the younger boy dropped into the hold, and the engine started.

"This whole deal is a fraud!" Whatley protested.

His wife looked up from her book and yawned.

"I don't know about you people," Qwilleran said, "but I'm ready to call it a day."

The boat picked up speed and headed for what he hoped would be dry land. On the return voyage he slumped in the canvas chair, engrossed in his own thoughts. Whatley had another swig and dozed off.

Qwilleran was no fisherman, but he had seen films of the sport, and his experience was hardly typical. His catch didn't fight like a fish; when it broke the surface it didn't splash like a fish; and it certainly didn't look like a fish.

Back in Mooseville he headed straightway for the tourist bureau. He was not feeling amiable, but first he had to engage in the weather amenities. "You were right about the fog, Roger. How long do you think it will last?"

"It should clear by noon tomorrow."

"Did your wife get home all right?"

"One-thirty this morning. Took her two hours to drive the last twenty miles. She was a basket case when she finally got in. What have you been doing in this fog, Qwill?"

"I've been trolling."

"What! You're hallucinating. The boats didn't go out today."

"The *Minnie K* went out. We were out for four hours, and that was three hours too many."

Roger reached for a file. "I never heard of the *Minnie K*. And she's not here on the list of registered trollers. Where did you find her?"

"A guest at the hotel lined up the expedition. His name is Whatley."

"Yeah, I know him. Overweight, short of breath. He's been in here three times, complaining. How much did they charge? I assume you didn't catch any fish."

"No, but I caught something else," Qwilleran said. "It didn't behave like a fish, and when I got it to the surface, the skipper cut my line and took off for shore in a hurry. He didn't like the look of it, and neither did I. It looked like the body of a man."

Roger gulped and stroked his black beard. "It was probably an old rubber tire or something like that. It would be hard to tell for sure in the fog. The boaters lash tires to the side of the wharf —to act as bumpers, you know. They can break loose in a storm. We had a big storm Tuesday night . . ."

"Knock it off, Roger. We all know the Chamber of Commerce writes your script. I'd like to report this—this *rubber tire* to the police? Where do I find the sheriff?"

Roger flushed and looked guilty but not contrite. "Behind the log church. The building with a flag."

"By the way, I got a surprise last night," Qwilleran continued in a more genial humor. "Your mother-in-law left some turkey and a note at my cabin, but she didn't sign her name. I don't know how to thank her."

"Oh, she's like that—scatter-brained. But she's nice. Laughs a lot. Her name's Mildred Hanstable, and she lives at Top o' the Dunes, east of you. I should warn you about something. She'll insist on telling your fortune an then expect a donation."

"Isn't that illegal?"

"It's for charity. She's helping to raise money for some kind of heart machine at the Pickax Hospital."

"Count me in," Qwilleran said. "I'll need the machine before this restful vacation is over."

When he returned to the cabin, it was still daylight, filtered through fog. Indoors he smelled vinegar, reminding him of the homemade brass polish used by antique dealers. Sure enough, the brass lantern hanging over the bar was newly polished. Tom had been there in spite of the stipulation; he had been told not to come to the cabin until called. Qwilleran had left his old watch and some loose change on the dresser in the bunkroom, and they were still there. He shrugged.

When he called to his friends, Yum Yum came running from the guest room, but Koko was too busily engaged to respond. He was perched on the moose head, fussing and talking to himself in small musical grunts that originated deep in his snowy chest.

"What are you doing up there?" Qwilleran demanded.

Koko was shifting positions on the antlers, standing on his hind legs and reaching up with a front paw as if searching for a toehold. The moose head was mounted on a varnished wooden plaque that was hung on the uneven log wall. Koko was trying to thrust his paw into one of the crevices behind the plaque. After some experimental footwork he finally braced himself well enough to reach the aperture. His paw ventured warily into the opening. Something rattled inside. Koko tried harder, stretched longer, still muttering to himself.

Qwilleran walked closer, and when the prize fell out of the crevice and bounced off the antler, he caught it. "What's this? A cassette!"

It was a blank tape that had been used for home-recording. Side *A* was inscribed *1930 Favorites* in what appeared to be Aunt Fanny's handwriting. Side *B* was labeled *More 1930 Favorites*. There was no dust on the clear plastic case.

Qwilleran took the cassette to the stereo and removed the Brahms concerto that had been in the player ever since he arrived. "Wait a minute," he said aloud. "This is not the way I left it." The cassette had been reversed, and the flip side, offering Beethoven, was faceup.

Koko's trophy produced bouncy music: renditions of *My Blue Heaven, Exactly Like You,* and others of the period, all with the dubious fidelity of old 78s. It was a strange collection to hide behind a moose head.

Qwilleran finished listening to Side *A* and then flipped it over. There was more of the same. Then halfway through *Little White Lies* a voice interrupted—an unprofessional voice—an ordinary man's voice, but forceful. After a brief and surprising message, the music resumed. He rewound the cassette and played it again.

The demanding voice cut in: "Now hear this, my friend. You get busy or you'll be sorry! You know what I'll do! You gotta bring up more stuff. I can't pay off if you don't come up with the loot. And we've gotta make some changes. Things are gettin' hot. You come and see me Saturday, you hear? I'll be at the boat dock after supper."

The tape had been used recently. It was only the day before that Koko had stepped on the buttons and played the Brahms. Someone had been there in the meantime and had either taped the message or listened to it, afterwards replacing the Brahms concerto upside-down. Someone had also stolen a gold watch and a gold pen, but that had happened earlier. Unidentified visitors were walking in and out of the cabin in the casual way that Aunt Fanny found so neighborly.

Someone had undoubtedly climbed on a bar stool to reach the moose head, and Qwilleran checked the four pine stools for footprints, but the varnished surfaces were clean.

Koko was watching intently as Qwilleran tucked the cassette into a dresser drawer. "Koko," the man said, "I don't like this open-door policy. People are using the place like a bus terminal. We've got to find a locksmith. . . . And if you are ever in danger, or if Yum Yum is in danger, you know what to do."

Koko blinked his eyes slowly and wisely.

SIX

Mooseville, Friday

DEAR ARCH,

I'm too tight to buy you an anniversary card, but here's wishing you and your beautiful bride a happy twenty-fourth and many more to come. It seems only yesterday that you dropped the wedding ring and I lost your honeymoon tickets.

Well, since coming to Mooseville I've discovered that all civilization is divided into two parts: Up Here and Down Below. We have friendly people up here who read the *Fluxion*—also mysterious incidents that they try to cover up. Yesterday I went fishing and hooked something that looked like a human body. When I reported it to the sheriff's office, no one seemed particularly concerned. I know it wasn't an accidental drowning. I have reason to believe it was homicide—manslaughter at least. I keep wondering: Who was that guy in the lake? Why was he there? Who tossed him in?

I got into some poison ivy, but I'm okay now. And early this morning I thought someone was stealing my tires, but it was a seagull making a noise like a car-jack.

The eateries up here are so-so. For a restaurant reviewer it's like being sent to Siberia.

Qwill

P.S.
   Koko has some new tricks—answering the phone and
playing the stereo. In a few years he'll be working for
NASA.

   The fog was lifting. From the windows of the cabin it was
possible to see nearby trees and the burial place of the septic
tank. Although Old Sam had filled the depression and leveled it
neatly, the cats had resumed their previous occupation of staring
in that direction.
   When the telephone rang on Friday morning Koko leaped
from the windowsill and raced to the bar. Qwilleran was close
behind but not fast enough to prevent him from dislodging the
receiver. It fell to the bar top with a crash.
   The man seized it. "Hello? Hello?"
   "Oh, *there* you are," said the gravel voice from Pickax. "I was
worried about you, dear. I called yesterday and the phone made
the most *unusual* noises. When I called back I got a busy signal. I
finally told the operator to cut in, and she said the phone was off
the hook, so I sent Tom out there to investigate. He said the
receiver was lying on the bar—and no one was home. You
should be more careful, dear. I suppose you're preoccupied with
your book. How is it progressing? Are you still . . ."
   "Aunt Fanny!"
   "Yes, dear?"
   "I spent the day in town, and my cat knocked the receiver off.
It's a bad habit he's developed. I'm sorry about it. I'll start keeping the phone in the kitchen cupboard, if the cord will reach."
   "Be sure to close the windows whenever you go out, dear. A
squall can come up suddenly and *deluge* the place. How many
chapters of the book have you written? Do you know when it will
be published? Tom says the big jack pine has been cut down.
He'll be out there tomorrow with a log-splitter. Have you noticed the canoe under the porch? The paddles are in the toolshed. Don't go out in rough weather, dear, and be sure to stay
close to shore. Now I won't talk any more because I know you

want to get back to your writing. Some day you can write my life story, and we'll both make a *fortune.*"

Wearing his orange cap, of which he was getting inordinately fond, Qwilleran drove to Mooseville to mail the letter to Arch. At the post office he sniffed warily but detected only fresh floor wax.

His next stop was the Cannery Mall, where he decided the aroma of smoked fish was not entirely unpleasant after all. At the medical clinic the young doctor was sitting at the reception desk, reading a gourmet magazine. He was right about her green eyes; they sparkled with youth and health and humor.

"Remember me?" he began, doffing his cap. "I'm the patient with the Cemetery Syndrome."

"Glad to see you're not as grouchy as you were yesterday."

"The shot took effect immediately. Do you get many cases like mine?"

"Oh, yes," she said. "Ivy poisoning, second-degree sunburn, infected heel blisters, rabid squirrel bites—all the usual vacation delights."

"Any drownings?"

"The police emergency squad takes care of those. I hope you're not planning to fall in the lake. It's so cold that anyone who falls overboard goes down once and never comes up. At least, that's the conventional wisdom in these parts." She closed her magazine. "Won't you sit down?"

Qwilleran settled into a chair and smoothed his moustache nervously. "I'd like to ask you a question about that shot you gave me. Could it cause hallucinations?"

"Extremely unlikely. Do you have a history of hallucinating?"

"No, but I had an unusual experience after the shot, and no one believes I saw what I saw. I'm beginning to doubt my sanity."

"You may be the one person in ten million who had an abnormal reaction," the doctor said cheerfully. "Congratulations!"

Qwilleran regarded her intently, and she returned his gaze with laughing eyes and fluttering eyelashes.

He said: "Can I sue you for malpractice? Or will you settle for a dinner date?"

"Make it a quick lunch, and I can go right now," she said,

consulting her watch. "I never refuse lunch with an interesting *older* man. Do you like pasties?"

"They'd be okay if they had flaky pastry, a little sauce, and less turnip."

"Then you'll *love* the Nasty Pasty. Let's go." She threw off the white coat that covered a Mooseville T-shirt.

The restaurant was small and designed for intimacy, with two rows of booths and accents of fishnet, weathered rope, and stuffed seagulls.

Qwilleran said: "I never thought I'd be consulting a doctor who is female and half my age and easy to look at."

"Better get used to the idea," she said. "We're in plentiful supply. . . . You're in good shape for your age. Do you exercise a lot?"

"Not a great deal," he said, although "not at all" would have been closer to the truth. "I'm sorry, doctor, but I don't know your name."

"Melinda Goodwinter."

"Related to the attorney?"

"Cousin. Pickax is loaded with Goodwinters. My father is a GP there, and I'm going to join his office in the fall."

"You probably know Fanny Klingenschoen. I'm borrowing her log cabin for the summer."

"Everyone knows Fanny—for better or worse. Maybe I shouldn't say that; she's a remarkable old lady. She says she wants to be my first patient when I start my practice."

"Why do you call her remarkable?"

"Fanny has a unique way of getting what she wants. You know the old country courthouse? It's an architectural gem, but they were ready to tear it down until Fanny went to work and saved it —single-handedly."

Qwilleran touched his moustache. "Let me ask you something, Melinda. This is beautiful country, and the people are friendly, but I have a gnawing suspicion that something is going on that I don't comprehend. Am I supposed to believe that Moose Country is some kind of Utopia?"

"We have our problems," she admitted, "but we don't talk about them—to outsiders. This is not for publication, but there's a tendency up here to resent visitors from Down Below."

"They love the tourists' dollars, but they don't like the tourists, is that right?"

She nodded. "The summer people are too smooth, too self-important, too aggressive, too condescending, too *different*. Present company excepted, naturally."

"You think *we're* different? You're the ones who are *different*," Qwilleran objected. "Life in the city is predictable. I go out on assignment, eat lunch at the Press Club, hurry back to the paper to write the story, have dinner at a good restaurant, get mugged on the way home . . . no surprises!"

"You jest. I've lived in the city, and country is better."

The pasties were a success: flaky, juicy, turnipless, and of comfortable size. Qwilleran felt comfortable with Melinda, too, and at one point he smoothed his moustache self-consciously and said: "There's something I'd like to confide in you, if you don't mind."

"Flattered."

"I wouldn't discuss it with anyone else, but since you're a doctor . . ."

"I understand."

"How shall I begin? . . . Do you know anything about cats? They have a sixth sense, you know, and some people think their whiskers are a kind of extrasensory antenna."

"Interesting theory."

"I live with a Siamese, and I swear he's tuned in to some abstruse body of knowledge."

She nodded encouragingly.

Qwilleran lowered his voice. "Sometimes I get unusual vibrations from my moustache, and I perceive things that aren't obvious to other people. And that's not all. In the last year or so my sense of smell has been getting unusually keen—disturbingly keen, in fact. And now my hearing is becoming remarkably acute. A few nights ago someone was walking on the beach a hundred feet away—on the soft sand—and I could hear the footsteps through my pillow: thud thud thud."

"Quite phenomenal," she said.

"Do you think it's abnormal? Is it something I should worry about?"

"They say elephants can hear the footsteps of mice."

"I hope you're not implying that I have large ears."

"Your ears are very well proportioned," Melinda said. "In fact, you're quite an attractive man—for your age."

On the whole Melinda Goodwinter was enjoyable company, although Qwilleran thought she referred to his age too frequently and even asked if he had grandchildren. Nevertheless he was feeling good as he drove home to the cabin; he thought he might start work on his book, or get some exercise.

The fog had all but disappeared. Intermittent gusts of offshore breeze were pushing it out to sea, and the lake had a glassy calm. Perfect canoeing weather, he decided.

Qwilleran had not been canoeing since he was a twelve-year-old at summer camp, but he thought he remembered how it was done. He found paddles in the toolshed and chose the longest one. It was easy to drag the aluminum canoe down the sandy slope to the beach, but launching it was another matter, involving wet feet and a teetering lunge into a wobbly and uncooperative craft. When he finally seated himself in the stern and glided across the smooth glistening water, he sensed a glorious mix of exhilaration and peace.

He remembered Aunt Fanny's advice and turned the high bow, which rose out of the water considerably, to follow the shore. A moment later a gust of offshore wind caught the bow, and the canoe swiveled around and headed for open water, but its course was quickly corrected when the breeze abated. He paddled past deserted beaches and lonely dunes topped with tall pines. Farther on was the Top o' the Dunes Club, a row of substantial vacation houses. He fancied the occupants watching and envying him. Two of them waved from their porches.

The offshore breeze sprang up again, riffling the water. The bow swung around like a weathervane, and the canoe skimmed in the direction of Canada a hundred miles away. Qwilleran summoned all his remembered skills, but nothing worked until the wind subsided again.

He was now farther from shore than appeared wise, and he tried to turn back, but he was out of the lee of the land, and the offshore gusts were persistent, swiveling the bow and making the canoe unmanageable. He paddled frantically, digging the paddle in the water without plan or purpose, desperately trying to turn the canoe. It only drifted farther out, all the while spinning crazily in water that was becoming choppy.

He had lost control completely. Should he jump overboard and swim for shore and let the canoe go? He was not a competent swimmer, and he remembered the reputation of the icy lake. There was no time to lose. Every second took him farther from shore. He was on the verge of panic.

"Back-paddle!" came a voice riding on the wind. "Back-paddle . . . back-paddle!"

Yes! Of course! That was the trick. He reversed his stroke, and while the bow still pointed north the canoe made gradual progress toward shore. Once in the lee of the land, he was able to turn the canoe and head for the beach.

A man and a woman were standing on the sand watching him, the man holding a bullhorn. They shouted encouragement, and he beached the canoe at their feet.

"We were really worried about you," the woman said. "I was about to call the helicopter." She laughed nervously.

The man said: "You need a little more practice before you try for the Olympics."

Qwilleran was breathing heavily, but he managed to thank them.

"You must be Mr. Qwilleran," the woman said. She was middle-aged, buxom, and dressed in fashionable resortwear. "I'm Mildred Hanstable, Roger's mother-in-law, and this is our next-door neighbor, Buford Dunfield."

"Call me Buck," said the neighbor.

"Call me Qwill."

They shook hands.

"You need a drink," Buck said. "Come on up to the house. Mildred, how about you?"

"Thanks, Buck, but I've got a meat loaf in the oven. Stanley is coming to dinner tonight."

"I want to thank you for the turkey," Qwilleran said. "It made great sandwiches. A sandwich is about the extent of my culinary expertise."

Mildred laughed heartily at that and then said: "I don't suppose you found a bracelet at your cabin—a gold chain bracelet?"

"No, but I'll look for it."

"Otherwise it could have dropped off when I was walking on the beach."

"In that case," Buck said, "it's gone forever."

Mildred gave a hollow laugh. "If the waves don't get it, *those girls* will."

The two men climbed the dune to the cottage. Buck was a well-built man with plentiful gray hair and an authoritative manner. He spoke in a powerful voice that went well with a bullhorn. "I'm sure glad to see that fog let up," he said. "How long are you going to be up here?"

"All summer. Do you get fog very often?"

"A bad one? Three or four times a season. We go to Texas in the winter."

The cottage was a modern redwood with a deck overlooking the lake and glass doors leading into a littered living room.

"Excuse the mess," the host said. "My wife went to Canada with my sister to see some plays about dead kings. The gals go for that kind of stuff. . . . What'll you have? I drink rye, but I've got Scotch and bourbon. Or maybe you'd like a gin and tonic?"

"Just tonic water or ginger ale," Qwilleran said. "I'm off the hard stuff."

"Not a bad idea. I should cut down. Planning on doing any fishing?"

"My fishing is on a par with my canoeing. My chief reason for being here is to find time to write a book."

"Man, if I could write I'd write a best-seller," Buck said. "The things I've seen! I spent twenty-five years in law enforcement Down Below. Took early retirement with a good pension, but I got restless—you know how it is—and took a job in Pickax. Chief of police in a small town! Some experience!" He shook his head. "The respectable citizens were more trouble than the lawbreakers, so I quit. I'm satisfied to take it easy now. I do a little woodworking. See that row of candlesticks? I turn them on my lathe, and Mildred sells them to raise money for the hospital."

"I like the big ones," Qwilleran said. "They look like cathedral candlesticks."

They were sitting at the bar. Buck poured refills and then lighted a pipe, going through the ritual that Qwilleran knew so well. "I've made bigger sticks than that," he said between puffs. "Come on downstairs and see my workshop." He led the way to a room dominated by machinery and sawdust. "I start with one of these four-by-fours and turn it on the lathe. Simple, but the tourists like 'em, and it's for a good cause. Mildred finished one pair in gold and made them look antique. She's a clever woman."

"She does a lot for the hospital, I hear."

"Yeah, she's got crazy ideas for fund-raising. That's all right. It keeps her mind off her troubles."

The pipe smoke was reaching Qwilleran's nostrils, and he remarked: "You get your tobacco from Scotland."

"How did you know? I order it from Down Below."

"I used to smoke the same brand, Groat and Boddle Number Five."

"Exactly! I smoked Auld Clootie Number Three for a long time, but I switched last year."

"I used to alternate between Groat and Boddle and Auld Barleyfumble."

Buck swept the sawdust from the seat of a captain's chair and pushed it toward his guest. "Put it there, my friend."

Qwilleran slid into the chair and enjoyed the wholesome smell of sawdust mixed with his favorite tobacco. "Tell me, Buck. How long did it take you to adjust to living up here?"

"Oh, four or five years."

"Do you lock your doors?"

"We did at first, but after a while we didn't bother."

"It's a lot different from Down Below. The surroundings, the activities, the weather, the customs, the pace, the attitude. I never realized it would be such a drastic change. My chief idea was to get away from pollution and congestion and crime for a while."

"Don't be too sure about that last one," Buck said in a confidential tone.

"What makes you say that?"

"I've made a few observations." The retired policeman threw his guest a meaningful glance.

Qwilleran smoothed his moustache. "Why don't you drop in for a drink this weekend? I'm staying at the Klingenschoen cabin. Ever been there?"

Buck was relighting his pipe. He puffed, shook his head, and puffed again.

"It's on the dune, about a half mile west of here. And I've got a bottle of rye with your name on it."

When Qwilleran paddled the canoe home through shallow water, he was thinking about the man who had saved his life with a bullhorn. Buck had denied ever being at the Klingenschoen cabin, and yet . . . On the evening when Mildred left her gift of turkey, two figures had disappeared into the fog, headed for the beach, and one of them had been smoking Groat and Boddle Number Five.

SEVEN

THE MUFFLED BELL of the telephone rang several times before
Qwilleran roused enough to answer it. The instrument was now
housed in a kitchen cupboard, and Koko had not yet devised a
means of unlatching the cupboard door.

Qwilleran was not ready for a dose of directives from Madame
President before his morning coffee, and he shuffled to the
phone reluctantly.

A gentle voice said: "Hello, Qwill dearest. Did I get you out of
bed? Guess what! I can drive up to see you if you still want me?"

"Want you! I'm pining away, Rosemary. When can you come?
How long can you stay?"

"I should be able to leave the store after lunch today and
arrive sometime tomorrow, and I can stay a week unless someone makes a firm offer for Helthy-Welthy. I'm being *very nice* to
Max Sorrell, hoping he'll offer cash."

Qwilleran's response was a disapproving grunt.

There was a pause. "Are you there, dearest? Can you hear
me?"

"I'm speechless with joy, Rosemary. I sent you the directions
to the cabin, didn't I?"

"Yes, I have them."

"Drive carefully."

"I can hardly wait."

"I need you."

He missed Rosemary in more ways than one. He needed a friend who would share his pleasures and problems. He was surrounded by friendly people, yet he was lonely.

He kept saying to the cats: "Wait till she sees the cabin! Wait till she sees the lake! Wait till she meets Aunt Fanny!" His only regret was the fishy odor wafting up from the beach. During the night the lake had deposited a bushel or more of silvery souvenirs, which began to reek in the morning sun.

When he drove into town for breakfast he waved breezy greetings to every passing motorist. Then, fortified by buckwheat flapjacks and lumbercamp syrup, he went in search of the candle shop at Cannery Mall. He detected the thirty-seven different scents even before he saw the sign: *Night's Candles*.

"Are you Sharon MacGillivray?" he asked a young woman who was arranging displays. "I'm Jim Qwilleran."

"Oh, I'm so glad to meet you! I'm Sharon Hanstable," she said, "but I'm married to Roger MacGillivray. I've heard so much about you."

"I like the name of your shop." He thought a moment and then declaimed: " 'Night's candles are burnt out, and jocund day stands tiptoe on the misty mountain.' "

"You're fabulous! No one else has ever noticed that it's a quote."

"Maybe fishermen don't read Shakespeare. How do they feel about scented candles?"

Sharon laughed. "Fortunately we get all kinds of tourists up here, and I carry some jewelry and woodenware and toys as well as candles."

Qwilleran browsed through the narrow aisles of the little shop, his sensitive nose almost overcome by the thirty-seven scents. He said: "Roger has a good-looking money clip. Do you have any more of them?"

"Sorry, they're all gone. People bought them for Father's Day, but I've placed another order."

"How much for the tall wooden candlesticks?"

"Twenty dollars. They're made locally by a retired policeman, and every penny goes to charity. It was my mother's idea."

"I met your mother on the beach yesterday. She's very likable."

Sharon nodded. "Everyone likes Mom, even her students. She teaches in Pickax, you know. We're all teachers, except Dad. He runs the turkey farm on Pickax Road."

"I've seen it. Interesting place."

"Not really." Sharon wrinkled her nose in distaste. "It's smelly and messy. I took care of the poults when I was in high school, and they're so *dumb!* You have to teach domesticated turkeys how to eat and drink. Then they go crazy and kill each other. You have to be a little crazy yourself to raise turkeys. Mom can't stand them. Has she offered to tell your fortune?"

"Not yet," Qwilleran said, "but I've got a few questions I'd like her to answer. And I've got one for you: Where can I find a locksmith?"

"I never heard of a locksmith in Mooseville, but the garage mechanic might be able to help you."

He left the store with a two-foot candlestick and a stubby green candle and drove home inhaling deep draughts of pine scent. When he placed the candlestick on a porch table, Koko sniffed every inch of it. Yum Yum was more interested in catching spiders, but Koko's nose was virtually glued to the raw wood as he explored all its shapely turnings. His ears were swept backward, and occasionally he sneezed.

It was mid-afternoon when the blue pickup truck snaked up the driveway. Tom was alone in the cab.

"Where's the log-splitter?" Qwilleran asked cheerily.

"In the back of the truck," Tom said with his mild expression of pleasure. "I like to split logs with a maul, but this is a big tree. A very big tree." He gazed out at the lake. "It's a very nice day. The fog went away. I don't like fog."

The log-splitter proved to be a gasoline-powered contraption with a murderous wedge that rammed the foot-thick logs to produce firewood. Qwilleran watched for a while, but the noise made him jittery and he retreated to the cabin to brush the cats' fur. Their grooming had been neglected for a week.

At the cry of "Brush!" Koko strolled from the lake porch where he had been watching the wildlife, and Yum Yum squirmed out from under the sofa where she had been driven by the racket in the yard. Then followed a seductive pas de deux as the two cats twisted, stretched, writhed, and slithered ecstatically under the brush.

When Tom had finished splitting the wood, Qwilleran went out to help stack it. "So you don't like heavy fog," he said as an opener.

"No, it's hard to see in the fog," Tom said. "It's dangerous to drive a car or a truck. Yes, very dangerous. I don't drive very much in the fog. I don't want to have an accident. A man in Pickax was killed in an accident. He was driving in the fog." Tom's speech was slow and pleasant, with a musical lilt that was soothing. Today there was something different about his face—a three-day growth on his upper lip.

Qwilleran recognized the first symptom of a moustache and smiled. Searching for something to say he remarked about the quality of sand surrounding the cabin—so fine, so clean.

"There's gold in the sand," Tom said.

"Yes, it sparkles like gold, doesn't it?"

"There's real gold," Tom insisted. "I heard a man say it. He said there's a gold mine buried under this cabin. I wish this was my cabin. I'd dig up the gold."

Qwilleran started to explain the real-estate metaphor but thought better of it. Instead he said: "I often see people picking up pebbles on the beach. I wonder what they're looking for."

"There isn't any gold on the beach," Tom said. "Only agates. The agates are pretty. I found some agates."

"What do they look like?"

"They look like little stones, but they're pretty. I sold them to a man in a restaurant. He gave me five dollars."

They worked in silence for a while. The tall tree had produced a huge amount of firewood, and Qwilleran was puffing with the exertion of stacking it. The handyman worked fast and efficiently and put him to shame.

After a few minutes Tom said: "I wish I had a lot of money."

"What would you do with it?"

"I'd go to Las Vegas. It's very pretty. It's not like here."

"Very true," Qwilleran said. "Have you ever been there?"

"No. I saw it on TV. They have lights and music and lots of people. So many people! I like nightclubs."

"Would you want to work in a nightclub if you went to Las Vegas?"

"No," Tom said thoughtfully. "I'd like to *buy* a nightclub. I'd like to be the boss."

After Tom had raked up the wood chips, Qwilleran invited him in for a beer. "Or would you rather have a shot? I've got some whiskey."

"I like beer," Tom said.

They sat on the back porch with their cold drinks. Koko was entranced by the man's soothing voice, and even Yum Yum made one of her rare appearances.

"I like cats," the handyman said. "They're pretty." Suddenly he looked embarrassed.

"What's the matter, Tom?"

"*She* told me to come up here and look at the telephone. That's why I came. You told me not to come. I didn't know what to do."

"That's perfectly all right," Qwilleran said. "You did the right thing."

"I always do what she tells me."

"You're a loyal employee, Tom, and a good worker. You can be proud of your work."

"I came up here to look at the telephone, and the big cat came out and talked to me."

"That's Koko. I hope he was polite."

"Yes, he was very polite." Tom stood up and looked at the sky. "It's time to go home."

"Here," Qwilleran said, offering him a folded bill. "Buy yourself some supper on the way home."

"I have my supper money. *She* gave me my supper money."

"That's all right. Buy two suppers. You like pasties, don't you?"

"Yes, I like pasties. I like pasties very much. They're good."

Qwilleran felt saddened and uneasy after the handyman's visit. He heated a can of Scotch broth and consumed it without tasting it. He was in no condition to start writing his novel, and he was relieved when another visitor arrived—this time from the beach.

Buck Dunfield, wearing a skipper's cap, climbed up the dune in the awkward way dictated by loose sand on a steep slope. "You promised me a drink," he called out, "and I'm collecting now while I'm still a bachelor. My wife gets home tomorrow. How's it going?"

"Fine. Come in on the porch."

"I brought you something. Just found it." He handed Qwilleran a pebble. "It was on your beach, so it's yours. An agate!"

"Thanks. I've heard about these. Are they valuable?"

"Well, some people use them to make jewelry. Everybody collects them around here. I brought you something else." Buck drew a foil package from his jacket pocket. "Meat loaf—from Mildred. Her husband never showed up last night." In a lower voice he added: "Just between you and me, she's better off without him."

They settled down in canvas chairs on the porch, with a broadside view of the placid lake. Buck said: "Let me give you a tip. If you use this porch much, remember that voices carry across the lake when the atmosphere is still. You'll see a fishing boat out there about half a mile, and you'll hear a guy say 'Hand me another beer' just as clear as on the telephone. But don't forget: He can hear you, too."

There were several boats within sight on the silvery lake, which blended into a colorless sky. The boats seemed suspended in air.

"Do you do much fishing, Buck?"

"A little fishing, a little golf. . . . Say, I see you've got one of my candlesticks."

"Picked it up this morning at Sharon's candle shop."

"I'll tell Mildred. She'll be tickled. Nice little shop, isn't it? Nice girl, Sharon. Roger's a good kid, too." He took out his pipe and began the business of lighting it. Pointing the stem at the beach he said: "You've got some dead fish down there."

"You don't need to tell me. They smell pretty ripe when the breeze is off the lake."

"You should bury them. That's what I do. The stink doesn't bother me; I've got chronic sinus trouble, but my wife objects to it, so I bury the fish under the trees. Good fertilizer!"

"If you don't have a good nose," Qwilleran said, "how can you enjoy that pipe? The aroma used to be the big attraction for me."

"Just a nervous habit." Buck watched two long-legged girls strolling down the beach with heads bowed, studying the sand underfoot. "See? What did I tell you? Everybody collects agates. In the middle of summer it's like a parade along this beach." He had another look at the girls. "They're a little twiggy for me. How about you?"

Qwilleran was thinking, smugly: Wait till he sees Rosemary! He said: "Do you know the woman who owns this cabin?"

Buck rolled his eyes expressively. "Lord, do I ever! She hates my guts. I got her license revoked after she rammed a hole in the Pickax police station. She didn't know forward from reverse. I hoped she's not your grandmother or something."

"No. No relation."

"Just because she's got all the money in the world, she thinks she can do anything she pleases. A woman of her age shouldn't be allowed to carry a firearm. She's crazy enough to shoot up a city council meeting some day." He puffed on his pipe aggressively. "Her name's Fanny, but she calls herself Francesca, and anybody who names their kid after her gets written in her will. There are more Francescas in Pickax than in Rome, Italy."

When the second drink was poured Buck leaned over and said confidentially: "All foolin' aside, how do you size up this place?"

"What do you mean?"

"Mooseville. Do you think everything is out in the open?"

From the man's conspiratorial manner it was clear that he was not talking about the landscape. Qwilleran stroked his moustache. "Well . . . they have a tendency, I would say, to gloss over certain situations and explain them away very fast."

"Exactly! It's their way of life. The *Picayune* didn't even report it when some tourists were mauled by bears at the village dump. Of course, the stupid jerks climbed the fence and teased the bears, and after that the town put up a double fence. But nothing was ever printed in the paper."

"I'm wondering if this vacation paradise is as free of crime as they want us to believe."

"Now you're talking my language." Buck glanced around quickly. "I suspect irregularities that should be investigated and prosecuted. You've worked on the crime beat; you know what I mean. I'm friendly with a few detectives Down Below, and they speak highly of you."

"Do you know Lieutenant Hames?"

"Sure do." Buck chuckled. "He told me about your smart cat. That's really far-out! I don't believe a word of it, but he swears it's true."

"Koko's smarter than I am, and he's sitting under your chair right now, so be careful what you say."

"Cats are all right," Buck said, "but I prefer dogs."

"Getting back to the subject," Qwilleran went on, "I think the authorities up here want to operate in their own way without any suggestions or embarrassing questions from outsiders."

"Exactly! The locals don't want any hotshot city-types coming up here and telling them what's wrong."

"What do you think is wrong?"

Buck lowered his voice again and looked over his shoulder twice. "I say there are crimes that are being conveniently overlooked. But I'm working on it—privately. Once a cop, always a cop. Did you ever eat at the FOO? The customers are a mixed bag, and the battleax that runs the joint has larceny in her heart, but it's hooked up to the best grapevine in the country. . . . Now, mind you, I'm not going to stick my neck out. I'm at the age when I value every day of my life. I've got good digestion, a good woman, and something useful to do. Know what I mean? Only . . . it would give me a lot of satisfaction to see a certain criminal activity cleaned up. I'm not saying the police are corrupt, but they're hogtied. Nobody wants to talk."

Qwilleran sat in silence, grooming his moustache with his knuckles as the panorama of his adventure on the *Minnie K* unreeled before his mind's eye.

"I had an interesting experience the other day," he began. "It might support your theory, although I have no actual evidence. How about you?"

"I've been doing some snooping, and I'm getting there. Something may break very soon."

"Okay. Let me tell you what happened to me. Did you ever hear of a boat called the *Minnie K*?" The newsman went on to recount the entire fog-bound tale, not missing a single detail.

Buck listened attentively, forgetting to relight his pipe. "Too bad we don't know the name of the boat where the guys were having the fight."

"It probably docks in the same godforsaken area where we boarded the *Minnie K*. It was a sleazy part of the shoreline. I haven't been back there since the fog lifted, so I don't know how much activity there is in the vicinity."

"I know that area. It's the slum of the waterfront. Mooseville would like to see it cleaned up, but it's beyond the village limits. Want to drive out there with me—some day soon?"

"Be glad to. I'm having company from Down Below for about a week, but I can work it in."

"Gotta be going," Buck said. "Thanks for the booze. I've gotta get rid of a sinkful of dirty dishes before the old gals get home and give me hell. I've got a wife *and* a sister on my tail all the time. You don't know how lucky you are." He looked at the sky. "Storm tonight."

He left the same way he had come, slipping and sliding down the dune to the beach. The leggy girls were returning from their walk, and Buck fell into step behind them, throwing an OK finger-signal to Qwilleran up on the porch.

Koko was still sitting under the chair, very quiet, folded into a compact bundle. There was something about the visitor that fascinated him. Qwilleran also appreciated this new acquaintance who spoke his language and enjoyed the challenge of detection. They would have a few investigative adventures together.

The day was unusually calm. Voices could be heard from the fishing boats: "Anybody wanna beer? . . . Nah, it's time to go in." There was something portentous about the closeness of the atmosphere. One by one the boats slipped away toward Mooseville. There was a distant rumble on the horizon, Koko started throwing himself at the legs of tables and chairs, while Yum Yum emitted an occasional shriek. By nightfall the storm was overhead. The rain pelted the roof and windows, claps of thunder shook the cabin, and jagged bolts of lightning slashed the night sky and illuminated the lake.

EIGHT

WHEN THE SIRENS went screaming down the highway, Qwilleran was having his morning coffee and one of Aunt Fanny's cinnamon buns from the freezer, thawed and heated to pudding consistency in the microwave. Several acres of woods separated the cabin from the main road, but he could identify the sound of two police cars and an ambulance speeding eastward. Another accident! Traffic was getting heavier as the vacation season approached. Vans, recreation vehicles, and boat trailers were turning a country road into a dangerous thoroughfare.

That morning Qwilleran had lost another round in his feud with the fireplace. Why, he asked himself, can a single cigarette butt start a forest fire when I can't set fire to a newspaper with eleven matches? When he finally managed to ignite the sports section, smoke billowed from the fireplace and flakes of charred newsprint floated about the room before settling on the white linen sofas, the oiled wood floors, and the Indian rugs.

After breakfast he began to clean house. He started by dusting the bookshelves and was still there two hours later, having discovered books on Indians, raccoons, mining history, and common weeds. The dissertation on poison ivy included a sketch of the sinister vine. At once Qwilleran left the cabin with book in hand to scout the woods beyond the septic tank—that particular area that monopolized the cats' attention.

All of nature was reacting ebulliently to the violence of the recent storm. Everything was cleaner, greener, taller, and more alive. Two little brown rabbits were gnawing pine cones. Small creatures rustled through the ground cover of pine needles and last year's oak leaves. There was no poison ivy, however. Back to the dusting, Qwilleran thought.

Then another opportunity for procrastination presented itself. He had never entered the toolshed except to select a canoe paddle. It was a cedar hut with a door, no window and no electric light. Immediately inside the entrance were the paddles, long-handled garden tools, and a ladder. The far end of the shed was in darkness, and Qwilleran went back to the cabin for a flashlight. As he expected, his activities were being monitored by two Siamese in the east window.

In the inner gloom of the shed the flashlight beam picked out paint cans, coils of rope, a garden hose, axes, and—against the far wall—a dingy cot with a limp pillow. On the wall above hung faded magazine pages with a two-year-old dateline and the unmistakable razzle-dazzle of Las Vegas. Mosquitoes were bounding off Qwilleran's neck and ears, and a loud buzzing suggested something worse. Qwilleran made a quick exit.

He had resumed his desultory housecleaning when he heard a rumbling in Koko's throat. The cat rushed to the windows overlooking the lake. Moments later a lone walker on the beach started to climb the dune. Mildred Hanstable's head was bowed, and she was dabbing her eyes with a tissue.

Qwilleran went out to meet her. "Mildred! What's wrong?"

"Oh, God!" she wailed. "It's Buck Dunfield."

"What's happened?"

"He's dead!"

"Mildred, I can't believe it! He was here yesterday and healthy as an ox." She all but collapsed in his arms, and he took her indoors and seated her on a sofa. "Can I get you something? Tea? A shot of whiskey?"

She shook her head and controlled herself with effort. Koko watched, his eyes wide with alarm. "Sarah and Betty got home—from Canada—a little while ago and—and found him in the basement—workshop." She put her hands over her face. "Blood all over. He'd been killed—beaten—with one of the—one of the big—candlesticks." Her words drowned in her tears, and Qwilleran held her hand and let her cry it out, while he coped with his own shock and outrage.

When she was calm she said, between fits of sniffling: "Sarah passed out—and Betty came screaming over to my house—and we called the police. I told them I hadn't heard anything—not even the machinery. The storm drowned everything out."

"Do you know if the motive was burglary?"

"Betty says nothing was touched. I'm shattered. I don't know what I'm doing. I'd better go home. Sharon and Roger are coming over as soon as they can."

"Let me walk you home."

"No, I want to walk alone—and straighten myself out. Thanks, though."

Qwilleran tried to straighten out his own thinking. First he had to deal with the bitter realization that violence like this could take place in Mooseville. Could it be someone from Down Below? The area was being inundated by outsiders. . . . Then there was genuine grief. He liked Buck Dunfield and had looked forward to a summer of good talk and shared adventures. . . . And there was anger at the senseless killing. Buck had been so glad to be alive and to be doing something useful. . . . After that came uneasiness. No matter what the local custom, locks on doors were now an imperative. He hurried to the phone and called Pickax.

"*Aunt Fanny!* This is Jim calling from Mooseville. I want you to listen carefully. This is important. I need to find a locksmith immediately. I *must have locks* on these doors, or keys for the existing locks. Someone entered my neighbor's house and killed him. Someone has also been using this cabin for some shady purpose. I know this is Sunday, but I want to be able to call a locksmith early tomorrow. The whole idea of leaving doors open to strangers is unsafe, absurd, and medieval!"

There was a long pause before the scratchy baritone response: "Bless my soul! My dear boy, I didn't realize a journalist could get so upset. You are always so *contained*. Never mind! Hang up, and I'll make some arrangements. How is the weather on the shore? Did you have thunder and lightning last night?"

Qwilleran replaced the receiver and groaned. "What do you bet," he asked Koko, "that she'll send Tom, the resident genius?" To Yum Yum, who came struggling out from under the sofa, he said: "Sorry, sweetheart, I didn't know I was shouting." To himself he said: Fanny didn't even ask who had been murdered.

Barely ten minutes elapsed before a car could be heard winding its careful way among the trees and over the rolling dunes. Koko rushed to his checkpoint on the porch. The visitor was a young man with curly black hair, dressed in Mooseville's idea of Sunday Best: a *string tie* with his plaid shirt and jeans, and *no cap*.

With deference in his tone and courteous manner he said: "Good afternoon, Mr. Qwilleran. I hear you have a problem."

"Are you the locksmith?"

"No, sir. Mooseville doesn't have a locksmith, but I know something about locks. I'm an engineer. My wife and I were having our usual Sunday dinner at the hotel, and Miss Klingenschoen tracked us down. She's a very persuasive woman. I came as soon as I finished my prime rib. Very good prime rib at the hotel. Have you tried it?"

"Not yet," Qwilleran said, trying to conceal his impatience. "We've been here just a few days."

"That's what my wife told me. She's postmistress in Mooseville."

"Lori? I've met her. Charming young lady." Qwilleran relaxed a little. "And your name?"

"Dominic. Nick for short. What seems to be the trouble?" After the situation was explained he said: "No problem at all. I'll bring some equipment tomorrow and take care of it."

"Sorry to bother you on a Sunday, but a man at Top o' the Dunes was murdered. It's been a great shock."

"Yes, it's too bad. Everyone is wondering what effect it will have on the community."

"You mean people know about it already? They didn't find the body until a couple of hours ago."

"My wife heard the news in the choir loft," Nick said. "She sings at the Old Log Church. I heard it from one of the ushers during the offering."

"Murder is not what I'd expect in Mooseville. Who would do such a thing? Some camper from Down Below?"

"Well-l-l," replied the engineer. "I could make a guess."

Qwilleran's moustache bristled. He sensed a source of information. "May I offer you a drink, Nick?"

"No, thank you. I'll get back to my wife **and** my dessert. We like the deep-dish apple pie at the hotel."

Qwilleran walked with him to the car. "So you're an engineer. What kind of work do you do?"

"I'm employed at the prison," Nick said. "See you tomorrow."

Qwilleran went back to his housecleaning—in the desultory manner that was his specialty. He was shaking the Indian rugs in the parking lot when he heard a sound that made his heart leap: a car with a faulty muffler. Rosemary had never found time to have it replaced. He caught a glimpse of her little car between the trees and gasped. She had a passenger! If she had brought Max Sorrel—that pushy opportunist, that viper with a shaved head and facile smile—there might be another murder in Mooseville. The car disappeared in a gully, then rumbled back into view. Seated next to the driver, mouth agape and eyes staring, was the polar bear rug from the apartment at Maus Haus.

Rosemary tumbled out of the car, laughing at Qwilleran's spluttering amazement. "How—what—how—"

"The former tenant offered to sell it for fifty dollars, and I thought you could afford that much," she said. "I had fun driving up here with the bear in the front seat, but the state troopers stopped me and said it was a motoring hazard. I pushed the head down under the dashboard, but it kept popping up. . . . What's the matter, dearest? You're rather subdued."

"There's been a shocking incident here," Qwilleran told her, "and if you want to turn around and go home, I won't blame you."

"What on earth—?"

"A murder, half a mile down the beach."

"Someone you know?"

He nodded sadly.

Rosemary raised her chin in the determined way she had. "Of course I'm not going home. I'm going to stay here and cheer you up. You've been too solitary, and you've probably been eating all the wrong food, and you've been spending too much time at the typewriter instead of getting exercise."

That was his Rosemary—not as young as some of the women he had been seeing; in fact, she was a grandmother. But she was an attractive brunette with a youthful figure, and she was comfortable to have around. Once, when he had made some foolish attempt at rigorous exercise, she had given him a remarkably skillful massage.

"Please bring in my luggage, dearest, and show me where I'm going to sleep. I'd love to have a shower and a change of clothes. Where are the beautiful cats? I've brought them some catnip."

Koko and Yum Yum remembered her from Maus Haus and reacted to her presence without feline wariness but also without overt friendliness. Occasionally, when she had visited Qwilleran's apartment, they had been locked in the bathroom.

Rosemary's vitality and dewy complexion and bright eyes were the result, she claimed, of eating the Right Food, some of which she had brought along in a cooler. With the Right Food warming in the oven and the bearskin rug grinning on the hearth, the cabin felt homey and comfortable. Koko walked across the cassette player, and they had music.

"*Aimez-vous* Brahms?" Qwilleran asked.

"What?" Rosemary often missed the point of his quips.

He inquired about the situation at Maus Haus.

"It's terrible. The cook has left. Hixie never says anything funny. Charlotte cries all the time. And one night the immaculate Max had a spot on his tie. You're so lucky to have this cabin for the summer, Qwill. It's so lovely. There are violets and trilliums all along the driveway, and I've never seen so many goldfinches, and the chipmunks are so cute."

Rosemary noted and commented on everything: the white linen slipcovers on the sofas, the mauve and turquoise tints of the lake as the sun sank, the tall oak candlestick on the porch, the moose head and crosscut saw over the mantel.

"The pickax! Where's the pickax?" Qwilleran exclaimed, jumping to his feet. "There was an antique pickax up there a week ago. I don't know, Rosemary. People walk in and out of this cabin like it's a bus terminal. It's considered unfriendly to lock doors. My good watch has disappeared and—worst of all—the gold pen you gave me. And now the pickax is missing."

"Oh, dear," she said sympathetically.

"Everything around here is strange. The police set up roadblocks just for fun. Nobody has a last name. There are footsteps on the roof in the middle of the night. The cats spend all their time staring at the septic tank."

"Oh, Qwill, you must be exaggerating. You're punchy from eating the wrong food."

"You think so? Well, this is a fact: Koko found a cassette hidden behind the moose head, with a threatening message recorded right in the middle of the music. And when I went fishing, I hooked the body of a man."

Rosemary gasped. "Who was it?"

"I don't know. It went back to the bottom of the lake, and everybody tries to tell me it was an old rubber tire."

"Qwill, dearest, are you sure you're getting enough fresh fruit and vegetables?"

"You're like all the others," he complained, "but there was one person who believed me, and now he's dead, with his skull bashed in."

"Oh, Qwill! Don't meddle with these things. You might be in danger yourself."

"We'll see about that," he said. "Let's eat. But first I want to feed the cats. A nice woman down the beach sent over some meat loaf, and I've conned them into thinking it's pâté de foie gras."

"Have you met many nice women down the beach?" Rosemary inquired sweetly. "I thought you were up here to write a book."

They talked far into the night. Qwilleran couldn't stop. He told her about the Nasty Pasty and the FOO, cherry blossoms and mosquitoes, agates and gravediggers, the Goodwinters and the Whatleys, shipwrecks and poachers, Little Henry and Big George, Night's Candles and Bob's Chop Shop.

Rosemary could no longer control her yawns, which she tried to disguise as laughs, coughs, and hiccups. "Dearest, I've been driving all day," she said. "Isn't it about time . . . ?"

After a prolonged good-night she escaped to the guest room and dislodged the Siamese from their favorite bunk. Qwilleran went to his own bed and thought about Rosemary for ten minutes, worried about the unlocked door for seven, and pondered the mystery of Buck Dunfield's murder for four and a half before falling into a deep sleep.

He was waked by horrendous screaming. He leaped out of bed. It was just outside his window. "Rosemary!" he shouted.

"What's that?" she cried.

Lights were turned on. Koko dashed about with his ears laid back. Yum Yum hid. Rosemary came running from the guest room in her red nightgown.

The sound of wordless struggle in the underbrush ceased, and the screams gradually diminished in volume, fading away into the night stillness.

Qwilleran grabbed a flashlight and a poker from the fireplace.

"Don't go out there, Qwill!" Rosemary cried. "Call the police!"

"It won't do any good. I reported one incident this week, and they made me feel like a fool."

"Please call them, Qwill. It could be murder, or rape, or abduction. Some woman walking on the beach. It was a woman screaming."

"It sounded like a banshee to me."

Succumbing to Rosemary's pleas he phoned the sheriff's office. He gave his name and location and described the episode as calmly and objectively as possible.

In answer to a question he said: "No, there's not another house for quarter of a mile, but people walk on the beach in the middle of the night. . . . Yes, it's heavily wooded. . . . There were sounds of struggling in the woods. No other voice—just the screams. . . . Very loud at first—utter panic. Then they got weaker and just died away. . . . A what? . . . Hmmm. Very interesting. Do you think that's what it was? . . . It certainly did. . . . Well, thank you, officer. Sorry to bother you."

Qwilleran turned to Rosemary. "It was an owl, swooping down on a rabbit and carrying it away."

"Is that what he said? Well, I don't care; it scared me out of my skin. I'm still shaking. I'd feel a lot safer in your room. Do you mind?"

"No, I don't mind," Qwilleran said, grooming his moustache.

"The cats would like it better, too," said Rosemary. "They seem to think I've taken their bed."

NINE

QWILLERAN WAS FEELING particularly happy and agreeable on Monday morning. Although he was not given to using affectionate appellations, he started calling Rosemary "honey." As the day progressed, however, his elation gradually deflated. The first setback occurred when Nick arrived to work on the locks before Qwilleran had had his coffee.

"I see you have a Siamese," Nick said after Koko had inspected him at the checkpoint. "We have three cats, just ordinary ones. My wife would love to see yours."

Recalling the engineer's cryptic remark about Buck Dunfield's murderer, Qwilleran said: "Why don't you bring your wife over some evening—to meet Koko and Yum Yum? I must apologize again for disturbing your meal yesterday."

"Think nothing of it. Glad to oblige. Besides, nobody ever says no to Miss Klingenschoen." Nick raised his eyebrows in a good-humored grimace.

When he left he was carrying one of Rosemary's catnip toys. "While you're here," he told her, "be sure to visit the flower gardens at the prison. The tulips are out now. Everything is later here than Down Below, you know."

After he had gone Rosemary said: "What a nice young man! I can visit the gardens this afternoon while you're working on your book. I'd also like to get my hair done if I can get an appointment."

The Siamese were delighted with their new plaything, catnip tied in the toe of a sock. Koko was especially dexterous, batting it with a paw, chasing it, tumbling with it, then losing it in some remote nook or crevice.

Qwilleran, on the other hand, was less than delighted with his late breakfast. It consisted of a fresh fruit compote sprinkled with an unidentified powder resembling cement, followed by a cereal containing several mysterious ingredients—some chewy, some gummy, some sandy. He knew it was all the Right Food, and he consumed everything without comment but refused to give up his morning caffeine in favor of brewed herbs.

Rosemary said: "I found some dreadful commercial rolls in your freezer, made with white flour and covered with sugary icing. You don't want to eat that junk, Qwill dearest. I threw them out."

He huffed into his moustache and said nothing.

After her noisy car had chugged down the drive and headed for Bob's Chop Shop, Qwilleran planned his own day. He set up his typewriter on the dining table, together with writing tools and scattered papers, in a realistic tableau of creative industry. Then he telephoned Mildred: "How are you doing?"

"I'm not as hysterical as I was yesterday," she said, "but I feel terrible. Do you realize what it's like to have your next-door neighbor murdered?"

"We've all got to start locking our doors, Mildred—the way they do Down Below."

"Buck and Sarah and Betty were such good friends of mine. We played bridge all the time. He'll be buried in his hometown, and the girls have taken off already, so it's quiet and gloomy. I miss hearing the woodworking machines. Would you like to drop in? I'll make a strawberry pie."

"I have a houseguest," Qwilleran said, "and I was going to suggest that you and your husband come for drinks and then be my guests at the hotel dining room."

"You're very sweet," she said, "but he's awfully busy on the farm right now. Why don't you bring your guest down here? I'll read the tarot cards for you."

Next on Qwilleran's agenda was a trip into Mooseville. Before leaving the cabin he checked the whereabouts of the Siamese, closed the windows, and enjoyed the familiar ritual of locking the door. Leaving the cabin without locking up was an unnatural act that had made him uneasy ever since coming to Mooseville.

For the last three days he had nursed a desire to take another look at the *Minnie K,* simply to convince himself that the boat really existed. He headed west, retracing the route taken with the unforgettable Whatleys. Beyond the Cannery Mall and beyond the FOO the landscape was dotted with ramshackle cottages, each with a junk car in the yard, a TV antenna on the roof, and gray laundry on the clothesline. Finally he turned down the lane alongside the trash-filled canal.

There at the end of the rotting wharf was the boat with the torn, gray, spotted canvas chairs on the deck. But it was no longer the *Minnie K;* it was the *Seagull,* according to the freshly painted stern board. There was no sign of a crew. Farther down the shore other boats of equal dilapidation were moored in Monday morning lassitude.

From one of those moldy decks, Qwilleran was sure, someone had been thrown into the icy lake.

On the return trip to Mooseville he stopped at the FOO for coffee and the Monday edition of the *Pickax Picayune.* The news item he sought was buried at the bottom of page five under the Euchre Club scores. It was headlined: *Incident on East Shore.* Qwilleran read it twice.

> Buford Dunfield, 59, retired police officer and long-time summer resident of Mooseville, was found dead in the basement workshop of his posh East Shore cottage Sunday morning, the apparent victim of an unknown assailant, who attacked him with a blunt instrument just a few hours before his wife, Sarah Dunfield, 56, and his sister, Betty Dunfield, 47, returned home from their annual summer visit to Canada, where they attended three Shakespearean plays. Police are investigating.

The restaurant was buzzing with conversation about fishing. Qwilleran suspected the customers switched to that subject automatically whenever an outsider walked in.

His next stop was the tourist bureau. Roger was seated at his desk, bantering with a visitor—a fresh-faced youth who lounged in a chair expertly balanced on two legs, with his feet propped on Roger's desk.

"Qwill! You're just in time to meet the managing editor of the *Pickax Picayune*," Roger exclaimed. "This is Junior Goodwinter, one of your admirers. We were just talking about you."

The young man jumped to his feet. "Wow! The great man in person!"

"And yet another of the famous Goodwinters," Qwilleran said. "I knew you were a journalist by the way you balanced that chair. Congratulations on your coverage of the Dunfield murder. That was the most succinct seventy-one-word sentence I've ever read."

"Wow! You counted!"

"You omitted only one pertinent fact: the titles of the plays that the ladies attended in Canada."

"Now you're putting me on," said Junior.

"At last I realize why you don't have any crime up here. You have 'incidents' instead. Brilliant solution to the crime problem."

"Aw, take the nails out, will you? I know we do things in a different way up here—different from what I learned in J school anyhow. We're country, and you're city. Would you mind if I interviewed you some day?"

"My pleasure. Maybe I'd learn something."

"Well, so long. I've got to get out and sell some ads," Junior said.

Qwilleran was shocked. "Don't tell me you sell advertising as well as edit the paper!"

"Sure, we all sell ads. My father owns the paper, and he sells ads and sets the type."

The managing editor loped out of the office in his jogging shoes, and Qwilleran's face registered amazement and amusement. "Isn't he young for a managing editor?" he said to Roger.

"He's been working at the paper since he was twelve. Worked his way up. Graduated from State last year. Ambitious kid."

"I've always wanted to own a small newspaper."

"You could buy the *Picayune* cheap, but it would take a lot of dough to drag it into the twentieth century. It was founded in 1859 and hasn't changed since. . . . Anything I can do for you today?"

"Yes. You have all the answers. Tell me who killed Buck Dunfield."

Roger flushed. "That's a tough one. I haven't heard any scuttlebutt. Sharon and I went over to see Mildred yesterday, and she was really shook up."

"Was it a random killing? Did Dunfield have enemies? Or was he involved in something we don't know about?"

Roger shrugged. "I don't know much about the summer people."

"He lived next door to your mother-in-law and made candlesticks to sell in your wife's store. You never met him?"

"I guess I met him on the beach a couple of times and had a few words."

"You're lying, Roger. Are you practicing to be a politician?"

Roger raised both hands. "Don't shoot!" Then he gave Qwilleran a mocking grin. "Been doing any fishing from the *Minnie K* lately?"

"Tell you something interesting," Qwilleran said. "I went back to have another look at the old scow this morning, and the name's been changed to *Seagull* with the *S* painted backward."

Roger nodded. "I can tell you why, if you want to know. The skipper was probably afraid you'd go around blabbing about a body in the lake, and you'd involve the *Minnie K*. Then he'd be fined for operating an illegal charter service. Boats have to be registered before they can take trolling parties. From what you say about the *Minnie K*, she'd never pass the inspection."

Qwilleran had one more mission to pursue that afternoon. His curiosity about the buried pail kept luring him back to the cemetery, and now that he could identify poison ivy he was ready for another expedition. Weekend activity in the lovers' lane had increased the amount of picnic litter, and the sunny days and rainy nights had done wonders for the weeds in the graveyard itself. He found the vicious vines with three pointed leaves around the small headstones, and he remembered how he had torn at them to read the inscriptions. Then he followed the faint foot-trail behind the Campbell monument.

The pail was still camouflaged by scattered weeds, and it was still empty. But it had been used for some purpose. There were bits of straw in the bottom of the pail, and the top-handle on the

lid, which Qwilleran had left at right angle to the headstone, was
now askew.

Qwilleran didn't linger. He hurried back to the cabin in order
to arrive before Rosemary. The whiffs of rotting fish, increasing
in pungency, aggravated his cheerless mood. Rosemary, on the
other hand, breezed into the cabin bubbling with enthusiasm
and carrying an armload of yellow, white, pink, red, and pur-
plish-black tulips.

"The prison gardens are lovely," she said. "You must go to see
them, Qwill dearest. A charming man gave me these to bring
home. How many pages did you write today?"

"I never count," Qwilleran said.

"It's a lovely new prison. A very friendly woman outside the
gate invited me to join PALS. That's the Prisoner Aid Ladies'
Society, or something like that. They write letters to the inmates
and send them little presents."

"Did you hear any gossip about the murder?"

"Not a word! Do you have any vases for these tulips? I have
some groceries in the car for our dinner. I picked up some fresh
fish and *lovely* parsnips and Brussels sprouts—and some carrots
for the kitty cats. You should grate a little carrot and mix it with
their food every day."

Brussels sprouts! Parsnips! Qwilleran had been thinking about
a sixteen-ounce steak and French fries with ketchup and Parker-
House rolls and a Roquefort salad and deep-dish apple pie with
cheddar cheese and three cups of coffee.

"Will the fish keep?" he asked. "I'd like to take you to the
Northern Lights Hotel for dinner. My day hasn't been produc-
tive, and I need a change of scene."

"Why, of course! That sounds lovely," Rosemary said. "Do I
have time to walk on the beach for an hour?"

"You won't like it. The beach is covered with dead fish."

"That won't bother me," she said. "It's part of nature."

Leaving tulips in a lemonade pitcher on the mantel, in a flour
canister on the dining table, and in an ice bucket on the bar,
Rosemary tripped jubilantly down the slope to the beach.

Qwilleran sprawled on one of the sofas. "Koko, I feel like an
idiot," he told the cat, who was studying him intently from the
back of the sofa. "I don't have a single clue. What are we working with? A dead body in the lake, the murder of a retired cop,

and a message on a cassette. Someone has been using this cabin for some kind of illicit or illegal purpose. Never mind *who*. We don't even know *what*."

"YOW!" said Koko, blinking his large blue eyes.

Qwilleran brought the cassette from his dresser drawer and once more played *Little White Lies*. The voice cut in: ". . . bring up more stuff . . . gotta make some changes . . . things are gettin' hot . . . at the boat dock after supper." It was a high-pitched nasal voice with a monotonous inflection.

"I've heard that voice before," Qwilleran said to Koko, but the cat was playing with his catnip toy. "Things were getting hot because Buck was closing in on his investigation. Some changes had to be made because the cabin was no longer available as a depot."

That voice! That voice! He had heard it at the post office, or at the FOO, or at the General Store, or in the hotel dining room.

No! Qwilleran snapped to attention. The voice on the cassette was the voice he had heard in the fog, when two men were brawling on another boat. One voice had a deep rumble and a British accent. The other man spoke with a piercing twang and a flat inflection. As he recalled, something had happened to the engine, and they were arguing, apparently, about the best way to get it started.

CLUNK!

Qwilleran recognized the clunk of a book being pushed from a bookshelf and landing on the floor. Koko had done it before. He was never clumsy; if he knocked something down it was for a good reason.

Koko was on the second shelf, digging behind a row of books to extricate his sockfull of catnip. The book he had dislodged was a treatise on historic shipwrecks. It was lying open on the floor—open to a page marked by a folded slip of paper.

There on page 102 was an account of the sinking of the *Waterhouse B. Duncan*, a freighter carrying a rich cargo of copper ingots. It went down in treacherous water north of Mooseville during a severe storm in November 1913. All lives were lost: three passengers and a crew of twenty-three, including a woman cook.

The folded slip that marked page 102 was a penciled agreement to rent a boat for thirteen summer weekends, terms to be decided. It was dated the previous year and was signed S. Hanst-able.

There was something about this information that jogged Qwil-leran's memory. Somewhere in one of her letters Aunt Fanny had mentioned . . . what? The recollection was a vague one. He delved into his correspondence file and groaned; not only were her letters cross-written but her handwriting was extremely individual, and the multitude of dashes made each page a daz-zling plaid.

He put on his reading glasses and squinted through half a dozen pages before he found the reference that was nagging his memory. On April third she had first offered him the use of the cabin. Written in her telegraphic style, the letter read:

> Charming little place—built entirely of logs—quite comfortable—I'm getting older—don't enjoy it so much —last summer decided to rent—two handsome young men—interested in marine history—came up on week-ends—their girlfriends stayed all week—horrid crea-tures—played games with spaghetti—threw it at the ceiling—unspeakable mess—two weeks to clean the place—never again!

Qwilleran's moustache bristled, the way it did when he thought he had found a clue. The bookmark raised other ques-tions: Did Roger's wife own a boat? Did she print like a kinder-garten teacher? Did she spell "decided" with an *s*?

TEN

BEFORE TAKING ROSEMARY out to dinner Qwilleran fed the cats, both of whom fastidiously avoided every shred of carrot that contaminated their corned beef.

He had made a reservation at the Northern Lights Hotel in order to get one of the high-backed booths constructed from the salvaged cabins of retired fishing boats. Diners in these booths had to be careful to avoid splinters, and in humid weather the booths exuded haunting reminders of their origin, but they were ideal for confidential conversation.

Rosemary was wearing a Mooseville T-shirt and a braided leather necklace from the prison gift shop, and she looked so youthful, so vibrant, so healthy that Qwilleran found it hard to believe she had a grandson old enough to be in medical school. She hung her shoulder-strap bag on a hook at the entrance to the booth. "Isn't it wonderful," she said, "not to worry about theft! At home, when I go to a restaurant, I put this bag on the floor, keep my foot on it, and wind the strap around my ankle."

The menu cover reproduced an engraving of a terrifying storm on the lake, and the paper placemats listed the dates of major shipwrecks plus the number of lives lost. *Bon appetit*, Qwilleran thought.

He said to Rosemary: "You can order the poached scrod with

cauliflower if you wish, but I'm going to have a large steak with fries. . . . Don't look so shocked. I know the Right Food has done wonders for you; you don't seem a day over thirty-nine. But it's too late for me. The only time I ever looked thirty-nine was when I was twenty-five."

"Truce! Truce!" she said, waving a paper napkin. "I didn't mean to be a nag, Qwill. You order whatever you want, and don't apologize. You're under creative pressure with your book, and you've earned a treat. How many chapters have you written? Would you read me a few pages tonight?"

"And another thing, Rosemary: Please don't keep asking about my progress. I don't have a daily quota or a deadline, and when I'm not sitting at my typewriter I want to forget about it entirely."

"Why, certainly, Qwill. I've never known an author personally. You'll have to tell me how to behave."

He kept glancing across the room toward a party of four seated beneath a large painting of a drowning sailor in shark-infested water. "Don't look now," he said, "but the two men over there are wreck-divers, I've been told. They loot sunken ships."

The men were tall, lean, and stony-faced. "They look like cigarette ads," Rosemary said, "and the girls with them look like models. How did they get those gorgeous tans so early in the season? And why don't they look happy? Their diet is probably inadequate."

"I've seen the girls walking on the beach," Qwilleran said. "I think they're staying at a cottage near ours. They may be the four who rented Fanny's cabin last year." He told how Koko had attracted his attention to the shipwreck book and how he had waded through the cross-written correspondence. "If you're looking for a quick way to get a headache," he added, "I'll lend you a few of Fanny's letters."

"When am I going to meet her?"

"Tomorrow or Wednesday. I'd like to ask her about these so-called marine historians and about her relationship with Buck Dunfield. There's one obstacle; it's hard to get her attention."

"Some types of deafness are caused by a diet deficiency," Rosemary said.

"She's not deaf, I'm sure. She simply chooses not to listen. Maybe you'll be able to get through to her, Rosemary. She seems to favor women. . . . Excuse me a moment. I want to catch those people before they leave."

He crossed the room to the wreck-divers and addressed the more formidable of the two. "Pardon me, sir. Aren't you a correspondent for one of the wire services?"

The man shook his head. "Sorry, you're on the wrong track," he said in a deep and less-than-cordial voice.

"But you're a journalist, aren't you? Didn't you do graduate work at Columbia? You covered the last presidential election."

"Sorry, none of the above."

Qwilleran made a good show of bewilderment and turned to the second man. "I was sure you were a press photographer, and you two worked together on big assignments."

More genially the other man said: "Nothin' like that, suh. We're jest a coupla bums up heah awn vacation."

Qwilleran apologized, wished them a pleasant holiday, and returned to the booth.

"What was that all about?" Rosemary asked.

"Tell you later."

On the way home he explained: "I think there's a syndicate operating around here. They've been using Fanny's cabin for an underground headquarters. It's secluded; the doors have always been unlocked; and there are three avenues of access or escape: from the beach, from the highway, and from the woods. The boss has been giving tape-recorded orders to his henchmen, hiding the cassette behind the moose head."

Rosemary laughed. "Qwill, dear, I know you're kidding me."

"I'm serious."

"Do you think it's drug-related?"

"I think it's shipwreck-looting. The lake is full of valuable wrecks, and there's a book at the cabin that pinpoints their location and describes their cargoes. Some of the boats went down more than a hundred years ago."

"But wouldn't the cargo be ruined by this time?"

"Rosemary, they weren't shipping automobiles and TV sets in 1850. They were shipping copper ingots and gold bullion. The shipping manifests tell exactly what was aboard each vessel when it sank—how many barrels of whiskey, how many dollars in banknotes and gold. At one time this part of the country was booming."

"Why did you talk to the men at the hotel?"

"I thought one of them might be the ringleader, but there's no similarity between their voices and the one on the cassette. None at all. But the ringleader is around here somewhere."

"Oh, Qwill! You have a fantastic imagination."

When they arrived at the cabin Qwilleran unlocked the door and Rosemary entered. He heard her yelp: "Oh! Oh! There are tulips all over the floor!"

"*Those cats!*" Qwilleran bellowed—loud enough to send both of them flying to the guest room.

"They pulled out all the *black* tulips, Qwill."

"I don't blame them. Tulips were never intended to be black."

"But you told me once that cats can't distinguish colors."

He picked up the flowers, and Rosemary rearranged the bouquets in the impromptu vases on mantel, bar, and dining table. Then they went to the lake porch to await the sunset, stretching out in varnished steamer chairs old enough to have sailed on the *Titanic*.

Seagulls soared and swooped and squabbled over the dead fish on the beach. Rosemary identified them as herring gulls. The flycatchers, she said, who were performing a nonstop aerial ballet were purple martins. Something brown and yellow that kept whizzing past the porch was a cedar waxwing.

"I hear an owl," Qwilleran said, to prove he was not totally ignorant about wildlife.

"That's a mourning dove," she corrected him. "And I hear a cardinal . . . and a phoebe . . . and I think a pine siskin. Close your eyes and listen, Qwill. It's like a symphony."

He touched his moustache guiltily. Perhaps he had been listening to the wrong voices. Here he was in the country, on vacation, surrounded by the delights of nature, and he was trying to identify miscreants instead of cedar waxwings. He should be reading the bird book instead of cross-written letters.

Rosemary interrupted his thought. "Tell me some more about Aunt Fanny."

"Ah—well—yes," he said, shifting his attention back to the moment. "For starters . . . she wears flashy clothes and bright lipstick, and she has a voice like a drill sergeant. She's spunky and bossy and full of energy and ideas."

"She must have a wonderful diet."

"She has a houseman who drives her around, runs errands, takes care of the garden, cleans the house, and knows how to repair everything under the sun."

Rosemary giggled. "He'd make a wonderful husband. How old is he?"

"But I have a suspicion he's also a petty thief."

"I knew there was a catch," Rosemary said. "How does Koko react to him?"

"Very favorably. Tom has the kind of gentle voice that appeals to cats."

Koko heard his name and wandered nonchalantly onto the porch.

"Have you been walking Koko on his leash?"

"No, but I've contemplated a reconnaissance maneuver. He spends a lot of time staring out the guest room window, and I'd like to know what he finds so interesting."

"Rabbits and chipmunks," Rosemary suggested.

"There's something more." Qwilleran stroked his moustache. "I have a hunch . . ."

"Let's take him out."

"Now?"

"Yes. Let's!"

On several occasions Koko had been strapped into his blue harness and taken for a walk. A twelve-foot nylon cord donated by a *Fluxion* photographer served as a leash and gave him a wide range. Frequently Koko's inquisitive nose and catly perception led to discoveries that escaped human observation.

The appearance of the harness produced a noisy demonstration, and when the buckles were tightened Koko uttered a gamut of Siamese sounds denoting excitement. Yum Yum thought he was being tortured and protested loudly.

For the first time since his arrival Koko left the cabin. Outside the porch he found the rope hanging from the brass bell, stretched until he could catch it with a claw, and gave the bell a peal or two. Without hesitation he then turned eastward—past the porch, beyond the cabin itself, around the sandy rectangle that covered the septic tank, and toward the woods. When he reached the carpet of pine needles, acorns, and dried oak leaves, every step was a rustling, crackling experience unknown to a city cat. Squirrels, rabbits, and chipmunks retired to safety. A frantic robin tried to distract him from her nest. Koko merely walked resolutely toward the woods on top of the dune. Behind a clump of wild cherry trees was the toolshed.

"How do you like that?" Qwilleran whispered to Rosemary. "He made a beeline for the toolshed."

He opened the door, and Koko hopped across the threshold. He gave a single sniff to a canoe paddle and two sniffs to the trash can. "Quick, Rosemary, run and get the flashlight. It's hanging inside the back door."

In the inner gloom of the shed Koko glanced at the collection of paint cans and went directly to Tom's cot. Jumping on the threadbare blanket he started pawing industriously, all the while making gutteral noises and flicking his tail in wide arcs. He pawed the sorry excuse for a pillow, pawed the wall with the faded Las Vegas pictures, and returned to pawing the blanket.

"What are you looking for, Koko?" Qwilleran pulled aside the blanket, and Koko dug into the thin mattress.

Rosemary was beaming the flashlight on the drab scene. "He's very determined."

"There might be a nest of mice in the mattress."

"Let's pull the whole dirty thing off onto the floor."

The mattress slid off the flat springs of the cot, and with it came a large manila envelope. Rosemary held the light closer. The envelope was addressed to Francesca Klingenschoen and postmarked two years before. The return address was that of a Florida real estate firm.

"Look inside, Qwill."

"Money! Mostly fifties."

"Here, let me count it. I'm used to counting money." She snapped the bills with professional speed. The total sum was almost twelve hundred dollars. "What shall we do with it?"

"It belongs to Fanny's houseman," Qwilleran said. "We'll put it back, and tidy the bed, and get out of here before the mosquitoes bring up their reserves."

Late that night he lay awake wondering about Tom's cache in the toolshed. Was the poor fellow saving up for a down payment on a Las Vegas nightclub? Where was he getting the money? Not from Aunt Fanny. It appeared that she doled out a few dollars at a time.

Qwilleran heard heavy footsteps on the roof. He hoped Roger was right. He hoped it was a raccoon.

ELEVEN

Tuesday morning Qwilleran drove to town before breakfast to buy eggs. Rosemary insisted there was nothing better than a soft-boiled egg for easy digestibility. Qwilleran couldn't remember eating a soft-boiled egg since the time he stayed home from second grade with a case of mumps. Nevertheless, he bought a dozen eggs, and when he returned Rosemary met him at the door. Her face was stern.

"Koko has been naughty," she said.

"Naughty!" No one had ever accused Koko of being naughty. Perverse, perhaps, or arrogant, or despotic. But naughtiness was beneath his dignity. "What has he done?"

"Pulled out all the black tulips again. I saw him do it. I scolded him severely and locked him in the bathroom. Yum Yum has been sitting outside the door whimpering, but Koko is very quiet inside. I'm sure he knows he did wrong."

Qwilleran opened the door slowly. The scene was like the aftermath of a blizzard. A roll of paper towels was reduced to confetti. The wastebasket was overturned and its contents scattered. A fresh box of two hundred facial tissues was empty, and the toilet tissue was unrolled and festooned about the room. Bath salts and scouring powder were sprinkled liberally over all.

Koko sat proudly on the toilet tank as if he had completed a work of conceptual art and was ready for a press conference.

Qwilleran drew his hand across his face to erase a wicked smile, but Rosemary burst into tears.

"Don't be upset," he said. "Go and boil the eggs, and I'll clean up this mess. I think he's trying to tell us something about black tulips."

Conversation was strained at the breakfast table. Rosemary asked meekly: "When are we going to see Aunt Fanny?"

"I'll phone her after breakfast. Today we should take your car to Mooseville to get the muffler fixed. While we're there we can visit the museum and have lunch at the Nasty Pasty. . . . I'd also like to suggest that we eliminate the black tulips."

The telephone call to Pickax required the usual patience.

"Of course, I would *adore* to see you and your lady friend tomorrow," said Aunt Fanny in her chesty voice. "You must come for lunch. We'll have pork chops or nice little veal collops. Do you like spinach soufflé? Or would you rather have cauliflower with cheese sauce? I have a splendid recipe for the soufflé. How's the weather on the shore? Is there anything Tom can do for you? I could make an orange chiffon pie for dessert if you . . ."

"*Aunt Fanny!*"

"Yes, dear?"

"Don't plan a big lunch. Rosemary has a small appetite. I could use Tom's services, though, if it isn't inconvenient. We have some dead fish on the beach that should be buried."

"Of course. Tom enjoys working on the beach. Are you making good progress with your book? I'm so eager to read it!"

Rosemary was unusually subdued all morning, and Koko—being a master of one-upmanship—devised a subtle way to press his advantage. He followed her around the cabin and repeatedly maneuvered his tail under her foot. His blood-curdling screeches after each incident reduced her to nervous confusion.

Qwilleran, though amused at Koko's ingenuity, began to feel sorry for Rosemary. "Let's get out of here," he said. "In a battle with a Siamese you never win."

They dropped off her car at the garage, and Qwilleran paid close attention to the mechanic's manner of speech. Compared with the voice on the cassette, he had the right pitch but the wrong timbre and wrong inflection.

The museum occupied an opera house dating from the nineteenth century, when loggers, sailors, miners, and millhands paid their dimes and quarters to see music hall acts. Now it was filled with memorabilia of the old lumbering and shipping industries. Rosemary pored over the cases containing scrimshaw and other seamen's crafts. Qwilleran was attracted to the scale models of historic ships that had gone to the bottom. So were two other men, whom he recognized. They studied the ship models and mumbled to each other.

A third man—young and enthusiastic—came hurrying over. "Mr. Qwilleran, I'm glad you've honored us with a visit. I'm the museum curator. Roger told me you were in town. If you have any questions, I'll try to answer them." Qwilleran noted that the pitch, timbre, and inflection were all wrong.

He said to Rosemary: "I've got to do an errand. I'll be back in half an hour, and we'll go to lunch."

He hurried to the visitors' center and waited impatiently while five tourists inquired about the bears at the dump. Then he threw a slip of paper on Roger's desk. "What can you tell me about this?"

Roger read the boat rental agreement. "That's my father-in-law's signature."

"Does he have a boat?"

"Everybody up here has a boat, Qwill. He likes to go fishing whenever he can get away from those stupid turkeys."

"Did he rent it to wreck-divers last summer?"

"I don't know for sure, but I think he'd do anything for a buck." Roger wriggled uncomfortably. "The truth is: He and I don't get along very well. Sharon was her daddy's girl, and I came along and stole her. Get the picture?"

"Too bad. I got into that situation myself. . . . Another question, Roger. What do you know about the people who run the FOO?"

"They're a weird couple. She's a hundred pounds overweight, and when she's at the cash register, you'd better count your change. He was in some kind of industrial accident Down Below. When he collected compensation, they came up here and bought the FOO. That was before the *D* dropped off."

"Is that her husband who does the cooking? Little man with thinning hair."

"No, Merle is a big guy. Spends all his time on his boat."

"Where does he keep it?"

"In the dock behind the restaurant. . . . Say, did you see the UFO last night?"

"No, I didn't see the UFO last night," Qwilleran said, starting for the door.

"We get a lot of them up here," Roger called after him. But Qwilleran was gone.

Here was the opportunity to check the voice of a likely suspect. The FOO had raised his suspicions from the beginning—for several reasons. Something that didn't look like coffee was frequently served in coffee cups. There were rooms for rent upstairs. Customers slipped money to Mrs. FOO surreptitiously and received a slip of paper. As for the little man with thinning hair, he shuffled about in a furtive manner and made ghastly pasties.

Now Qwilleran wanted to meet Merle. Still leaving Rosemary at the museum he drove to the FOO, parked in the lot, and ambled down to the dock. A good-sized boat in shipshape condition was bobbing alongside the pier, but no one was in sight. He called to Merle several times, but there was no response.

As he returned to his car, the cook sidled out of the back door, smoking a cigarette. "Lookin' for sumpin'?" he inquired.

"I want to see Merle. Know where he is?"

"He went somewheres."

"When will he be back?"

"Anytime."

Qwilleran returned to town and took Rosemary to the Nasty Pasty. She had recovered from her tiff with Koko and was brimming with conversation. The museum was so interesting; the curator was so friendly; the restaurant was so cleverly decorated.

Qwilleran, on the other hand, was disappointed at missing Merle, and he jingled three pebbles in his sweater pocket.

"What's the matter, Qwill? You seem nervous."

"I'm just revving up my good luck tokens." He threw the pebbles on the table. "The green one is polished jade that a collector gave me. The ceramic bug is a scarab that Koko found. The agate is one that Buck Dunfield picked up on our beach—last agate he ever found, poor guy."

"And here's another one for your collection," Rosemary said, producing a dime-size disc of yellowed ivory with the face of a cat etched in the surface. "It's scrimshaw, and quite old."

"Great! Where did you find it?"

"In the antique shop behind the museum. The curator told me about it. Have you been there?"

"No. Let's go after lunch."

"An old sea captain runs it, and I'm warning you: It's a terrible place."

The Captain's Mess was an apt name for the jumble of antiquities and fakes that filled the shop behind the museum. A little storefront, it was older than the opera house itself, and the next nor-easter would be sure to blow it down. The building was so loose and out-of-joint that only the solid oak door held it upright. When the door was open, the building slouched to one side, and it was necessary to push the door jamb back into position before the door could be closed. Qwilleran sniffed critically. He detected mildew and whiskey and tobacco.

There were marine lanterns, bits of rigging, unpolished brass objects, ships in dusty bottles, water-stained charts, and—sitting in the midst of the clutter—an old man with a stubby beard and well-worn captain's cap. He was smoking a carved pipe from some far-off place, but his tobacco was the cheapest to be found in the corner drug store. Qwilleran knew them all.

"Ye back again?" shrilled the captain when he spied Rosemary. "I told ye—all sales final. No money back."

Qwilleran asked: "Do you still go to sea, captain?"

"No, them days is over."

"I suppose you've sailed around the globe more times than you can remember."

"Yep, I been about a bit."

"How long have you had your shop?"

"Quite a piece."

The pitch of the man's voice was right; the timbre was right; the inflection was almost right, but the delivery lacked the force of the voice on the cassette. The captain was too old. Qwilleran was looking for someone younger, but not too young. He rum-

maged among the junk and bought a brass inkwell guaranteed
not to slide off a ship captain's desk in a rolling sea.

They returned to the cabin, and Rosemary suggested a walk
on the beach. While she changed clothes Qwilleran ambled
around the property. He knew Tom had been there; the brass
bell had a fresh sheen, and the putrid little carcasses on the
beach had been buried.

Rosemary appeared in a turquoise sundress. "I wanted to
wear my new apricot jumpsuit, but I can't find my coral lipstick."

"You look beautiful," Qwilleran said. "I like you in that color."

Koko glared at them silently when they went down the slope
to the beach.

Rosemary said: "I think he wants me to go home."

"Nonsense," Qwilleran said, and yet the same idea had
crossed his mind. Koko had never approved of the women in his
life.

Heading eastward they trudged through deep sand in silence,
the better to enjoy the peacefulness of the lonely beach. Then
came the row of summer houses on top of the dune. One resem-
bled the prow of a ship. Another, sided with cedar shakes,
looked like a bird with ruffled feathers. Some of the cottagers
were burying their dead fish. Two girls were sunning on the
deck of a rustic A-frame.

"They're the models we saw at the hotel," Rosemary said,
"and they're not wearing tops *or* bottoms."

Qwilleran pointed out the redwood house where Buck had
been murdered. "Now it's even more of a mystery," he said. "At
first I thought there was some connection between Buck's private investigation and the message on the cassette, but he was on
the track of a *crime*, and the wreck-divers are not criminals.
They're shrewd opportunists operating for private gain and not
in the public interest, but they're not breaking the law."

Next they passed Mildred's yellow house and traversed another half mile of desolate beach until a creek, bubbling across a
bed of stones on its way to the lake, sliced through the sand and
barred their way. As they retraced their steps, Mildred waved to
them from her porch, beckoning them up the dune and offering
them coffee and homemade apple pie. "It's in the freezer," she
said. "It won't take a minute to thaw."

The interior of the bungalow was muffled in handmade quilts, hanging on the walls and covering the furniture.

"Did you make all these? They're lovely," Rosemary exclaimed. "You've got a lot of time invested here."

"I've had a lot of spare time to invest," Mildred said with a small sigh. "Did you see the UFO last night?"

"No, but I heard about it," Qwilleran said. "What do you think it was?"

Mildred looked surprised. "Why, everyone *knows* what it was."

It was Qwilleran's turn to look surprised. "Do you actually believe it was an extraterrestrial visitor?"

"Of course. They come here all the time—usually at two or three in the morning. I see them because of my insomnia. I had standing orders to phone the Dunfields at any hour, so they could get up and watch."

Making a mental note to follow up this local idiosyncrasy, Qwilleran said: "Have you heard from Buck's wife and sister?"

"They phoned once—to ask if I'd adopt their geraniums and throw the perishables out of the refrigerator. They don't know when they'll be back."

"Any developments in the case?"

"The men from the police lab have been working at the house. Betty told me that Buck must have been working in his shop when the murderer sneaked in and took him by surprise. There was a candlestick on the lathe and a lot of sawdust. Those power tools make so much noise, Buck wouldn't hear anyone come in, I suppose."

"Can we assume that the killer turned the machine off afterward? That was thoughtful of him."

"No one mentioned it, and I never thought of it."

"He must have tracked sawdust out of the house."

"I don't know. I suppose so."

"Did Buck ever talk about the shipwreck-diving that goes on up here? Or did he hint at any criminal activity?"

Mildred shook her head and lowered her eyes and lapsed into a reverie.

To snap her out of it Qwilleran said: "Okay, Mildred, how about reading the tarot cards? I have a couple of questions?"

She drew a deep breath. "Come over to the card table. I'll read for you one at a time. Who wants to go first?"

"Are you serious about this?" Qwilleran asked. "Or is it a gimmick for the hospital fund?"

"I'm serious. Quite serious," she said, "and I have to be in the right state of mind, or it doesn't work. So . . . no fooling around, please."

"Would the cards reveal anything about the murder?"

Her face turned pale. "I wouldn't want to ask them. I wouldn't want to get into that."

Rosemary said: "The cards are spooky—such strange pictures! Here's a man hanging upside-down."

"The symbols are ancient, but the symbols only unlock thoughts and insights. Do you have a question, Rosemary?"

Rosemary wanted to know about her business prospects. She sat across the table from Mildred and shuffled the cards. Then Mildred arranged a dozen of the cards in a pattern and meditated at length.

"The cards are in sync with your question," she murmured, "and with some of the questions you didn't ask. Everything points to change. Business, home, romance—all subjects to change in the near future. You have had partnerships in the past, and you have lost them, in one way or another. Your present business partner is a woman, I think. That will change. You have always welcomed change, but now you are reluctant to face something new. A broken contract has disappointed you. Don't let it affect your energy and enthusiasm. You will make an inspiring contact soon. And expect good news from a young male of great ambition. I see another figure in the cards—a mature male of great intelligence. You may take a long journey with him. Be alert for two dangers: Avoid conflict between business and personal life, and beware of treachery. All will end happily if you use your natural gifts and maintain an even course." She stopped and drew a deep breath.

"Wonderful!" Rosemary said. "And all so true!"

"Will you excuse me for a moment?" Mildred said weakly. "I want to step outdoors and do some deep breathing before the next reading."

She drifted from the room, and Qwilleran and Rosemary looked at each other. "What do you think about that, Qwill?" she said. "The broken contract is my lease at Maus Haus. My partner at Helthy-Welthy is a woman. The ambitious young man is my grandson, I know. He's trying for a very desirable internship in Montreal."

"How about the other guy? Mature and intelligent. That rules out Max Sorrel."

"Now you're mocking. You're supposed to be serious."

By the time Mildred returned, Qwilleran had composed his face in an expression of sincerity. He shuffled the cards and asked his questions: "Will I accomplish my goal this summer? Why am I balked in everything I try to do in this north country?"

"The cards show a pattern of confusion, which could result in frustration," Mildred said quietly. "This causes you to scatter your forces and waste your energy in trivial detail. You have skills but you are not using them. Change your tactics. Your stubbornness is the obstacle. Be receptive to outside help. I see a male and a female in the cards. The woman is good-hearted and fair in coloring, and she has taken a liking to you. The man is young, dark-complexioned, and intelligent. Let him help you. The cards also see a new emotional entanglement. There may be some bad news, involving you in legal matters, but you will make the best of it. Your summer will be successful, although not as you planned it."

Qwilleran squirmed in his chair. "I'm impressed, Mildred. You're very good!"

She nodded absently and drifted from the room again, after placing a fishbowl on the table. It was labeled *Hospital Donations* and contained a ten-dollar bill. Qwilleran said: "My treat, Rosemary," and added two twenties, a generous sum that would have amazed his friends at the *Fluxion*.

Rosemary said: "I don't like the idea of your new entanglement. It's probably that blonde she mentioned."

"Did you notice that card? The blonde had a black cat. It sounds like the postmistress. The dark male sounds like her husband."

"Or Koko," Rosemary said.

The return walk along the beach was in silence, as each pondered the advice of the cards. One could hear the squeaking of the sand underfoot. Qwilleran made one observation: "Mildred has lost her nervous laugh since the tragedy next door."

At the porch entrance they clanged the brass bell for the sheer pleasure of hearing its pure tone, and when Qwilleran unlocked the door and threw it open for Rosemary, Koko was on the threshold, with Yum Yum not far behind. Koko was carrying a single red tulip in his mouth.

"It's a peace offering," Qwilleran told Rosemary, but he knew very well that Koko never apologized for anything. The cat was trying to convey information, and it was not in the field of horticulture. . . . Tulips . . . Tulips . . . Qwilleran's moustache was sending him signals. The tulips came from the prison gardens. Nick was employed at the prison. . . . He glanced at his watch and grabbed the phone.

Lori answered. "You caught me just in time, Mr. Qwilleran. I was about to lock up and go home."

"You mean you actually *lock* the post office in Mooseville?"

"Seems silly, doesn't it?" she said. "But it's federal regulations."

He made the requisite remarks about the weather and then said: "Would you and Nick like to come over tomorrow evening to have a drink and meet the cats and watch the sunset? I have a charming guest from Down Below, and I don't know how much longer she can stay."

Lori's acceptance was almost too effusive, and Qwilleran said to Rosemary later: "You'd think it was an invitation to the White House or Buckingham Palace."

She raised her eyebrows. "Did I hear you say that your charming guest might not stay much longer?"

"Merely an innocent social prevarication intended to lend convincing authenticity to an alarmingly abrupt invitation."

"You must be feeling good," Rosemary said. "You always get wordy when you're feeling good."

TWELVE

"WHAT SHALL I WEAR to visit Aunt Fanny?" Rosemary asked on Wednesday morning. "I'm all excited."

"You look nice in your white suit," Qwilleran said. "She'll be dressed like Pocahontas or the Empress of China. I'm going to wear my orange cap." He knew Rosemary was not enthusiastic about his new headgear.

On the road to Pickax he pointed out the turkey farm. "Mildred brought us some turkey from the farm one day, and it was the best I've ever tasted."

"That's because it was raised naturally," Rosemary explained. "And it was fresh. No preservatives."

Near the old Dimsdale Mine he pointed out a dilapidated boxcar doing business as a diner. "I call it the Dismal Diner. We're having dinner here tonight."

"Oh, Qwill! You're kidding."

As they neared Pickax he said: "I have a hunch Aunt Fanny will like you. You might find out why she rented to those divers last summer. And tell her the pickax disappeared from the cabin."

"Why me?"

"I'm going to take a walk and let you girls get acquainted. You could mention the murder of Buck Dunfield and see how she reacts. I'm also curious to know why an eighty-nine-year-old woman with a live-in bodyguard carries a handgun in a county that has no crime."

"Why don't you ask the questions and I'll take a walk," Rosemary suggested. "I'm no good at snooping."

"With me she's evasive. With another woman she might open up. She likes women lawyers and women doctors, I happen to know."

They drove past crumbling buildings that had been shaft houses for the mines, past old slag heaps that made unnatural bumps in the landscape, past rows of stone rectangles that had been the foundations of miners' cottages. Then the road reached the crest of a hill, and Pickax City lay in the valley below, with the circular park in dead center.

"Fanny lives on the circle," Qwilleran said. "Best location in town. Her ancestors made a pile of money in mining."

When they pulled into the driveway of the great fieldstone house, Tom was working on the perfectly groomed lawn and his blue pickup was parked in front of the carriage house. Qwilleran waved to him and noticed that the growth on the young man's lip was beginning to resemble a moustache.

Aunt Fanny greeted them in a flowing purple robe of Middle Eastern design with borders embroidered in silver. A purple scarf was knotted about her head, and her long dangling earrings were set with amethysts. Rosemary was spellbound, and Aunt Fanny was volubly cordial.

Qwilleran brought up an insignificant rear as the hostess swept them into the large pretentious dining room for lunch. He tried hard to pretend he was enjoying his cup of tomato soup, half a tuna sandwich, and weak coffee. He listened in amazement as Rosemary gushed and twittered and Aunt Fanny proved she could answer questions in a normal way.

"When was this lovely old house built?" Rosemary asked.

"Over a hundred years ago," Aunt Fanny said. "In horse-and-buggy days it was considered the grandest house in town. Would you like me to show you around after lunch? Grandfather brought over Welsh stonemasons to build the house, and there's an English pub in the basement that was imported from London, piece by piece. The third floor was supposed to be a ballroom, but it was never finished."

"While you ladies are taking the grand tour," Qwilleran said, "I'd like to walk downtown, if you'll excuse me. I want to see the *Picayune* offices."

"Oh, you journalists!" Aunt Fanny said with a coy smirk. "Even when you're on vacation you can't forget your profession. I admire you for it!"

Leaving the house, Qwilleran looked for Tom, but the handyman and the blue truck had gone.

The commercial section of Main Street extended for three blocks. Stores, restaurants, a lodge hall, the post office, the home of the *Picayune,* a medical clinic, and several law offices were all built of stone with more exuberance than common sense. Cotswold cottages nestled between Scottish castles and Spanish forts. Qwilleran gave the *Picayune* office a wide berth and turned into the office of Goodwinter and Goodwinter.

"I don't have an appointment," he told the gray-haired secretary, "but I wonder if Mr. Goodwinter is available. My name is Qwilleran."

The secretary was undoubtedly a relative; she had the narrow Goodwinter face. "You've just missed him, Mr. Qwilleran," she said pleasantly. "He's on his way to the airport and won't be back until Saturday. Would you like to speak to his partner?"

The junior partner bounded out of her office in a cloud of expensive perfume, extending a well-manicured hand, and smiling happily. "Mr. Qwilleran! I'm Penelope. Alex has told me about you. He's attending a conference in Washington. Won't you come in?"

She too had the long intelligent face that Qwilleran had learned to recognize, but it was softened by a smile that activated tantalizing dimples.

Qwilleran said: "I just dropped in to report on something your brother discussed with me."

"About the mysterious liquor purchases?"

"Yes. I don't find any evidence that our elderly friend is tippling."

"I agree with you," said the attorney. "That's my brother's private theory. He thinks she's developing a whiskey voice. I says it's hormones."

"How do you account for the houseman's liquor purchases?"

"He must buy it to treat friends. He has an apartment in the carriage house, and he must have some social life of a sort, or it would be a very lonely life."

"He's a strange young man."

"But gentle and rather sweet," Penelope said. "He's a good worker and carries out orders perfectly, and some of our affluent families would *kill* to get him."

"Know anything about his background?"

"Only that a friend of Fanny's in New Jersey arranged for Tom to come out here and help her. Isn't she a remarkable woman? She amassed her fortune in the days before women were supposed to have brains."

"I thought she inherited her money."

"Oh, no! Her father lost everything in the Twenties. Fanny saved the family property and went on to make her own millions. She'll be ninety next month, and we're giving a party. I hope you'll join us. How are you enjoying Mooseville?"

"It's never dull. I suppose you know about the murder."

She nodded without any emotion, as if he had said: "Do you know it's Wednesday?"

"It was a shocking thing to happen in a place like Mooseville," he said. "Do you have any theories?"

She shook her head.

She knows something, Qwilleran thought, but the Legal Curtain has descended. "Wasn't Dunfield the police chief who was feuding with Fanny a few years ago? What was the trouble?"

The attorney looked up at the ceiling before answering cooly. "Simply small-town politics. It goes on all the time."

Qwilleran liked her style. He enjoyed his half hour in the company of an intelligent young woman with dimples and chic. Rosemary was attractive and comfortable to be with, but he had to admit he was captivated by career women in their thirties. Fondly he remembered Zoe the artist, Cokey the interior designer, and Mary the antiques dealer.

On his way back to the stone house he spotted another Goodwinter face. "Dr. Melinda, what are you doing here?" he said. "You're supposed to be repairing tourists at the Mooseville Limp-in Clinic."

"My day off. Buy you a cup of coffee?" She guided him around the corner to a luncheonette. "Second worst coffee in the county," she warned him, "but everybody comes here."

He tested the coffee. "Who's in first place? They'd have to try hard to beat this."

"The Dimsdale Diner takes top honors," Melinda said with a flourish. "They have the *worst* coffee in the county and the worst *hamburgers* in northeast central United States. You should try it. It's an old boxcar on the main highway, corner of Ittibittiwassee Road."

"You're not going to make me believe *Ittibittiwassee.*"

"No joke. It's the road to the Ittibittiwassee River. The Indians had a village there at one time. Now it's time-sharing condos."

"Tell me something, Melinda. I've seen the remains of the Dimsdale Mine and the Goodwinter Mine. Where's the Klingenschoen Mine?"

Melinda studied his eyes to see if he could possibly be serious. Finally she said: "There is no Klingenschoen Mine. There *never* was a Klingenschoen Mine."

"How did Fanny's grandfather make his money? In lumbering?"

She looked amused. "No. He was a saloonkeeper."

Qwilleran paused to digest the information. "He must have been highly successful."

"Yes, but not highly respected. The K Saloon was notorious for half a century before World War I. Fanny's grandfather built the most luxurious house in town, but the Klingenschoens were never accepted socially. In fact, they were ridiculed. The miners had a marching song that went like this: *We mine the mines and the K mines us, but who Mines Minnie when the something something something.* I don't know the punch line, and I'm not sure I want to know."

"Then Minnie K was . . ."

"Fanny's grandmother, a very friendly lady, according to the stories. You can read about it in the local history section of the public library. Fanny's father inherited the saloon but went bankrupt during Prohibition. Fortunately Fanny had her grandfather's talent for making money, and when she came back here at the age of sixty-five, she could buy and sell anyone in the county."

As Qwilleran returned to the stone house he walked with a springier step. There was nothing like a juicy morsel of news to buoy his spirit, even when he was not on assignment.

Rosemary was equally exhilarated when he picked her up for the ride home. She had had a *lovely* visit. The house was *lovely*—full of antiques. Francesca had given her a Staffordshire pitcher from her collection, and Rosemary thought it was *lovely*. Qwilleran thought it was ugly.

He said: "I've been hungry ever since lunch, and we ought to have an early dinner because Nick and Lori are coming at seven. Let's try the Old Stone Mill."

The restaurant was an authentic old mill with a water wheel, and the atmosphere was picturesque, but the menu was ordinary —from the chicken noodle soup to the rice pudding.

"All I want is a salad," Rosemary said.

"I'm going to order the mediocre pork chops, a soggy baked potato, and overcooked green beans," Qwilleran said. "That's the Moose County specialty. Why don't you have the chicken julienne salad? It's probably tired lettuce and imitation tomatoes with concrete croutons and slivers of invisible chicken. No doubt they serve it with bottled dressing from Kansas City and a dusting of grated Parmesan that tastes like sawdust. This used to be a sawmill, you know."

"Oh, Qwill! You're terrible," Rosemary admonished.

"What did you two emancipated females talk about while I was taking my walk?"

"You. Aunt Fanny thinks you are so talented, so sincere, so kind, so sensitive. She even likes your orange cap. She says it makes you look dashing."

"Did you tell her about the missing pickax?"

"Yes. She said the Historical Society wanted it for their museum, so she had Tom pick it up."

"She might have let me know. And what about the divers?"

"They wrote to a real estate firm in Mooseville, asking for a summer house to rent. They turned out to be very undesirable tenants. Especially the girls who spent the summer with them. She called them a name that I wouldn't repeat."

"Aw, c'mon. Tell me."

"No."

"Spell it."

"No, I won't. You're just teasing me."

Qwilleran chuckled. He liked to tease Rosemary. She was the epitome of the Perfect Lady circa 1902.

She said: "I have a lot more to tell you, but I don't want to talk here."

When they resumed their drive north he said: "Okay, let's have it. You and Fanny seemed to hit it off pretty well."

"She thinks you and I are engaged, and I didn't dispute it because I wanted her to talk. It was really flattering, the way she took me into her confidence."

"Good girl! What did she confide?"

"Her method of getting what she wants. She manipulates people with big promises and little threats. She says everybody *wants* something or is *hiding* something. The trick is to find their weakness. I think she makes it a kind of *hobby*."

"The little old rascal! That's the carrot-and-stick technique."

"Of course, it works better if you have a lot of money."

"Of course. What doesn't?"

"She showed me a little gold pistol that she carries. That's to intimidate people. It's just a joke."

"She has a quaint sense of humor. What did she say about Dunfield's murder?"

"Oh my! She really hated that man. She got so mad I thought she was going to have a stroke."

"Buck was the only one she couldn't manipulate."

Rosemary giggled. "He accused her of growing marijuana in her backyard. Can you imagine that?"

"Yes, I can."

"About his murder, she said that people who play with fire can expect to get burned, and then she used some *very bad language.* I was shocked."

Qwilleran smiled into his moustache. He reminded himself that Rosemary shocked easily.

"Such a nice little old lady," Rosemary went on. "Where did she pick up such a vocabulary?"

"In New Jersey, probably."

There was more to relate: about the library with four thousand leather-bound books, unread; the four closets filled with Aunt Fanny's spectacular wardrobe; the Staffordshire collection in the breakfast room, the envy of three major museums; the Georgian silver in the dining room . . .

"Stop!" Rosemary cried as they approached the turkey farm. "I'll run in and see if they have a dressed turkey. Then I can cook it for you before I leave."

Qwilleran pulled in the farmyard alongside the inevitable blue pickup. "Make it snappy. It's getting close to seven o'clock."

Alongside the row of poultry coops there was a metal shed with a sign on the door: *Retail and Wholesale*. Someone was moving about inside.

Rosemary ran into the building and in two minutes flat she was out again, carrying a bulbous object in a plastic sack. She looked green. She tossed the bundle into the back seat. "Get me out of here before I throw up! The odor was incredible!"

"No one said a turkey farm is supposed to smell like a rose garden," Qwilleran said.

"You don't need to tell me about barnyards," she said indignantly. "I grew up on a farm. This was something different."

She was unusually quiet until they reached the parking lot of the cabin. "I want to change clothes before they come," she said. "I feel like wearing something red."

Qwilleran handed her the key. "You go in and start changing. I'll bring the bird. I hope it'll fit in the refrigerator."

She hurried toward the cabin and stepped onto the porch. A moment later she screamed.

"Rosemary! What is it?" Qwilleran shouted, running after her.

"Look!" she cried, staring toward the locked door.

Dangling there was a small animal, hanging by the neck, the rope looped over one of the porch beams.

"Oh my God!" Qwilleran groaned. He felt sick. Then he said in astonishment: "It's a wild rabbit!"

"At first I thought it was Yum Yum."

"So did I."

It was one of the little brown rabbits that gnawed pine cones near the toolshed. It had been shot and then trussed up in a hangman's noose.

Qwilleran said: "You go down to the beach and calm down, Rosemary. I'll take care of this." He wondered: Is this a threat? Or a warning? Or just a prank? Someone had come out of the woods on the crest of the dune—the thicket that the cats were always watching. Anyone approaching the cabin by stealth would come from that direction.

He left the sad bit of fur hanging there and went to the other side of the cabin to let himself in. Koko and Yum Yum came running in a high state of nervous excitement, dashing about without direction or purpose, Koko growling and Yum Yum shrieking. They had seen the prowler from their favorite window. They had heard the shot. They had smelled the presence of the dead animal.

"If only you could talk," Qwilleran said to Koko.

A vehicle was chugging over the roller-coaster terrain of the driveway, and he went out to meet the visitors. His face was so solemn that Nick's happy smile faded instantly.

"Is anything wrong, Mr. Qwilleran?"

"Let me show you something unpleasant."

"Oh, no! That's a dirty trick!" Nick exclaimed. "Lori, come and look at this!"

She gasped. "A poor little cottontail! For a moment I thought it was one of your cats, Mr. Qwilleran."

Nick advised calling the sheriff. "Where's your phone? I'll call him myself. Don't touch the evidence."

While Nick was phoning, Lori was on her hands and knees, crooning to the disturbed Siamese. Gradually they responded to her soothing voice and even played games with her golden hair, which she was wearing in two long braids tied with blue ribbons. Rosemary served raw vegetables and a yogurt dip, and Qwilleran took orders for drinks. Lori thought she would like a Scotch.

"Watch it, kid," her husband warned her, with one hand covering the mouthpiece of the phone. "You know what the doctor told you."

"I'm trying to get pregnant," she explained to Rosemary, "but so far we haven't had anything but kittens."

Nick replaced the phone in the kitchen cupboard. "Okay. The sheriff's coming. And I'll have a bourbon, Mr. Qwilleran."

"Call me Qwill."

They sat on the porch and enjoyed the tranquilizing effect of the placid blue lake. Koko, who was not inclined to be a lap cat, jumped onto Lori's lap and went to sleep.

"I'm not sure I want to stay around Mooseville," Qwilleran suddenly announced. "If I leave the cabin, and the cats are sitting on the windowsill, what's to prevent that maniac from taking a shot through the glass? This incident might be a warning. He might come again."

"Or she," said Lori quietly.

Three questioning faces were turned in her direction, and Qwilleran asked: "Do you have a reason for switching genders?"

"I'm only trying to be broadminded."

"I suppose you know everyone at the Top o' the Dunes Club," he said to her.

"My wife knows everyone in the whole postal district," Nick said proudly, "including how many stamps they buy and who gets stuff in plain brown wrappers."

Qwilleran said: "I know the Hanstables and the Dunfields. Who are the others?"

Lori counted on her fingers. "There are three retired couples. And an attorney from Down Below. And a dentist from Pickax. Don't go to him; he's a butcher. Then there are two cottages for sale; they're empty. Another is in probate, and its being rented to two *very good-looking men.*" She threw a sly glance at her husband. "I think they're professors from somewhere, doing research on shipwrecks. The school superintendent from Pickax lives in the shingled house, and an antiques dealer lives in the one that looks like a boat."

"That fraud!" Nick interjected. "And how about the people who own the FOO?"

"Their place is up for sale. They lost it. The bank owns it now. . . . By the way," she said to Qwilleran, "the homeowners on the dune are worried about the future of this property. Miss Klingenschoen said she might leave it to the county for a park. That would be good for business in Mooseville, but it would hurt property values on the dune. Do you know what your aunt intends to do?"

"She's not my aunt," Qwilleran said, "and I don't know anything about her will, but if the subject ever comes up, I'll know what the local sentiments are." He was pouring the third round of drinks. "It doesn't look as if the sheriff's coming. He probably thinks I'm a nut. I called him about an owl the other night, and last week I reported a dead body in the lake, which everybody seemed to think was a rubber tire."

Nick turned to him abruptly. "Where did you see this body?"

"I was trolling and brought it up on my fishhook." Qwilleran

related the story of the *Minnie K* with relish, appreciating the
rapt attention of his listeners.

Nick asked: "What was the date? Do you remember?"

"Last Thursday."

"How about the voices on the other boat? Could you hear
them distinctly?"

"Not every word, but well enough to know what was going on.
The engine had conked out, and they were arguing about how
to fix it, I think. One guy had a high-pitched unmusical voice.
The other guy's name was Jack, and he had what I would call a
British working-class accent."

Nick glanced at Lori. She nodded. Then he said: "Englishmen
are always called Jack up here. It's a custom that started way
back in mining days. Last week one of the inmates went over the
wall. He was a fellow with a Cockney accent."

Qwilleran looked at him in amazement mixed with triumph.
"He was trying to escape to Canada! Someone was ferrying him
across—in the fog!"

"They all try it," Nick said. "It's suicide, but they try it. . . .
This is off-the-record, Qwill. Everybody knows about the ferry
racket, but we don't want it getting in the papers. You know the
media. They blow everything up."

"Do many inmates escape?"

"The usual percentage. They never head south. A poor bastard gives a local skipper good money to ferry him to Canada,
and when they're a few miles out . . . *splash!* Just like you said.
The water's so cold that a body goes down once and never comes
up."

"Incredible!" Qwilleran said. "That's assembly-line murder.
Do you think there are many guys working in the racket?"

"Everything points to one skipper, who happens to have a
good contact inside. But so far they've never been able to appre-
hend him."

"Or her," Lori said softly.

"I see," Qwilleran said, smoothing his moustache. "No bodies
—no evidence—no trace."

"Frankly," Lori said, "I don't think the authorities are trying
very hard to catch anybody."

Nick snapped at her: "Lori, don't shoot off."

"How about the drug problem inside?" Qwilleran asked.

"No more than what they expect. It's impossible to stop the smuggling entirely."

His wife piped up again. "They don't want to stop it. Pot and pills make the inmates easier to control. It's the liquor that causes trouble."

A car door slammed. "That's one of the sheriff's men," Nick said, jumping to his feet. Qwilleran followed.

Lori said to Rosemary: "Don't you just love the hats the deputies wear—with the two little tassels in front? I'd love to have one."

THIRTEEN

WHEN THE TELEPHONE rang, Koko and Yum Yum were sitting on the polar bear rug, washing up after their morning can of crabmeat. Rosemary was in the kitchen, preparing the turkey for the oven. Qwilleran was having his third cup of coffee on the porch when the phone bleated its muffled summons from the kitchen cupboard.

He was trying to organize his wits. The dead rabbit was one more mismatched piece of the Mooseville Puzzle. Nick's revelation about escaped convicts reassured him, however, that he could still tell a human body from an automobile tire. Now it was clear that the ferry racket—and not wreck-looting—was the focus of Buck's do-it-yourself investigation; if one could identify the cold-blooded skipper, it would undoubtedly solve the mystery of Buck's murder. He (or she, as Lori would say) was someone who was used to killing.

Qwilleran had no way of knowing what clues the police had found in the sawdust or what progress they were making in the investigation. At the *Daily Fluxion* he could count on the police reporter to tip him off, but in Mooseville he was an outsider who registered alarm over a marauding owl or a dead rabbit or a body snagged by a fishhook. One thing was certain: The voice in the fog matched the voice on the cassette. If he could find that voice in Mooseville, he would have useful information for the investigators. Yet, the *message* on the cassette seemed to have nothing to do with the premeditated drownings.

Rosemary appeared on the porch. "Telephone for you, Qwill. It's Miss Goodwinter."

He thought at once of perfume and dimples, but the pleasurable tremor subsided when he heard the attorney's grave voice.

"Yes, Miss Goodwinter. . . . No, I haven't had the radio turned on. . . . No! How bad? . . . Terrible! I can't believe it! . . . What is being done? . . . Is there anything I can do? . . . Yes, I certainly will. Right away. Where shall we meet? . . . In about an hour."

"What's happened?" Rosemary demanded.

"Bad news about Aunt Fanny. Sometime last night she fell down a flight of stairs."

"Oh, Qwill! How terrible! Is she . . . She can't have survived."

He shook his head. "Tom found her at the bottom of the stairs this morning. Poor Aunt Fanny! She was so spirited—had such a youthful outlook. She enjoyed life so much. She never complained about being old."

"And she was so generous. Imagine giving me a Staffordshire pitcher! I'm sure it's valuable."

"Penelope wants me to meet her at the house as soon as possible. There are things to discuss. You don't have to go with me, but I'd appreciate it if you would."

"Of course I'll go with you. I'll put the turkey back in the fridge."

Before leaving for Pickax, Qwilleran latched all the windows and closed the interior shutters so that the cats could not be seen by a prowler. He locked front and back doors to keep them from the screened porches. "I'm sorry to do this to you guys," he said, "but it's the only safe way."

To Rosemary he said: "Who would think such security measures would be necessary in a place like this? I'm going to move back to the city next week. Now that Aunt Fanny's gone, the cabin might not be available to me anyway. That's probably what the attorney wants to discuss."

"It was too good to be true, wasn't it?"

"It would have been ideal—without the complications. But the simple country life is not all that simple. They'll razz me when I show up at the Press Club next week. I'll never live it down."

When they arrived at the stone house in Pickax, Tom was working in the yard, but his head was bowed and he didn't wave his usual eager greeting.

Penelope answered the doorbell, and Qwilleran introduced his houseguest. "This is Rosemary Whiting. We were both stunned by the news."

Rosemary said: "We lunched with her yesterday, and she was so *chipper!*"

"One would never guess she would be ninety next month," the attorney said.

"Is this where it happened?" Qwilleran pointed to the staircase.

Penelope nodded. "It was a terrible tumble, and she was such a fragile little person. She had been having fainting spells, and Alex and I urged her to move into a smaller place, all on one floor, but we couldn't convince her." She shrugged in defeat. "Would you like a cup of tea? I found some teabags in the kitchen."

Rosemary said: "Let me fix the tea while you two talk."

"Very good of you, Miss Whiting. We'll be in the conservatory."

They went into the room with the French doors and the rubber plants and Aunt Fanny's enormous wicker rocking chair. Qwilleran said: "Fanny called this the sun parlor."

Penelope smiled. "When she moved back here after years on the East Coast, she took great pains to conceal her sophistication. She tried to talk like a little old granny, although we knew she was nothing of the sort. . . . I phoned Alex in Washington this morning, and he told me to contact you, as next of kin. He can't possibly return until Saturday."

"Fanny and I were not related. She was a close friend of my mother's, that's all."

"But she referred to you as her nephew, and she had great affection and admiration for you, Mr. Qwilleran. She has no other relatives, you know." The attorney opened her briefcase. "Our office handled all of Fanny's affairs—even her mail, to protect her from hate mail and begging letters. She deposited a sealed envelope in our file, detailing her last wishes. Here it is.

No funeral, no visitation, no public display, just cremation. The *Picayune* is running a full-page obituary tomorrow, and we plan a memorial service on Saturday."

"Did she have a church affiliation?"

"No, but she made annual contributions to all five churches, and the service will probably be held at the largest. It will be very well attended, I'm sure—people coming from all over Moose County."

During the conversation the telephone rang frequently. "I'm not answering," Penelope said. "They're just curiosity-seekers. Legitimate inquiries will go to the office."

Qwilleran asked: "What about the open-door policy that seems to prevail in these parts? Won't people walk into the house?"

"Tom has instructions to turn them away."

Then Rosemary served the tea, and conversation drifted into polite reminiscences. Penelope pointed out Fanny's favorite rocker. Qwilleran commented on her flair for exotic clothes.

Finally he said: "Well, everything seems to be under control here. Are you sure there's nothing we can do to help?"

"There is one little matter that Alex said I should discuss with you." She paused dramatically. "We don't have Fanny's will."

"What! With all that money and all that real estate—she died intestate? I can't believe it!"

"We are positive that a holographic will exists. She insisted in writing it herself to protect her privacy."

"Is that a legal document?"

"In this state, yes . . . if it's written in her own hand and signed and dated. Witnesses are not required. That was the way she wanted it, and one didn't argue with Fanny! Naturally we advised her on the terminology to avoid ambiguity and loopholes. It's location should have been noted in her letter of instructions, but unfortunately . . ."

"And now what?"

Penelope looked hopefully at Qwilleran. "All we have to do is find it."

"Find it!" he said. "Is that what you want me to do?"

"Would you object strenuously?"

Qwilleran looked at Rosemary, and she nodded enthusiastically. She said: "Fanny gave me a tour of the house yesterday, and I don't think it would be difficult."

"Call me at the office if you have any problems," Penelope said, "and don't answer the phone; it will only prove a nuisance."

Then she left them alone, and Qwilleran confronted Rosemary. "All right! If you think it's so easy, where do we begin?"

"There's a big desk in the library and a small one in Fanny's sitting room upstairs. Also an antique trunk in her bedroom."

"You're amazing! You notice everything, Rosemary. But has it occurred to you that they might be locked?"

She ran to the kitchen and returned with a handful of small keys. "These were in the Chinese teapot I used for the tea. Why don't you start in the library? I'd like to tackle the trunk."

That was a mistake, considering Qwilleran's obsession with the printed word. He was awed by the rows of leather-bound volumes from floor to ceiling. He guessed that Grandfather Klingenschoen tucked away a few pornographic classics on the top shelf. He guessed the library housed a fortune in first editions. On one shelf he found a collection of racy novels from the Twenties, with Aunt Fanny's personal bookplate, and he was absorbed in *Five Frivolous Femmes* by Gladys Gaudi when Rosemary rushed into the room.

"Qwill, I've made a terrific discovery!"

"The will?"

"Not the will. Not yet. But the trunk is filled with Fanny's scrapbooks as far back as her college days. Do you realize that dear Aunt Fanny was once an exotic dancer in New Jersey?"

"A stripper? In burlesque houses?"

Rosemary looked gleeful. "She saved all the ads and some 'art photographs' and a few red hot fan letters. No wonder she wanted you to write a book! Come on upstairs. The scrapbooks are all dated. I've just started."

They spent several hours exploring the trunk, and Qwilleran said: "I feel like a voyeur. When she told me she was in clubwork, I visualized garden clubs and hospital auxiliaries and afternoon study clubs."

Actually her career had been pursued in Atlantic City nightclubs, first as an entertainer, then as a manager, and finally as an owner, with her greatest activity during the years of Prohibition.

There were excerpts from gossip columns, pictures of *Francesca's Club*, and photos of Francesca herself posing with politicians, movie stars, baseball heroes, and gangsters. There was no mention of a marriage, but there was evidence of a son. His portraits from babyhood to manhood appeared in one scrapbook until—according to newspaper clippings—he was killed in a mysterious accident on the New York waterfront.

But there was no will.

Qwilleran telephoned Penelope to say they would continue the search the next day. He made the chore sound tedious and depressing. In fact, the excitement of Fanny's past life erased the sadness of the occasion, and both he and Rosemary were strangely elated.

She said: "Let's do something reckless. Let's eat at the Dismal Diner on the way home."

The boxcar stood on a desolate stretch of the highway with not another building in sight—only the rotting timbers of the Dimsdale shaft house. There were no vehicles in the pasture that served as a parking lot, but a sign in the door said *OPEN,* contradicting another sign in one window that said *CLOSED.*

The side of the boxcar was punctuated with windows of various sorts, depending on the size and shape available at some local dump. The interior was papered with yellowing posters and faded menus dating back to the days of nickel coffee and ten-cent sandwiches. Qwilleran raised his sensitive nose and sniffed. "Boiled cabbage, fried onions, and marijuana," he reported. "I don't see a maître d'. Where would you like to sit, Rosemary?"

Along the back wall stretched a worn counter with a row of stools, several of them stumps without seats. Tables and chairs were Depression-era, probably from miners' kitchens. There was only one sign of life, and that was uncertain. A tall, cadaverous man, who may not have eaten for a week, came forward like a sleepwalker from the dingy shadows at the end of the diner.

"Nice little place you've got here," Qwilleran said brightly. "Do you have a specialty?"

"Goulash," the man said in a tinny voice.

"We were hoping you'd have veal cordon bleu. Do you have any artichokes? . . . No? . . . No artichokes, Rosemary. Do you want to go somewhere else?"

"I'd like to try the goulash," she said. "Do you suppose it's real Hungarian goulash?"

"The lady would like to know if it's real Hungarian goulash," Qwilleran repeated to the waiter.

"I dunno."

"I think we'll both have the goulash. It sounds superb. And do you have any Bibb lettuce?"

"Cole slaw is all."

"Excellent! I'm sure it's delicious."

Rosemary was eyeing Qwilleran with that dubious, disapproving look she reserved for his playful moments. When the waiter, who was also the cook, shambled out of his shadowy hole with generous portions of something slopped on chipped plates, she transferred the same expression to a study of the food. She whispered to Qwilleran: "I thought goulash was beef cubes cooked with onions in red wine, with sweet paprika. This is macaroni and canned tomatoes and hamburger."

"This is Mooseville," he explained. "Try it. It tastes all right if you don't think about it too much."

When the cook brought the dented tin coffeepot, Qwilleran asked genially: "Do you own this delightful little place?"

"Me and my buddy."

"Would you consider selling? My friend here would like to open a tearoom and boutique." He spoke without daring to look at Rosemary.

"I dunno. An old lady in Pickax wants to buy it. She'll pay good money."

"Miss Klingenschoen, no doubt."

"She likes it a lot. She comes in here with that quiet young fellah."

When Qwilleran and Rosemary continued their drive north, she said: "There's an example for you. Fanny made irresponsible promises to the poor man, and you're just as bad—with your jokes about tearooms and artichokes."

"I wanted to check his voice against the cassette," Qwilleran said. "It doesn't fit the pattern I'm looking for. When you stop to think about it, he doesn't fit the role of master criminal either . . . although he could be arrested for that goulash. My chief suspect now is the guy who owns the FOO."

When they turned into the private drive to the cabin, Rosemary said: "Look! There's a Baltimore oriole." She inhaled deeply. "I love this lake air. And I love the way the driveway winds between the trees and then suddenly bursts into sight of the lake."

Qwilleran stopped the car with a jolt in the center of the clearing. "The cats are on the porch! How did they get out? I locked them in the cabin!"

Two dark brown masks with blue eyes were peering through the screens and howling in two-part harmony.

Qwilleran jumped out of the car and shouted over his shoulder: "The cabin door's wide open!" He rushed indoors, followed by a hesitant Rosemary. "Someone's been in here! There's a bar stool knocked over . . . and blood on the white rug! Koko, what happened? Who was in here?"

Koko rolled over on his haunches and licked his paws, spreading his toes and extending his claws.

From the guest room Rosemary called: "This window's open! There's glass on the floor, and the shutter's hanging from one hinge. The screen's been cut!"

It was the window overlooking the septic tank and the wooded crest of the dune.

"Someone broke in to get the cassette," Qwilleran said. "See? He set up a bar stool to reach the moose head. He fell off—or jumped off in panic—and gave the stool a back-kick. I'll bet Koko leaped on the guy's head from one of the beams. His eighteen claws can stab like eighteen stilettoes, and Koko isn't fussy about where he grabs. There's a lot of blood; he could have sunk his fangs into an ear."

"Oh, dear!" Rosemary said with a shudder.

"Then the guy ran out the door—maybe with the cat riding on his head and screeching. Koko's been licking his claws ever since we got home."

"Did the man get the cassette?"

"It wasn't up there. I have it hidden. Don't touch anything. I'm going to call the sheriff—again."

"If my car had been parked in the lot, this wouldn't have happened, Qwill. He'd think someone was home."

"We'll pick up your car tomorrow."

"I'll have to drive home on Sunday. I wish you were coming with me, Qwill. There's a dangerous man around here, and he knows you've found his cassette. What are you going to tell the sheriff?"

"I'm going to ask him if he likes music, and I'll play *Little White Lies.*"

Later that evening Rosemary and Qwilleran sat on the porch to watch the setting sun turn the lake from turquoise to purple. "Did you ever see such a sky?" Rosemary asked. "It shades from apricot to mauve to aquamarine, and the clouds are deep violet."

Koko was pacing restlessly from the porch to the kitchen to the guest room and back to the porch.

"He's disturbed," Qwilleran explained, "by his instinctive savagery in attacking the burglar. Koko is a civilized cat, and yet he's haunted by an ancestral memory of days gone by and places far away, where his breed lurked on the walls of palaces and temples and sprang down on intruders to tear them to ribbons."

"Oh, Qwill," Rosemary laughed. "He smells the turkey in the oven, that's all."

FOURTEEN

Rosemary picked up her car at the Mooseville garage, and Qwilleran picked up his mail at the post office.

"I heard the bad news on the radio," Lori said. "What a terrible way to go!"

"And yet it was in character," Qwilleran said. "You've got to admit it was dramatic—the kind of media event that Fanny would like."

"Nick and I want to go to the memorial service tomorrow."

He said: "We're on our way to Pickax now, and we're taking the cats. There was a break-in at the cabin yesterday, and we think Koko attacked the burglar and drove him away."

"Really?" Lori's blue eyes were wide with astonishment.

"There was blood on the rug, and Koko was licking his claws with unusual relish. If one of your postal patrons turns up with a bloody face, tip me off. Anyway, I'm not leaving Koko and Yum Yum at the cabin alone until this thing is cleared up. They're out in the car right now, disturbing the peace on Main Street."

Rosemary drove her car back to the cabin and parked it in the clearing. Then the four of them headed for Pickax at a conservative speed that would not alarm Yum Yum.

Rosemary mentioned that the garage mechanic was going to the memorial service.

"Fanny had a real fan club in Moose County," Qwilleran said. "For a name that used to be despised, *Klingenshoen* has made a spectacular comeback."

He swerved to avoid hitting a dead skunk, and the Siamese raised noses to sniff-alert, with ears back and whiskers forward.

Rosemary said: "I've been thinking about that odor at the turkey farm. It wasn't a barnyard smell; it was a bad case of human B.O. I think the farmer has a drastic diet deficiency. I wish I could suggest it to his wife without offending her."

Next the car hit a pothole, and Yum Yum launched a tirade of Siamese profanity that continued all the way to Pickax.

Qwilleran parked in the driveway of the imposing stone house with its three floors of grandeur. "Here we are, back at Mandalay," he quipped.

"Oh, is that the name of the place?" Rosemary asked innocently.

The two animals were shut up in the kitchen with their blue cushion, their commode, and a bowl of water, while Qwilleran and Rosemary continued their search for the will.

The library desk was a massive English antique, its drawers containing tax records, birth and death documents, insurance policies, real estate papers, investment information, paid bills, house inventories, and hundred-year-old promissory notes . . . but no will. The desk in Aunt Fanny's sitting room was a graceful French escritoire devoted to correspondence: love letters from the Twenties; silly chit-chat about "beaux" written by Qwilleran's mother when she and Fanny were in college; brief notes from Fanny's son at boarding school; and recent letters typed on *Daily Fluxion* letterheads. But still no will.

"Here's something interesting, Qwill," Rosemary said. "From someone in Atlantic City. It's about Tom, asking Fanny to hire him as a man-of-all-work." She scanned the lines hastily. "Why, Qwill! He's an ex-convict! It says in this letter he's about to be paroled . . . but he needs a place to go . . . and the promise of a job. He's not real sharp, it says . . . but he's a hard worker . . . obeys orders and never makes any trouble. . . . Listen to this, Qwill. He took a rap and got ten years . . . but he's being released for good behavior. . . . Oh, Qwill! What kind of people did Fanny know in New Jersey?"

"I can guess," Qwilleran said. "Let's go to lunch."

He checked the Siamese; they were perched on their blue cushion on top of the refrigerator and were as contented as could be expected under the circumstances. He found the handyman working in the yard.

"Hello, Tom," he said sadly. "This is an awful thing that has happened."

Tom had lost his bland, boyish expression and looked twenty years older. He nodded and stared at the grass.

"Are you going to the memorial service tomorrow?"

"I never went to one. I don't know what to do."

"You just go in and sit down and listen to the music and the speeches. It's a way of saying goodbye to Miss Klingenschoen. She'd like to know that you were there."

Tom leaned on his rake and bowed his head. His eyes brimmed.

Qwilleran said: "She was good to you, Tom, but you were also a great help to her. Remember that. You made the last years of her life easier and happier."

The handyman smeared his wet face with his sleeve. His grief was so poignant that Qwilleran felt—for the first time since hearing the news—a constriction in his throat. He coughed and started talking about the broken window at the cabin. "I've got a piece of cardboard in the window now, but if it rains hard and the wind blows from the east . . ."

"I'll fix it," Tom said quietly.

The luncheonette that served the second worst coffee in Moose County was crowded at the lunch hour and buzzing with chatter about the Klingenschoen tragedy. No church was large enough for the expected crowd, so the memorial service would be held in the high school gymnasium. Pastors of all five churches would give eulogies. The Senior Citizens' Glee Club would sing. A county commissioner would play taps on a World War I bugle. Fanny Klingenschoen's favorite wicker rocker would be on the platform, and kindergarten children would file past, each dropping a single rosebud in the empty chair.

There was, of course, much speculation about the will. The great stone house had been promised to the Historical Society for a museum, and the carriage house had been promised to the Art Society for a gallery and studio. It was rumored that a lump sum would go to the Board of Education for an Olympic-size swimming pool. Altogether there was an atmosphere of mingled sorrow and excitement and gratitude among the customers at the luncheonette, especially the younger ones, several of whom were named Francesca.

Qwilleran said to Rosemary: "I hope she remembered Tom in her will. I hope she left him the blue truck. He takes care of it like a baby."

"What if we don't find the will?"

"The government and the lawyers will get everything."

After lunch the search continued in the drawing room, where a Chinese lacquer desk was stuffed with photographs: tintypes, snapshots, studio portraits, and glossy prints from newspapers. Qwilleran wanted to guess which whiskered chap was Grandfather Klingenschoen, and which bright-eyed girl with ringlets was Minnie K, but Rosemary dragged him away.

Upstairs there were marble-topped dressers, tall chests, and wardrobes. Rosemary organized the search, taking Fanny's suite herself and directing Qwilleran to the other rooms. Then they compared notes, sitting on the top stair of the long flight that had been the scene of the accident.

Rosemary said: "All I found was clothing. Real silk stockings and silk lingerie, imagine! White linen handkerchiefs by the gross . . . lots of white kid gloves turning yellow . . . everything smelling of lavender. What did you find?"

Qwilleran's list was equally disappointing. "Sheets by the tons. Blankets an inch thick, smelling of cedar. Enough white towels for a Turkish bath. And tablecloths big enough to cover a squash court."

"Where do we go from here?"

"There might be a safe," he said. "It could be built into a piece of furniture or set in a paneled wall or hidden behind a picture. If Fanny was so concerned about concealing the nature of her will, she'd keep it in a safe."

"It could take weeks to find it. You'd have to pull the whole house apart."

A distant howl echoed through the quiet rooms. "That's Koko," Qwilleran said. "He objects to being shut up for so long. You know, Rosemary, that little devil has a sixth sense about things like this. We could let him walk through the house and see what turns him on."

As soon as Koko was released from the kitchen, he stalked through the butler's pantry into the dining room with the dignity of a visiting monarch, head held regally, ears worn like a coronet, tail pointing aloft. He sniffed ardently at the carved rabbits and pheasants on the doors of the mammoth sideboard, but it stored only soup tureens and silver serving pieces. In the foyer he was entranced by a spot on the rug at the foot of the stairs, until Qwilleran scolded him for bad taste. In the drawing room he examined the keys of the old square piano and rubbed against the bulbous legs. There was nothing to interest him in the library or conservatory, but he found the basement stairs and led the way to the English pub.

It was a dark paneled room with a stone floor and several tavern tables and crude wooden chairs. The bar was ponderous, and there was a backbar elaborately carved and set with leaded glass. Koko nosed about behind the bar, then struck a rigid pose. In slow motion he approached a cabinet under the bar. He waited, staring at the bottom of the cabinet door. Qwilleran put his finger to his lips. Neither he nor Rosemary dared to move or even breathe. Then Koko sprang. There were tiny squeaks of terror, and Koko pranced back and forth in frustration.

"A mouse," Qwilleran mouthed in Rosemary's direction. He tiptoed behind the bar and opened the cabinet door. A tiny gray thing flew out, and Koko took off in pursuit.

"Let him go," Qwilleran said. "This is it!" Inside the cabinet was an old black-and-gold safe with a combination lock. "Only one problem. How do we open it?"

"Call Nick."

"Nick and Lori are coming into town for the service tomorrow. The safe can wait until then. Let's go home and eat that turkey."

They bought a copy of the *Pickax Picayune* and found that Fanny's obituary filled the front page. Even the classified ads that usually occupied column one of page one were omitted. The text of the obituary was set in large type in a black-bordered box in the center of the page, surrounded by white space and then another wide black border. In fine print at the bottom on the page it was mentioned that the obituary was suitable for framing.

Rosemary read it aloud on the way back to Mooseville, and

Qwilleran called it a masterpiece of evasion and flowery excess. "They wrote obituaries like that in the nineteenth century. Wait till I see the editor! It's not easy to write a full-page story without saying anything."

"But there are no pictures."

"The *Picayune* has never acknowledged the invention of the camera. Read it to me again, Rosemary. I can't believe it."

The headline was simple: *Great Lady Called Home*.

Rosemary read:

Elevated to the rewards of a well-spent life, without enduring the pangs of decay or the sorrow of parting or pain of sickness, and happy in her consciousness of having completed to the best of her ability her work for mankind, Fanny Klingenschoen at the advanced age of eighty-nine, slipped suddenly into the sleep from which there is no waking, during the midnight hours of Wednesday at her palatial residence in downtown Pickax. In the few brief moments when The Reaper called her home, she passed from the scene of her joy and happiness, closed her eyes to the world, and smiled as the flickering candle of life went out, casting a gloom over the county such as rarely, if ever, has been felt on a similar occasion.

No pen can describe the irreparable loss to the community when the cold slender fingers of death gripped the heart strings that inspired so many of her fellow creatures—inspired them for so many years—inspired them with an amplitude of leadership, poise, refined taste, cultivated mind, forthrightness, strength of character and generous nature.

Born to Septimus and Ada Klingenschoen almost nine decades ago, she was the granddaughter of Gustave and Minnie Klingenschoen, who braved the trackless wilderness to bring social betterment to the rugged lives of the early pioneers.

Although her spirit has taken flight, her forceful presence will be felt Saturday morning at eleven o'clock when a large number of county residents representing every station of life will assemble at Pickax High School

to do honor to a woman of sterling qualities and unas-
suming dignity. Business in Pickax will be suspended
for two hours.

Rosemary said: "I don't know what you object to, Qwill. I
think it's beautifully written—very sincere—and rather touch-
ing."

"I think it's nonsense," Qwilleran said. "It would make Fanny
throw up."

"YOW!" said Koko from the back seat.

"See? He agrees with me, Rosemary."

She sniffed. "How do you know if that's a yes or a no?"

They arrived at the cabin in time to hear the telephone struggling for attention inside a kitchen cupboard.

"Hello, there," said a voice that Qwilleran despised. "Have
you got my girl up there? This is your old pal, Max Sorrel."

Qwilleran bristled. "I have several girls here. Which one is
yours?"

After Rosemary had talked with Max she was moody and
aloof. Finally she said: "I've got to start driving home tomorrow
right after the memorial service."

"YOW!" Koko said with more energy than usual, and it
sounded so much like a cheer that both Qwilleran and Rosemary
looked at him in dismay. The cat was sitting on the mantel, peril-
ously close to the Staffordshire pitcher. One flick of the tail
would . . .

"Let's move your pitcher to a safe place," Qwilleran suggested. Then: "Did Max say something to upset you, Rosemary?"

"He's decided to buy me out and go through with the restaurant deal, and I'm nervous."

"You don't like him much, do you?"

"Not as much as he thinks I do. That's what makes me nervous. I'd like to go for a walk on the beach and do some thinking."

With some concern Qwilleran watched her go. Reluctantly he
admitted he was not entirely sorry to see her move to Toronto.
He had been a bachelor for too long. At his age, he could not
adjust to a supervised diet and Staffordshire knickknacks. He
had given up his pipe at Rosemary's urging, and he often longed

for some Groat and Boddle, despite his attempts to rationalize. Although she was attractive—and companionable when he was tired or lonely—he had other moods when he found younger women more stimulating. In their company he felt more alive and *wittier*. Rosemary was not tuned in to his sense of humor, and she was certainly not tuned in to Koko. She treated him like an ordinary cat.

The cooling of the relationship was only one development in a vacation that had hardly been a success. It had been two weeks of discomfort, mystification, and frustration—not to mention guilt; he had not written a word of his projected novel. He had not enjoyed evenings of music or walked for miles on the beach or lolled on the sand with a good spy story or paid enough attention to the sunsets. And now it was coming to an end. Even if the executors of the estate did not evict him, he was going to leave. Someone had been desperate enough to break into the cabin. Someone had been barbarous enough to club a man to death. A rabbit-hunter could come out of the woods with a rifle at any moment.

The cabin was quiet, and Qwilleran heard the scurrying of little feet. Koko was playing with his catnip toy, dredged up from some remote corner. He batted it and sent it skidding across the floor, pounced on it, clutched it in his front paws and kicked it with his powerful hind legs, then tossed it into the air and scampered after it.

Qwilleran watched the game. "Koko bats to rightfield . . . he's under it . . . he's got it . . . throws wild to second . . . makes a flying catch . . . he's down, but he's got the ball . . . here comes a fast hook over the plate. . . . foul to left."

The catnip ball had disappeared beneath the sofa. Koko looked questioningly at the precise spot where it had skidded under the pleated skirt of the slipcover. The sofa was built low; only Yum Yum was small enough to struggle under it.

"Game's over," Qwilleran said. "You've lost by default."

Koko flattened himself on the floor and extended one long brown leg to grope under the sofa. He twisted, squirmed, stretched. It was useless. He jumped to the back of the sofa and scolded.

"Tell your sidekick to fish it out for you," the man said. "I'm tired."

Koko glared at him, his blue eyes becoming large black orbs. He glared and said nothing.

Only a few times had Qwilleran seen that look, and it had always meant serious business. He hoisted himself off the comfortable sofa and went to the porch for the crude pitchfork hanging there. With the handle he made a swipe under the piece of furniture and brought forth some dustballs and one of his navy blue socks. He made another swipe and out rolled Rosemary's coral lipstick and a gold ballpoint pen.

Both cats were now standing by, enjoying the performance.

"Yum Yum, you little thief!" Qwilleran said. "What else have you stolen?"

Once more he raked under the sofa with the handle of the pitchfork. The catnip ball appeared first—and then his gold watch—and then some folded bills in a gold money clip. "Whose money is this?" he said as he counted the bills. Thirty-five dollars were tucked into what looked like a jumbo paper clip in shiny gold.

At that moment Rosemary climbed up the dune from the beach and wandered wearily into the cabin.

"Rosemary, you'll never believe what I found," Qwilleran said. "The gold pen you gave me! I thought Tom had stolen it. And your lipstick! Yum Yum has been stashing things under the sofa. My watch, one of my socks, and some money in a gold money clip."

"I'm so glad you found the pen," she said quietly.

"Are you okay, Rosemary?"

"I'll be all right after a good sleep. I'd like to go to bed early."

"We haven't even had dinner."

"I'm not hungry. Will you excuse me? I'll have a long drive tomorrow."

Qwilleran sat on the porch alone, hardly noticing the foaming surf and the gliding seagulls. The money clip, he reflected, was the kind that Roger used. Had Roger been in the cabin? If so, for what purpose? The place had been locked for several days. No, he refused to believe that his young friend was involved in any devious operation. Certainly it was not his voice on the cassette.

He sat on the porch until dusk, then made himself a turkey

sandwich and a cup of coffee. He chopped a little turkey for the cats also. Yum Yum devoured her share, but—surprisingly— Koko was not in the least interested. There was no way to predict, understand, or explain the moods of a Siamese.

FIFTEEN

THERE WERE FOUR documents in Aunt Fanny's safe. Three were envelopes sealed with red wax and labeled *Last Will and Testament* in her unmistakable handwriting. These Qwilleran turned over to Goodwinter and Goodwinter along with some velvet cases of jewelry to put in the attorneys' safe. The fourth item was a small address book bound in green leather, which he slipped into his pocket.

Nick and Lori had arrived at the stone house an hour before the memorial service, giving Nick time to crack the safe and giving Rosemary time to show Lori the handsome rooms with their antique furnishings. Then, leaving Koko and Yum Yum on top of the refrigerator, all four of them joined the crowd at the Pickax High School.

Everyone was there. Qwilleran saw Roger and Sharon and Mildred, the fraudulent sea captain who sold fake antiques, Old Sam, Dr. Melinda Goodwinter in a sea-green suit to match her eyes, the two boys from the *Minnie K,* a.k.a. the *Seagull,* the museum curator, the Mooseville garage mechanic—everyone. The emaciated cook from the Dismal Diner arrived by motorcycle, riding behind a burly man wearing a large diamond ring and a leather jacket with cut-off sleeves. Tom was there, huddled shyly in the back row. Even the proprietors of the FOO were there with their furtive cook.

The managing editor of the *Pickax Picayune* was standing on the front steps, making note of important arrivals.

"Junior, you've surpassed yourself!" Qwilleran said in greeting. "You hit seventy-eight in a single sentence! That must be a record. What genius writes your obituaries?"

The young editor laughed off the question. "I know it's weird, but they've been written that way since 1859, and that's what our readers like. A flowery obit is a status symbol for the families around here. I told you we do things our own way."

"You weren't serious, I hope, when you said Fanny's obit was suitable for framing."

"Oh, sure. A lot of people up here collect obits as a hobby. One old lady has more than five hundred in a scrapbook. There's an Obituary Club with a monthly newsletter."

Qwilleran shook his head. "Answer another question, Junior. How does the Dimsdale Diner stay in business? The food's a crime, and I never see anyone there."

"Didn't you ever see the coffee crowd? At seven in the morning and then at eleven o'clock the parking lot's full of pickups. That's where I go to gather news."

At that moment the FOO delegation arrived, and Qwilleran grasped the chance to speak to the elusive Merle. He was a mountain of a man—tall, obese, forbidding, with one eye half-shut and the other askew.

"Excuse me, sir," Qwilleran said. "Are you the owner of the FOO restaurant?"

His wife, the beefy woman who presided at the cash register, said: "He don't talk no more. He had a accident at the factory." She made a throat-cutting motion with her hand. "And now he don't talk."

Qwilleran made a fast recovery. "Sorry. I just wanted to tell you, Merle, how much I enjoy your restaurant, especially the pasties. My compliments to the cook. Keep up the good work."

Merle nodded and attempted to smile but only succeeded in looking more sinister.

While the preachers and politicians paid glowing tribute to Fanny Klingenschoen, Qwilleran fingered the little green book in his pocket. It was indexed alphabetically and filled with names, but instead of addresses there were notations of small-town malfeasance: shoplifting, bad checks, infidelity, graft, conflict of interest, errant morals, embezzlement. Nothing was documented, but Fanny seemed to know. Perhaps she too was a regular patron of the coffee hour at the Dismal Diner. It was her hobby. As others collected obituaries, Fanny had collected the skeletons in local closets. How she used her information, one could only guess. Perhaps the little green book was the weapon she used in saving the courthouse and getting new sewers installed. Qwilleran decided he would build a fire in the fireplace before the day was over.

After the service Rosemary said: "I've had a lovely time, Qwill. Sorry I can't stay for lunch, but I have a long drive ahead."

"Did you remember to take the Staffordshire pitcher?"

"I wouldn't forget that for anything!"

"It's been good to have you here, Rosemary."

"Write and tell me how the estate is settled."

"Send me your address in Toronto, and don't get too involved with our friend Max."

There was a note of friendly affection in their farewell, but none of the warmth and intimacy there had been a week ago. Too bad, Qwilleran thought. He collected the Siamese and drove back to the cabin. It was clear that Koko had disliked Rosemary. He had always been a man's cat. The night before, Koko had refused to eat the turkey that Rosemary had so thoughtfully purchased and roasted.

"Okay, Koko," Qwilleran said when they reached the cabin. "She's gone now. We'll try the turkey once more."

A tempting assortment of white meat and dark meat was arranged on the cats' favorite raku plate—a feast that would send any normal Siamese into paroxysms of joy. Yum Yum attacked it ravenously, but Koko viewed the plate with distaste. He arched his back and, stepping stiffly on long slender legs, circled the repast as if it were poison—not once but three times.

Qwilleran stroked his moustache vigorously. In the few years he had known Koko, the Siamese had performed this ritual twice. The first time he pranced around a dead body; his second macabre dance had been the clue to a ghastly crime.

The telephone emitted its stifled ring.

"Hello, Qwill. It's me. I'm calling from Dove Lake."

"Oh-oh. Car trouble?"

"No, everything's fine."

"Forget something?"

"No, but I remembered something. You know that money you found under the sofa. The money clip looked familiar, and now I know why."

"The candle shop carried them. Roger has one, and I tried to buy one myself," Qwilleran said.

"Maybe so, but the one I remember was at the turkey farm. That man with the terrible problem got out his money clip to give me a dollar in change, and it looked like a big gold paper clip."

Qwilleran combed his moustache with his fingertips. Rosemary had bought the turkey on Wednesday. The break-in was Thursday. The money clip could have popped out of a pants pocket when the man jumped or fell from the bar stool and fled from those eighteen claws.

"Did you hear me, Qwill?"

"Yes, Rosemary. I'm putting two and two together. There's something about that turkey you bought—it's turning Koko off. He's getting vibrations. Yum Yum thinks it's great, but Koko still refuses to touch it. I think he's steering me to that turkey farm."

"Be careful, Qwill. Don't take any chances. You know what almost happened to you at Maus Haus when you meddled in a dangerous situation."

"Don't worry, Rosemary. Thanks for the information. Drive carefully, and stop if you get sleepy."

So that was the clue! Turkey! Qwilleran grabbed the money clip with the thirty-five dollars, locked the cats in the cabin, and hurried to his car.

It was only a few miles to the turkey farm. The bronze backs were pitching and heaving as usual. The blue pickup was in the yard. He parked and headed for the door that invited retail and wholesale trade. The wind was from the northwest, so there was very little barnyard odor, but once he stepped inside the building he was staggered by the stench.

There was nothing to account for it. The premises were spotless: the white-painted walls, the scrubbed wooden counter with its stainless steel scales and shiny knives, the clean saw-dust on the floor in the manner of old butcher shops. There was a bell on the counter: *Ring for service.* Qwilleran banged it three times, urgently.

When the tall, hefty man stepped out of a walk-in cooler, Qwilleran tried to control his facial reaction of revulsion. It was the post office experience all over again, but there was more. The man's face and neck were covered with red, raw scratches. There was an adhesive bandage on his throat. One ear was torn. He was wearing the inevitable feed cap, and its visor had apparently protected his eyes when Koko attacked, but the sight was worse than Qwilleran had imagined, and the odor was nauseating.

He stared at the farmer, and the man returned the stare, impassively, defensively. Someone had to say something, and Qwilleran brought himself to make the natural comment: "Looks like you had a bad accident."

"Damn turkeys!" the man said. "They go crazy and kill each other. I should learn to stay outa the way."

That was all that was necessary for Qwilleran's practiced ear. It was the voice on the cassette.

He threw the money and the gold clip on the counter. "Does this belong to you? I found it in my cabin. I also have a cassette that might be yours." He looked the disfigured farmer squarely in the eye.

The man's expression turned hostile; his eyes flashed; his jaw clenched. With a yell he leaped over the counter, grabbing a knife.

Qwilleran bolted for the door but tripped over a doorstop and went down on one knee—his bad knee. He sensed an arm raised above him, a knife poised over his head. It was a frozen pose, a freeze-frame from a horror movie. The knife did not descend.

"You drop that," said a gentle voice. "That's a very bad thing to do."

The knife fell to the sawdust-covered floor with a muffled clatter.

"Now you turn around and hold your hands up."

Tom was standing in the doorway, pointing a gun at the farmer, a small pistol with a gold handle. "Now we should call the sheriff," he said to Qwilleran mildly.

"You idiot!" his prisoner screamed. "If you talk, I'll talk!"

There was no doubt about it; that was the voice: high pitch, metallic timbre, flat inflection.

Two deputies took Hanstable away, and Qwilleran agreed to go to the jail later to sign the papers.

"How did you happen to stop here?" he asked Tom.

"I went to fix your window. The door was locked. I couldn't get in. Then I went to Mooseville to buy a pasty. I like pasties."

"And then what?"

"I was going home. I saw your car here. I came in to get the key."

"Come on back to the cabin and have a beer," Qwilleran said. "I don't mind telling you, I've never been so glad to see anyone in my life! That's a nice little gun you've got there." How a pistol from Fanny's handbag happened to be in Tom's pocket was a matter of interest that Qwilleran did not pursue at the moment.

"It's very pretty. It's gold. I like gold."

"How can I repay you, Tom? You saved my life."

"You're a nice man. I didn't want him to hurt you."

Qwilleran drove back to the cabin, the handyman following in his blue truck, shining like new. They sat on the south porch in the shelter of the building because the northwest wind was blowing furiously, lashing trees and shrubs into a green frenzy.

Qwilleran served a beer and made a toast. "Here's to you, Tom. If you hadn't come along, I might have ended up as a turkey hot dog." The quip, such as it was, appealed to the handyman's simple sense of humor. Qwilleran wanted to put him at ease before asking too many questions. After a while he asked casually: "Do you go to the turkey farm often, Tom?"

"No, it smells bad."

"What did the farmer mean when he said he would talk if you talked?"

A sheepish smile flickered across the bland face. "It was about the whiskey. *He told me* to buy the whiskey."

"What was the whiskey for?"

"The prisoners."

"The inmates at the big prison?"

"I feel sorry for the prisoners. I was in prison once."

Qwilleran said sympathetically: "I can see how you would feel. You don't drink whiskey, do you? I don't either."

"It tastes bad," Tom said.

The newsman had always been a sympathetic interviewer, never pushing his questions too fast, always engaging his subjects in friendly conversation. To slow down the interrogation he got up and killed a spider and knocked down a web, commenting on the size of the spider population and their persistence in decorating the cabin, inside and out, with their handiwork. Then:

"How did you deliver the whiskey to the prisoners?"

"*He* took it in."

"Excuse me, Tom. I hear the phone."

It was Alexander Goodwinter calling. He had just returned from Washington and was at a loss to express his sadness at the death of the gallant little lady. He and Penelope were about to drive to Mooseville and would like to call on him in half an hour to discuss a certain matter.

Qwilleran knew what that certain matter would be. As executors of the estate they would want a thousand a month for the cabin. He returned to the porch. Koko had been conversing with Tom in his absence.

"He has a loud voice," the handyman said. "I stroked him. His fur is nice. It's soft."

Qwilleran made a few remarks about the characteristics of Siamese, mentioned Koko's fondness for turkey, and then sidled into the inquiry again. "I suppose you had to deliver the whiskey to the turkey farm."

"I took it to the cemetery. He told me to leave it in the cemetery. There's a place there."

"I hope he paid you for it."

"He gave me a lot of money. That was nice."

"It's always good to have a little extra money coming in. I'll bet you stashed it away in the bank to buy a boat or something."

"I don't like banks. I hid it somewhere."

"Well, just be sure it's in a safe place. That's the important thing. Are you ready for a beer?"

There was time out for serving and for comments on the velocity of the wind and the possibility of a tornado. The temperature was abnormally high, and the sky had a yellow tone. Then:

"Did you buy the liquor in Mooseville? They don't have a very good selection."

"He told me to buy it in different places. Sometimes he told me to buy whiskey. Sometimes he told me to buy gin."

Qwilleran wished he had a pipeful of tobacco. The business of lighting a pipe had often filled in the pauses and softened the edges of an interview when the subject was shy or reluctant. He said to Tom: "It would be interesting to know how the farmer got the liquor into the prison."

"He took it in his truck. He took it in with the turkeys. He told me to buy pint bottles so they would fit inside the turkeys."

"That's a new way to stuff a turkey," Qwilleran said, getting a hilarious reaction from the handyman. "If you didn't go to the farm, how did you now what kind of liquor to buy?"

"He came here and talked into the machine. I listened to it when I came here to work. That was nice. I liked that." Something occurred to Tom and he giggled. "He left it behind the moose."

"I always thought that moose looked kind of sick, and now I know why."

Tom giggled some more. He was having a good time.

"So you played the cassette when you came here."

"It had some nice music, too."

"Why didn't the farmer just leave you a note?" Qwilleran performed an exaggerated pantomime of writing. *"Dear Tom, bring five pints of Scotch and four pints of gin. Hope you are feeling well. Have a nice day. Love from your friend Stanley."*

The handyman found this nonsense highly entertaining. Then he sobered and answered the question. "I can't read. I wish I could read and write. That would be nice."

Qwilleran had always found it difficult to believe the statistics on illiteracy in the United States, but here was a living statistic, and he was struggling to accept it when the telephone rang again.

"Hello, Qwill," said a voice he had known all his life. "How's everything up there?"

"Fine, Arch. Did you get my letters?"

"I got two. How's the weather?"

"You didn't call to ask about the weather, Arch. What's on your mind?"

"Great news, Qwill! You'll be getting a letter from Percy, but I thought I'd tip you off. That assignment I told you about—investigative reporting—Percy wants you to come back and start right away. If the *Rampage* gets someone first, Percy will have a heart attack. You know how he is."

"Hmmm," Qwilleran said.

"Double your salary and an unlimited expense account. Also a company car for your own use—a new one. How's that for perks?"

"I wonder what the *Rampage* is offering?"

"Don't be funny. You'll get Percy's letter in a couple of days, but I wanted to be the first . . ."

"Thanks, Arch. I appreciate it. You're a good guy. Too bad you're an editor."

"And something else, Qwill. I know you'll need a new apartment, and Fran Unger is giving up hers and getting married. It's close to the office, and the rent is reasonable."

"And the walls are papered with pink roses and galloping giraffes."

"Keep it in mind anyway. Be seeing you soon. Say hello to that spooky cat."

Qwilleran was dizzy with shock and elation, but Tom was starting to leave and he had to thank him once more. He picked up the antique brass inkwell from the top of the bar.

"Here's something I'd like you to have, Tom. It needs polishing, but I know you like brass. It's an inkwell that traveled around the world on sailing ships a hundred years ago."

"That's very pretty. I never had anything like that. I'll polish it every day."

The handyman measured the broken window and drove into Mooseville to buy glass, while Qwilleran sat down to contemplate the offer from the *Fluxion*. Now that he was leaving this beautiful place he was filled with regret. He should have spent more time enjoying the verdure, the moods of the lake, the dew glistening on a spider web. Now he could look forward to the daily irritations of the office: the pink memos from Percy; electric pencil sharpeners always out-of-order; six elevators going up when a person wanted to go down; VDTs that made the job harder instead of easier. Suddenly he realized how much his knee was paining him.

He propped his leg on a chaise. From the back of a nearby

chair, where a hawk had once perched, he was being watched intently by a pair of blue eyes in a brown mask.

"Well, Koko," Qwilleran said, "our vacation didn't turn out the way we expected, did it? But the time hasn't been wasted. We've cracked a one-man crime operation. Too bad we couldn't have stopped him before he got Buck Dunfield. . . . Too bad no one around here will ever know you deserve all the credit. Even if we told them, they wouldn't believe it."

Howling wind and crashing surf drowned out the sound of the Goodwinter car as it pulled into the clearing. Qwilleran hobbled out to greet them—Alexander looking impeccably well-groomed and Penelope looking radiant and a trifle flushed. When they shook hands she added an extra squeeze, and in addition to her perfume there was a hint of mint breath-freshener.

"You're limping," she said.

"I tripped over a toadstool. . . . Come in out of the wind. I think we're going to have a tornado."

Alexander went directly to his previous seat on Yum Yum's sofa. Penelope went to the windows overlooking the turbulent lake and rhapsodized about the view and the cabin's desirable location.

Qwilleran thought: The rent just went up to twelve hundred. Won't they be surprised when I break the news!

"It is regrettable," Alexander was saying, "that I was in Washington when this unfortunate incident occurred. My sister tells me you were of great assistance, making many trips back and forth and spending long hours searching through the Klingenschoen archives. It cannot have been a pleasant task."

"There was a lot of material to sift through," Qwilleran said. "Luckily I had a houseguest from Down Below who was willing to help." He refrained from mentioning Koko's contribution; he doubted whether the Goodwinters were ready for the idea of a psychic cat.

"I regret I could not get a return flight in time to attend the memorial service, but it appears that Penelope organized it efficiently and tastefully, and it was well attended."

His sister had wandered over to the table that presented such a convincing picture of authorial industry, and now she dropped onto the other sofa. "Alex, why don't you get to the point? You're keeping Mr. Qwilleran from his writing."

"Ah, yes. The will. A problem has arisen in connection with the will."

"I don't envision any problem," Penelope retorted. "You're inventing one before it arises."

The senior partner threw a remonstrative glance in her direction, cleared his throat, and opened his briefcase. "As you know, Mr. Qwilleran, Fanny left three wills in the safe, written in her own hand. She had written many wills during the years, changing her mind frequently. Only the last three wills were saved (this on our recommendation). They were dated, of course, and only the most recent is valid. Having the three wills gives us an enlightening overview of the lady's feelings in the last few years."

Qwilleran's gaze dropped from the attorney's face to his shoe; the little brown triangle of a face was appearing under the skirt of the sofa. Koko, on the other hand, was perched on the moose head with the authority of a presiding judge.

"The oldest will, which is invalid, bequeathed Fanny's entire estate to a foundation in Atlantic City, for the purpose of rehabilitating a certain section of the city which apparently had nostalgic significance for her. Although it would be considered by most of us to be—ah—unsavory."

Yum Yum's paw was reaching out from her hiding place with stealth. Penelope had noticed the maneuver, and her face reflected a heroic effort to control mirth.

Goodwinter went on. "The second will, which is also invalid, I am mentioning merely to acquaint you with the change in Fanny's sympathies. This document bequeathed half her estate to the Atlantic City foundation and the other half to the schools, churches, cultural and charitable organizations, health care facilities, and civic causes in Pickax City. Considering the extent of her holdings there was plenty to distribute equitably, and she had promised sizable sums to all of the aforementioned."

Qwilleran checked Yum Yum's progress and glanced at Penelope, who returned his glance and exploded with laughter.

"Penelope!" her brother said in consternation. "Please allow me to conclude. . . . The most recent will leaves the sum of one dollar to each of the beneficiaries heretofore named—a wise precaution in our estimation, inasmuch as . . ."

"Alex, why don't you come to the point of this discussion," said Penelope, waving a hand gaily, "and tell Mr. Qwilleran that he gets the whole damned thing."

"YOW!" came a howl from the vicinity of the moose head.

Goodwinter cast a quick disapproving eye at Penelope and then at Koko. "Excepting only the token bequests I have indicated, Mr. Qwilleran, you are indeed the sole heir to the estate of Fanny Klingenschoen."

Qwilleran was stunned.

"That," the attorney said, "sums up the intent and purpose of the most recent will, dated April first of this year, thus revoking all prior documents. The formal reading of the will is scheduled to take place Wednesday afternoon in our office."

Qwilleran shook his head like a wet dog. He could think of nothing to say. He looked at Penelope for help, but she merely grinned in an idiotic way.

Finally he said: "It's an April Fools' joke."

Goodwinter said: "I assure you it is legitimate. The problem, as I see it, might be that the bequest will be challenged by the numerous organizations expecting generous sums."

"They were verbal promises that Fanny made to everyone in town," Penelope reminded her brother. "Mr. Qwilleran's claim is the only legal one."

"Nevertheless, one might foresee a class action suit on behalf of the Pickax charities and civic institutions, questioning Fanny's testamentary capacity, but I assure you . . ."

"Alex, you neglected to mention the proviso."

"Ah, yes. The assets—bank accounts, investments, real estate, etc.—are held in trust for five years with the entire income going to you, Mr. Qwilleran, provided you consent to make Pickax your residence for that period of time and maintain the Klingenschoen mansion as your address—after which time the trust is dissolved and the estate is transferred to you in toto."

There was silence in the room, and stares all around. A window slammed in the guest room.

Goodwinter looked startled. "Is there someone else in the house?"

"Only Tom," Qwilleran said. "He's fixing a broken window."

"Well?" Penelope asked. "Don't keep us in suspense."

"What happens if I decline the terms?"

"In that case," Goodwinter said, "the will specifies that the entire estate goes to Atlantic City."

"And if it goes to Atlantic City," Penelope added, "there will be rioting in the city of Pickax, and you will be lynched, Mr. Qwilleran."

"I still think you're pulling my leg," he said. "There's no reason why Fanny should make this . . . this incredible gesture. Until a couple of weeks ago I hadn't seen her for forty years or more."

Goodwinter reached into his briefcase and drew out a paper covered with Fanny's idiosyncratic handwriting. "She claims you as her godchild. Your mother was a friend she regarded as a sister."

Penelope giggled. "Come on, Alex, tie your shoelace and let's go. I have a dinner date tonight."

Tom's pickup truck had already gone when the attorneys drove away, following handshakes and congratulations. Penelope had staggered a little, Qwilleran thought. Either she had been celebrating something, or she had been drowning her disappointment.

Thu-rump. . . . thu-rump . . . thu-rump. It was the familiar sound of a cat jumping down from the moose head in three easy stages.

"Well, Koko," Qwilleran said, "what do you think about that?"

Koko rolled over on the base of his spine and licked his tail assiduously.

SIXTEEN

IN A DAZE Qwilleran prepared a dish of turkey for the Siamese. He was so preoccupied with the bombshells dropped by Arch Riker and Alexander Goodwinter that he prepared a cup of instant coffee for himself minus the essential ingredient. Then he carried his coffee mug to the lakeside window and sipped the hot water without noticing that something was lacking.

Foaming white breakers pounded the shore; the beach grasses rippled in the wind; the trees waved their branches frantically; even the little wildflowers bobbed their heads bravely under the tumultuous sky. He had never seen anything so violent and yet so beautiful. This could be mine, he thought. Had anyone ever faced such a crucial career choice? His two selves argued the case:

The Dedicated Newsman said: It's the opportunity of my entire career. Investigative reporting—what I've always wanted to do.

The Canny Scot countered: *Are you crazy? Would you pass up Fanny's millions for a job with a midwestern newspaper? The first time the* Fluxion *gets slapped with a lawsuit, Percy will change his mind. Then where will you be? Back on the restaurant beat—or worse.*

But I'm a newsman. Reporting is my life. It's not a job; it's what I *do.*

So buy your own newspaper with Fanny's money. Buy a chain of newspapers.

I never wanted to be a newspaper tycoon. I like to get out in the field, dig up stories, and bang them out with two fingers on an old black manual typewriter.

If you own the paper, you can do anything you damn please. You can even set the type, like the guy at the Picayune.

And I don't *need* a lot of money or possessions. I've always been satisfied, with what I earned.

But you're not getting any younger, and all you've got in the bank is $1,245.14. Forget the Fluxion *pension; it won't keep the cats in sardines.*

I'd have to live in Pickax, and I need the stimulation of a big city. I've never lived in a small town.

You can fly to New York or Paris or Tokyo any time you feel like it. You can even buy your own plane.

"YOW!" cried Koko in his most censorious voice. He was still waiting for his evening meal. Qwilleran had absentmindedly put the plate of turkey in the cupboard with the telephone.

"Sorry, kids," he said. He waited for Koko's reaction to the food. Twice this remarkable cat had rejected turkey from Stanley Hanstable's farm—until he succeeded in getting his message across. Now he devoured it with gusto. "Yow . . . gobble gobble . . . yow," Koko said as he gulped the white meat, leaving the dark meat for Yum Yum.

Qwilleran felt the need to talk to someone with a larger vocabulary and he telephoned Roger MacGillivray. "What time are you through at the office? . . . Why don't you run out here for a drink? . . . No, don't bring Sharon. Not this time. I want to speak to you privately."

Koko had finished his repast and was doing his well-known busybody act—restless meandering accompanied by grunts and chirps and squeals and mutterings. He inspected the fireplace, the stereo, the bathroom faucets. He pressed two keys on the typewriter (*x* and *j*) and sniffed a title on the lowest bookshelf (the bird book). When he ambled into the guest room, Qwilleran followed.

The lower birth of the double-decker was the spot where Koko and Yum Yum liked to sleep. During Rosemary's visit they had been banished to the upper level. Now Koko explored the lower bunk, muttering to himself and pawing the bedcover industriously. The bunk abutted the log wall, and soon he was reaching down between the mattress and the logs, trying first one paw and then the other, stretching to the limit until he dredged up a prize—a pair of sheer pantyhose. Still he was not satisfied. He fished in the narrow crevice until he retrieved a gold chain bracelet.

Qwilleran grabbed it. "That's Mildred's! How did it get down there?"

Mildred had said it might have fallen off her wrist when she delivered the gift of turkey the week before. Mildred had been there on that occasion with someone who smoked Groat and Boddle, although Buck Dunfield claimed he had never visited the cabin.

Qwilleran found Fanny's green leather address book, still in his jacket pocket, and flipped it open to the page indexed *H*.

HUNT, R.D.—Bought three farms while commissioner; sold for airport six months later.

HANSTABLE, S—Low bidder for prison turkey contract. *Too low.*

HANSTABLE, M—Sleeping around.

Qwilleran turned to the page indexed *Q* and found himself described as a former alcoholic. There was nothing under *M* for Roger, but Dunfield was labeled a womanizer, and there were two pages of Goodwinters, who appeared to have committed every sin in the book.

Qwilleran tossed the thing in the fireplace, emptied his wastebasket on top of it, added some twigs from the coal scuttle, and opened the damper. Just as the brass bell clanged at the back door, he struck a match and threw it in the grate. Almost immediately he had second thoughts about losing such a choice compendium of scandal. If he decided to move to Pickax, it might be useful. Too late! The tremendous draft of a windy day had whipped the debris into an instant blaze.

It was a subdued young man who waited at the door. Roger's white skin was whiter, and his black beard seemed blacker.

"Come in and make yourself comfortable," Qwilleran said. "It's too noisy to sit on the porch. The wind must be fifty miles an hour, and the surf is deafening."

Roger slumped on one of the sofas and stared into the fire, saying nothing.

"I saw you and Sharon and Mildred at the memorial service. What did you think of the turnout?"

"About what I expected," the young man said in a monotone. "Everyone there was expecting to inherit something. The Queen of Pickax went around making promises."

"Had she made any promises to you?"

"Oh sure. A couple of hundred thousand to start an underwater preserve. . . . I suppose I should congratulate you."

"For what?"

"For inheriting half of Pickax and three quarters of Moose County."

"How did you find out? They didn't open the will until a couple of hours ago."

"I have my sources," Roger said testily.

Qwilleran huffed into his moustache. He suspected that the Goodwinters' secretary was Junior's mother or aunt; she had the family resemblance. And Junior had undoubtedly rushed to phone Roger. "Well, Roger my boy, I haven't accepted the terms of the will, as of now. If you're lucky, I'll go back to the *Fluxion,* and half of Pickax and three quarters of Moose County will belong to Atlantic City."

"Sorry," Roger said. "I didn't mean to be snotty, but we're all miffed about your aunt's broken promises."

"She wasn't my aunt, and furthermore I wouldn't live up here for any amount of money. Your newspaper is a farce. The radio station should be put off the air. The restaurants massacre the food. And the whole county is insular and probably inbred. I won't even mention what I think about the mosquitoes."

"Wait a minute! Don't get excited," Roger said. "We'd rather see the money stay here with you than end up in New Jersey, restoring some red-light district."

"All right, let's have a drink and bury the hatchet. Scotch? Beer?"

They talked politely about the amenities of the cabin. "It's neat," Roger said. "Sharon and I want a place like this some day. Mildred's cottage is okay, but it's like the houses in town. This cabin is perfect for the woods. I wonder who shot that moose."

Suddenly he stiffened. "My God! There's a cat up there! I'm leery of cats. I got bitten by a barn cat when I was a kid."

"You were probably pulling its tail and deserved what you got," Qwilleran said. "You're looking at Koko up there. He's harmless if you behave properly. I suppose you know what happened to your father-in-law."

Roger shook his head dolefully. "I know he's in jail. It was inevitable, of course. Stanley has been on the skids for ten years."

"It's a strange thing," Qwilleran admitted. "Just because he's your father-in-law and Mildred's husband, I felt guilty about turning him in. But he came after me with a knife. . . . And still I hated to do it."

Roger agreed without enthusiasm. "That's the way it is up here. Everyone knows what's going on, but no one wants to do anything about it. Everyone is a relative or an old school chum or a war buddy or a member of the lodge."

"The sheriff's deputy apologized to Stanley for arresting him. They'd known each other since kindergarten. If you don't mind my saying so, it makes a perfect climate for corruption." Qwilleran poked the fire and threw two more logs into the grate. "What happened to Stanley ten years ago?"

"I was just beginning to date Sharon when it started. He'd been living high and suddenly got this incredible B.O. It was like a curse. His own family couldn't tolerate it. Mildred couldn't live in the same house. Sharon and I had to elope because the father-of-the-bride couldn't be stomached at a regular wedding. The guy became an outcast, that's all."

"Did he consult any doctors?"

"All kinds. They suspected abscessed lungs, infection of the sweat glands, chronic uremic poisoning, and you-name-it. But nothing checked out, and nothing seemed to help. Dr. Melinda —you know her—told me some people just have an idiopathic stink."

"Didn't Mildred consider divorce?"

"She was afraid to divorce him. He said he'd kill her, and she believed it. For a healthy, loving woman that was a helluva way to live, you know, so she was wide open for male companionship."

"Meaning Buck Dunfield?"

"He wasn't the first—only the unluckiest."

"Is that why Stanley killed him?"

"Well, it was no secret that he hated Buck. He knew what was going on."

"The real reason, I suspect—he found out Buck was snooping into his racket. The ferry racket."

"One thing I don't understand," Roger said. "How could Stanley *sneak up* on Buck undetected? That's what happened, they say."

"I know how. Buck had lost his sense of smell. Even the dead fish on the beach didn't bother him. Did Mildred suspect he was a killer?"

"Everyone knew. The police had a good idea, but they hadn't collected enough evidence. They were waiting for something to break."

"Everyone knows! The motto of Moose County ought to be *Omnes Sciunt.* What was Stanley's connection at the prison?"

"He made the lowest bid to supply turkeys. Pretty good contract. They have five thousand inmates."

"It had to be more than just a low bid, chum. He had a clientele inside for liquor and maybe drugs. He could also smuggle out an inmate in his truck-bed, rolled up in a tarpaulin. Did you know he was transporting escapees halfway to Canada?"

"There was gossip, but no one would blow the whistle. It had to be an outsider like you."

Qwilleran told Roger about the cassette and his efforts to match it with voices around town. He wondered if he should reveal Koko's role in solving the mystery. The cat had found the cassette, directed attention to the prison connection and later to the turkey farmer, attacked the man when he broke into the cabin, and brought the final clue to light: the money clip.

No, Qwilleran thought. Roger wouldn't buy such a fantastic story. Aloud he said: "Let's drop this depressing subject. . . . Have you seen any extraterrestrial aircraft lately?"

Just before leaving, Roger said: "I almost forgot. Some woman from Down Below phoned the visitors' center. She wanted to know how to reach you. I took her number. You're supposed to call her soon as possible."

He handed over a slip of paper with the phone number of the

Morning Rampage and the name of the woman who was managing editor.

Qwilleran returned her call, then drove into Mooseville—first for the formalities at the jail and then for dinner at the Northern Lights Hotel. He sat alone in a booth and longed for his pipe. If he decided to accept the terms of Fanny's will, his first act would be to order a couple of tins of Groat and Boddle Number Five. And if he accepted the new assignment at the *Fluxion* or *Morning Rampage* he would soon regard these two weeks in Moose County as a visit to another planet. Already his orange cap was beginning to look ridiculous.

After dinner he drove back to the cabin slowly, savoring every picturesque stand of birch, every grotesque jack pine, every sudden view of the raging lake as the highway dipped in and out of the woods. All the beauties of the landscape that he had ignored during the last two weeks now became treasures to stow away in his memory. He might never see this wild and wonderful country again, and he had not even taken the trouble to watch for the Northern Lights. Or a UFO.

A sheriff's car with the siren wailing sped past him, followed by the red truck of the volunteer fire department. Qwilleran's throat choked with dread and he pressed the accelerator. The cabin! The fire in the fireplace! *The cats!*

By the time he reached the Klingenschoen driveway the firefighters were working on a burning truck that had run off the road near the site of the old log schoolhouse. Several cars had stopped.

"Anyone hurt?" he asked the onlookers. No, they said. No sign of a driver, they said. Lucky it didn't start a forest fire, they said, considering the force of the wind.

As Qwilleran started up the long driveway a chilling thought occurred to him. The charred hulk looked like a blue pick-up.

As soon as he parked the car he heard Koko howling inside the cabin. As soon as he unlocked the door the cat rushed onto the porch and dashed crazily from one side to the other, stopping only to jump at the rattail latch of the screened door.

Qwilleran found the harness in a hurry and buckled it around the taut belly of the Siamese. Then he played out the long leash and opened the door. Koko immediately bounded toward the toolshed, forcing Qwilleran into a painful run.

The door of the shed was open; that was unusual. The interior of the windowless building was murky, but Qwilleran could see money blowing around on the floor. Stealthily the cat stalked the deep shadows of the shed, unearthly moans coming from the depths of his chest. A gust of wind stirred up another flurry of bills, and Qwilleran kicked an empty whiskey bottle. Then Koko started to howl—not his usual emphatic statement but a prolonged high-pitched wail. Qwilleran looped up the slack of the leash and edged warily into the shadows.

There was one bright spot in the gloom. Lying on the floor was a small handgun with a Florentine gold handle. The body of the handyman was sprawled on the shabby cot.

Snatching Koko, Qwilleran hobbled back to the cabin and phoned the sheriff's dispatcher.

In a matter of minutes a deputy's car pulled into the clearing. "We were right down there on the highway," the officer said. "Pickup on fire. Total loss. Looks like arson."

After the body had been carried away in the ambulance, Koko prowled through the cabin with long purposeful strides, wandering everywhere, a portrait of indecision. Yum Yum huddled with her haunches elevated and watched him with concern.

Qwilleran stood at the front windows, staring at a hundred miles of water. Who could fathom the moods and motives of a poor fellow like Tom? He was so willing to do anything suggested, so easily exploited, so pleased to be given a job to do, a pasty, or even a kind word. Fanny had bossed him and given him a home; Hanstable had given him orders and a regular payoff that encouraged that unrealistic dream of buying a nightclub. Without them, it seemed to Qwilleran, Tom had felt suddenly cut adrift.

A burst of music interrupted his uncomfortable reverie. It was the forceful introduction to Brahms' Double Concerto followed by the cello's haunting melody. Abruptly, in the middle of a phrase, the music was replaced by the spoken word—a gentle voice:

"I did it. . . . I pushed her. . . . She was a nice old lady. She was my friend." There was a choked sob. *"He told me* to do it. He said I would get a lot of money to buy a nightclub. He said we would be partners. . . . She promised me the money. She promised to leave me everything. She said I was like her son. . . . Why did she say it? She didn't mean it."

The voice trailed away, and the mike picked up the roar of the wind and waves and the cry of a cat. Then it cut out, and the music resumed with the plaintive theme and the solo violin.

Qwilleran coughed to dispel the lump in his throat. The cat was sitting alongside the stereo, studying the little red light. Qwilleran stroked Koko's head. "Did he say anything to you, Koko? Did he say goodbye?"

Mooseville, Sunday

Dear Arch,

Your news on the telephone has left me in a state of terminal shock. Now I have news for you! The *Rampage* has made a better offer, and they have a prettier managing editor. Do you think Percy is prepared to meet their terms?

There's been a little excitement here. We had a B-and-E at the cabin, and Koko bloodied the burglar. I almost got knifed by the same man. He killed one of our neighbors last weekend. Aunt Fanny died suddenly on Thursday, and her houseman shot himself yesterday —in my toolshed. Otherwise it has been a quiet vacation.

There is one little problem. The new assignment sounds great, but I've just found out that I'm the sole heir to Aunt Fanny's sizable fortune. Naturally there's a catch. I have to live in Pickax. What to do? What to do?

You won't believe a word of this, and I don't blame you.

Qwill

As he ripped the sheet out of the typewriter the two nagging voices in his head were still debating. Be true to your profession, said the Dedicated Newsman. *Take the money and run,* said the Canny Scot.

Koko was sitting on the table studying the keys and levers of the machine, while Yum Yum made playful passes at his tail.

"Tell me what to do, Koko," the man said. "You're always right. Shall I take the new assignment?"

Yum Yum was licking Koko's ears now, and both cats were cross-eyed with enjoyment. "Yow," he murmured weakly.

Qwilleran huffed into his moustache. Was that *yes* or *no?*

The Cat Who
Played Post Office

ONE

A Caucasian male—fiftyish, six-feet-two, weight two-thirty, graying hair, bushy moustache—opened his eyes and found himself in a strange bed in a strange room. He lay still, in a state of peculiar lassitude, and allowed his eyes to rove about the room with mild curiosity. Eyes that might be described as mournful surveyed the steel footboard of the bed, the bare window, the hideous color of the walls, the television on a high shelf. Beyond the window a tree was waving its branches wildly.

He could almost hear his mother's musical voice saying. "The tree is waving to you, Jamesy. Wave your hand like a polite little boy."

Jamesy? Is that my name? It doesn't sound—exactly—right. . . . Where am I? What is my name?

The questions drifted across his consciousness without arousing anxiety—only a vague perplexity.

He had a mental picture of an old man with a Santa Claus beard standing at his bedside and saying, "You haff scarlet fever, Jamesy. Ve take you to the hospital and make you vell."

Hospital? Is this a hospital? Do I have scarlet fever?

Although undisturbed by his predicament, he was beginning to have an uncomfortable feeling that he had neglected something of vital importance; he had failed someone close to him.

His mother, perhaps? He frowned, and the wrinkling of his brow produced a slight hurt. He raised his left hand and found a bandage on his forehead. Quickly he checked other parts of his anatomy. Nothing was missing and nothing seemed to be broken, but the movement of his right knee and right elbow was restricted by more bandages. There was also something unusual about his left hand. He counted four fingers and a thumb, and yet something was wrong. It was baffling. He sighed deeply and wondered what it could possibly be that he had neglected to do.

A strange woman—plump, white haired, smiling—bustled into the room with noiseless steps. "Oh, you're awake! You had a good night's sleep. It's a beautiful day, but windy. How do you feel, Mr. Cue?"

Cue? Jamesy Cue? Is that my name?

It sounded unlikely, if not absurd. He passed his hand over his face experimentally, feeling a familiar moustache and a jaw he had shaved ten thousand times. As a voice test he said aloud to himself, "I remember the face but not the name."

"My name? Toodle," the woman said pleasantly. "Mrs. Toodle. Is there anything I can do for you, Mr. Cue? Dr. Goodwinter will be here in a few minutes. I'll take your jug and bring you some fresh water. Are you ready for brekky?" As she left the room with the jug in hand, she called over her shoulder, "You have bathroom privileges."

Bathroom privileges. Brekky. Toodle.

They were foreign words that made no sense. The old man with a beard had told him he had scarlet fever. Now this woman was telling him he had bathroom privileges. It sounded like some kind of embarrassing disease. He heaved another sigh and closed his eyes to wait for the old man with a Santa Claus beard. When he opened them again, a young woman in a white coat was standing at his bedside, holding his wrist.

"Good morning, lover," she said. "How do you feel?"

The voice had a familiar ring, and he remembered her green eyes and long eyelashes. Around her neck hung a tubular thing, the name of which escaped him. Hesitantly he asked, "Are you my doctor?"

"Yes, and more—much more," she said with a wink.

He began to feel familiar sensations. *Is she my wife? Am I a married man? Am I neglecting my family?* Again he felt a twinge of guilt about the responsibility he was shirking, whatever it might be. "Are you—are you my wife?" he asked in a faltering voice.

"Not yet, but I'm working on it." She kissed an unbandaged spot on his forehead. "You still feel groggy, don't you? But you'll be A-OK soon."

He looked at his left hand. "Something's missing here."

"Your watch and ring are in the hospital safe until you're ready to go home," she explained gently.

"Oh, I see. . . . Why am I here?" he asked fearfully, worrying about the indelicate nature of his disease.

"You fell off your bicycle on Ittibittiwassee Road. Do you remember?"

Ittibittiwassee. Bathroom privileges. Brekky. Groggy. What language, he wondered, were these people speaking? He ventured to ask, "Do I have a bicycle?"

"You *did* have a bike, lover, but it's totaled. You'll have to buy a ten-speed now."

Totaled. Ten-speed. Toodle. He shook his head in dismay. Clearing his throat, he said, "That woman who came in here said I have bathroom privileges. What is that? Is it—is it some kind of—"

"It means you can get out of bed and walk to the bathroom," said the doctor with a smile twitching her lips. "I'll be back when I've finished my rounds." She kissed him again. "Arch Riker is coming to see you. He's flying up from Down Below." Then she walked from the room with a long leggy stride and a chummy wave of the hand.

Arch Riker. Down Below. What was she talking about? And who was she? To ask her name would have been embarrassing under the circumstances. He shrugged in defeat, hoisted himself out of bed, and hobbled to the bathroom. There in the mirror were sad eyes, graying temples and an oversized pepper-and-salt moustache that he recognized. Still, the name eluded him.

When the woman who called herself Toodle brought a tray of what she called brekky, he ate the blob of something soft and yellow, the two brown patties that were salty and chewy, the triangular slabs of something thin and crisp, which he smeared with something red and sweet. But he was glad to lie down again and close his eyes and stop trying to think.

He opened them suddenly. A man was standing at his bedside

—a paunchy man with thinning hair and a ruddy face that he had seen many times before.

"You dirty bird!" the visitor said genially. "You gave us a scare! What were you trying to do? Kill yourself? How do you feel, Qwill?"

"Is that my name? I can't remember."

The man gulped twice and turned pale. "All your friends call you Qwill. Short for Qwilleran. Jim Qwilleran, spelled with a *Q-w.*"

The patient studied the information and nodded slowly.

"Don't you remember me, Qwill? I'm Arch Riker, your old sidekick."

Qwilleran stared at him. *Sidekick.* Another baffling word.

"We grew up together in Chicago, Qwill. For the last few years I've been your editor at the *Daily Fluxion.* We've had a million lunches at the Press Club."

The light began to penetrate Qwilleran's foggy mind. "Wait a minute. I want to sit up."

Riker pressed a button that raised the head of the bed and pulled up a straight chair for himself. "Melinda called me and said you fell off your bike. I came right away."

"Melinda?"

"Melinda Goodwinter. Your latest girl, Qwill. Also your doctor, you lucky dog."

"What is this place?" Qwilleran asked. "I don't know where I am."

"This is the Pickax Hospital. They brought you here after your accident."

"Pickax? What kind of a hospital is that?"

"Pickax City—four hundred miles north of everywhere. You've been living here for the last couple of months."

"Oh. . . . Is that when I left Chicago?"

"Qwill, you haven't lived in Chicago for twenty years," Riker said quietly. "You've lived in New York, Washington—all around the country since then."

"Wait a minute. I want to sit in that big chair."

Riker picked up a red plaid bathrobe with ragged edges. "Here, get into this. It looks like yours. It's the Mackintosh tartan. Does that ring a bell? Your mother was a Mackintosh."

Qwilleran's face brightened. "That's right! Where is she? Is she all right?"

Riker drew a deep breath. "She died when you were in college, Qwill." He paused to formulate a plan. "Look here, let's go back to the beginning. I've known you ever since kindergarten. Your mother called you Jamesy. We called you Snoopy. Do you remember why?"

Qwilleran shook his head.

"You were always snooping into other kids' lunch boxes." He searched Qwilleran's face for a glimmer of recollection. "Do you remember our first-grade teacher? She was thin at the top and fat at the bottom. You said, 'Old Miss Blair looks like a pear.' Remember that?"

There was a slight nod and half smile in response.

"You were always good with words. You were playing with words when the rest of us were playing with water pistols." With patience Riker went on with the nostalgic recital, hitting the highlights of his friend's life. "You were spelling champ for three years. . . . In junior high school you discovered girls. . . . In high school you played baseball—outfield, good slugger. And you edited the school paper."

"The *North Wind*," Qwilleran murmured.

"That's it! That's the name! . . . After graduation you went into the service and came out with a trick knee, so that was the end of baseball. In college you sang in the glee club and got interested in acting." The years rolled by in a matter of minutes. "We both went into journalism, but you got the glamour assignments. You were tops as a crime reporter, and whenever there was any trouble overseas, they sent you to cover the hot spots."

With each revelation Qwilleran's mind became sharper, and he responded with more awareness.

"You won journalism prizes and wrote a book on urban crime. It actually got on the best-seller list."

"For about ten minutes."

Relief showed in Riker's face. His friend was beginning to sound normal. "You were my best man when I married Rosie."

"It rained all day. I remember the wet confetti."

"You were in Scotland when you married Miriam."

Again Qwilleran felt the vague uneasiness. "Where is she? Why isn't she here?"

"You were divorced about ten years ago. She's somewhere in Connecticut."

The mournful eyes gazed into space. "And after that everything fell apart."

"Okay, let's face it, Qwill. You developed a drinking problem and couldn't hold a job, but you snapped out of it and came to work for the *Daily Fluxion,* writing features. You turned out some good stuff. You could write about art, antiques, interior design—anything."

"Even if I didn't know anything about it," Qwilleran put in.

"When you started writing restaurant reviews, you could make food sound as interesting as crime."

"Wait a minute, Arch! How long have I been away from my desk? I've got to get back to work!"

"Hey, man, you quit several weeks ago!"

"What! Why did I quit? I need the job!"

"Not anymore, my friend. You inherited money—a bundle of it—the Klingenschoen fortune."

"I don't believe it! What am I doing? Where do I live?"

"Here in Pickax City. Those were the terms of the will. You have to live in Moose County for five years. You inherited a big house in Pickax with a four-car garage and a limousine and—"

Qwilleran grabbed the arms of his chair. "The cats! Where are the cats? I haven't fed the cats!" *That* was the thing that had been troubling the edges of his mind. "I've got to get out of here!"

"Don't get excited. You'll split your stitches. The brats are okay. Your housekeeper is feeding them, and she's making up a room for me so I can stay overnight."

"Housekeeper?"

"Mrs. Cobb. I wouldn't mind going there right now for a little shut-eye. I've been up since four o'clock this morning."

"I'll go with you. Where are my clothes?"

"Sit down, sit down, Qwill. Melinda wants to run a few tests. I'll check back with you later."

"Arch, no one but you could have dredged up all that ancient history."

Riker grabbed his friend's hand. "Are you feeling like yourself now?"

"I think so. Don't worry."

"See you later, Qwill. God! I'm glad to see you functioning again. You gave me a bad scare."

After Riker had left, Qwilleran tested himself. *Sidekick, shut-eye, brekky.* Now he knew the meaning of all the words. He could remember his own telephone number. He could spell *onomatopoeia.* He knew the names of his cats: Koko and Yum Yum, a pair of beautiful but tyrannical Siamese.

Yet, there was a period of a few hours that remained a blank. No matter how intensely he concentrated, he could not recall anything immediately before or immediately after the accident. Why did he fall off his bike? Did he hit a pothole or some loose gravel? Or did he pass out while pedaling? Perhaps that was Melinda's reason for wanting to run tests.

He was too tired to concentrate further. Recollecting his entire past had been an exhausting chore. In a single morning he had relived more than forty years. He needed a nap. He needed some *shut-eye.* Smiling to himself because he now knew all the words, he fell asleep.

Qwilleran slept soundly, and he had a vivid dream. He was having lunch in a sunny room, all yellow and green. The housekeeper was serving macaroni-and-cheese flecked with green pepper and red pimiento. He could picture everything distinctly: the brown casserole, the housekeeper's bright pink sweater. In the dream the colors were so vibrant they were disturbing.

Qwilleran was telling Mrs. Cobb that he might take a bike ride on Ittibittiwassee Road.

"Be careful with that rusty old crate," she said in a cheerful voice. "You really ought to buy a ten-speed, Mr. Q . . . a ten-speed, Mr. Q . . . a ten-speed, Mr. Q . . . ."

Suddenly he was awake; his bandaged brow was cold and wet. The sequence had been so real, he refused to believe it was a dream. There was only one way to be sure.

He reached for the telephone and dialed his home number, and when he heard his housekeeper's cheery hello he marveled at the audio-fidelity of his dream. "Mrs. Cobb, how's everything at the house? How are the cats?"

"Oh, it's *you*, Mr. Q," she squealed. "Thank goodness you're all in one piece! The cats? They miss you. Koko won't eat, and Yum Yum cries a lot. They know something's wrong. Mr. Riker is here, and I sent him upstairs to take a nap. Is there anything you want, Mr. Q? Anything I can send you?"

"No, thanks. Not a thing. I'll be home tomorrow. But just answer a couple of questions, if you will. Did you serve macaroni-and-cheese yesterday?"

"Oh Lord! I hope it wasn't the lunch that caused your spill."

"Don't worry. Nothing like that. I'm just trying to recall something. Were you wearing a pink sweater yesterday?"

"Yes, the one you gave me."

"Did I discuss my plans for the afternoon?"

"Oh, Mr. Q! This sounds like one of your investigations. Do you have some suspicions?"

"No, just curious, Mrs. Cobb."

"Well, let me think. . . . You said you were going to take the old bike out for a ride, and I said you ought to buy a new ten-speed. You'll have to buy one now, Mr. Q. The sheriff found your old one in a ditch, and it's a wreck!"

"In a ditch?" That's strange, Qwilleran thought, stroking his moustache thoughtfully. He thanked the housekeeper and suggested some delicacies to tempt Koko's appetite. "Where is he, Mrs. Cobb? Put him on the phone."

"He's on top of the refrigerator," she said. "He's listening to every word I say. Let me see if the phone cord will reach."

There was an interlude in which Mrs. Cobb could be heard making coaxing noises, while Koko's familiar yowl came through with piercing clarity. Then Qwilleran heard a snuffling sound coming from the receiver.

"Hello there, Koko old boy," he said. "Are you taking care of Yum Yum? Are you keeping the house safe from lions and tigers?"

A throaty purr came over the line. Koko appreciated intelligent conversation.

"Be a good cat and eat your food. You've got to keep up your strength to fight off all those jaguars and black buffalos. So long, Koko. I'll be home tomorrow."

"YOW!" came a sharp cry that stabbed Qwilleran's eardrum.

He replaced the receiver and turned to find Mrs. Toodle standing there in wide-eyed astonishment. Her voice was wary. "I came to see . . . if you'd like to have . . . your lunch now, Mr. Q."

"If there's no objection," he replied, "I'd prefer to go down to the cafeteria. Do you suppose they're serving consommé with poached plover eggs or a salpicon of mussels today?"

Mrs. Toodle looked alarmed and hurried out. Qwilleran chuckled. He was feeling euphoric after his brief brush with amnesia.

Before going in search of food he combed his hair and thought about Mrs. Cobb's remark: *The sheriff found the bicycle in the ditch!* The drainage ditch was a good thirty feet from the pavement to allow for future widening of the new highway. If he had blacked out or if he had hit some obstruction, he and his bike would have toppled over on the gravel shoulder. How did the bicycle end up in the ditch? It was a question he might pursue later, but first he needed food.

Wearing his Mackintosh bathrobe, Qwilleran headed for the elevator, walking with a slow dignified step dictated by his legful of bandages. He was thankful he had not landed on his bad knee. On second thought, he realized he now might have two bad knees.

Everyone in the corridor seemed to know him. Orderlies and ambulatory patients greeted him by name—or, rather, by initial —and one of the nurses said, "Sorry about your room, Mr. Q— the color of the walls, I mean. It was supposed to be antique pink, but the painters got their signals crossed."

"It's not very appetizing," Qwilleran agreed. "It looks like raw veal, but I can live with it for another twenty-four hours."

In the cafeteria he was greeted with applause from the nurses, technicians, and doctors who were lunching on cottage cheese salads, bowls of chili, and braised cod with poached celery. He acknowledged their greetings with courtly bows and exaggerated salutes before taking his place in line. Ahead of him was a white-haired country doctor with two claims to fame: He was Melinda's father, and he had swabbed throats, set bones, and delivered babies for half of Moose County.

Dr. Halifax Goodwinter turned and said, "Ah! The celebrated cyclist! Glad to see you're still among the living. It would be a pity if my daughter lost her first and only patient."

A nurse standing behind Qwilleran nudged his elbow. "You should wear a helmet, Mr. Q. You could've been killed."

He carried a tray of chili and corn muffins to a table occupied by three men he had met at the Pickax Boosters Club: the hospital administrator, a genial urologist, and a banker who served on the hospital board of trustees.

The doctor said, "Planning to sue anybody, Qwill? I can steer you to a couple of ingenius ambulance chasers."

The banker said, "You can't sue the manufacturer. That kind of bike hasn't been made for fifty years."

The administrator said, "We're taking up a collection to buy you a new bike—and maybe a new bathrobe."

Patting the lapels of his ratty red plaid, Qwilleran said in his best declamatory style, "This is a vintage robe with a noteworthy provenance, gentlemen. The distress marks merely add to its associative value." The truth was that Koko had gone through a wool-eating phase, nibbling chair upholstery, neckties, the Mackintosh robe, and other handy items.

Qwilleran felt at ease with the hospital badinage. It was the same kind of jocular roasting he had enjoyed at the *Daily Fluxion*. Everyone in Pickax City seemed to like him, and why not? He was an affable companion, a sympathetic listener, and the richest man in the county. He had no delusions on that score. As a feature writer for the *Fluxion* he had been courted by lobbyists, politicians, businessmen, and media hounds. He accepted their attentions graciously, but he had no delusions.

After lunch the lab took blood samples, and Qwilleran had an EKG, followed by another nap and another dream.

Again it was vivid—painfully so. He was climbing out of a ditch near a lonely highway. His clothing was soaked; his pants were torn; his legs were bleeding. Blood was trickling into his right eye as he stumbled onto the highway and started to walk. Soon a red car stopped, and someone in a blue shirt jumped out. It was Junior Goodwinter, the young managing editor of the *Pickax Picayune*. Junior gave him a ride back to town and talked incessantly on the journey, but Qwilleran could say nothing. He struggled to answer Junior's questions, but he could find no words.

The dream ended abruptly, and the dreamer found himself sitting up in bed, sweating and shivering. He mopped his face and then reached for the telephone and called the newspaper office.

"Qwill! You pulled through!" shouted Junior into the phone.

"When I picked you up yesterday, you weren't exactly dead, but you weren't alive either. We had the type all set up to print an obit if you kicked off."

"Thanks. That was decent of you," Qwilleran said.

"Are you hitting on all eight? You sound okay."

"They sewed me together, and I look like the Spirit of '76. Where was I when you picked me up, Junior?"

"On Ittibittiwassee Road, beyond the Buckshot mineshaft. You were wandering around in the middle of the pavement in a daze —going in the wrong direction. Your clothes were all ripped and muddy. Your head was bleeding. You really had me worried, especially when you couldn't talk."

"Did you see my bike?"

"Tell the truth, I wasn't looking for it. I just concentrated on getting you to the hospital. I hit a hundred ten."

"What were you driving?"

"My Jag, luckily. That's why I could kick it up to one-ten so fast."

"Thanks, Junior. Let's have lunch next week. I'll buy."

Another dream checked out! Even the color of the car was accurate. Qwilleran knew that Junior's Jaguar was red.

He discussed his dreams with Melinda Goodwinter and Arch Riker that evening when they came to the hospital to have dinner with him in the cafeteria. Without her white coat and stethoscope Melinda looked more like the young woman he had been dating for the last two months.

Qwilleran asked her, "Do you kiss all your bedridden male patients?"

"Only those of advanced age," she retorted with a sweetly malicious look in her green eyes.

"Funny thing," he said, "but some of the details I couldn't remember came back to me in dreams this afternoon. There's only one blank left in my memory—the actual circumstances that caused the accident."

"It wasn't a pothole," Melinda said. "That's a brand-new highway, smooth as glass."

Riker said, "It's my guess that you swerved to avoid hitting something, Qwill, and skidded on the shoulder. A skunk or raccoon, perhaps, or even a deer. I saw a lot of dead animals on the road, coming in from the airport."

"We'll never know for sure," Qwilleran said. "How's everything at the house? Did you get some sleep? Did Mrs. Cobb give you lunch? Did you see Koko?"

"Everything's fine. Koko met me at the front door and gave me a military inspection. I guess I passed muster, because he allowed me to enter."

Late that night, when the hospital corridor was silent, Qwilleran dreamed his final dream. It was the missing link between the macaroni-and-cheese and the red Jaguar. He saw himself pedaling at a leisurely pace along a deserted highway, appreciating the smooth asphalt and the lack of traffic and the gently rolling hills. Pedaling uphill was easy, and coasting down was glorious.

He passed the abandoned Buckshot Mine with its rotting shaft house and ominous signs: *Danger . . . Keep Out . . . Beware of Cave-ins*. The deserted mines that dotted the lonely landscape around Pickax City were a source of endless fascination for Qwilleran. They were mysterious—silent—dead.

The Buckshot was different, however. He had been told that, if one listened intently, one could hear an eerie whistling sound coming from the shaft where eighteen miners had been buried alive in 1913.

In the dream he pedaled slowly and silently past the Buckshot. Only a tick-tick in the rear wheel and a grinding sound in the sprocket broke the stillness. He turned his head to gaze at the gray ghost of the shaft house . . . the sloping depression at the site of a cave-in . . . the vibrant green weeds that smothered the whole scene. He was staring so intently that he was unaware of a truck approaching from the opposite direction—unaware until its motor roared. He looked ahead in time to see its burst of speed, its sudden swerve into the eastbound lane, a murderous monster bearing down upon him. In the dream he had a vivid picture of the grille, a big rusty thing that seemed to be grinning. He yanked the handlebars and plunged down toward the roadside ditch, but the front wheel hit a rock and he went sailing over the handlebars. For an interminable moment he was airborne.

Qwilleran wrenched himself from sleep in a fright and found himself sitting up in bed, sweating and shouting.

An orderly hurried into the room. "Mr. Q! Mr. Q! What's the problem? A bad dream?"

Qwilleran shook himself in an effort to dispel the nightmare. "Sorry. Hope I didn't disturb the other patients."

"Want a drink of water, Mr. Q?"

"Thanks. And will you raise the bed? I'd better sit up for a while."

Qwilleran leaned back against his pillow, reliving the dream. It was as graphic as the others. The sky was blue. The weeds around the deserted mine were poison green. The truck had a rusted grille.

Like the other dreams, it had actually happened, he realized, but there was no one he could phone for verification.

One thing was clear. What happened on Ittibittiwassee Road was no accident. He thought, I'm well liked in Pickax . . . but not by everyone.

TWO

IT WAS MIDSUMMER when the richest man in Moose County fell off his antiquated bicycle. Two months before that incident he was far from affluent. He was an underpaid feature writer working for a large midwestern newspaper noted for its twenty-four-point bylines and meager wage scale. As a frugal bachelor he lived in a one-room furnished apartment and was making payments on a used car. He owned a fifty-year-old typewriter with a faulty shift key, and his library consisted of the odd titles found on the twenty-five-cent table in secondhand bookstores. His wardrobe, such as it was, fitted comfortably in two suitcases. He was perfectly content.

Jim Qwilleran's sole extravagance was the care and feeding of two Siamese cats who shunned catfood, preferring beef tenderloin, lobster, and oysters in season. Not only did they have aristocratic sensibilities and epicurean appetites, but Koko, the male, showed unusual intelligence. Tales of his extrasensory perception had made him legendary at the *Daily Fluxion* and the Press Club, although nothing of the cat's remarkable attribute was mentioned outside the profession.

Then, without ever buying a lottery ticket, Qwilleran became a multimillionaire virtually overnight. It was a freak inheritance, and he was the sole heir.

When the astonishing news reached him, Qwilleran and his feline companions were vacationing in Moose County, the northern outpost of the state. They were staying in a lakeshore cabin near the resort town of Mooseville. As soon as he recovered from the shock he submitted his resignation to the *Daily Fluxion* and made arrangements to move to Pickax City, the county seat, thirty miles from Mooseville.

But first he had to clean out his desk at the *Fluxion* office, say goodbye to fellow staffers, and have one last lunch with Arch Riker at the Press Club.

The two men walked to the club, mopping their brows and complaining of the heat. It was the first hot spell of the season.

Qwilleran said: "I'm going to miss you and all the other guys, Arch, but I won't miss the hot weather. It's ninety-five degrees at City Hall."

"I suppose the photographers are frying their annual egg on the sidewalk," Arch remarked.

"In Moose County there's always a pleasant breeze. No need for air-conditioning."

"That may be, but how can you stand living four hundred miles from civilization?"

"Are you under the impression that today's cities are civilized?"

"Qwill, you've spent less than a month in that northern wilderness," Arch said, "and already you're thinking like a sheep farmer. . . . Okay, I'll rephrase that question. How can you stand living four hundred miles from the Press Club?"

"It's a gamble," Qwilleran admitted, "but those are the terms of Miss Klingenschoen's will: Live in Moose County for five years or forfeit the inheritance."

At the club, where the air conditioner was out of commission, they ordered corned beef sandwiches, gin and tonic for Riker, and iced tea for Qwilleran.

"If you forfeit the inheritance," Riker went on, "who gets it?"

"Some outfit in New Jersey. I don't mind telling you, Arch, it was a tough decision for me to make. I wasn't sure I wanted to give up a job on a major newspaper for *any* amount of money."

"Qwill, you're unique—if not demented. No one in his right mind would turn down millions."

"Well, you know me, Arch. I like to work. I like newspapering and press clubs. I've never needed a lot of dough, and I've never wanted to be encumbered by possessions. It remains to be seen if I'll be comfortable with money—I mean Money with a capital *M*."

"Try!" Riker advised. "Try real hard. What are the encumbrances that might ruin your life?"

"Some complicated investments. Office buildings and hotels on the East coast. A couple of shopping malls. Acreage in Moose County. Half of Main Street in Pickax City. Also the Klingenschoen mansion in Pickax and the log cabin in Mooseville where we spent our vacation."

"Rotten luck."

"Do you realize I'll need a housekeeping staff, gardeners, maintenance men, and probably a secretary? Not to mention an accountant, a financial adviser, two attorneys, and a property management firm? That's not my style! They'll expect me to join the country club and wear tailor-made suits!"

"I'm not worried about you, Qwill. You'll always be your own man. Anyone who's convinced his cat is psychic will never conform to conventional folkways. . . . Here's the mustard. Want horseradish?"

Qwilleran grunted and squirted a question mark of mustard on his corned beef.

Riker went on. "You'll never be anything but what you are, Qwill—a lovable slob. Do you realize every one of your ties is full of moth holes?"

"I happen to like my ties," Qwilleran countered. "They were all woven in Scotland, and they're not moth-eaten. Before Yum Yum came to live with us, Koko was frustrated and started chewing wool."

"Are those two cats playing house? I thought they were both neutered."

"Yes, but Siamese crave companionship. Otherwise they get neurotic. They do strange things."

"If you ask me," Riker said, "Koko is still doing some very strange things."

At that moment two photographers from the *Fluxion* stopped at the table to commiserate with Qwilleran. "Man, do you know what you're getting into up north?" one of them said. "Moose County is a *low-crime* area!"

"No problem," Qwilleran replied. "They import an occasional felon from down here, just so the cops won't get bored."

He was accustomed to being ribbed about his interest in crime. Everyone at the Press Club knew he had helped the police crack a few cases, and everyone knew that it was Koko who actually sniffed out the clues.

Qwilleran applied his attention to his sandwich again, and Riker resumed his questioning. "What's the population of Pickax?"

"Three thousand persons and four thousand pickup trucks. I call it Pickup City. The town has one traffic light, fourteen mediocre restaurants, a nineteenth-century newspaper, and more churches than bars."

"You could open a good restaurant and start your own paper, now that you're in the bucks."

"No thanks. I'm going to write a book."

"Any interesting people up there?"

"Contrary to what you think, Arch, they're not all sheep farmers. During my vacation I met some teachers and an engineer and a lively blond postmistress (married, unfortunately) and a couple of attorneys—brother and sister, very classy type. Also there's a young doctor I've started dating. She has the greenest eyes and longest eyelashes you ever saw, and she's giving me the come-on, if I'm reading the signals right."

"How come you always attract women half your age? Must be the overgrown moustache."

Qwilleran stroked his upper lip smugly. "Dr. Melinda Goodwinter, M.D. . . . not bad for a Saturday night date."

"Sounds like a character in a TV series."

"Goodwinter is the big name in Moose County. There's half a page of them in the telephone directory, and the whole phone book is only fourteen pages thick. The Goodwinters go back to the days when fortunes were being made in mining."

"What supports the economy now?"

"Commercial fishing and tourism. A little farming. Some light industry."

Riker chewed his sandwich in somber silence for a while. He was losing his best writer as well as his lunchtime companion. "Suppose you move up there, Qwill, and then change your mind before the five years are up? What happens then?"

"Everything goes to the people in New Jersey. The estate is held in trust for five years, and during that time all I get is the income . . ."

"Which amounts to . . ."

"After taxes, upwards of a million, annually."

Riker choked on the dill pickle. "Anyone should . . . be able to . . . scrape by with that."

"You and Rosie ought to come up for a week. Fresh air—no hustle—safe environment. I mean, they don't have street crime and random killings in Pickax." He signaled the waitress for the check. "Don't expect me to pay for your lunch today, Arch. I haven't seen a penny of that inheritance yet. Sorry I can't stay for coffee. Gotta get to the airport."

"How long does it take to fly up there?"

"Forever! You have to change planes twice, and the last one is a hedgehopper."

After some quick handshaking and backslapping with denizens of the Press Club, Qwilleran accepted a sizable doggie bag from the kitchen and said a reluctant farewell to his old hangout. Then he caught the three o'clock plane.

In flight his thoughts went to Arch Riker. They had been friends long enough to have genuine concern for each other, and today Arch had been unduly morose. The editor usually exhibited the detached cool of a veteran deskman, punctuated with good-natured raillery, but today something was bothering him. Qwilleran sensed that it was more than his own departure for the north country.

The flight was uneventful, the landing was smooth; and in the pasture that served as the airport's long-term parking lot, his car was waiting as he had left it. No one had slashed the tires or jimmied the trunk. Driving from the airport he knew he was back in Moose County; pickup trucks—many of them modified for rough terrain—outnumbered passenger cars two to one.

The temperature was ideal. Qwilleran was glad to escape the city heat and city traffic. As he neared Mooseville, however, he began to feel the familiar anxiety: What might have happened in his absence?

He had left Koko and Yum Yum alone in the cabin on the lakeshore. A cat-sitter had promised to visit twice a day to feed them, give them fresh drinking water, and make polite conversation. But how reliable was the woman? Suppose she had broken a leg and failed to show up! Would the cats have enough water? How long could they live without food? Suppose she had carelessly let them out of the cabin and they had run away! They were indoor cats—city cats. How would they survive in the woods? What defense would they have against a predatory owl or hawk? Suppose there were wolves in the woods! Koko would fight to the death, but little Yum Yum was so timid, so helpless . . .

It was a highly nervous man who arrived at the cabin and unlocked the door. There they were—both cats sitting on the hearth rug, rump to rump, like bookends. They looked calm and contented and rather fat around the middle.

"You scoundrels!" he shouted. "You conned her into giving you too much food! You've been gorging!"

It was July, and the strong evening sun slanted into the cabin, backlighting the cats' fur and giving each of the reprobates an undeserved halo. With brown legs tucked confidently under fawn bodies, with brown ears cocked at an impudent angle, with blue eyes gazing inscrutably from brown masks, Koko and his accomplice defied Qwilleran to criticize their Royal Catnesses.

"You don't intimidate me in the slightest," he said, "so wipe that superior look off your face—both of you! I have news for you two characters. We're moving to Pickax in the morning."

The Siamese were staunch supporters of the status quo and always resented a change of address. Nevertheless, early the next morning Qwilleran packed them and their belongings into the car and drove them—protesting at the rate of forty howls per mile—to the Klingenschoen mansion, thirty miles inland.

The historic K mansion, as the locals called it, was situated on the Pickax Circle, that bulge in Main Street that wrapped around a small park. On the perimeter were two churches, the Moose County Courthouse, and the Pickax Library, but none was more imposing than the hundred-year-old Klingenschoen residence.

Large, square, and solidly built of glistening fieldstone, it rose regally from well-kept lawns. A circular driveway served the front entrance, and a side drive led to the carriage house in the rear, also built of fieldstone with specks of quartz that sparkled in the sun.

Qwilleran drove to the back door of the house. He knew it would be unlocked, according to the friendly Pickax custom.

Hurriedly he carried two squirming animals into the big kitchen, placed their blue cushion on top of a refrigerator, and pointed out the adjoining laundry room as the new location of their drinking water and their commode. Cautioning them to be good, he closed both kitchen doors and then brought in the rest of the baggage, glancing frequently at his watch. He carried his two suitcases upstairs, and piled his writing materials on the desk in the library, including his ancient typewriter and a thirteen-pound unabridged dictionary with a tattered cover.

Previously Qwilleran had been impressed by the lavish furnishings of the mansion, but now he saw it with a proprietary eye: the high-ceilinged foyer with grandiose staircase; the dining room that could seat sixteen; the drawing room with its two fireplaces, two giant crystal chandeliers, and ponderous antique piano; the solarium with its three walls of glass. The place would cost a fortune to heat, he reflected.

Precisely at the appointed hour the doorbell rang, and he admitted the attorneys for the estate: Goodwinter & Goodwinter, a prestigious third-generation law firm. The partners—Alexander and his sister Penelope—were probably in their mid-thirties, although their cool magisterial manner made them appear older. They shared the patrician features and blond hair characteristic of Goodwinters, and they were conspicuously well dressed for a town like Pickax, dedicated to jeans, T-shirts, and feed caps.

"I just arrived myself," said Qwilleran, breathing hard after his recent exertion. "We're now official residents of Pickax. I flew up from Down Below last night." In Pickax parlance, Down Below referred loosely to the urban sprawl in the southern half of the state.

"May we welcome you to Moose County," Alexander Goodwinter said pompously, "and I believe I speak for the entire community. By establishing yourself here without delay, you do us a great favor. Your presence will ameliorate public reaction to the Klingenschoen testament, a reaction that was not exactly—ah—favorable. We appreciate your thoughtful cooperation."

"My pleasure," Qwilleran said. "Shall we go into the library to talk?"

"One moment!" Alexander raised a restraining hand. "The

purpose of our visit," he continued in measured tones, "is simply to make your transition as comfortable as possible. Unfortunately I must emplane for Washington, but I leave you in the capable hands of my sister."

That arrangement suited Qwilleran very well. He found the junior partner a fascinating enigma. She was gracious, but haughtily so. She had a dazzling smile and provocative dimples, but they were used solely for business purposes. Yet, on one occasion he had found her quite relaxed, and the only clue to her sudden friendliness had been a hint of minty breath freshener. Penelope piqued his curiosity; she was a challenge.

In making his departure Alexander concluded, "Upon my return you must break bread with us at the club, and perhaps you will allow me to recommend my barber, tailor, and jeweler." He cast a momentary glance at his client's well-worn sweatshirt and untrimmed moustache.

"What I really need," Qwilleran said, "Is a veterinarian—for preventive shots and dental prophylaxis."

"Ah . . . well . . . yes, of course," said the senior partner.

He drove away to the airport, and Qwilleran ushered Penelope into the library, enjoying the scent she was wearing—subtly feminine yet not unprofessional. He noted her silky summer suit, exquisitely tailored. She could pass for a fashion model, he thought. Why was she practicing law in this backwoods town? He looked forward to researching the question in depth.

In the library the warm colors of Bokhara rugs, leather seating, and thousands of books produced a wraparound coziness. The attorney look a seat on a blood-red leather sofa, and Qwilleran joined her there. Quickly she placed her briefcase on the seat between them.

"This will be an inspiring place in which to do your writing," she said, glancing at the bookshelves and the busts of Shakespeare and Homer. "Is that actually your typewriter? You might consider treating yourself to a word processor, Mr. Qwilleran."

Being frugal by nature, he resented advice on how to spend his own money, but his irritation was lessened by Penelope's dimpled smile.

Then she frowned at the big book with tattered cover. "You could use a new dictionary, too. Yours seems to have had a great deal of use."

"That happens to be the cats' scratching pad," Qwilleran said. "There's nothing better than an unabridged dictionary, third edition, for sharpening the claws."

The attorney's aplomb wavered for an instant before she recovered her professional smile and opened her briefcase. "The chief reason for this meeting, Mr. Qwilleran, is to discuss financial arrangements. Point One: Although the estate will not be settled for a year or more, we shall do everything in our power to expedite the probate. Meanwhile, our office will handle all expenses for household maintenance, employee wages, utilities, taxes, insurance, and the like. Invoices will come directly to us, obviating any inconvenience to you.

"Point Two: You have been good enough to sever ties with the *Daily Fluxion* and take up residence here immediately, and in so doing you have curtailed your income from that source. Accordingly we have arranged with the bank to provide a drawing account of several thousand a month until such time as the estate is settled—after which the monthly cash flow will be considerably greater. We can work out the terms of the drawing account with Mr. Fitch, the trust officer at the bank. If you have need of a new car, he will arrange it. Is that agreeable, Mr. Qwilleran?"

"It seems fair," he said casually.

"Point Three: Our offices will arrange for landscape and maintenance services, but you will need a live-in housekeeper plus day help, and the choice of such personnel should be your own. Our secretary will be glad to send you applicants for these positions."

Qwilleran sat facing the door, and he was surprised to see a cat walk past the library with perpendicular tail and purposeful step. Both animals had been penned in the kitchen, and yet Koko had easily opened a door and was exploring the premises.

"Point Four: The servants' quarters in the carriage house have been neglected and should be renovated—at the expense of the estate, of course. Would you be willing to work with our interior designer on the renovation?"

"Uh . . . yes . . . that would be fine," said Qwilleran. He was taking a mental inventory of breakables in the house and expecting to hear a shattering crash at any moment.

"Do you have any questions, Mr. Qwilleran? Is there anything we can do for you?"

"Yes, Miss Goodwinter," he said, wrenching his attention away from the impending catastrophe. "I would like to make my position clear. Point One: I have no desire for a lot of money. I don't want a yacht or private jet. I'm not interested in reading the fine print or watching the bottom line. All I wish is time to do some writing without too much interruption or annoyance."

The attorney appeared cautiously incredulous.

"Point Two, Miss Goodwinter: When the estate is settled, I intend to establish a Klingenschoen Foundation to distribute the surplus income within Moose County. Organizations and individuals would be eligible to apply for grants, scholarships, business development loans—you know the kind of thing."

"Oh, Mr. Qwilleran! How incredibly generous!" cried the attorney. "What a brilliant idea! I can hardly express what this will do for the morale and economic health of the county! And it will pacify the groups that had been promised bequests and then disappointed. May we announce your proposal in the newspaper at once?"

"Go ahead. I'll count on your office to work out the details. We might start with an Olympic-size swimming pool for the high school, and I know the marine history buffs want backing for an underwater preserve, and the public library hasn't had a new book since *Gone with the Wind*."

"When Alex returns, your proposal will be the first item on our agenda. I'll telephone him in Washington tonight to break the good news."

"That brings me to Point Three," Qwilleran said genially. "May I take you to lunch?"

"Thank you, Mr. Qwilleran. I would enjoy it immensely, but unfortunately I have a previous luncheon engagement." The dimpling process had subsided abruptly.

"How about dinner some evening next week?"

"I wish I could accept, but I'll be working late while Alex is out of town. Double work load, you know. Another time, perhaps."

As she spoke a snatch of music came from the drawing room—a few clear notes played on the antique piano.

"Who is that?" she inquired sharply.

"One of my feline companions," Qwilleran said with amusement. "That's just the white keys. Wait till he discovers the black ones."

The attorney glanced at him askance.

The sound had not surprised Qwilleran. He knew that Koko would never jump on the keyboard with a discordant crash. That approach was for ordinary cats. No, Koko would stand on his hind legs on the piano bench and stretch to reach the keys, pressing a few of them experimentally with a slender velvet paw. Having satisfied his curiosity, he would jump down and go on to his next investigation.

What Koko had played was a descending progression of four notes; G, C, E, G. Qwilleran knew the notes of the scale. As a boy he had practiced piano when he would have preferred batting practice. Now he recognized the tune as the opening phrase of *"A Bicycle Built for Two."*

"That piano rendition leads me to Point Four," he said to the attorney. "The doors in this house are so old that they don't latch securely. I'd like to be able to confine the Siamese to the kitchen on occasion."

"No problem at all, Mr. Qwilleran," she said. "We'll send Birch Trevelyan to do the necessary repairs. You will find him an excellent workman, but you must be patient. He would rather go fishing than work."

"Another thing, Miss Goodwinter. I know Pickax considers it unfriendly to lock the back door, but this house is filled with valuables. Now that tourists are coming up here from Down Below, you never know who will prowl around and get ideas. You people in the country are entirely too trusting. The back door here had a lock but no key."

"A new lock should be installed," she said. "Discuss it with Birch Trevelyan. Feel free to ask him about any problem that arises."

Later Qwilleran wondered about her real reason for declining to dine. Most young women welcomed his invitations. He preened his moustache at the recollection of past successes. Was Penelope maintaining professional distance from a client? His doctor was eager for his invitations; why not his attorney? He also wondered why she flicked her tongue across her lips whenever she mentioned Birch what's-his-name.

After she left, he found Koko in the dining room, sniffing the rabbits and pheasants carved in deep relief on the doors of the huge sideboard. Yum Yum had crept cautiously from the kitchen and was exploring the solarium with its small forest of rubber plants, cushioned wicker chairs, and panoramic view of birdlife.

Qwilleran himself went to inspect the fieldstone building that had once stabled horses and housed carriages. Now there were stalls for four automobiles. Besides his own small car and the Klingenschoen limousine there was a rusty bicycle with two flat tires, and there was a collection of garden implements completely foreign to an apartment dweller from the Concrete Belt.

Climbing the stairs to the loft, he found two apartments. In the days when servants were plentiful, these rooms would have been occupied by two couples—perhaps butler and cook, housekeeper and chauffeur. In the first apartment the drab walls and shabby furniture made a sorry contrast with the grandeur of the main house. . . . But the second apartment!

The second apartment burst upon the senses like an explosion. The walls and ceiling were covered with graffiti in every color available in a spray can. Giant flowers that looked like daisies were sprayed on every surface, intertwined with hearts, initials, and references to "LUV."

There was so much personality expressed in this tawdry room that Qwilleran half expected to meet the former occupant coming out of the shower. What would she look like? "Dizzy blonde" was the phrase that came instantly to mind, but he dismissed it as archaic. No doubt she dyed her hair green and wore hard-edge makeup. On second thought, it was difficult to imagine green hair in Pickax, and certainly not on a housemaid at the K Mansion.

How could anyone live in such a cocoon of wild pattern? Still, there was artistry in its execution. The motifs were organized as thoughtfully as a paisley shawl or Oriental rug.

Qwilleran knew that the previous owner had employed only a houseman, so . . . who was this unknown artist? How long ago had she painted these supergraphic daisies?

He touched his moustache; it always bristled when he made a discovery of significance. And now he was recalling the tune Koko had played on the piano. He hummed the four notes, and the lyric ran through his mind. *Daisy, Daisy!* An amazing coincidence, he thought. Or was it a coincidence?

THREE

THE THREE NEW residents of the K mansion were systematically adjusting to their drastically altered environment. Qwilleran found a bedroom suite to his liking—eighteenth-century English with Chippendale highboys and lowboys and a canopied bed— and he was learning to heat water for instant coffee in the vast, well-equipped kitchen. Yum Yum claimed the solarium as her territory. Koko, the investigator, after inspecting the luxurious precincts upstairs and downstairs, finally selected the staircase as his special domain. From this vantage point he could watch the front door, keep a constant check on the foyer, monitor traffic, guard the approach to the second floor, and listen for promising sounds in the kitchen. He was sitting on the stairs in a comfortable bundle when applicants for the housekeeping position began to arrive.

Qwilleran, during his career in journalism, had interviewed prime ministers, delivery boys, Hollywood starlets, vagrants, elderly widows, rock stars, convicted rapists, and—he had forgotten what else. He had never interviewed, however, a prospective employee.

"You've got to help me screen them," he said to Koko. "She should be fond of cats, cook fairly well, know how to care for antiques, and be agreeable. But not *too* agreeable."

Koko squeezed his eyes shut in approval and assent.

The first applicant was a white-haired woman with an impressive resumé and excellent references, but she could no longer lift anything, walk up stairs, or stand on her feet for any length of time.

The second interviewee took one look at the staircase and screamed, "Is that a cat? I can't stand cats!"

"So far we're batting zero," Qwilleran said to his monitor on the stairs, and then the third applicant arrived.

She was a rosy-cheeked, clear-eyed young woman in jeans and T-shirt, obviously strong and healthy in every way. Her plodding gait indicated she was more accustomed to walking over a plowed field than an Oriental rug. Qwilleran could picture her milking a herd of cows, feeding a kitchenful of farmhands at harvesttime, and frolicking in the hayloft.

The interview took place in the reception area of the foyer, where French chairs were grouped around the ornate console table under a carved gilt mirror. The young woman sat quietly on the edge of a Louis XV rococo bergère, but her eyes were in constant motion, taking in every detail of the foyer and its furnishings.

She gave her name as Tiffany. "This is a pretty house," she said.

"Do you have a surname?" Qwilleran inquired. "A last name?" he added when she hesitated.

"Trotter."

"And what experience have you had as a housekeeper?"

"I've done everything." Her eyes roamed up the staircase, around the amber-colored tooled leather walls of the foyer, and up and down the eight-foot tall case clock.

Qwilleran surmised that she was either a spy for the assessor's office or the advance woman for a ring of thieves from Down Below, disguised as a farmer's daughter. If anything dire happened in the near future, Tiffany Trotter would be the first suspect. The name was undoubtedly an alias.

"How long have you been doing housekeeping?" He guessed her age at not more than twenty.

"All my life. I kept house for my dad before he got married again."

"Are you working now?"

"Part-time. I'm a cow-sitter, and I help my dad with the haying."

"A cow-sitter?' Qwilleran was reluctant to appear naive. "Do you have many clients?"

She shrugged. "Off and on. Some people keep a family cow, and when they go on vacation I go twice a day to milk her and feed her and clean out. I'm taking care of the Lanspeaks' Jersey now. They went to Hawaii." For the fist time during the interview Tiffany showed enthusiasm, looking Qwilleran full in the face with her eyes sparkling. "I like Jerseys. This one has lots of personality. Her name is Stephanie."

The family she mentioned owned the local department store. "Why would the Lanspeaks want to keep a cow?" Qwilleran asked.

"Fresh milk tastes better," she replied promptly and with conviction. "And they like homemade butter and homemade cheese."

Tiffany left her telephone number and drove away in a pickup truck.

Next came a Mrs. Fulgrove, a scrawny woman who virtually vibrated with energy or nervousness. Without waiting for questions she said, "I ain't aimin' to be a live-in housekeeper 'cause 'twouldn't be right, you bein' a single man and me a widow, but seein' as how they said you ain't a drinkin' man, I'd be willin' to clean and iron three days a week, which I worked here when the Old Lady was alive and I had to do the work of two seein' as how the reg'lar girl wouldn't lift a finger if I didn't snitch on her to the Old Lady, which the young ones today drink and smoke and dance and all that, and I'm glad I was born when folks had some self-respect, so I always work six days a week and go to church three times on Sunday."

Qwilleran said, "Your industry and dedication are to your credit, Mrs. Fulgrove. What did you say was the name of the regular girl who was so lazy?"

"She was one of them Mull girls, which the Mulls was never respectable, not that I want to gossip, bein' a charitable woman if I do say it myself, and the Old Lady was fixin' to fire her, but she up and left of her own will, leavin' her rooms in an awful mess and the devil's own pictures painted all over the walls and dirt most everywhere, which the Old Lady was mad as a hornet, but 'twas good riddance, not that I'm sayin' she was wild, like others do, but she gallivanted around and stayed up late and wouldn't work, which I had to clean out her rooms after she run away."

After the woman had given a telephone number—a neighbor's, not her own—she left the house with a determined step, looking neither this way nor that. Immediately Qwilleran felt a strong desire to revisit the apartment with the devilish pictures. He knew there was an island of Mull off the coast of Scotland, and if the young woman happened to be Scottish, she couldn't be totally reprehensible.

In the garage loft he studied the initials scattered among the daisies and hearts on walls and ceilings: BD, ML, DM, TY, RR, AL, WP, DT, SG, JK, PM, and more. If these were the men in her life, she had been a busy girl. On the other hand, they might be the fabric of fantasy. RR might be a movie star, or a president.

Back at his desk in the library he looked up Mull in the fourteen-page telephone directory, but the name was not listed. Forty-two Goodwinters but no Mulls. He telephoned Penelope.

"Miss Goodwinter, you're right about the servants' quarters. How do I get in touch with your interior designer?"

"Her name is Amanda Goodwinter, and our secretary will ask her to call you for an appointment," the attorney said. "Did you see the announcement of the Klingenschoen Foundation in yesterday's *Picayune?*"

"Yes, and it was very well stated. Have you had any reaction?"

"Everyone is delighted, Mr. Qwilleran! They call it the best news since the K Saloon closed in the 1920s. When my brother returns, we shall explore the ramifications. Meanwhile, have you interviewed any prospective housekeepers?"

"I have, and will you tell your secretary not to send us anymore octogenarians or ailurophobes or cow-sitters? By the way, do you know who painted the graffiti in the servants' quarters?"

"Oh, that atrocity!" Penelope exclaimed. "It was one of those girls from Dimsdale. She was housemaid for a short time."

"What happened to her? Did she get a job painting subway trains?"

"I heard she left town after defacing her apartment," the attorney said briskly. "Speaking of transportation, Mr. Qwilleran, wouldn't you like to replace your little car with something more . . . upscale? Mr. Fitch at the bank will cover the transaction."

"There's nothing wrong with the car I have, Miss Goodwinter. There's no rust on the body, and it's economical to operate."

Qwilleran ended the conversation hurriedly. While Penelope was talking he became aware of unusual noises coming from another part of the house—a miscellany of plopping, pattering, fluttering, swishing, and skittering. He rushed out of the library to track it down.

Beyond the foyer with its majestic staircase there was a vestibule of generous proportions, floored with squares of creamy white marble. Here was the rosewood hall stand with hooks for top hats and derbies, as well as a rack for walking sticks. Here was a marble-topped table with a silver tray for calling cards. And here was the massive front door with its brass handle and escutcheon, its brass doorbell that jangled when one turned a key on the outside, and its brass mail slot.

Through this slot were shooting envelopes of every size and shape, dropping in a pile on the floor. Sitting on the cool marble and watching the process with anticipation were Koko and Yum Yum. Now and then Koko would put forth a paw and scoop a letter from the pile, and Yum Yum would bat it around the slick floor.

As Qwilleran watched, the cascade of envelopes stopped falling, and through the sidelights he could see the mail carrier stepping into her Jeep and driving away.

His first impulse was to call the post office and suggest some other arrangement, but then he observed the pleasure that the event afforded the cats. They jumped into the pile like children in a snowbank, rolling over and skidding and scattering the mail. Nothing so wonderful had ever happened in their young lives! Letters slithered across the marble vestibule and into the parquet foyer, where Yum Yum tried to push them under the Oriental rug. Hiding things was her specialty.

One letter was gripped in Koko's jaw, and he paraded around with an air of importance. It was a pink envelope.

"Here, give me that letter!" Qwilleran commanded.

Koko ran into the dining room with Qwilleran in pursuit. The cat darted in and out of the maze of sixty-four chair legs, and the man chasing and scolding. Eventually Koko tired of the game and dropped the pink envelope at Qwilleran's feet.

It was a letter from the postmistress he had met in Mooseville during his vacation. Beautifully typed, it put to shame his own two-fingered efforts, which had not improved despite twenty-five years of filing news stories. The letter read:

> Dear Qwill,
>   Congratulations on your good fortune! You and the Siamese will be a wonderful addition to Moose County. We hope you will enjoy living up here.
>   Nick and I have some exciting news, too. I'm pregnant at last! He wants me to quit my job because I'm on my feet so much (the doctor says I must be careful), so here's an idea. Could you use a part-time secretary? It would be fun to be a secretary to a real writer.
>   Say hello to Koko and Yum Yum for me.
>   Catfully yours,
>   Lori Bamba

It was obvious what had happened. Koko had selected the pink letter from the pile of mail because it carried the scent of someone he knew. Lori had established a rapport with the cats during their visit in Mooseville; they were entranced by her long golden braids tied with blue ribbons.

In a moment or two Koko appeared with another letter and bounded away when Qwilleran reached for it. Then the chase was on—again.

"You think this is a game," Qwilleran shouted after him, "but it could get to be a bore! I'll start picking up my mail at the post office."

This time the letter was from a former landlady Down Below. One memorable winter Qwilleran had rented an apartment above her antique shop, in an old building that smelled of baked potatoes when the furnace was operating. Koko had recognized the scent of his former residence. The hand-written note read:

> Dear Mr. Qwilleran,
>   Rosie Riker told me about your inheritance, and I'm very happy for you, although we'll all miss your column in the *Daily Fluxion*.
>   Don't drop dead when I tell you I've sold my antique shop! My heart wasn't in the business after my husband

died, so Mrs. Riker is taking over. She's a smart collector, and she'd always wanted to be a dealer.

My son wants me to move to St. Louis, but he's married now, and I might be in the way. Anyway, I got a crazy idea yesterday and stayed awake all night thinking about it. Here goes—

Mrs. Riker says you inherited a big house full of antiques and will need a housekeeper. I can cook pretty well, you remember, and I know how to take care of fine antiques. Also—I have my appraiser's license now and could do some up-to-date appraisals for you—for insurance purposes. I'm serious! I'd love to do it. Let me know what you think.

> Yours truly,
> Iris Cobb

P.S. How are the cats?

Qwilleran's salivary glands went into action as he remembered Mrs. Cobb's succulent pot roasts and nippy macaroni-and-cheese. He remembered other details: cheerful personality—dumpy figure—fabulous coconut cake. She believed in ghosts; she read palms in a flirtatious way; she left a few lumps in her mashed potatoes so they'd taste like the real thing.

He immediately put in a phone call to the urban jungle Down Below. "Mrs. Cobb, your idea sounds great! But Pickax is a very small town. You might find it too quiet after the excitement of Zwinger Street."

Her voice was as cheerful as ever. "At my age I could use a little quiet, Mr. Qwilleran."

"Just the same, you ought to look us over before deciding. I'll buy your plane ticket and meet you at the airport. How's the weather down there?"

"Sweltering!"

Koko had listened to the conversation with a forward tilt to his ears, denoting disapproval. Always protective of Qwilleran's bachelor status, he had resented the landlady's friendly overtures in the past.

"Don't worry, old boy," Qwilleran told him. "It's strictly business. And you'll get some home-cooked food for a change. Now let's open the rest of the mail."

The envelopes scattered about the vestibule included messages of welcome from five churches, three service clubs, and the mayor of Pickax. There were invitations to join the Ittibittiwassee Country Club, the Pickax Historical Society, the Moose County Gourmets, and a bowling league. The administrator of the Pickax Hospital asked Qwilleran to serve on the board of trustees. The superintendent of schools suggested that he teach an adult class in journalism.

Two other letters had been pushed under the rug in the foyer. The Volunteer Firefighters wished to make Qwilleran an honorary member, and the Pickax Singing Society needed a few more male voices.

"There's your chance," he said to the cat. Koko, as he grew older, was developing a more expressive voice with a gamut of clarion yowling, guttural growling, tenor yodeling, and musical yikking.

That afternoon Qwilleran met another Goodwinter. While writing about "beautiful living" for the *Daily Fluxion*, he had met all kinds of interior designers—the talented, the charming, the cosmopolitan, the fashionable, the witty, and the scheming, but Amanda Goodwinter was a new experience.

When he answered the doorbell—after three impatient rings —he found a scowling gray-haired woman in a baggy summer dress and thick-soled shoes, peering over her glasses to examine the paint job on the front door.

"Who painted this door?" she demanded. "They botched it! Should've stripped it down to the wood. I'm Amanda Goodwinter." She clomped into the vestibule without looking at Qwilleran. "So this is the so-called showplace of Pickax! Nobody ever invited me here."

He ventured to introduce himself.

"I know who you are! You don't need to tell me. Penelope says you need help. The foyer's not too bad, but it needs work. What fool put that tapestry on those chairs?" She prowled from room to room, making comments. "Is this the drawing room I've heard about? The draperies have got to go; they're all wrong. . . . The dining room's too dark. Looks like the inside of a tomb."

Qwilleran interrupted politely. "The attorney suggested that you might redecorate the rooms over the garage."

"What!" she screeched. "You expect me to do servants' quarters!"

"As a matter of fact," he said, "I want to use one of the garage apartments myself—as a writing studio—and I'd like it done in good contemporary."

The designer was pacing back and forth in the foyer like a caged lioness. "There's no such thing as *good* contemporary! I didn't do contemporary. I loathe the damn stuff."

Qwilleran cleared his throat diplomatically. "Are there any other designers in town who are competent to work with contemporary?"

"I'm perfectly competent, mister, to work in any style," she snapped.

"I don't want to upset you . . ."

"I'm *not* upset!"

"If you feel uncomfortable with contemporary, I know designers Down Below who will undertake the entire commission, including the mansion itself after the garage apartments are finished."

"Show me the garage," she said with a scowl. "Where is it? How do we get out there?"

He showed her to the rear of the house. As she passed the library she gave a grunt of begrudging approval. She sniffed at the yellow and green breakfast room and called it gaudy. Poking her head into the kitchen, she stared without comment at the top of the refrigerator, where the Siamese were striking sculptural poses on their blue cushion.

In the garage they climbed the stairs to the loft, and Qwilleran pointed out the drab apartment he wanted converted to a studio.

"Hasn't been touched for twenty years," she grumbled. "Plaster's all shot. Needs a lot of work."

"If you think this one needs a lot of work," he said, "wait until you see the other suite."

Amanda gave one look at the daisy extravaganza and groaned. "Don't tell me! Let me guess! It was the Mull girl who did this. What a mess! She came to work here after I let her go."

"Did she work for you?"

"I paid her wages, dammit, but she didn't work! Her art teacher wanted me to take her on. Big mistake. Cute girl, but not a brain in her head. Her scruffy friends were always hanging around the studio, too. Then she got sticky fingers, so I gave her the sack. Those Mulls! Not a one of them ever amounted to anything. . . . Look at this abomination! It'll take three coats to cover it, maybe four."

Koko's tune rang through Qwilleran's mind. *Daisy, Daisy.* "Hold everything," he said. "Forget this apartment for the time being and concentrate on my studio."

"You'll have to come downtown to pick out colors and look at samples," she said irritably.

"Let's make it easy. Just rip out the rugs and furniture and cart the whole shebang to the dump. Then carpet the floor in dark brown, like my shoes."

"Hmmm, you're a casual cuss," the designer said.

"And paint the walls the color of my pants."

"Mojave beige?"

"Whatever you call it. And let's have some of those adjustable blinds with thin slats. After that we'll talk about furniture."

After the designer had stomped down the stairs, mumbling to herself, Qwilleran had another look at the intricate daisy design and regretted the artist had left town. During his career as a crime reporter he had won the confidence of many characters outside the law—or on the borderline—and this girl, with her talent and her questionable reputation, interested him.

Daisy, Daisy. Fingering his moustache in perplexity, he wondered why and how Koko had touched those particular keys on the piano. True, the cat was fascinated by push buttons, switches, and typewriter keys, but this was the first piano Koko had ever seen, and he had played a recognizable tune.

Returning to the house, Qwilleran found something else to ponder. Koko, guarding the house from his post on the grand staircase, was sitting on the third stair. Out of a flight of twenty-one stairs, he always chose the third.

FOUR

No JETS LANDED at the Pickax airport. There was no VIP lounge in the terminal—not even a cigarette machine for nervous passengers. Moose County travelers were grateful to have shelter and a few chairs.

While waiting for Mrs. Cobb's plane, Qwilleran recalled that much of his education about antiques had come from the Cobbs' establishment when he was covering the "junk beat" for the *Daily Fluxion*. What he remembered of the lady herself was a composite of bustling exuberance, plump knees, and two pairs of eyeglasses dangling from ribbons around her neck.

When she stepped off the plane in her travel-weary pink pantsuit, he found her thinner and somewhat subdued, and her glasses had new frames studded with rhinestones.

"Oh, Mr. Qwilleran, how good to see you!" she cried. "What lovely weather you have here! It's suffocating in the city. Isn't this a quaint airport!"

"Everything's quaint in Pickax, Mrs. Cobb. Do you have luggage?"

"Only this carryon. It's all I need for an overnight."

"You're welcome to stay longer, you know."

"Oh, thank you, Mr. Qwilleran, but I have to go back tomorrow to close the deal with Mrs. Riker. She's going to live in your old apartment over the shop."

"*She* is going to live there?" Qwilleran repeated. "What about her husband? What about their house in the suburbs?"

"Didn't you know? She's getting a divorce."

"I had lunch with Arch a few days ago, and he didn't say a word about it . . . but I remember he looked troubled. I wonder what happened."

"I'll let him tell you the story," Mrs. Cobb said, and she pursed her lips with finality.

On a relentlessly straight highway they drove across the lonely landscape of Moose County—through evergreen forests and rockbound wasteland, past abandoned mines and unnatural hillocks that had once been slag heaps.

"Very rocky," Mrs. Cobb observed.

"Pickax is built almost entirely of stone," said Qwilleran.

"Is it really? Tell me about your house. Is it sumptuous?"

"It's a big chunk of fieldstone three stories high. I call it Alcatraz Provincial," he began. "All the rooms are huge. The foyer would make a good roller rink if we took up the Oriental rugs. . . . Every bedroom has a canopied bed and its own sitting room, dressing room, and bath. . . . There's an English pub in the basement, and the top floor was supposed to be a ballroom, but it was never finished. . . . The kitchen is so big you have to walk a mile to prepare a meal. It includes a butler's pantry, a food storage room, a laundry, a half bath, and a walk-in broom closet. The whole service area, as well as the solarium, is floored in square tiles of red quarry stone."

"Any ghosts?" Mrs. Cobb asked with some of the old twinkle in her eyes. "Every old house should have a ghost. Maybe you remember the one we had on Zwinger Street. She never materialized, but she moved things around in the middle of the night. She was very prankish."

"I remember her very well," Qwilleran said. "She put salt shakers in your bedroom slippers." He also remembered that her ghostly pranks were an ongoing practical joke that C. C. Cobb had played on his gullible wife.

"How's Koko?" she asked.

"He's fine. He's taking piano lessons."

"Oh, Mr. Qwilleran," she laughed. "I never know whether to believe what you say."

They approached Pickax via Goodwinter Boulevard, lined with the stately stone houses that wealthy mining pioneers had built in the heyday of the city. Then came Main Street, the circular park, and the majestic K mansion.

Mrs. Cobb gave a little scream. "Is this it? Oh! Oh! I want the job!"

"You don't know how much it pays," Qwilleran said. "Neither do I."

"I don't care. I want the job."

When they entered the foyer, the amber walls were glowing and the brass-and-crystal chandelier was sparkling. The furnishing looked almost self-consciously pedigreed.

"Why, it's like a museum!"

"It's a little rich for my taste," Qwilleran admitted, "but everything is the real thing, and I have respect for it."

"I could do a real museum catalogue for you. That rosewood-and-ormolu console is Louis XV, and I'll bet it's a signed piece. The clock is a Burnap—brass works, moonphase, late eighteenth."

"Are you ready for the dining room?" Qwilleran switched on the twenty-four electric candles mounted on two staghorn chandeliers. It was a dark room, richly paneled, and the furniture was massive.

"Linenfold paneling!" Mrs. Cobb gasped. "Austrian chandeliers! The furniture is German, of course."

"That's the original furniture," Qwilleran said, "before the Klingenschoens became serious collectors and switched to French and English."

When they crossed the foyer to the drawing room, she stared in awed silence. Chandeliers festooned with crystal were ablaze in the afternoon sun. Mellowed with age, the red walls made a handsome background for oil paintings in extravagant frames: French landscapes, Italian saints, English noblemen, and one full-length, life-size portrait of an 1880 beauty with bustle and parasol. On the far wall a collection of Chinese porcelains filled the shelves in two lofty arched niches.

"I think I'm going to faint," Mrs. Cobb said.

"You should rest for a while," Qwilleran suggested. "There

are four suites upstairs, each done in a different period. I'll bring your overnight bag up to the French suite in a few minutes."

While she climbed the stairs in a daze, he dashed off a note to his friend Down Below.

> Dear Arch,
>   Mrs. Cobb just broke the bad news. I don't need to tell you how terrible I feel about it. Why don't you take a week off and fly up here? It'll be a change of scene, and we can talk.
>
>   Qwill

He was addressing the envelope when he heard cries of alarm upstairs. "What are they doing? *What are they doing?*"

Mrs. Cobb came rushing down the stairs, babbling incoherently, and he ran to meet her.

"That truck in the back drive!" she cried. "I looked out the window. They're stealing things from the garage. Stop them! Stop them!"

"Don't get excited, Mrs. Cobb," Qwilleran said. "This isn't Zwinger Street. Those are porters from the design studio, cleaning out the junk before we redecorate."

"It's not junk! Stop them!"

They both hurried to the garage, where a truck was being loaded with rolled rugs, an old mattress, and odds and ends of furniture.

"That's a Hunzinger!" Mrs. Cobb shouted, pointing to an odd-looking folding chair. "And that's a real Shaker rocker!" She rushed about—from an early trestle table to a Connecticut dower chest to a Pennsylvania German *schrank*.

Qwilleran stopped the porters. "Take it all back except the mattress. Put everything in one of the garage stalls until we can sort it out."

Mrs. Cobb was weak with shock and excitement. "What a narrow escape," she said, over a cup of tea. "You know, there was a period when Americana wasn't appreciated. These people must have moved their heirlooms to the garage when they bought their French and English antiques. It's strange that your decorator didn't recognize their current value."

Maybe she did, Qwilleran thought.

Later in the afternoon he conducted the prospective house-keeper on a walking tour of downtown Pickax. "How do you like the French suite?" he asked.

"I've never seen anything so grand! There's a Norman bonnet-top armoire that must be early eighteenth century!" Hesitantly she added, "If I come to work here, would you mind if I did a few appraisals for other people on the side?"

"Not at all. You can even open a tearoom in the basement and tell fortunes."

"Oh, Mr. Qwilleran, you're such a joker."

Downtown Pickax was a panorama of imitation Scottish castles, Spanish fortresses, and Cotswold cottages. "All real stone," he pointed out, "but somehow it looks fake, like a bad movie set."

They passed Amanda's studio (pure Dickens) and the offices of the *Pickax Picayune* (early monastery). Then he steered her into the office (Heidelberg influence) of Goodwinter & Goodwinter.

The junior partner was conferring with a client but consented to step out of her private office for a moment.

Qwilleran said, "I want to introduce Iris Cobb. I've convinced her to move up here from Down Below and manage our household. Mrs. Cobb, this is Penelope Goodwinter, attorney for the estate."

"Pleased to meet you," said the housekeeper, extending her hand. Penelope, glancing at the rhinestone-studded glasses, was a fraction of a second slow in shaking hands and saying, "How nice."

Qwilleran went on. "Mrs. Cobb is not only experienced in household management, but she's a licensed appraiser and will catalogue the collection for us."

His former landlady beamed, and Penelope said, "Oh really? We must discuss salary, of course. When do you wish to start your employment, Mrs. Cobb?"

'Well, I'm flying home tomorrow, and I'll drive up here in my van as soon as I pack my reference books."

"I suggest," the attorney said, "that you defer your arrival until your apartment is redecorated. At present it's in deplorable condition."

"No problem," Qwilleran interjected. "Mrs. Cobb will have

the French suite in the house. I plan to fix up the garage apartment for myself."

The attorney's reaction started with shock, faded into disapproval, and recovered enough to muster a half smile. "I hope you will both be comfortable. Let us talk about terms and contracts tomorrow."

"I'm taking Mrs. Cobb to dinner at the Old Stone Mill tonight," Qwilleran said. "Would you care to join us?"

"Thank you. Thank you so much, but I have a previous engagement. And now . . . if you will excuse me . . ."

"Oh my!" Mrs. Cobb said afterward. "She's a very smart dresser, isn't she? I didn't know they had clothes like that in Pickax."

Qwilleran reported the incident to Melinda Goodwinter after putting the housekeeper on the plane the next day. The young doctor with green eyes and long eyelashes telephoned to invite him to dinner.

"My treat," she said. "I'd like to take you to Otto's Tasty Eats."

"Never heard of it. How's the food?"

"Ghastly, but there's lot of it. It's a family restaurant—no liquor—and you can sit in the smoking section or the screaming section, depending on whether you want to ruin your lungs or your eardrums."

"You make the invitation irresistible, Melinda."

"To tell the truth, I have an ulterior motive. I want to see your house. I've never seen the interior. The Klingenschoens and the Goodwinters weren't on the same wavelength socially. Could you meet me at Otto's at six-fifteen? I'll reserve a booth."

At the appointed hour Qwilleran was wedging his green economy-model car into the crowded parking lot when Melinda pulled up in a silver convertible.

"When are you going to buy a gold-plated Rolls?" she greeted him.

"Do I look like a sheikh? Don't let the moustache mislead you."

"You really made a hit when you proposed giving away your money," she said. "There's a rumor that Pickax will be renamed Qwillville. All the women in Moose County will be chasing you, but remember—I found you first."

Otto's Tasty Eats occupied a former warehouse in the industrial area of Pickax. The wrinkled carpet suggested old army blankets. Long institutional tables—at least an acre of them— were covered with sheets of stiff white paper. Lights glared. Noise reverberated. Customers flocked in by the hundreds.

In the center of the room was a veritable shrine to gluttony: twelve-gallon crocks of watery soup, bushels of torn iceberg lettuce, mountains of fried chicken and fried fish, tubs of reconstituted mashed potatoes, and a dessert table that was a sea of white froth masquerading as whipped cream.

"Do you come here often?" Qwilleran asked.

"Only when I entertain supercilious urban types."

Overstuffed diners were making three or four trips to the buffet, but Melinda insisted on ordering from the menu and having table service.

"I don't imagine," Qwilleran said, "that your cousins from the law office are frequent diners at Otto's Tasty Eats." He described the meeting between the attorney and Mrs. Cobb. "Penelope was a trifle perturbed when I told her the housekeeper would occupy the French suite and I'd live over the garage."

Melinda's green eyes brimmed with merriment. "She probably went into shock. She and Alex are the last of the hard-line Goodwinter snobs. They consider themselves the superior branch of the family. Did you know that Penny is the one with brains? Alex is just a tiresome bore with an inflated ego, and yet she defers to him as if he were the mastermind."

"He's a good-looking guy. Is he involved in politics? He seems to go to Washington a lot."

"Well, it's like this," Melinda explained. "There's a lot of Old Money in Moose County, and Alex steers campaign donations to friendly pols. He loves the importance it gives him in the Capitol and at Washington parties. Have you met any other Goodwinters?"

"Junior at the newspaper, for one. He's a bright kid, and he majored in journalism, but he's wasted at the *Picayune*. It looks like an antebellum weekly. I told him he's got to get the classified ads off the front page."

"I hear that cousin Amanda is going to redecorate your garage apartment. Did she kick you in the shins or just call you a twelve-letter word?"

"I don't understand how that woman stays in business. She has the personality of a hedgehog."

"She has a captive clientele. There's no other decorator within four hundred miles."

They could talk freely. Their booth was an island of privacy in a maelstrom of ear-splitting noise. The animated conversation of happy diners and the excited shrieks of children bounced off the steel girders and concrete walls, and the din was augmented by the Tasty Eats custom of pounding the table with knife handles to express satisfaction with the food.

The waiter was deferential. Melinda was not only a Goodwinter; she was a doctor. He brought a lighted candle to the table—a red stub in a smoky glass left over from Christmas. He persuaded the kitchen to *broil* two orders of pickerel *without breading*, and he found a few robust leaves of spinach to add to the sickly salad greens.

Qwilleran said to Melinda, "We've been here for five generations. My great-great-grandfather was an engineer and surveyor. His four sons made fortunes in the mines. Most speculators grabbed their money and went to live abroad, so their daughters could marry titles, but the Goodwinters stayed here, always in business or the professions."

"Too bad none of them ever opened a good restaurant. Are there any black sheep in the family?"

"Occasionally, but they're always persuaded to move to Mexico or change their name."

"Change it to Mull, I suppose."

Melinda gave him an inquiring glance. "You've heard about the Mulls? That's an unfortunate social problem. They worked in the mines a hundred years ago, and their descendants have lived on public assistance for the last three generations. They lack motivation—drop out of school—can't find jobs."

"Where did they emigrate from originally?"

"I don't know, but they were miners when the pay was a dollar and a half a day. They worked with *candles* in their caps and had to buy their own candles from the company store. The miners were exploited by the companies and by the saloons. You can read about it in the public library."

"Did any of the Mulls ever break out of the rut?"

"The young ones often leave town, and no one ever hears

about them again—or cares. There's a lot of poverty and unemployment here. Also a lot of inherited wealth. Have you noticed the cashmeres at Scottie's Men's Store and the rocks at Diamond Jim's Jewelry? Moose County also has more private planes per capita than any other county in the state."

"What are they used for?"

"Mostly convenience. Commercial airlines have to route passengers in roundabout ways through hub cities. My dad flew his own plane before he became diabetic. Alex Goodwinter has a plane. The Lanspeaks have two—his and hers."

Melinda bribed the waiter to find some fresh fruit for dessert, and after coffee Qwilleran said, "Let's go to my place. I'd like to show you my graffiti."

Melinda brightened, and she batted her long lashes. "The evening begins to show promise."

They drove both cars to the K mansion, and she asked if she might park the silver convertible in the garage. "It would be recognized in the driveway," she explained, "and people would talk."

"Melinda, haven't you heard? This is the last quarter of the twentieth century."

"Yes, but this is Pickax," she said with raised eyebrows. "Sorry."

When Qwilleran escorted his guest upstairs to the servants' quarters, she walked into the jungle of daisies in a state of bedazzlement. "Ye gods! This is stupendous! Who did it?"

"A former housemaid. One of the Mulls. Worked for Amanda before she came here."

"Oh, *that one!* I guess she was a one-woman disaster at the studio. Amanda fired her for pilfering."

"After doing these murals she left town," Qwilleran said. "I hope she found a way to use her talent."

"It's really fantastic! It's hard to believe it was done by Daisy Mull."

"Daisy?" Qwilleran echoed in astonishment. "Did you say *Daisy* Mull?"

A melody ran through his mind, and he wondered if he should mention it. Previously he had hinted to Melinda about Koko's extrasensory perception, but a piano-playing cat seemed too radical a concept to share even with a broad-minded M.D.

"You've never met Koko and Yum Yum," he said. "Let's go over to the house."

When he conducted his guest into the amber-toned foyer, she gazed in wonder. "I had no idea the Klingenschoens owned such fabulous things!"

"Penelope knew. Didn't she ever tell you?"

"Penelope would consider it gossip."

"The rosewood-and-ormolu console is Louis XV," Qwilleran mentioned with authority. "The clock is Burnap. Koko is usually sitting on the staircase to screen arriving visitors, but this is his night off."

Melinda commented on everything. The sculptured plaster ceilings looked like icing on a wedding cake. The life-size marble figures of Adam and Eve in the solarium had a posture defect caused by a calcium deficiency, she said. The Staffordshire dogs in the breakfast rooms were good examples of concomitant convergent strabismus.

"Want to see the service area?" Qwilleran asked. "The cats often hang out in the kitchen."

Yum Yum was lounging on her blue cushion on top of the refrigerator, and Melinda stroked her fur adoringly. "Softer than ermine," she said.

Koko was conspicuously absent, however.

"He could be upstairs, sleeping in the middle of a ten-thousand-dollar four-poster-bed," Qwilleran said. "He has fine taste. Let's go up and see."

While he hunted for the cat, Melinda inspected the suites furnished in French, Biedermeier, Empire, and Chippendale. Koko was not to be found.

Qwilleran was beginning to show his nervousness. "I don't know where he can be. Let's check the library. He likes to sleep on the bookshelves."

He ran downstairs, followed by Melinda, but there was no sign of the cat in any of his favorite places—not behind the biographies, not between the volumes of Shakespeare, not on top of the atlas.

"Then he's got to be in the basement."

The English pub had been imported from London, paneling

and all, and it was a gloomy subterranean hideaway. They turned on all the lights and searched the bar, the backbar, and the shadows.

No Koko!

FIVE

FRANTICALLY QWILLERAN SCOURED the premises for the missing Koko, with Melinda tagging along and offering encouragement.

"He'll be in one of four places," he told her. "A soft surface, or a warm spot, or a high perch, or inside something."

None of these locations produced anything resembling a cat. Calling his name repeatedly, they peered under sofas and beds, behind armoires and bookcases, and into drawers, cupboards, and closets.

Qwilleran dashed about with increasing alarm, looking in the refrigerator, the oven, the washer, the dryer, then the oven again.

"Slow down, Qwill. You're stressing." Melinda put a hand on his arm. "We'll find him. He's around here somewhere. You know how cats are."

"He's got to be in the house . . . unless . . . you know, the back door can't be locked. Someone could come in and snatch him. Or he might have eaten something poisonous and crawled away in a corner."

Melinda, wandering in aimless search, stepped into the back entry and called, "What's this stairway? Where does it go?"

"What stairway? I never noticed any stairway back there."

Hidden by the broom closet and closed off by a door that

latched poorly, it was the servants' stairs to the second floor—a narrow flight with rubberized treads. Qwilleran bounded to the top, followed by Melinda, and they emerged in a hallway with a series of doors. Two doors stood ajar. One opened into a walk-in linen closet. The second gave access to another flight of ascending stairs, wide but unfinished and dusty. "The attic!" Qwilleran exclaimed. "It was supposed to be a ballroom. Never finished." Flipping wall switches, he scrambled to the top, sneezing. Melinda ventured up the stairs cautiously, shielding her mouth and nose with her hand.

The staircase ended in a large storage room illuminated faintly by fading daylight through evenly spaced windows and by eight low-wattage light bulbs dangling from the ceiling.

Qwilleran called the cat's name, but there was no answer. "If he's up here, how will we find him among all this junk?"

The space was littered with boxes, trunks, cast-off furniture, framed pictures, rolls of carpet, and stacks of old *National Geographics*.

"He could be asleep, or sick, or worse," he said.

"Could we lure him out with a treat?" Melinda suggested.

"There's a can of lobster in the food pantry. Open it and bring it up."

When she had run downstairs, Qwilleran stood still and listened. The floorboards had stopped creaking. The hum of traffic on Main Street seemed far away. He held his breath. He could hear a familiar sound. What was it? He strained to listen. It was scratching—the whisper of claws gliding over a smooth surface. He followed the sound noiselessly.

There, in a far corner of the attic, stood a large carton, and Koko was on top of it with his hind end elevated and his front assembly stretched forward as he scratched industriously.

"Koko! What are you doing up here?" Qwilleran demanded in the consternation that followed his unnecessary panic. Then a prickling sensation on his upper lip caused him to investigate the scene of the action. A corrugated carton that had once contained a shipment of paper towels was tied with twine and labeled with a tag on which was a name in excellent handwriting: Daisy Mull.

By the time Melinda returned with the lobster, Qwilleran had untied the carton and was tossing out articles of clothing. "This is astonishing!" he shouted over his shoulder. "There's something important about this box, or Koko wouldn't have found it."

Out of the carton came a musty-smelling jacket of fake fur in black and white stripes unknown to any animal species, along with a woolly stocking hat that had once been white and a pair of high red boots with ratty fur trim. There were faded flannel shirts, well-worn jeans, two maid's uniforms, and a sweatshirt printed with the message: TRY ME. A small item wrapped in a wad of newspaper proved to be an ivory elephant with Amanda's studio label on the bottom of the teakwood base.

Qwilleran said, "Obviously she went south when she cleared out—to some climate where she wouldn't need winter clothing. Probably California. Dreamers always head for California, don't they? And she left her uniforms behind, so she didn't plan a career as a domestic."

"But why would she leave the elephant? If she liked it enough to steal it, wouldn't she like it enough to take it along? You can tell it's valuable."

"Smart question," Qwilleran said as he piled the clothing back into the carton. "You take the elephant; I'll carry Koko—if I can find him. Where did he go?"

Having finished the can of lobster, the cat was cleaning his mask, whiskers, ears, paws, chest, underside, and tail.

"Either he was trying to tell us something about Daisy Mull," Qwilleran said, "or he thought of a sneaky way to get an extra meal."

The three of them returned to the main floor, carefully closing the door to the attic stairs. It immediately popped open.

"That's typical of old buildings," Qwilleran complained. "The doors never fit properly. There are too many places for an inquisitive animal to get lost."

"He wasn't lost," Melinda said with a smug smile. "It's simply that you couldn't find him."

"For that astute observation you'll be rewarded with a nightcap. Would you like Scotch, bourbon, white grape juice, a split of champagne? I also have beer, in case Penelope's maintenance man ever shows up to fix the doors."

"What are you drinking?"

"Club soda with a twist."

"I'll have a split."

Qwilleran carried the tray of drinks into the library and slipped the ivory elephant into a desk drawer. "Would you enjoy some music? There's a prehistoric stereo here, and an odd assortment of records that you could use for paving a patio. This house came equipped with seven television sets, and I'd like to trade in six of them for a new music system."

"Don't you like TV?"

"I'm a print man. The printed word does more for me than the small screen."

After some grinding and humming and a loud *clunk* the record changer produced some romantic zither music, and they sat on the blood red leather sofa that Qwilleran had recently shared with Penelope Goodwinter, but there was no briefcase between them and considerably less space.

He said, "Koko has an uncanny talent for finding objects of significance. I don't usually mention it because the average person wouldn't believe it, but I feel I can confide in you."

"Any time," Melinda said with an agreeable inflection in her voice.

"It's good to have a confidante." His mournful eyes met her inviting green gaze and the world stood still, but the magic moment was interrupted by a simulated catfight in the foyer. Qwilleran huffed into his moustache, and Melinda sipped her champagne and looked at the three walls of bookshelves.

"Nice library," she said.

"Yes. Good bindings."

"Mostly classics, I suppose."

"It appears so."

"Did the Klingenschoens read these?"

"I doubt it . . . Melinda, did you ever see Daisy Mull? What did she look like?"

"Hmmm . . . tiny . . . reddish hair . . . pouty mouth. Daisy was quite visible in Pickax. She and her girlfriend used to stand outside the music store and giggle when cars tooted their horns. Her clothes were flashey by Pickax standards, but that was a few years ago. Things have changed. Today even the middle-aged women in Pickax have given up lavender sweater sets and basket bags."

Qwilleran draped an arm over the back of the sofa, musing

that a firm, shiny, slippery upholstery left something to be desired. A loungy, down-filled, velvety sofa would be more seductive; at least, that had been his experience in the past.

"Why did you name your cats Koko and Yum Yum?" Melinda asked. "Are you a Savoyard?"

"Not especially, although I like Gilbert and Sullivan, and in college I sang in *The Mikado*."

"You're an interesting man, Qwill. You've lived everywhere and done everything."

He groomed his moustache self-consciously. "It helps if you've been around as long as I have. You've always dated young squirts from medical school."

"Not true! I'm always attracted to older men. Eyelids with a middle-aged droop turn me on."

He leaned closer to add champagne to her glass. There was a sense of pleasurable propinquity, and then the tall case clock started to bong eleven times and Koko walked into the library. Walking with a stiff-legged gait and tail at attention, he looked at the pair on the sofa and uttered an imperious "YOW!"

"Hello, Koko," Melinda replied. "Are you and I going to be friends?"

Without a reply he turned and left the scene, and a moment later they heard another insistent howl.

"Something's wrong," Qwilleran said. "Excuse me." He followed the cat and found him in the vestibule, staring at the front door.

"Sorry, Koko. Wrong time of day. The mail comes in the afternoon."

Returning to the library, Qwilleran explained the cats' obsession with the mail slot. Casually he was maneuvering to resume the intimate mood that had been interrupted, when Koko stalked into the room a second time. Looking sternly at Melinda, he said, "nyik nyik nyik YOW!" And again he marched to the front door.

"Does he want to go out?"

"No, he's an indoor cat."

"He has a noble face, hasn't he?" She glanced at her watch.

"Siamese are a noble breed."

The third time Koko made his entrance, scolding and glaring at the guest, she said, "He's trying to tell me something." She jumped up and trailed after the determined animal, who plodded resolutely toward the front of the house, stopping at intervals and looking back to be sure she was following. In the vestibule he stared pointedly at the door handle.

"Qwill, I believe he's telling me to go home."

"This is embarrassing, Melinda."

"That's okay. I have the early shift at the clinic tomorrow."

"My apology! He likes the lights turned out at eleven. Next time we'll lock him up somewhere."

"Next time," she corrected him, "we'll go to my place—if you don't mind sitting on the floor. I don't have any furniture yet. Only a bed," she added with a sidelong glance.

"How soon is next time?"

"After the medical conference. When I come back from Paris I'm leaving the Mooseville clinic. I'm tired of taking fishhooks out of tourists' backsides."

"What do you plan to do?"

"Join my father's office in Pickax."

"I'll be your first patient. Can you check cholesterol, heart, and all that?"

"You'll be surprised what I can do!" She threw him another of her provocative green-eyed glances.

Qwilleran escorted Melinda to her silver convertible parked discreetly in the garage—not a bad idea, as it turned out.

When she finally drove away, he walked back to the house with a buoyant step and found Koko waiting for him with a smug look of accomplishment.

"You're not as smart as you think you are," Qwilleran said to him, preening his moustache with satisfaction.

Early the next morning he walked downtown to Amanda's studio to order a sofa. The crotchety designer was out on a house call, but a friendly young assistant produced some catalogues of contemporary furniture. Within five minutes Qwilleran had ordered a slouchy sofa in rust-colored suede, a brown lounge chair and ottoman, and some reading lamps—for his new studio.

"You have good taste," the assistant said, "and I've never seen a client make such speedy decisions. I'd love to see your carriage house when it's finished."

"And what is your name?" he asked.

"Francesca Brodie. My father knows you—by reputation, that is. He's the police chief. Aren't you sort of a detective?"

"I like to solve puzzles, that's all," Qwilleran said. "Did you ever know a Daisy Mull who worked here?"

"No, I've only been here four months."

For the next two days Qwilleran spent most of his time answering the letters that came shooting through the mail slot in great number, much to the delight of the Siamese. Koko personally delivered an envelope addressed in red ink, and he was not surprised that it came from a building in which they had recently lived. The letter was written by another tenant, a young woman who used to speak French to Koko and who was subject to problems with weight and problems with men. She wrote:

> Dear Qwill,
>   Arch Riker gave me your address. Congratulations on striking oil! We miss you.
>   Want to hear my good news? I'm dating a chef now, and he's not married—or so he says. The bad news is that I've gained ten pounds. I'm still hacking copy at the ad agency, but I'd kill to get into the restaurant business. If you'd like to open a restaurant in Pickax, let me know. Have chef; will travel. Say bonjour to Koko.
>   Hixie Rice

Other letters arrived faster than Qwilleran could poke out answers on his old typewriter. The telephone rang constantly. And there were other interruptions, as when a young man in white coveralls suddenly appeared at the door of the library, carrying a six-pack of diet cola.

"Hi!" he said. "Mind if I put this in your fridge? This is a big job. Lots of spackling and patching and scraping, and some of the woodwork's bleeding."

He had the wholesome look of a Moose County native, raised on bushels of apples, milk right from the cow, vegetables from the garden, and unlimited fresh air.

"I assume you're a painter employed by Amanda Goodwinter," Qwilleran said.

"Yeah, I'm Steve. She's always telling people I'm slow, but I do good work. My grandfather worked on this house when the Old

Lady was alive. He showed me how to paint without laps or drips or sags or pimples. Hey, do you really live in this joint? I live in a mobile home on my father-in-law's farm."

There were other reasons for Qwilleran's discontent. Mrs. Cobb had not arrived. There was no sign of anyone to fix the doors. Melinda had left for Paris. And an exasperating melody kept running through his mind: *Daisy, Daisy.*

Then a schoolteacher he had met in Mooseville telephoned and said, "Hi, Qwill, this is Roger. How does it feel to be filthy rich?"

"Arduous, frustrating, and annoying—so far. But give me another week to get used to it. How's everything at the lake?"

"Oh, you know . . . lots of tourists and happy merchants."

"Is business good at your wife's shop?"

"Not bad, but she puts in long hours. Say, want to meet me for dinner somewhere tonight? Sharon's working late."

"Sure. Why don't you drive down here to the Bastille?" Qwilleran suggested. "I'll give you a conducted tour of the dungeons and pour you a drink. Then we can find a restaurant."

"Great! I'd like to see inside that rockpile. We can eat at the Hotel Booze."

"That's a new one to me."

"Oldest flophouse in the county. They have a twelve-ounce bacon cheeseburger with fries that's the greatest!"

Roger MacGillivray, whose Scottish name appealed to Qwilleran, arrived in the early evening. He was a young man with a clipped black beard and vigorous opinions, and he exclaimed about the size of the rooms, the number of the windows, the height of the ceilings, and the extent of the property. "It'll cost an arm and a leg to maintain this place," he predicted. "Who's going to clean all those windows and dust all those books?"

"The landscape service alone costs more than I earned at the *Daily Fluxion*," Qwilleran informed him. "There's always a green truck in the driveway and a guy in a green jumpsuit riding around on a little green tractor."

He poured Scotch for his guest and white grape juice for himself, and they sat in the big wicker chairs in the solarium.

Roger stared at Qwilleran's stemmed glass. "What are you drinking?"

"Catawba grape juice. Koko likes it, so I bought a case of it."

"You really pamper that animal." Roger glanced around apprehensively. "Where is he? I'm not comfortable with cats."

Koko, hearing his name, sauntered into the solarium and positioned himself in Roger's view.

"He won't bother you," Qwilleran said. "He enjoys listening to our conversation, that's all. He likes the tone of your voice."

Koko moved a little closer.

"Who looks after these rubber plants, Qwill? They look healthier than I do."

"The green jumpsuit comes in and sticks a meter in the soil and takes a reading," Qwilleran said. "The whole horticultural scene is too esoteric for me. I've spent all my life in apartments and hotels."

"I think your gardener is Devin Doone, a former student of mine. He goes to Princeton now and does gardening during summer vacation. You've got a pretty good-sized lot."

"Half a block wide and half a mile long, I estimate. There's an orchard back there and an old barn that would make a good summer theater."

Roger gripped the arms of his chair. "Why is he looking at me like that?"

"Koko wants to be friends. Say something to him."

"Hello, Koko," Roger said in a weak voice.

The cat blinked his eyes shut and emitted a squeaky, non-threatening "ik ik ik."

"He's smiling," Qwilleran said. "He likes you. . . . How's your mother-in-law, Roger?"

"She's fine. She's gung ho about a new craft project now—designing things with a Moose County theme, for Sharon to sell in her shop. Pot holders and toys and stuff. The idea is to have the Dimsdale women make them by hand—sort of a cottage industry. She wanted to get a grant from the state, but there was too much red tape. Besides that, the people in Dimsdale don't want to work. Do you know that place?"

"I've seen the remains of the Dimsdale Mine," Qwilleran said, "and I've eaten at the decrepit diner at the intersection, but I thought it was mainly a ghost town."

"Officially Dimsdale doesn't exist, but there's a bunch of shanties back in the woods—squatters, you know. In fact, I think they're on Klingenschoen property, your property. You'd never believe it, Qwill, but a hundred years ago Dimsdale was a thriving town with hotels, a sawmill, housing for miners, stores, even a doctor."

"You know a lot about local history, Roger."

"I ought to! That's what I teach. . . . Say, he's a good-looking animal, isn't he? Very well behaved."

"His real name is Kao K'o Kung. He was named after a thirteenth-century Chinese artist."

Knowing he was the topic of conversation, Koko casually ambled over to Roger's chairside.

"If you've never stroked a Siamese," Qwilleran said, "You don't know what fur is all about."

Cautiously Roger extended a hand and patted the silky fawn-colored back. "Good boy!" he said. "Good boy!"

The cat looked at Qwilleran, slowly closing one eye, and Qwilleran thought, Score another one for Koko.

The two men finished their drinks and then drove from the palatial splendor of the K mansion to the stolid ugliness of the Hotel Booze. It was a stone building three stories high, with the plain shoebox architecture typical of hotels in pioneer towns. A sign, almost as big as the hotel itself, advertised booze, rooms, and food.

"In this hotel," Roger said, "a miner could get a man-sized dinner and a bed on the floor for a quarter, using his boots for a pillow, or a sack of oats if he was lucky."

The dim lighting in the dining room camouflaged the dreary walls and ancient linoleum floor and worn plastic tables. Nevertheless, the room hummed with the talk of customers wearing feed caps and wolfing down burgers and beer.

Qwilleran tried three chairs before finding one with all its legs and rungs. "I've have the Cholesterol Special," he told the waitress, a homey-looking woman in a faded housedress.

"Make it two, Thelma," said Roger.

The sandwich proved to be so enormous that she served it with her thumb on top of the bun to hold it all together.

"We call her Thumbprint Thelma," Roger whispered.

Qwilleran had to admit that the burger was superior and the fries tasted like actual potatoes. "Okay, Roger, how about a history lesson to take my mind off the calories? Tell me about the abandoned mines around here."

"There were ten of them in the old days—all major operations. Shafts went a thousand feet deep, and the miners had to climb down on a *ladder!* After a long day underground, with water dripping all around, it took half an hour to climb back up to the surface."

"Like climbing a hundred-story building! They must have been desperate for work."

"Most of them came from Europe—left their families behind —and hoped to send money home. But—what with payday binges at the saloon and buying on credit at the company store— they were always in hock."

Thelma brought coffee, and Roger—without much difficulty —persuaded Qwilleran to try the wild thimbleberry pie.

"Picked the berries myself this morning," the waitress said.

The men savored each forkful in the reverent silence that the pie merited and ordered second cups of coffee.

Qwilleran said, "I suppose the old saloons had gambling in the back room and girls upstairs."

"Right! And a bizarre sense of fun. When a customer drank too much and passed out, his pals carried him outside and nailed his boots to the wooden sidewalk. And there was always an old soak hanging around the saloon who would do anything for a drink. One of these characters used to eat poison ivy. Another would bite the head off a live chipmunk."

"This isn't the best dinner-table conversation I've ever heard, Roger."

"I'm telling it like it was! The K Saloon was notorious."

"Is that what you teach in your history classes?"

"Well, it grabs their attention. The kids eat it up!"

Qwilleran was silent for a moment before he asked, "Did you ever have a student by the name of Daisy Mull?"

"No, she dropped out before I started teaching, but my mother-in-law had her in art class. She said Daisy was the only Mull who would ever amount to anything—if she applied herself. She was kind of goofy."

Qwilleran told him about the graffiti—then about his plans for a studio over the garage—and then about his search for a housekeeper.

"How do you figure you'll adjust to a live-in housekeeper?"

Roger asked him. "I suppose it's like having a wife, without the fringe benefits."

"Speak for yourself, Roger."

"Are you getting along okay with G&G?"

"So far, so good. Penelope is the one handling the estate. I haven't figured her out yet."

"She's the bright one in the family. What do you think of her brother?"

"Alexander hasn't been around much. He's gone to Washington again."

Roger lowered his voice. "There's a rumor he's got a woman down there. If he's serious, it's big news. Alex has always been a confirmed bachelor."

"Is Penelope involved with anyone?"

"Why? Are you interested?"

"No thanks. I've got all I can handle at the moment."

"She never bothers with guys," Roger said. "Strictly careerist. Too bad. She's really got it together."

Qwilleran picked up the check and paid the cashier on the way out. She was a large woman in a patterned muumuu splashed with oversize black-eyed Susans. Qwilleran found himself whistling *Daisy, Daisy.*

Instantly the hubbub in the dining room dissolved into silence, and the cashier wagged a finger at Qwilleran. "That's a no-no." She pointed to a sign over the cash register: *No credit. No checks. No spitting. No whistling.*

"Sorry," Qwilleran said.

"It's bad luck," Roger explained. "It used to be considered unlucky to whistle in the mines, and the superstition stuck. There's no whistling in Pickax—by city ordinance."

SIX

He had never been much of a whistler, but as soon as Qwilleran learned that whistling was forbidden in Pickax he felt a compulsion to whistle. As he prepared the cats' breakfast he whistled an air from *The Mikado,* causing Koko to twist his ears inside out and run into the back entry hall. Yum Yum went slinking into the laundry room and crouched behind their commode.

The cats' commode was an oval roasting pan containing a layer of kitty gravel—an unorthodox but substantial piece of equipment that worked well. Their water dish was an Imari porcelain bowl that Qwilleran had found in the butler's pantry. Their food he arranged on a porcelain dinner plate with a wide blue and gold border—appropriate because the border matched the ineffable blue of Yum Yum's eyes, and because the gold-embellished crest bore a *K.*

Qwilleran put a plate of canned red salmon on the floor in the laundry room and called the cats. Yum Yum reported immediately, but there was no response from Koko.

"Drat him! He's gone up to the attic again," Qwilleran muttered. It was true. The door to the attic stairs stood ajar, and Koko was on the third floor, sharpening his claws on a roll of carpet.

Qwilleran made a lunge for him, but the cat eluded his grasp and bounded to the top of an Art Nouveau chifforobe, where he assumed a challenging posture. Then it was an insane chase around the dusty storeroom—Koko streaking over a General Grant bed, under a bowlegged Chinese table, around a barricade of steamer trunks, with Qwilleran breathing heavily in stubborn pursuit.

Koko finally allowed himself to be caught, while crouching defiantly on a cheap cardboard suitcase patterned to resemble tweed. Qwilleran's moustache sent him a signal: another item of significance! He grabbed an unprotesting cat in one hand and the suitcase in the other and descended to the kitchen, where Yum Yum was washing up after finishing the whole can of salmon.

Attached to the broken handle of the luggage there was a tag written in the perfect penmanship he had seen before: *Daisy Mull*. The contents had the same musty odor he remembered from opening her carton of winter clothing. This time the collection included sandals, T-shirts, cutoffs, a faded sundress, underpants dotted with red hearts, and the briefest of swimsuits.

Qwilleran could explain why the girl had abandoned her cold-weather gear, but why had she left her summer wearables as well? Perhaps she had lined up a situation that would provide an entirely new wardrobe—either a job or a generous patron. Perhaps a tourist from some other part of the country had come up here and staked her to a getaway—for better or worse. Qwilleran wished the poor girl well.

There were other items in the suitcase: a paper bag containing tasteless junk jewelry as well as one fourteen-karat gold bracelet, heavy enough to make one wonder. Had she stolen it? And if so, why had she left it behind? Another paper bag was stuffed with messy cosmetics and a toothbrush; she had left in a hurry!

There was one more surprise in the suitcase. In a shopping bag with the Lanspeak's Department Store logo Qwilleran found a pathetic assortment of baby clothes.

He sat down in a kitchen chair to think about it. Had she left town hurriedly to have an abortion? After starting a sentimental collection of bootees and tiny sweaters with rosebuds crocheted into the design, why had she decided to end her pregnancy? And what had happened to her? Why had she not returned? Did her family know her fate? Did they know her present whereabouts? Did she even have a family? If so, did they live in that shantytown near the old Dimsdale Mine site? Unanswered questions tormented Qwilleran, and he knew he would never stop probing this one until he had an answer.

His ruminations were interrupted by the sound of a vehicle in the service drive. Dropping the gold bracelet into his pocket, he stuffed the rest of Daisy's belongings back into the sad excuse for a suitcase—broken handle, torn lining, scuffed corners. Then he went outdoors to greet Mrs. Cobb. Her van was filled to the roof with boxes of books, which he began to carry into the house.

She was happy to the point of tears. "I'm so thrilled, I don't know where to begin."

"Get yourself settled comfortably," he said. "Then make a list of what you need for the refrigerator and pantry. The cats are looking forward to your Swedish meatballs and deviled crab."

"What do you like to eat, Mr. Qwilleran?"

"I eat everything—except parsnips and turnips. I'll take you out to lunch this noon, and then I have an appointment at my attorney's office."

The meeting that Penelope had scheduled included Mr. Fitch from the bank and Mr. Cooper, accountant for the estate. The banker was well tanned; Mr. Cooper was ghastly pale in spite of the sunshine that was parching Moose County. Mr. Fitch graciously congratulated Qwilleran on his proposal to start an eleemosynary foundation. He also inquired if Qwilleran golfed.

"I'm afraid I'm a Moose County anomaly," was the answer. "Non-golfing, non-fishing, non-hunting."

"We'll have to do something about that," said the banker cordially. "I'd like to sponsor you for the country club."

The first order of business concerned the opening of a drawing account at the bank. Then Penelope suggested to Qwilleran that he start sifting through any documents he might find in the house. "It would be wise," she said, "to acquaint yourself with insurance coverages, taxes, household inventories, and the like before turning them over to our office."

He squirmed uncomfortably. He despised that kind of paperwork.

"Is everything progressing smoothly?" she asked, smiling and dimpling.

"The housekeeper arrived this morning," he said, "and she agrees we should have some day help."

"I recommend Mrs. Fulgrove. She works for us a few days a week and is very thorough. Has Birch Trevelyan made contact with you?"

"Never showed up. All the doors need attention, and we definitely need a lock on the back door."

"That Birch is a lazy dog," said the banker. "You have to catch him at one of the coffee shops and twist his arm."

Penelope threw Mr. Fitch a reproving glance. "I'll handle it, Nigel. I think I can put a little diplomatic pressure on the man. . . . Do you have any questions, Mr. Qwilleran?"

"When does the city council meet? Sitting in on a meeting is a good way to get acquainted with a new community. Mrs. Cobb might like to go, too."

"In that case," Penelope said quickly, "I'll take the lady as my guest. It wouldn't be appropriate for you to escort her."

"Oh, come on, Penny," said the banker with a half laugh, and she threw him one of her sharp glances.

Turning to the silent accountant, she asked, "Do you have anything to add, Mr. Cooper?"

"Good records," he said. "It's important to have good records. Do you keep good records, Mr. Qwilleran?"

Qwilleran had visions of more paperwork. "Records of what?"

"Personal income, expenditures, deductions. Be sure to keep receipts, vouchers, bank statements, and such."

Qwilleran nodded. The accountant had given him an idea. After the meeting he drew the man aside. "Do you have the records of domestic help at the Klingenschoen house, Mr. Cooper? I'd like to know the dates of employment for one Daisy Mull."

"It's all in the computer," the accountant said. "I'll have my secretary phone you with the information."

In the ensuing days Qwilleran enjoyed the housekeeper's home cooking, answered letters, and bought new tires for the bicycle in the garage. He also telephoned the young managing editor of the *Picayune*. "When are you going to introduce me to coffee shop society, Junior? You promised."

"Any time. Where do you want to go? The best place is the Dimsdale Diner."

"I had lunch there once. I call it the Dismal Diner."

"You're not kidding either. I'll pick you up tomorrow morning at ten. Wear a feed cap," the editor advised, "and you'd better practice drinking coffee with a spoon in the cup."

Although Junior Goodwinter looked like a high school sophomore and always wore running shoes and a Pickax varsity letter, he had graduated from journalism school before going to work for his father's newspaper. They drove to the diner in his red Jaguar, the editor in a baseball cap and Qwilleran in a bright orange hunting cap.

"Junior, this country has the world's worst drivers," he said. "They straddle the centerline; they make turns from the wrong lane; they don't even know what turn signals are for. How do they get away with it?"

"We're more casual up here," Junior explained. "You people Down Below are all conformists, but we don't like anybody telling us what to do."

They parked in the dusty lot at the diner, among a fleet of vans and pickup trucks and one flashy motorcycle.

The Dismal Diner was an old railroad freight car that had been equipped with permanently dirty windows. The tables and chairs might have been cast-offs from the Hotel Booze when it redecorated in 1911. For the coffee hour, customers pushed tables together to seat clubby groups of eight or ten—all men wearing feed caps. They helped themselves to coffee and doughnuts on the counter and paid their money to a silent, emaciated man in a cook's apron. Cigarette smoke blurred the atmosphere. The babble of voices and raucous laughter was deafening.

Qwilleran and Junior, sitting at a side table, caught fragments of conversation:

"Never saw nothin' like what they put on TV these days."

"How's your dad's arthritis, Joe?"

"Man, don't try to tell me they're not livin' together."

"We need rain."

"The woman he's goin' with—they say she's a lawyer."

"Ever hear the one about the little city kid who had to draw a picture of a cow?"

Qwilleran leaned across the table. "Who are these guys?"

Junior scanned the group. "Farmers. Commercial fishermen. A branch bank manager. A guy who builds pole barns. One of them sells farm equipment; he's loaded. One of them cleans septic tanks."

Pipe smoke and the aroma of a cigar were added to the tobacco haze. Snatches of conversation were interwoven like a tapestry.

"Durned if I didn't fix my tractor with a piece of wire. Saved a coupla hundred, easy."

"Always wanted to go to Vegas, but my old lady, she says no."

"Forget handguns. I like a rifle for deer."

"My kid caught a bushel of perch at Purple Point in half an hour."

"We all know he's got his hand in the till. Never got caught, that's all."

"Here's Terry!" several voices shouted, and heads turned toward the dirty windows.

One customer rushed out the door. Picking up a wooden palette, he slanted it across the steps to make a ramp. Then a man in a feed cap, who had eased out of a low-slung car into a folding wheelchair, waited until he was pushed up the ramp into the diner.

"Dairy farmer," Junior whispered. "Bad accident a few years ago. Tractor rollover . . . Milks a hundred Holsteins an hour in a computerized milking parlor. Five hundred gallons a day. Eighteen tons of manure a year."

The talk went on—about taxes, the commodities market, and animal waste management systems. There was plenty of laughter —chesty guffaws, explosive roars, cackling and bleating. "Baa-a-a" laughed a customer behind Qwilleran.

"We all know who she's makin' eyes at, don't we? Baa-a-a!"

"Ed's new barn cost three quarters of a million."

"They sent him to college and dammit if he didn't get on dope."

"That which is crooked cannot be made straight, according to Ecclesiastes One-fifteen."

"Man, he'll never get married. He's got it too good. Baa-a-a!"

"We need rain bad."

"If he brings that woman here, there's gonna be hell to pay."

A sign over the doughnut tray read: "Cows may come and cows may go, but the bull in here goes on forever."

"I believe it," Qwilleran said. "This is a gossip factory."

"Nah," Junior said. "The guys just shoot the breeze."

Toward eleven o'clock customers began to straggle out, and a man with a cigar stopped to give Junior a friendly punch in the ribs. He had a big build and arrogant swagger, and he bleated like a sheep. He rode off on the flashy motorcycle in a blast of noise and flying gravel.

"Who's that?" Qwilleran asked.

"Birch Tree," Junior said. "It's really Trevelyan, an old family name in Moose County. His brother's name is Spruce, and he has two sisters, Maple and Evergreen. I told you we're individualists up here."

"That's the guy who's supposed to do our repairs, but he's taking his own sweet time."

"He's good, but he hates to work. Hikes his prices so people won't hire him. Always has plenty of dough, though. He's part owner of this diner, but that would never make anyone rich."

"Unless they're selling something besides food," Qwilleran said.

On the way back to Pickax he asked if women ever came to the coffee hour.

"Naw, they have their own gossip sessions with tea and cookies. . . . Want to hear the eleven o'clock news?" He turned on the car radio.

Ever since arriving in Moose County Qwilleran had marveled at the WPKX news coverage. The local announcers had a style that he called Instant Paraphrase.

The newscaster was saying, ". . . lost control of his vehicle when a deer ran across the highway, causing the car to enter a ditch and sending the driver to the Pickax Hospital, where he was treated and released. A hospital spokesperson said the patient was treated for minor injuries and released.

"In sports, the Pickax Miners walloped the Mooseville Mosquitoes thirteen to twelve, winning the county pennant and a chance at the play-offs. According to Coach Russell, the pennant gives the Miners a chance to show their stuff in the regional play-offs."

Suddenly Junior's beeper sounded, and a siren at City Hall started to wail. "There's a fire," he said. "Mind if I drop you at the light? See you later."

His red Jaguar varoomed toward the fire hall, and Qwilleran walked the few remaining blocks. On every side he was hailed by strangers who seemed happy to see him and who used the friendly but respectful initial customary in Pickax.

"Hi, Mr. Q."

"Morning, Mr. Q."

"Nice day, Mr. Q."

Mrs. Cobb greeted him with a promise of meatloaf sandwiches for lunch. "And there's a message from Mr. Cooper's office. The person you inquired about terminated her employment five years ago on July seventh. She started April third of that year. Also, a very strange woman walked in and said she'd been hired to clean three days a week. She's upstairs now, doing the bedrooms. And another thing, Mr. Qwilleran—I found some personal correspondence in my desk upstairs, and I thought you should sort it out. It's on your desk in the library."

The correspondence filled a corrugated carton, and perched on top of the conglomeration of papers was Koko, sound asleep with his tail curled lovingly around his nose. Either the cat was developing a mail fetish, or he knew the carton had once contained a shipment of canned tuna.

Qwilleran removed the sleeping animal and tackled the old Klingenschoen correspondence. There was no order or sense to the collection, and nothing of historic or financial importance. Mail that should have been thrown into a wastebasket had been pigeon-holed in a desk. A letter from a friend, dated 1921, had been filed with a solicitation for a recent Boy Scout drive.

What caught Qwilleran's attention was a government postal card with two punctures in one corner, looking suspiciously like the mark of feline fangs.

The message read:

"Writing on bus. Sorry didn't say goodbye. Got job in Florida —very sudden. Got a lift far as Cleveland. Throw out all my things. Don't need anything. Good job—good pay."

It was signed with the name that had been haunting Qwilleran for the last ten days, and it was dated July 11, five years before. Curiously enough, there was a Maryland postmark. Why the girl was traveling from Cleveland to Florida by way of Maryland was not clear. Qwilleran also noted that the handwriting bore no resemblance to the precise penmanship on Daisy's luggage tags.

He ripped the tag from the suitcase in the kitchen and went in search of Mrs. Fulgrove. He found her in the Empire suite, furiously attacking a marble-topped, sphinx-legged table with her soft cloths and mysterious potions.

"This place was let go somethin' terrible," she said, "which don't surprise me, seein' as how the Old Lady didn't have no decent help for five years, but I'm doin' my best to put things to rights, and it ain't easy when you're my age and pestered with a bad shoulder, which I wouldn't wish it on my worst enemy."

Qwilleran complimented her on her industry and principles and showed her the luggage tag. "Do you know anything about this?"

"Course I do, it's my own writin', and nobody writes proper anymore, but the nuns taught us how to write so's anybody could read it, and when the Old Lady told me to put that girl's things in the attic, I marked 'em so's there'd be no mistake."

"Why did the Old Lady keep Daisy's clothing, Mrs. Fulgrove? Was the girl expected to return?"

"Heaven knows what the Old Lady took it in her head to do. She never throwed nothin' away, and when she told me to pack it all in the attic, I packed it in the attic and no questions asked."

Qwilleran disengaged himself from the conference and let Mrs. Fulgrove return to her brass polish and marble restorer and English wax. He himself went back to answering letters. The afternoon delivery brought another avalanche spilling into the vestibule, to be distributed by the two self-appointed mail clerks. Koko delivered a card announcing a new seafood restaurant, as well as a letter from Roger's mother-in-law. She wrote:

Dear Qwill,
   Are you enjoying your new lifestyle? Don't forget you're only thirty miles from Mooseville. Drop in some afternoon. I've been picking wild blueberries for pies.
                                        Mildred Hanstable

She had been Qwilleran's neighbor at the beach, and he remembered her as a generous-hearted woman who loved people. He seized the phone and immediately accepted the invitation—

not only because she made superb pies but because she had been
Daisy Mull's art teacher.

Driving up to the shore the next afternoon he sensed a difference in the environment as he approached the lake—not only
the lushness of vegetation and freshness of breeze but a general
air of relaxation and well-being. It was the magic that lured tourists to Mooseville.

The Hanstable summer cottage overlooked the lake, and an
umbrella table was set up for the repast.

"Mildred, your blueberry pie is perfection," Qwilleran said.
"Not too gelatinous, not too viscous, not too liquescent."

She laughed with pleasure. "Don't forget I teach home ec as
well as art. In our school district we have to be versatile, like
coaching girls' volleyball and directing the senior play."

"Do you remember a student named Daisy Mull?" he asked.

"Do I ever! I had great hopes for Daisy. Why do you ask?"

"She worked for the Klingenschoens a while back, and I found
some of her artwork."

"Daisy had talent. That's why I was so disappointed when she
didn't continue. It's unusual for that kind of talent to surface in
Moose County. The focus is on sports, raising families, and
watching TV. Daisy dropped out of school and eventually left
town."

"Where did she go?"

"I don't know. She never kept in touch, to my knowledge—
not even with her mother, although that's easy to understand.
What kind of artwork did you find?"

Qwilleran described the murals.

"I'd love to see them," Mildred said. "In fact I'd like to see the
whole house, if you wouldn't mind. Roger says it's a showplace."

"I think we can arrange that. . . . Didn't Daisy get along with
her mother?"

"Mrs. Mull has a drinking problem, and it's hard for a young
girl to cope with an alcoholic parent. . . . Please help yourself
to the pie, Qwill."

He declined a third helping, reminding himself that Mrs.
Cobb was planning lamb stew with dumplings for dinner, with
her famous coconut cake for dessert.

He drew a postal card from his pocket. "I found this at the
house, dated five years ago. Daisy was on her way to Florida."

Mildred looked at the address side of the card, frowning a little. Then she turned it over and read the message twice. She shook her head. "Qwill, this is definitely not Daisy's handwriting."

SEVEN

QWILLERAN SAT IN a deck chair on the Hanstable terrace overlooking the lake. Clouds scudded across the blue sky and waves lapped the beach, but his mind was elsewhere. Why would anyone forge a communication to Daisy's employer? He could make a guess or two, but he needed more information.

"How do you know?" he asked his hostess, "that this card wasn't written by Daisy?"

"It's not her handwriting or her spelling," Mildred said with assurance. "She'd never put a *w* in 'writing' or an *e* in 'goodbye' or an apostrophe in anything. She could draw, but she couldn't spell."

"You knew her very well?"

"Let me tell you something, Qwill. For a teacher—a *real* teacher—the biggest reward is to discover raw material and nurture it and watch it develop. I worked hard with Daisy—tried to raise her sights. I knew she could get a scholarship and go into commercial art. It would have been a giant step forward for anyone with the name of Mull. She had invented an individual style of handwriting—hard to read but pleasing to the eye—so I know that *no way* did she write that postcard."

"Any idea who might have written it?"

"Not the faintest. Why on earth would anyone . . ."

Qwilleran said, "Was there any reason why she might want people in Pickax to *think* she had gone to Florida? Was she afraid of someone here? Afraid of being followed and brought back? Were the police looking for her? Had she stolen something? She may have gone out west but arranged for someone else to mail the card in Maryland. Was she clever enough to figure that out? Did she have an accomplice?"

Mildred looked distressed as well as bewildered. "She took a rather pricey object from the decorating studio, but Amanda didn't prosecute. Honestly, I can't imagine Daisy being involved in a serious theft."

"What kind of guys did she go around with?"

"Not the most respectable, I'm afraid. She started . . . *hanging out* after she left school."

"Would her mother know her friends?"

"I suspect her mother would neither know nor care."

"I'd like to talk with that woman."

"It might not be easy. The Mulls are suspicious of strangers, and Della isn't sober very often. I could try to see her when I go to Dimsdale to check on my craft workers. Della does nice knitting and crochet, and she could make items for Sharon's shop, but she can't get herself together."

"You could tell her I've found her daughter's belongings," Qwilleran said, "including a valuable piece of gold jewelry. Stress 'valuable,' and see how she reacts. Ask if I might deliver Daisy's luggage to her."

"Did she really have some good jewelry?" Mildred asked.

"It was in her suitcase in the attic. The question is: why did she leave it behind? She disappeared in the month of July and left both summer and winter clothing, including her toothbrush and . . . Did you know she was pregnant?"

"I'm not surprised," Mildred said sadly. "She never got any love at home. How do you know she was pregnant?"

"She'd been buying baby clothes from Lanspeak's—that is, buying or shoplifting. She left those behind, too. My first hunch was that she was running away to have an abortion."

"She could have had a miscarriage. That can unhinge a woman, and Daisy wasn't the most stable girl in the world—or the healthiest."

"To tell you the truth, Mildred," said Qwilleran, "I'm getting some unsavory vibrations about this case. But I can't say any more—just yet."

Driving back to Pickax he made a detour at the Dimsdale intersection. Just as Roger had said, a dirt road led back into the woods, and among the trees were flat-roofed shacks and old travel trailers. The number of small outhouses suggested a lack of plumbing in this shantytown. Junk was scattered everywhere: bedsprings, an old refrigerator without a door, fragments of farm machinery, rusted-out cars without wheels. The only vehicles that looked operative were trucks in the last stages of dilapidation. Here and there a dusty vegetable garden was struggling to survive in a clearing. Gray washing hung on sagging clotheslines. Flocks of small children played among the rubbish, shrieking and tumbling and chasing chickens.

Comparing the scene with his own lavish residence, Qwilleran cringed—and put the Dimsdale squatters on his mental list for the K Foundation: decent housing, skill training, meaningful jobs, something like that.

At the K mansion he was surprised to see a motorcycle parked at the back door. The service drive was usually occupied by a pickup or two. The green jumpsuit was constantly mowing, edging, watering, spraying and pruning, and Amanda's crew was always coming and going on obscure missions. This afternoon there was a black motorcycle—long in the wheelbase, wide in the tank, voluptuous as to fairings, and loaded with chrome.

Qwilleran stepped into the entry hall and heard voices:

"Whaddaya see, Iris baby? Gimme the bad news."

"Your palm is very good, very easy to read. I see a long lifeline and—oh my!—many love affairs."

"Baa-a-a-a!"

There was no mistaking the laugh or the motorcycle.

In the kitchen the scene was casual, to say the least, Birch Trevelyan in his field boots and feed cap sprawled in a chair at the kitchen table, a T-shirt stretched across his beefy chest and a leather jacket with cutoff sleeves hanging on a doorknob. Mrs. Cobb, apparently dazzled by this macho glamour, was holding his hand and stroking the palm. Koko was monitoring the situation from the top of the refrigerator, not without alarm. Yum Yum was under the table sniffing the man's boots. And on the table were the remains of the three-layer, cream-filled coconut cake that Mrs. Cobb had baked for Qwilleran's evening meal.

She jumped to her feet, looking flushed and guilty. "Oh, there you are, Mr. Qwilleran. This is Birch Tree. He's going to solve all our repair problems."

"Howdy," said Birch in the coffee-shop style, loud and easy. "Pull up a chair. Have some cake. Baa-a-a!" His mismatched eyes—one brown, one hazel—had an evil glint, but he had a disarming grin showing big square teeth.

Qwilleran accepted a chair that Birch shoved in his direction and said, "That's some classy animal you've got tethered out there."

"Yeah, it's a mean rig. Y'oughta get one. You can hit a hundred-fifty in sixth on the airport road, if it's clear. Ten miles of straight, there. Ittibittiwassee—you get four straight but you rev up to ten grand and it's all over."

Tactfully Qwilleran slipped into the topic of primary interest. "There's something wrong with the doors in this house, Birch. They don't latch properly. Even the cat can open them."

"Lotta muscle in one of them small packages," Birch said with authority.

"We've got about twenty doors that won't stay shut. What can be done?"

The expert tucked his thumbs in his belt, rocked his chair on two legs, and nodded wisely. "Old house. Building settles. Door-frames get out of whack. Doors shrink. I can fix 'em, but it'll cost ya."

For a man who hated to work, he seemed most agreeable. New lock for the back door? "Easy!" Twenty doors refitted? "Piece o' cake!"

He said he would start the next morning—early. Qwilleran surmised that Mrs. Cobb had bribed him with a promise of huckleberry pancakes and sausages.

After Birch had roared away on his motorcycle, the housekeeper said, "Isn't that a wonderful machine?"

Qwilleran grunted noncommittally. "How is he going to transport tools with that thing?"

"Oh, he told me he has a couple of trucks, and an ORV, and one of those big campers. He likes wheels. He wants to take me for a ride on the motorbike. What do you think?"

Qwilleran exhaled audibly into his moustache. "Don't rush into anything with that guy. I think he's an opportunist."

"He seems very nice. When I told him that smoke was harmful to antiques, he chucked his cigar without a word. And he *loved* my coconut cake."

"That's obvious. He ate most of it."

"Even little Yum Yum liked him. Did you see her sniffling his boots?"

"Either he'd been walking around a barnyard or she was looking for a shoelace to untie. It wasn't necessarily a character endorsement. . . . By the way, have you noticed Koko sitting on the main staircase a lot?"

She nodded. "That's his favorite perch, except for the refrigerator."

"The strange thing is that he always sits on the *third stair*. I don't understand why."

The housekeeper looked warily at Qwilleran. "I have something strange to report, too, but I'm afraid you'll laugh at me."

"Mrs. Cobb, I always take you seriously."

"Well, you remember I mentioned ghosts when I came here. I was only kidding, sort of, but now I'm beginning to think this house is haunted—not that I'm afraid, you understand."

"How did you get that idea?"

"Well, sometimes when I come into the kitchen at night I see a white blur out of the corner of my eye, but when I turn to look, it's gone."

"I'm always seeing white blurs, Mrs. Cobb. One's called Koko and the other's called Yum Yum."

"But things also move around mysteriously—mostly in the kitchen. Twice it was the kitchen wastebasket, right in the middle of the floor. Last night that old suitcase was shoved across the doorway. Do you know anything about the people who lived here, Mr. Qwilleran? Were there any unexplained deaths? I don't know whether you really believe in ghosts."

"These days I'll believe in anything."

"It's dangerous. I almost fell over the suitcase in the dark. What's it doing here? It seems to be full of musty clothes."

"I'll put it in the broom closet—get it out of your way. And you must promise to turn on lights when you come in here after dark."

"I guess I'm used to saving electricity."

"Forget about that. The estate owns a big chunk of the electric company. And please don't walk around without your glasses, Mrs. Cobb. How's your eye problem these days?"

She held up two crossed fingers. "I still see the eye doctor twice a year."

"Is everything else working out all right? Any questions?"

"Well, I took some cookies over to the painter in the garage—he's a nice young man—and he showed me the huge daisies all over the walls. Who painted those?"

"A girl named Daisy, by a strange coincidence. She used to work here. I hope you're not planning to paint irises all over the kitchen."

"Oh, Mr. Qwilleran," she laughed.

"Have you started to catalogue the collection?"

"Yes, and I'm terribly excited. There's a silver vault in the basement with some eight-branch silver candelabra about three feet high. The butler's pantry has china to serve twenty-four, and the linen closet had damask and Madeira banquet cloths like you wouldn't believe! You ought to give a big dinner party, Mr. Qwilleran. I'd be glad to cook for it."

"Good idea," he said, "but don't try to do too much. Save some time for yourself. You might want to join the Historical Society, and when you're ready to take on appraisal jobs we'll run an ad in the *Picayune*—even get you some publicity on WPKX."

"Oh, that would be wonderful!"

"And how would you like to attend a city council meeting? I intend to go, and the attorney suggested you might enjoy it, too."

"Wasn't that sweet of her! Yes, I'd love to go," Mrs. Cobb said, her eyes shining. "We had so much trouble with bureaucrats in the city; I'd like to see how a small town operates."

"Okay, it's a date. Now I'm going to take a bike ride before dinner."

"Mr. Qwilleran," the housekeeper said hesitantly, "It's none of my business, but I'd like to say something if it won't offend you."

"Fire away!"

"I wish you'd get a new bicycle. That old one is such a rattle-trap! It's not safe."

"The bike's perfectly safe, Mrs. Cobb. I've cleaned it and oiled it and bought new tires. It has a few squeaks, but it's good enough for my purposes."

"But there are so many trucks, and they travel so fast! They could blow you right off the road."

"I do most of my biking on country roads, where there's very little traffic. Don't worry."

The housekeeper set her mouth primly. "But it doesn't *look right* for a man in your position to be riding a—riding a piece of junk, if you'll pardon the expression."

"And if you'll pardon my saying so, Mrs. Cobb, you're beginning to sound like Penelope Goodwinter. Those eight-branch candelabra have gone to your head."

She smiled sheepishly.

"While I'm gone," he said, "Miss Goodwinter might call to say when she's picking us up for the council meeting. Also, a Mrs. Hanstable might phone. She wants a tour of the house. Tell her that any time tomorrow will be okay. I'm going to start charging twenty bucks for these tours."

"Oh, Mr. Qwilleran, you must be kidding."

In order to bike on country roads he had to negotiate four blocks of downtown traffic, five blocks of old residential streets, and then six blocks of suburbia abounding in prefabricated ranch houses, children, plastic tricycles, dogs, and barbecue smoke. After that came the lonely serenity of open country— pastureland, old mine sites, patches of woods, and an occasional farmhouse with a bicycle-chasing dog.

As he pedaled along the four straight miles on Ittibittiwassee Road he thought of many things: lamb stew and dumplings for dinner . . . Melinda coming home soon . . . the loungy sofa he had ordered . . . Arch Riker's pending visit . . . a tick-tick-tick in the rear wheel . . . a dinner party with three-foot silver candelabra . . . poor Mrs. Cobb, too long a widow . . . a new grinding noise in the sprocket . . . *Daisy, Daisy* . . . the police chief with a good Scottish name . . . cream-filled coconut cake.

"The nerve of that guy!" he said aloud, and a lonely cow on the side of the road turned her head to look at him benignly.

Nerve was Birch Tree's outstanding trait. Early the next morning he arrived with a truckful of tools, an appetite for breakfast, and a portable radio. Qwilleran was half awake when a blast of noise catapulted him from his bed. Raucous music was augmented by a concert of caterwauling.

Grabbing his old plaid robe, he bolted downstairs and found the maintenance man happily at work on a kitchen door. Yum Yum was screeching like the siren at City Hall, and Koko was exercising his full range of seven octaves as the music pulsed out of a radio with satellite speakers and a control panel like a video game.

"Cut the volume!" Qwilleran shouted. "It's hurting their ears!"

"Throw 'em a fish head and they'll shut up," Birch yelled. "Baa-a-a-a!"

Qwilleran made a dive for the controls. "If you want to know, Birch, that blaster hurts *my* ears, too."

Mrs. Cobb beckoned him into the laundry room. "Let's not discourage him," she whispered. "He's touchy, and we want to keep him on the job."

For the next few days Birch Tree was always underfoot, modifying the volume of his radio in proportion to Mrs. Cobb's supply of food, compliments, and beer. The whine of power tools turned the cats' ears inside out, but Qwilleran learned to accept the chaos as a positive indication of progress.

On the afternoon that Mildred Hanstable came to see the house, the tour started in the garage, where the slow-motion painter was spreading Mojave beige in Qwilleran's future studio. They picked their way among buckets, ladders, and drop cloths to reach Daisy's apartment.

At the sight of it the art teacher caught her breath. "It's remarkable! A *tour de force!* A poor girl's Sistine Chapel!" Tears came to her eyes. "That sad little creature! I wonder if she'll ever return."

Qwilleran fingered his moustache uncertainly. "Frankly, I'm beginning to doubt that Daisy's alive."

"What are you trying to tell me, Qwill?"

"We don't know if she ever really left town, do we?"

"Do you suspect something . . . *awful?*"

"I don't know. It's just a hunch, but it's a strong one." How could he tell her about the tremor on his upper lip and the tune that kept running through his mind? "Let's go to the house, Mildred, and you can tell me what Daisy's mother said."

As they turned to leave the apartment the congenial Steve was standing in the doorway, holding a paint roller and shaking his head. "I'd hate to hafta paint this room. Did she do it all by herself? Crazy Daisy! That's what we called her in school."

"Just go back and push that roller, Speedo," Qwilleran said with a fraternal punch on the shoulder. "No laps, no sags, no drips, no pimples."

In the main house he conducted Mildred through the rooms with the finesse of a professional guide. "Opposite the fireplace you see a *pietra dura* cabinet, late seventeenth century. The Regency desk is laburnum with kingswood banding." Mrs. Cobb was training him well.

"All this art! All this splendor!" Mildred exclaimed. "You don't expect it in Moose County."

"Very few people knew what this house contained," Qwilleran said. "The Klingenschoens never entertained, although they owned a boxcarful of china and silver. . . . Would you like a drink?"

"Do you have any fruit juice?"

He served white grape juice from Koko's private stock, and they sat in the solarium, where Mildred critiqued the marbled sculptures. It was mercifully quiet, except for an occasional "Baa-a-a!" Birch had turned off his radio and was having a beer with Mrs. Cobb in the kitchen. Either the housekeeper was totally smitten, or she was a master strategist. The work was being done, and it was being done well.

"And now," Qwilleran said to Mildred, "Tell me about Mrs. Mull."

"She was fairly sober and quite agreeable. I gave her your message, and when I mentioned the gold jewelry she perked up noticeably."

"Did she have any news of her daughter?"

"None, but here's something interesting. She too received a postcard shortly after Daisy left. Something like 'Going to Florida . . . never coming back . . . forget about me . . . you never loved me.' Della was quite bitter about it."

"Did you see the card?"

"She hadn't kept it. And naturally she didn't remember the postmark or the handwriting or the date. That was five years ago, and she's been in a fog most of the time."

Qwilleran said, "I went to the police station and met Chief Brodie. Pleasant guy, very cooperative. Daisy had no record—no arrests, no complaints. I gave him the date when she left, but there was no report to Missing Persons."

"I'm relieved to know she has a clean slate," Mildred said. "She wasn't a *bad* girl, but the odds were against her. She used to come to school in rags. I kept some of Sharon's old clothes in the art room, and I'd make Daisy put them on. Yesterday I looked up some of the old yearbooks. She was a sophomore when she left school, but her picture wasn't in the book. Couldn't afford to have a photo taken, I guess. There was a comment about each student, and for Daisy they said she'd marry a rich husband. I don't know whether they were being kind or cruel."

"I think I'll visit Della Mull tomorrow while she's in a good mood."

"Good. She lives in an old trailer with a big daisy painted on the door."

"Excuse me a minute," Qwilleran said. "I want to show you something." He went to the broom closet and returned with the baby clothes in a Lanspeak's shopping bag.

Mildred examined them thoughtfully.

"These aren't from Lanspeak's. They're handmade. It looks like Della's work."

"Then she knew Daisy was pregnant, didn't she? We may be getting somewhere. I'll know better tomorrow."

The next morning Qwilleran overheard a conversation that gave him an idea. Birch was again on the job, snacking with Mrs. Cobb in the kitchen and describing the culinary delights of the Dimsdale Diner: corned beef and cabbage on special every Tuesday; foot-longs with chili every Wednesday. Qwilleran decided to take Della Mull to lunch. Women, he found, liked to be lunched. They became friendly and talkative. To Della, the Dismal Diner would be *haute cuisine*.

With the gold bracelet in a buttoned pocket, and with Daisy's suitcase and carton of clothing in the trunk of his car, he started for Dimsdale shortly before noon. Halfway there he turned on the twelve o'clock newscast from WPKX:

". . . and you'll save dollars on top quality at Lanspeak's. Now for the headlines . . . The mayor of Pickax has assured local merchants that the downtown business district will have a new municipal parking lot before snow flies. In a speech before the Chamber of Commerce, Mayor Blythe said downtown would definitely have a new parking lot before snow flies.

"A Pickax restaurant has announced an expansion project that will increase seating capacity by fifty percent and create seven new jobs. Otto Geb, the proprietor of Otto's Tasty Eats, told WPKX that the new addition will serve fifty percent more customers and add seven employees to the payroll.

"A Dimsdale woman was found dead in her trailer home early this morning, a victim of accidental substance abuse. The body of Della Mull, forty-four, was found by a neighbor seeking to borrow a cigarette. The coroner's office ascribed death to alcohol and pills. According to Dr. Barry Wimms, the ingestion of alcohol and pills was the cause of death.

"And now a friendly word from the folks at Lanspeak's."

EIGHT

"WHEN ARE WE going to have your memorable macaroni?" Qwilleran asked Mrs. Cobb as they waited for Penelope Goodwinter to pick them up.

"As soon as I find some good nippy cheese. It has to be aged cheddar, you know," the housekeeper said. "By the way, I forgot to tell you—a woman phoned you and wants to come to see you. I told her to call back tomorrow. It's about Daisy, she said."

"Did you get her name?"

"It sounded like 'Tiffany Trotter,' but I'm not sure. She sounded young."

Mrs. Cobb was wearing her no-iron pink pantsuit, and Qwilleran had thrown his wash-and-wear summer blazer over a club shirt. When the attorney drove up in her tan BMW, she was wearing a crisp linen suit in pin stripe mauve with a mauve silk shirt and mauve pearls. In a cordial but authoritative tone, Penelope instructed Mrs. Cobb to sit in the back seat.

"My brother has returned," she told Qwilleran, "and we are discussing a plan of organization for the Klingenschoen Foundation. Everyone endorses the idea heartily. I have never seen such unanimity in this city. Usually there are several warring factions, even if the issue is only flowerboxes on Main Street."

The City Hall was a turreted stone edifice of medieval inspiration, lacking only a drawbridge and moat. With its parking lot, fire hall, police station, and ambulance garage, it occupied an entire city block, just off Main Street.

In the council chamber Mayor Blythe and the council members were assembling at a long table on a dais, and they included —to Qwilleran's surprise—two persons he knew: Amanda Goodwinter with her built-in scowl and Mr. Cooper with his perpetually worried expression. Ten rows of chairs for the general public were already filled, except for three reserved seats in the front row. Penelope took care to seat herself between Qwilleran and his housekeeper.

The mayor's gavel rapped the table, and he intoned, "All rise for the Pledge of Allegiance."

Chairs were scraping the floor and the audience was struggling to its collective feet when a loud voice in the back of the room called out, "I object!"

Mrs. Cobb gasped audibly. The audience groaned and sat down again. Council members fell back into their chairs with assorted grimaces of impatience, exasperation, and resignation. Looking around for the source of the disturbance, Qwilleran spotted a belligerent-looking middle-aged man with an outdated crew cut, standing and waiting to be recognized by the chair.

With stoic calm the mayor said, "Will you please state your objection, Mr. Hackpole?"

"That's not the official flag of these United States," the man announced in a booming voice. "It's got forty-eight stars, and the federal government retired that piece of cloth in 1959."

The audience uttered another groan, and individuals shouted, "Who's counting? . . . Sit down!"

"Order!" Mayor Blythe banged the gavel. "Mr. Hackpole, this flag has been saluted in this chamber for more than a quarter of a century without offending the tax-payers of Pickax or the federal government or the residents of Hawaii and Alaska."

"It's a violation of the flag code," insisted the objector. "What's right is right. What's wrong is wrong."

An elderly councilwoman said in a sweetly reasonable voice, "Many of us remember fondly that this flag was presented to the city of Pickax by the late Miss Klingenschoen, and it would be a mark of disrespect to remove it so soon after her untimely death."

"Hear! Hear!" was the response from the audience.

The somber accountant said, "This is an expensive flag. We couldn't afford to replace it with anything of like quality in today's market."

Scowling over her glasses, Amanda Goodwinter added, "It would have to be custom-made. This flag is one-hundred percent virgin wool, lined with silk—very unusual. The stripes are individually stitched, and the stars are embroidered on the blue field. It was ordered through my studio."

"Don't forget the gold fringe," piped up a tremulous voice from the end of the table. "You don't see many flags with gold fringe." The speaker was an old man so small that he virtually disappeared behind the council table.

A councilman of enormous girth, who occupied two armless chairs placed side by side, said, "Looks to me like the flag's got some moth holes in it."

"The holes could be darned," said the elderly woman sweetly. "I would do it myself if my eyesight were better."

"Darning is ridiculous," said Amanda with her usual bluntness. "Professional reweaving—that's what you need. But we'd have to send it Down Below, and we wouldn't get it back for two months."

"It should be sprayed with something," the little old man suggested helpfully.

Again the overweight councilman spoke up. "All that reweaving and all that spraying, and you've still got a flag with forty-eight stars. You're not facing up to the issue as stated by Mr. Hackpole."

Three of his peers glared at him, and Mr. Cooper said, "I, for one, am opposed to the purchase of a costly flag to satisfy a single taxpayer. It's not in the budget."

A lively discussion ensued.

"We wouldn't have to buy an expensive one."

"Who needs embroidered stars?"

"Yes, but would a cheap flag project the image we want for the city of Pickax?"

"To heck with image!"

"Why not embroider two more stars on the flag we have? I would be glad to undertake it myself if my eyesight—"

"Where do you think you'd put them? On a red stripe? That would look god-awful!" This was Amanda's comment.

"It would not be legal."

"We'd be defacing the flag of the United States."

"Why not get an ordinary printed flag? It doesn't have to be as fancy as this one."

"That solution doesn't eliminate the affront to the donor, rest her soul." This was the elderly councilwoman.

"Then buy a fancy one with gold fringe and send the bill to Hawaii and Alaska. They're the ones with all the money."

There were cheers from the audience.

Mayor Blythe wielded the gavel. "We have a four-horned dilemma here. We can keep the present flag and offend Mr. Hackpole. We can replace it and offend the memory of the original donor. We can buy a cheap substitute and sully the city's image. Or we can buy an expensive flag with funds that might better be applied to the new municipal parking lot. I would entertain a motion to table this issue and proceed with further business, assuring Mr. Hackpole that his objection will be given due consideration." The flag issue was tabled; the forty-eight stars and thirteen stripes were saluted by all except Mr. Hackpole, and the council applied its brainpower to more important matters: barking dogs, the watering of the downtown flowerboxes, and a request from the waterbed store for permission to install a Cuddle Room in which prospective customers might test the product.

At the conclusion of the business meeting the mayor said, "Before we adjourn I would like to introduce a distinguished guest and new resident to Pickax—Mr. James Qwilleran."

The benevolent heir to the Klingenschoen fortune— impressively tall and hefty and moustached—rose and bowed graciously. He was greeted by applause and cheers, but no whistles, this being Pickax.

"Mr. Mayor, members of the council, ladies and gentlemen," he began, "it is a pleasure to join a community imbued with such sensitive concern, cogent awareness, and vigilant sense of responsibility. I have listened with rapt attention to the flag discussion, and I should like to propose a solution. First I suggest that you preserve the present flag as a memorial to the donor and as a historic artifact, mounting it on the wall under glass. Second, I urge you to accept my gift of a new custom-made, all-wool, silk-lined, floor-standing flag with hand-stitched stripes, embroidered stars, and gold fringe, to be ordered through Amanda's Studio of Interior Design."

The cheers were vociferous, and the demonstration ended with a standing ovation. Qwilleran raised his hand for silence. "You are all aware of the historic Klingenschoen mansion on the Circle. It is my intention that it will eventually be donated to the city of Pickax as a museum." More cheers. "Meanwhile, its priceless treasures are being preserved professionally by our new house manager, who will function as conservator, registrar, and curator of the collection. She is an authority with impeccable credentials, who comes to us from Down Below. May I present Iris Cobb? Mrs. Cobb, will you please stand!"

Mrs. Cobb's eyes glistened more brightly than the rhinestones on her glasses as she took her bow. And when the meeting adjourned, Penelope said in slightly crisp tones, "Indeed, Mr. Qwilleran, you were a wellspring of surprises this evening."

She drove them home but declined to join them in a celebratory nightcap. "My brother is waiting for me at the office," she explained. "We are pleading a case in court tomorrow, and there are momentous decisions to make before we call it a day."

Mrs. Cobb also excused herself. "You'll think I'm silly, Mr. Qwilleran, but I want to have a good cry. If only my husband was alive and could hear the applause tonight and see me taking a bow! And your wonderful introduction! It was all so—so thrilling!" She ran upstairs.

Qwilleran went to the library to gaze in panic at the growing pyramid of mail on his desk. Fearing that his gift of a flag would result in even more saccharine letters of commendation, he telephoned the Mooseville postmistress at her home. Her husband answered.

"Hi, Nick. How's everything in Mooseville?"

"Perfect temperature, Qwill, but we need rain. I saw you out biking the other day. Where'd you get that relic?"

"It could use a paint job," Qwilleran admitted, "but it works. I like biking. It gives me time to think. What I don't like is a dog barking at my heels."

"They're not allowed to run loose in this county. You could make a complaint to the police. That's a violation."

"Well, I always bellow a few choice words, and so far I haven't lost a foot. How's Lori? Is she still working?"

"Not for long," Nick said. "She's put in her resignation."

"She wrote to me about part-time secretarial work."

"Sure thing. I'll put her on."

A vivacious Lori came on the line. "Hello, Qwill. Did you get my letter?"

Immediately Koko was on the desk, nudging the phone and trying to bite the cord. He knew who was on the other end of the line. Qwilleran pushed him away.

"I did indeed, Lori, and there are two bushels of letters here, waiting for you. If Nick wants to pick them up, you can answer them at home."

"Super!"

"You're an expert typist, and your machine is much better than mine."

"Thank you. Nick gave me an electronic for my birthday. I really wanted some little diamond earrings, but he's so practical. An engineer, you know."

"I also want to ask a question, Lori, since you're so knowledge-able about cats." Qwilleran was fighting for possession of the telephone. "Koko likes to sit on the grand staircase, but only on the third stair. How do you explain that behavior?" He gave Koko another shove.

Lori said, "Cats leave their individual scent wherever they go, and they like to return to the same spot. It's like their private territory."

"Hmmm," Qwilleran mused. "Perhaps you're right."

It was still only ten-thirty, and he was finishing a letter to the Pickax Thespians, declining their invitation to play the role of Teddy in *Arsenic and Old Lace,* when he heard a snatch of music.

From the drawing room came three distinct notes: E, D, C. Koko was playing the piano again. At least, Qwilleran presumed it was Koko at the keyboard, although he had never actually witnessed the cat pressing the keys. No doubt Mrs. Cobb would attribute the performance to the resident ghost.

Going to investigate, he found Koko ambling around the

drawing room with conspicuous nonchalance. Qwilleran picked him up and plunked him without ceremony on the piano bench. "Now let's hear you play something."

Koko said, "ik ik ik," in a pleasant voice and rolled over to lick his nether parts.

"Don't be modest. Show me what you can do." Qwilleran set the cat back on his four feet and then guided one paw to the keyboard. Twisting like a pretzel, Koko squirmed out of the man's grasp, jumped to the floor, and walked away with stiff-legged hauteur, returning to his perch on the third stair.

Was it coincidence that the notes coming from the piano had been the opening phrase of "Three Blind Mice"? Qwilleran felt the familiar tickle on his upper lip. There was some significance, he felt, to the number three. Three-base hit . . . three-dollar bill . . . three sheets to the wind . . . the three Weird Sisters . . . three-mile limit. Clues eluded him completely.

The next morning Qwilleran was having his third cup of coffee when Amanda Goodwinter arrived unexpectedly, giving the doorbell her three impatient rings.

She barged into the vestibule, wearing an unkempt khaki suit and canvas golf hat, with wisps of hair escaping from underneath the brim. "Came to see if my painter is loafing on the job," she announced.

Qwilleran marveled that Penelope could look so sleek in a suit and Amanda could look so frumpy—the sleeves too long, one shoulder drooping, and the blouse collar half-in and half-out.

"What's that infernal racket?" she demanded.

"Birch Tree is doing some repairs for us," Qwilleran said. "Excuse me a moment. I have something to give you." From a locked drawer in the library desk he brought an ivory elephant. "I think this belongs to you."

"Where the devil did you find this?" She turned the carving over to verify the label.

"Among Daisy Mull's belongings. I was cleaning out the attic."

"It must be six years since this disappeared from the studio," the designer said. "Daisy was working for me then, but it was an election year, and I thought some sneaky Republican made off with it." She handed the carving back to Qwilleran. "Here! It's yours. It's a good one—old—can't import them anymore."

"No! No! It's your property, Amanda."

"Shut up and keep it," she barked at him. "I've already taken a loss on the books. What did you think of the meeting last night?"

"It was refreshing to hear public servants speaking English. No prioritizing. No inpacticizing. No decontextualizing."

"Your speech was a corker—all that bosh about vigilant awareness and cogent concern. It gave me a bellyache, but they fell for it."

"By the way, who's Mr. Hackpole?" Qwilleran asked.

"He gives *everybody* a bellyache. Always throwing a monkey wrench in the works. Steer clear of Hackpole. He's bad news."

"The overweight councilman seemed to side with him in the flag dispute."

"That's Scott Gippel—scared to death of Hackpole. They're next-door neighbors. Hackpole never pulled a shotgun on anybody *yet*, but he can get gol-durned mad if somebody steps on his grass or complains about his dogs."

"What's his problem?"

"Wife ran off with a beer-truck driver, and he went bonkers. Didn't affect his financial savvy, though. He sells used cars. Sharp operator! . . . Well, let's go and look at the paint job. You ought to keep this back door locked. Bloody tourist season, you know. Town's full of creeps, stoned to the gills. They broke into Dr. Hal's office. Took drugs and needles."

As they approached the garage Qwilleran said, "Look at this big wardrobe. I thought it was junk, but Mrs. Cobb says it's a Pennsylvania *schrank* and highly collectible."

Amanda snorted. "Looks like junk to me."

"Well, I'd like your porters to move it into the house when they have time. I'd like to put it just outside the library."

"Arrgh!" she growled. Puffing and grunting, she climbed the stairs to inspect the apartment under renovation. After threatening to fire Steve if he didn't show some signs of life, she had another incredulous look at Daisy's murals and then said to Qwilleran, "Walk me to my car."

As they walked down the driveway under ancient maple trees, Qwilleran remarked about the glorious weather.

"Wait till you've spent a winter here, mister!" Then she added, "Got some advice for you. Watch your step in Pickax. The town likes to gossip. Somebody's always listening. Seems like the whole town's bugged. Wouldn't be surprised if they bugged the flowerboxes on Main Street. I don't trust our mayor either. Nice fella, but I don't trust him as far as I can spit. So keep your eyes and ears open, and don't say anything you don't want repeated."

"At the coffee shop, you mean?"

"Or at the country club. Or on the church steps."

Amanda climbed into the driver's seat with some awkward maneuvering of knees, elbows, and hips. She gunned the motor and her car shot down the driveway, stopped short with squealing tires, and backed up. "And watch out for my cousins! Don't be fooled by the phoney Goodwinter charm."

She took off again, barreling recklessly into the traffic flow around the Circle.

Qwilleran was baffled. Pickax was full of Goodwinters, and they were all cousins. There was nothing phony about Melinda. He liked her humor—sometimes cynical, usually irreverent. She had just returned from Paris, and he had made a date with her, anticipating a relaxing evening of conversation, if not more. Melinda had been aggressively seductive from the beginning.

"Is that good or bad?" he said aloud when he returned to the house to feed the cats. "What would you guys like for breakfast? Veal Oscar? *Coq au vin?* Shrimp deJonghe?" He diced some of Mrs. Cobb's pot roast and arranged it on a Royal Worcester plate with pan juices, a little grated carrot, and a sprinkling of hard-cooked egg yolks. *"Voilà,"* he said.

Both cats attacked the meal with gusto, carefully avoiding the grated carrot.

His next visitor was Tiffany Trotter, the same wholesome, robust country girl who had interviewed for the job of housekeeper. This time they talked in the library to avoid the noise of Birch's hammering and sawing and radio; he was now building shelves for Mrs. Cobb's reference books.

In the library Tiffany swiveled her eyes over the book-filled shelves and sculptured plaster ceiling. "This is a pretty room," she said.

"You wanted to speak to me about Daisy," Qwilleran reminded her.

"She used to work here."

"I'm aware of that. Are you a friend of Daisy's?"

"We were very good friends, and—" She shrugged for want of the right words. "I thought it was kinda funny when she left town without telling me—didn't even write." She searched Qwilleran's face for reaction.

"Did you make inquiries at that time?"

"I asked the old lady she worked for, and she said Daisy moved to Florida. She acted as if she was mad about something."

"That was five years ago. How long had you been friends?"

"Since ninth grade. The Dimsdale kids were bused to Pickax, and the other kids made fun of Daisy because she was a Mull. I kinda liked her. She was different. She could draw."

"Did she have boyfriends?"

"Not till she left school. She didn't finish. She didn't like school."

"Do you know who her friends were?"

"Just guys."

"She was pregnant when she left. Did you know that?"

"Mmmm . . . yes."

"Did she say anything about getting an abortion?"

"Oh, no!" Tiffany was emphatic for the first time during the interview. "She wanted the baby. She wanted to get married, but I don't think the guy wanted to."

"Who was the father?"

"Mmmm . . . I dunno."

"What did Daisy's mother think about all of this?"

Tiffany shrugged. "I dunno. She never talked about her mother. They didn't get along."

"Mrs. Mull died a few days ago. Did you know?"

"Somebody told me."

It was one of those moments when Qwilleran would have relished a smoke. Puffing a Scottish blend in his old quarter-bend bulldog would have sharpened his mental processes, would have given him pauses in which to organize his questions. But Melinda had urged him to give up his comfortable old pipe.

He asked the girl if she would like a beer, thinking it would help her relax; she was sitting on the edge of the blood red leather sofa.

"I guess not," she said. "I hafta go and do the milking."

"Do you think something bad might have happened to your friend?"

Tiffany moistened her lips. "I dunno. I just thought it was funny when she went away and didn't tell me. Nobody else cared, so that's why I came."

As Qwilleran accompanied her to the front door, Birch was shifting his tools and radio to another place of operation. "Whatcha doin' here, sweetheart?" he called out in his hearty voice. "Lookin' for a job? Whatsa matter with that big bozo you married? I thought you'd be knocked up by now. Baa-a-a-a!"

Tiffany gave the man a sideways glance and a timid smile, and Qwilleran said to him, "Skip the social pleasantries, Birch. Just tell us when we're going to get a lock on the back door."

"Came in yesterday—airmail from Down Below," Birch said. "You'll have it tomorrow. No lie."

Qwilleran watched Tiffany leave. She crossed the little park and drove away in a pickup that had been parked on the far side of the Circle. Why hadn't she parked in the driveway? There was ample space. Her wordless reaction to Birch's remark had been equally puzzling.

"Dammit!" Qwilleran said aloud. He should have asked her why she came to see him. Who told her he was interested?

There's something going on here that I don't know about, he thought, and she knows something she's not telling. That's the way it is in a small town. It's all very friendly and open on the surface, but underneath it's a network of intrigue and secrecy.

NINE

QWILLERAN AND MELINDA dined at the Old Stone Mill, a former gristmill converted into a restaurant by dedicated preservationists who cared more about historic landmarks than about the seasoning of the soup. Yet, the atmosphere was inviting and conducive to intimate conversation. He ordered champagne, to celebrate her return, and something innocuous for himself.

"How was Paris?" he asked.

"Full of Americans. The next conference will be in Australia. You should go with me, lover."

Too expensive, he thought. Then he realized the words no longer belonged in his vocabulary. He was finding it difficult to adjust to his new financial status.

"I don't like traveling alone," Melinda was saying. "I don't even like living alone." Her green eyes flickered invitingly.

"Watch those fluttering eyelashes," Qwilleran said. "We haven't even had the soup yet."

"Any excitement while I was away?"

In graphic detail he described the Great Flag Controversy. "I'm curious about Blythe," he said. "He's articulate and conducts a meeting exceptionally well. Who is he? What's his background?"

"He's an investment counselor. His mother was a Goodwinter.

He was principal of the high school until the scandal a few years ago."

"What happened?" As a journalist Qwilleran felt professionally privileged to pry.

"He was involved with some girl students, but he got off with a slap on the wrist and an invitation to resign. Anyone else would have left town in disgrace, but he's got the Goodwinter Guts. He ran for mayor and won by a landslide."

At Melinda's urging they ordered ravioli. "It's the specialty of the house. They buy it frozen, and it's the only thing on the menu that the cook can't ruin."

"This town really needs a good restaurant."

"The Lanspeaks are opening one—haven't you heard? They travel a lot and appreciate good food, so it should be an oasis in a desert of French fries and ketchup. . . . How's everything at the Pickax Palace?"

"Mrs. Cobb finally arrived. And I've ordered a suede sofa for my studio. And at last we have a lock on the back door. Birch Tree comes almost every day to do the repairs and play his obscene radio. Today he went fishing, and it was so quiet the cats walked around on tiptoe."

"Is Koko still throwing your female guests out of the house at eleven P.M.?"

"That's his bedtime," Qwilleran explained apologetically. "Not only can that cat tell time, but I believe he can count. He sits on the *third stair* of the staircase all the time."

"Third from the top or third from the bottom? If he's counting from the top, it's more likely he's sitting on the eighteenth stair." The green eyes were impudent.

Then Qwilleran told her about the three-foot candelabra in the silver vault. "If I decide to give a dinner party, will you consent to be my hostess?"

"Or anything else, lover," she said with a green-eyed wink.

"My editor from the *Fluxion* is flying up to spend a few days, and I thought I might invite Penelope and Alexander and a few others from Pickax and Mooseville. Mrs. Cobb has offered to cook."

"Is she good?"

"Well, she does the world's best pot roast and coconut cake and macaroni-and-cheese."

"Darling, you can't serve macaroni-and-cheese with three-foot silver candelabra on the table. You should have something elegant: six courses, starting the *escargots* . . . a butler serving cocktails in the solarium . . . two footmen to serve in the dining room . . . a string trio going crazy behind the potted palms."

"You're not serious, I hope," Qwilleran said warily.

"Of course I'm serious. There's no time to send out engraved invitations, so you'll have to telephone everyone, although it's not good form for a formal dinner."

"Who'll know the difference?"

"*Penelope* will know," Melinda said with a mocking grin. "Penelope still eats ice cream with a fork. Socially she's a throwback to the Edwardian era. My great-grandmother owned sixteen etiquette books. In those days people didn't worry about losing weight or getting in touch with their feelings; they wanted to know if they should eat mashed potatoes with a knife."

She declined dessert and finished the bottle of champagne, but Qwilleran ordered French-fried ice cream, a cannonball of pastry reposing in a puddle of chocolate sauce. No matter how he attacked the impenetrable crust, the ball merely rotated in the slippery sauce and threatened to bounce to the floor.

With each sip of champagne Melinda was becoming more elated about the party. "To impress your editor we ought to serve foods indigenous to this area, starting with terrine of pheasant and jellied watercress consommé. There's a secret cove on the Ittibittiwassee—accessible only by canoe—where one can find watercress. Do you canoe?"

"Only in reverse," Qwilleran said.

"How about Chinook salmon croquettes for the first course?" She took another sip of champagne. "The entree could be lamb *bûcheronne* with tiny Moose County potatoes and mushrooms. It's too dry to find morels." Another sip. "Then a salad of home-grown asparagus vinaigrette. How does that sound?"

"Don't forget dessert. Preferably not French-fried ice cream."

"How about a wild raspberry trifle? We'll need two or three wines, but I can steal those from Dad's wine cellar."

"I hope butlers and footmen are indigenous to Moose County," Qwilleran said.

"That poses a problem," Melinda admitted, "but . . . we

might get actors from the Pickax Thespians. Larry Lanspeak played the title role in *Jeeves*, and he'd make a perfect butler."

"You don't mean the owner of the department store, do you?"

"Sure! He'd love it! The Fitch twins are home from Yale, and they could wear their costumes from *The Student Prince* and play the footmen. We'd have a rehearsal, of course, and they'd play their roles with a straight face. . . . Penelope will have a fit!"

Qwilleran believed not a word of it, but he was enjoying Melinda's champagne fantasy. "Where will we get a string trio?"

She closed her eyes in thought. "Dad talks about three musicians who used to play Strauss waltzes behind the potted palms at the Pickax Hotel before World War Two."

"By now they're all dead, Melinda."

"Not necessarily. People live a long time in Moose County."

As they left the restaurant he said, "Your scenario has been a lot of fun. I only wish we could swing it."

"Of course we can swing it!" she said indignantly. "I have my mother's recipes, and I'll work out the details with Mrs. Cobb. All you have to do is pay the bills."

They went to Melinda's condo to look at her great-grandmother's etiquette books, and Qwilleran arrived home at a late hour, humming a tune from *The Student Prince*. As he turned the key in the new back-door lock, he could hear Koko scolding severely.

"You mind your own business," Qwilleran told him. "Go and fraternize with Yum Yum."

Before retiring he made his nightly house check, turning on lights in all the rooms, inspecting windows and French doors, taking a hasty inventory of French bronzes, Chinese porcelains, Venetian glass, and Georgian silver. Everything was in order except in the kitchen, where the step stool was situated unaccountably in the center of the room.

When Qwilleran reported this manifestation to Mrs. Cobb the next morning, she said, "I told you something spooky was happening. Now you'll believe me! What's more, I heard someone fooling around with the piano keys last night after the lights were out."

Qwilleran was scheduled to address a luncheon meeting of the Pickax Boosters Club at noon and then pick up Arch Riker at the airport. But first he telephoned his dinner invitations. Everyone accepted with pleasure, despite the short notice.

Penelope said, "My brother returns from Washington this evening. We shall be delighted to attend. Black tie?"

"Optional," Qwilleran said. "Melinda wants you to know she's wearing a long dress."

"Splendid!"

When he called Amanda she was exultant. "Nobody's invited me to cocktails and dinner in a coon's age! I'll drag my long dress out of the cedar closet."

To Junior Goodwinter he said, "Don't bring your notebook. You're invited as a guest, not a reporter. And see if you can borrow a tie somewhere."

Before going to his luncheon meeting Qwilleran himself bought a new tie at Scottie's Men's Shop, although he thought the price exorbitant.

There were no feed caps at the Boosters luncheon. All the influential men of the community gathered in a private room at the Old Stone Mill for frozen ravioli á la microwave. Among those he recognized were Mayor Blythe, Dr. Halifax Goodwinter, Chief Brodie, and the dour Mr. Cooper. Since President Goodwinter was still in Washington and Vice-President Lanspeak had trans-Pacific jet lag, Nigel Fitch introduced the guest speaker with flowery accolades.

"Gentlemen," Qwilleran began, "it was my previous understanding that Down Below referred to a geographic location. Now I realize it's something else. While we enjoy perfect temperature in Moose County, it's hot as hell Down Below." There was hearty applause from the Boosters.

"Fine weather," he went on, "is not the only reason I'm happy to be here. Since arriving I have not once been mugged, or asphyxiated by carbon monoxide, or knocked down by a truck." (More applause.) "On the debit side, I have had to give up whistling." (Laughter from all except Cooper.)

"Having worked all my life, I feel the need to engage in some worthwhile enterprise in this area. I have considered opening an exercise studio next door to Otto's Tasty Eats." (Chuckles.) "Or I might acquire the mosquito-repellant franchise for Mooseville." (Loud laughter.) "Or start a driver's training school." (Roars of laughter.)

He then went on to explain the aims of the Klingenschoen Foundation, and as he bowed to the final applause Mayor Blythe presented him with a genuine pickax in good working order.

After adjournment the hardware merchant introduced himself. "I understand you're starting to lock your back door, Mr. Qwilleran. Not a bad idea, the way things are going. I special-ordered your lock from Down Below. Beautiful mechanism! Top of the line!"

Then the police chief led Qwilleran aside. "You were talking to me about that girl who disappeared five years ago. You said she was last seen on July seventh."

"That's the last day she worked, according to our employment records."

"There was something about that date that rang a bell," Brodie said. "I was a sheriff's deputy then. There was a big cave-in at one of the mines on the night of July seventh. We had it roped off, I remember, until they could put up a fence. Kept a deputy there twenty-four hours a day. Just thought I'd mention it."

A smooth-looking sand-haired man introduced himself as Sam Gafner, a real estate broker. Qwilleran knew he was a salesman before he opened his mouth. "Interested in a business opportunity, Mr. Q? I happen to know this restaurant is going on the block very soon. Beautiful piece of property; all it needs is some good food management."

With applause and compliments elevating his mood, Qwilleran drove to the airport to meet Arch Riker.

The editor stepped off the plane and looked around in dismay. "Is this the airport? Is that the terminal? I thought we'd made an emergency landing on a softball field and the shack with a wind sock was the dugout."

Qwilleran grabbed his hand. "Good to see you, Arch. How was the flight?"

"Like flying with the Wright brothers."

Qwilleran steered him to the Klingenschoen limousine. "I hope you brought your dinner jacket, Arch."

With Riker's luggage stowed in the trunk, the sleek black vehicle purred down the long stretch of Airport Road.

"Ten miles of straight road without a curve, hill, crossroad, or habitation," Qwilleran boasted. "Nothing to worry about except deer, elk, raccoons, skunks, and the state police. There's a lot of wild game around here. Everybody goes hunting, pronounced *'huntn.'* Everybody has a *huntn* rifle and *huntn* dogs. . . . Where you see warning signs, those are abandoned mines."

"Spooky-looking places," Riker said. "I'll bet the kids use the old shaft houses for their wild parties. How do you like living in the wilderness?"

Qwilleran thought, Wait till he sees the butler and the string trio. "Fine! I like it fine! And the cats are going crazy, chasing around the big rooms. Koko can fly up twenty-one stairs in two leaps."

"Has he learned any new tricks?"

"Arch, that crazy animal has started playing post office. When the mail comes, he sorts it out and brings me the letters he considers important."

"Nobody else would believe that, but I do."

"It's a fact. He seems to detect certain scents. He's brought me letters from persons he knows, households that have cats, and places where he used to live."

"I hear Mrs. Cobb is working for you," Riker said, verging on a touchy subject.

"We'll talk about that when we get home and settle down with a drink," Qwilleran said. "How's everything at the *Flux?*"

"I'm just serving time until I can collect my pension."

"Wait till you see the *Pickax Picayune!* You need a magnifying glass to read the headlines. They cover all the ice cream socials and chicken dinners."

"What do you do for news?"

"Fortunately the state edition of the *Flux* is distributed up here, and that keeps us in touch with reality—wars, disasters, assassinations, riots, mass murders, all the worthwhile news. WPKX keeps us informed of car accidents, hunting mishaps, and barn fires." He turned on the radio. "We've just missed the six o'clock news, I'm afraid."

The announcer was saying, ". . . when she fell from a tractor on a farm owned by her father, Terence Kilcally, forty-eight. The tractor then entered a ditch and overturned. Sheriff deputies told WPKX that the tractor continued to travel until it entered a ditch and rolled over. . . . Present temperature in Pickax, a pleasant seventy-five degrees."

"Pickax doesn't need air-conditioning," Qwilleran said as he pointed out the important houses on Goodwinter Boulevard. "These stone buildings stay cool all summer. They have walls two feet thick."

And then they reached the K mansion. Riker, jaded after twenty-odd years of editing sensational news, was nonetheless stunned by its grandeur. "Nobody lives like this, Qwill! Least of all you! It's a little Versailles! It's the Buckingham Palace of the north woods!"

"Quit writing headlines, Arch, and tell me what you want to drink."

"I'm back on martinis, but I'll mix my own. Since you've been on the wagon you've lost your touch."

Qwilleran poured white grape juice for himself and a thimbleful for Koko.

"He remembers me," said Riker as the cat rubbed against his ankles.

"He knows you have cats at home. How's old Punky? How's old Mibs?"

"Let's go and sit down," Riker said with sudden weariness. They took their drinks to the solarium. "Well, it's like this," he said in a tremulous voice. "We had them put to sleep. It was a rough decision to make, but Rosie didn't want them, and the house was up for sale, and I moved to a hotel. Nobody wants to adopt old animals, so . . . I asked the vet to put them away. They were beautiful longhairs, and he didn't want to do it, but . . . I had no choice."

Both men were silent as Koko and Yum Yum sauntered into the room, nestled together on a cushioned wicker chair, and started licking each other.

"Where's Mrs. Cobb?" Riker asked finally.

"She went to a meeting of the Historical Society. I was surprised to hear she'd sold her antique shop."

"*You* were surprised? How do you think I felt? Rosie got a little inheritance, and next thing I knew, she bought out the Cobb business and announced she was going to live over the store—on Zwinger Street! That crummy neighborhood!"

"What happened to Rosie, Arch? I knew she went back to school after the kids left home."

"She took a few college courses and got in with a young crowd —got some new ideas, I guess. Young people have always liked

Rosie; she's full of life. But there's something sad about mature people who suddenly try to return to their youth—especially a middle-aged woman with a young lover."

Qwilleran combed his moustache with his knuckles. "What about middle-aged men with young partners?"

Riker thought about it. "That's different, somehow."

Qwilleran suggested the Old Stone Mill for dinner. "Don't expect great food, but the atmosphere's pleasant, and we can have a little privacy."

They sat at a window table overlooking the great mill wheel, which still turned and creaked without benefit of a millstream. It was powered electrically, with taped sound effects giving the impression of rushing water.

Riker relaxed. "Bucolic tranquillity! Makes one wonder why we live in cities. Don't you miss the criminal activity Down Below? You always enjoyed a good murder."

Qwilleran lowered his voice. "To tell the truth, Arch, there's a situation here that's got me wondering. A girl disappeared from the K mansion five years ago, and I've been getting the old familiar vibrations."

He told Riker about the murals, the four notes played on the antique piano, and Koko's discovery of Daisy's luggage in the attic. "The real tip-off was a postal card supposed to be from Daisy but not in her handwriting. I found out the girl was pregnant and the guy wouldn't marry her."

"Nowadays it doesn't matter a whole lot, does it? My daughter wants a child but no husband. We're an endangered species."

"This case was different, Arch. Here was a girl from the *wrong side* of the wrong side of the tracks, and marriage would be a chance to change her name. Just as I was about to visit her mother and ask a few questions, the woman died of accidental substance abuse—or so the coroner decided."

"You always get mixed up in these things," Riker said, "and I don't know why. Who played the piano? Don't tell me it was the cat!"

"Who knows? I also heard the opening notes of *Three Blind Mice*. And if it wasn't Koko, we've got an apparition on the premises. Take your pick."

They returned to the house shortly after dark. Flickering blue lights in an upstairs window indicated that Mrs. Cobb had retired to watch television.

"Nightcap?" Qwilleran suggested to his guest.

At that moment they both heard four notes played on the piano in the drawing room: E, E, E, C—loud and clear.

Riker was startled. "What was that?"

"Beethoven's Fifth," Qwilleran said. "Now will you believe me?"

They sat at the kitchen table and listened to the eleven o'clock news on WPKX:

"The annexation battle between city and county became a slugging match at a public hearing this evening when a township supervisor was assaulted by an angry resident. Clem Wharton declined to press charges against his assailant, Herb Hackpole.

"The school board tonight voted unanimously in favor of quality education. Board president Nimkoff told WPKX, 'We've put ourselves on the line in favor of quality education.'

"It was earlier reported that a Pickax Township woman was killed in a fall from a tractor on her father's farm. According to the coroner's report, Tiffany Trotter, twenty-two, was killed by a gunshot wound. Police are investigating."

TEN

QWILLERAN PASSED a sleepless night. He was concerned about his friend's marital breakup. He was apprehensive about hosting an ambitious dinner party. And he felt uneasy about the murder of Tiffany Trotter.

He had told Riker about her interest in Daisy, adding, "If there's a connection between her visit here and her murder, it means I'm on a hot scent."

"It also means you could be on the hit list yourself," the editor had said. "Better cool it, Qwill."

At an early hour the telephone rang, and Amanda Goodwinter plunged into the conversation with her usual brashness. "Got a problem. Got to find another painter to finish your apartment. Not easy to do these days. Nobody wants to work."

"What happened?" Qwilleran asked in the early-morning stupor that followed an unsatisfactory sleep.

"Didn't you hear the news? Tiffany Trotter was shot."

He was slow in putting two and two together. "Uh . . . yes . . . I heard it on the radio."

"That's Steve's wife," Amanda shouted impatiently. "Steve, my painter! He won't be back on the job for a while."

"I didn't get the connection," Qwilleran said. "That's a terrible thing. We don't expect that in Moose County, do we?"

"Tourists! That's what's wrong," the designer grumbled. "Coming up here in their fancy painted vans. They're all *stoned,* I tell you!"

"Is that what the police think? I haven't heard any details."

"Francesca says—that's my assistant; her father is chief of police—Francesca says they think it was a sniper—some psycho who just happened to be driving past the farm with a high-powered rifle. These kooks from Down Below have been known to shoot cows, but this is outrageous!"

"Is Brodie handling the investigation?"

"It's the sheriff's turf, but the Pickax police cooperate."

As Amanda rambled on, conjectures raced through Qwilleran's mind: Not necessarily a tourist; everyone in the county has a hunting rifle. . . . The husband is always the first suspect. There could be a dozen different reasons why an enemy or a neighbor or even a relative might pull the trigger. . . . Who are these Trotters? Are they involved in anything shady?

Amanda was saying, "So I'm trying to get Steve's cousin to finish the job."

"No hurry. It can wait till Steve comes back."

"Shucks, I want the job finished so I can get my money! Carpet's waiting to be laid. The blinds are ready. . . . Say, I'm all excited about your party. Hope you've got some good bourbon."

Qwilleran said, "I think you'll like our visitor from Down Below. Arch Riker is an editor from the *Daily Fluxion.*"

"I'll be on my good behavior, unless my cousins provoke me, and then *look out!*"

"May we pick you up? I'll send Arch over with the limousine."

"Hot damn!" said Amanda.

Qwilleran and Riker took a walk downtown during the morning hours, to view the bizarre street scene—eight centuries of Old World architecture condensed into two commercial blocks. The department store posed as a Byzantine palace. The gas station looked like Stonehenge.

At the *Picayune* office they introduced themselves to Junior's father, owner and publisher of the newspaper. Senior Goodwinter was a mild-mannered man, wearing a leather apron and a square paper cap made of folded newsprint.

"Is it true you hand-set most of the type yourself?" Qwilleran asked.

"Been doing it since I was eight. Had to stand on a stool to reach the typecases," Senior said proudly. "It's the best part of the business."

Riker said, "The *Picayune* is the only paper I know that has successfully resisted twentieth-century technology and new trends in journalism."

"Thank you," said the publisher. "It hasn't changed in any way since it was founded by my great-grandfather."

From there the two men walked to the office of Goodwinter & Goodwinter. Qwilleran apologized to Penelope for dropping in without an appointment. "I simply wanted to introduce Mr. Riker and request some information."

"Come into the conference room," she said graciously, but her automatic smiles and dimples faded when he put his question:

"Do you know anything about the Trotter girl who was murdered?"

"What do you mean?" she asked sharply.

"Do you have any inside information about the young woman, her family, her activities? Any theories about the murder? Was it a random killing or is there some local intrigue, some shady connection?"

"I'm afraid you've come to the wrong place, Mr. Qwilleran. This is a law firm—not a detective agency or a social services office." There was a sarcastic edge to her voice. "May I inquire why you ask these peculiar questions?"

"Sorry. I should have explained," Qwilleran said. "My first impulse, on hearing about the murder, was to establish a scholarship for farm youth as a memorial to Tiffany Trotter. I'm assuming she was an innocent victim. If there is anything unsavory about her character or connections, my idea would not be exactly appropriate."

The attorney relaxed. "I see what you mean, but I'm unable to give you an immediate answer. My brother and I will take it under advisement. We are both looking forward to your dinner tomorrow evening."

Walking away from the Goodwinter office Qwilleran said to Riker, "I've never seen her quite so edgy. She's working too hard. Her brother spends half his time in Washington—doing God-knows-what—and she has to handle the practice single-handed."

Exactly at noon the siren on the roof of City Hall blasted its hair-raising wail. At that signal everything in Pickax closed for an hour, allowing workers to go home to lunch. No taxes or traffic tickets were paid; no automobiles or candy bars were sold; no prescriptions or teeth were filled. Only emergency services and one small downtown restaurant continued to operate.

Qwilleran and Riker went into the luncheonette for a sandwich and listened to the buzz of voices. There was only one topic of conversation:

"They weren't married more than a year. She made her own wedding dress."

"Tiff made more kills last year than anybody in the volleyball league."

"My brother was Steve's best man. All the fellas wore white tailcoats and white top hats. Really cool!"

When the two men returned home there was an unfamiliar truck parked near the garage. Its body mounted high over the chassis.

"What's that ugly thing doing there?" Riker asked.

"Don't knock it," Qwilleran said. "A terrain vehicle up here has the *éclat* of a private jet Down Below. Farmers and sportsmen love 'em. I'll go and see whose it is."

In the loft above the garage he found a substitute painter putting the finish coat on the doorframes. "Are you Steve's cousin?"

"Yeah, I'm fillin' in till he gets back."

"I feel very bad about Tiffany."

"Yeah, it's tough. And you wanna know what? The police took Steve in for questioning! Ain't that a kick in the head?"

"It's only routine," Qwilleran assured him. "The police think the sniper was a tourist."

The painter looked wise and said in a lowered voice, "I could tell 'em a few things, but I know when to keep my mouth shut."

Typical small-town reaction, Qwilleran thought. Everyone knows the answers, or thinks he does, or pretends to. But no one talks.

Riker had found a hammock in the backyard and was reading the *Picayune*. Mrs. Cobb was in the kitchen, pounding boned pheasant for the terrine.

"The police were here!" she announced. "They wanted to

know if Steve was on the job yesterday afternoon, and I was able to give him an alibi. He was having a beer with me at the time of the shooting. He's a nice young man. I feel very sorry for him."

"It's abnormally quiet. Where's Birch?"

"Gone fishing. He's catching the salmon for the croquettes."

"Is everything progressing to your satisfaction?"

"Everything's getting done, but Koko's been acting funny, scratching the broom closet door and jumping up to reach the handle."

"I put that musty suitcase in the closet, and he can smell it. He doesn't miss a thing. It's time I got rid of all that junk."

Koko heard his name and came running, saying, "ik ik ik," in a businesslike tone.

"Okay, okay, I'm throwing the smelly things out." Qwilleran carried the large carton of Daisy's winter clothing to the trash bin in the garage and then returned for the suitcase. He was halfway to the back door when he heard an emphatic yowl. It was not the kind of cat-talk that meant "Time for dinner" or "Here comes the mail" or "Where's Yum Yum?" It was a vehement directive.

Qwilleran stopped. Why, he asked himself, had Koko suddenly resumed interest the suitcase? Not the carton, just the suitcase. Without further hesitation he turned around and carried the piece of luggage to the library. Koko followed in great excitement.

Once again Qwilleran inspected the contents of the suitcase, examining each pathetic item, hoping to find a clue or start a train of thought. He emptied the case right down to the sleazy torn lining.

"Yow!" said Koko, who was supervising the process.

Torn lining! A twinge on Qwilleran's upper lip was telling him something. Speculatively he passed a hand over the bottom of the case. There was the outline of something flat and rectangular beneath the cheap, shiny, stained cloth. When he reached into the rip it tore further and exposed an envelope—a blank white envelope. Inside it was a wad of currency—new bills—hundred-dollar bills—ten of them.

"Yow!" said Koko.

Where, Qwilleran wondered, did she get this much money?

Did she steal it? Was it a payoff? A bribe to leave town? The wherewithal for an abortion?

Daisy might not have realized the value of the ivory elephant. She might have forgotten the gold bracelet in her hurry to get away. But if she happened to have a thousand in cash, she would hardly leave town without it . . . that is, if she *had* left town.

After the dinner party, Qwilleran promised himself, he would have another chat with the police chief.

ELEVEN

ON THE DAY of the party the house was in turmoil, and the Siamese were banished to the basement—until their indignant protests became more annoying than their actual presence underfoot.

Mrs. Cobb was rolling croquettes and slivering lamb with garlic. Mrs. Fulgrove was ironing table linens, polishing silver, and writing place cards and gentlemen's envelopes in her flawless penmanship, flattered beyond words when asked to do so. The florist delivered a truckload of flowers. The end sections of the long dinner table had been removed in order to seat ten comfortably, and Melinda was using a yardstick to measure the correct distance between dinner plates.

All this frenzied activity made Qwilleran nervous. He had never hosted a formal dinner; all his entertaining had been done in restaurants and clubs. So, when Riker borrowed the car and went sightseeing, Qwilleran set out for a tranquilizing bike ride.

Having completed the loop that constituted his daily ten-mile workout, he was just within the city limits when a menacing dog with a full set of repulsive teeth bounded from a backyard and charged the bicycle, barking and nipping at his heels. Qwilleran bellowed and swerved to the left and heard a screeching of tires as a motorist behind him jammed on the brakes.

Someone called to the dog, and the animal ran back into the yard, where two others were barking and straining at their chains.

In spluttering fury Qwilleran approached the driver of the car. "That dog—did you see him come at me?"

The woman at the wheel said, "I'm all shook up. I thought sure I was going to hit you. It was terrible! It shouldn't be allowed."

"Allowed! It's not allowed! It's prohibited by law. I'm going to make a formal complaint. May I have your name as a witness?"

She shrank away from him. "I'd really like to help, but . . . my husband wouldn't want me to get involved. I'm terribly sorry."

Qwilleran said no more but biked directly to the police station, where he found Chief Brodie on the desk, growling about a complaint of his own. "Too much paperwork! They invent computers to make life easier, and everything gets complicated. What can I do for you, Mr. Q?"

Qwilleran related his experience with the unchained dog, giving the name of the street and the number of the house. "That dog might be rabid," he said, "and I might have been killed."

Brodie made a helpless gesture. "Hackpole again! It's a problem. He's had a lot of warnings. There's nothing more we can do unless you want to go to the magistrate and sign a complaint. Nobody else will stick his neck out."

"Who is Hackpole, anyway? Was he ever a New York cabdriver?"

"He was born here, but he worked in the East for a long time —Newark, I think. Came back a few years ago. Runs a used-car lot and a garage."

"Will it do any good if I sign a complaint?"

"The sheriff will deliver a summons, and there'll be a show-cause hearing in two or three weeks."

"I'll do it!" Qwilleran said. "And tell the sheriff to get an antirabies shot and wear dogproof pants."

When he returned home from his bike ride he was less tranquil than before, but the magnificence of the interior calmed his tensions.

In the dining room, crystal and silver glittered on white damask, and two towering candelabra flanked a Victorian epergne, its branches filled with flowers, fruit, nuts, and mints.

By seven o'clock Melinda had changed into a chiffon dinner dress in a green that enhanced her eyes. Qwilleran, wearing the better of his two suits and his new tie, looked almost well dressed; his hair and moustache were trimmed, and two weeks of biking had given him a tan as well as an improved waistline.

Riker had been dispatched to pick up Amanda. As for the Siamese, it was decided that they be allowed to join the company. Otherwise their nonstop wailing would drown out the efforts of the three elderly men who were tuning their stringed instruments in the foyer.

Playing the role of butler, the genial owner of the department store was rehearsing with starched dignity and a stony countenance. As the footmen, the banker's sons were practicing obsequious anonymity—not easy for Yale undergaduates, Melinda remarked. The Fitch twins would be stationed at the front door to admit guests and conduct them to the solarium, where Lanspeak would announce them and serve cocktails. Later, in the dining room, the footmen would serve from the left and remove plates from the right, while the butler poured wine with a deft twist of the wrist.

"Remember," Melinda told them. "No eye contact."

How did I get mixed up in this? Qwilleran wondered.

First guest to ring the doorbell was the fresh-faced young managing editor of the *Picayune*, looking like a high school student on graduation day. Roger and his wife and mother-in-law arrived in high spirits. Sharon in an Indian sari and Mildred in something she had woven herself, with much fringe. Equally merry were Arch Riker and his blind date, leading Qwilleran to assume they had stopped at a bar. Amanda's floral print dinner dress had the aroma of a cedar closet and look of a thrift shop.

Finally, making their quiet but grand entrance, were Penelope and her brother, Alexander—a tall impressive pair with the lean, high-browed Goodwinter features and an elegant presence. Alexander looked cool and important in a white silk suit, and his sister was cool and chic in a simple white dinner dress. She moved in a cloud of perfume, an arresting fragrance that seemed to take everyone by surprise.

"The Duke and Duchess have arrived," Amanda whispered to Riker. "Mind your manners or it's *off with your head!*"

Qwilleran made the introductions, and Alexander said to Riker in his courtroom voice, "We trust you will find our peaceful little community as enjoyable as we find your—ah—stimulating newspapers."

"I'm certainly enjoying your—ah—perfect weather," said the editor.

Qwilleran inquired about the weather in Washington.

"Unbearably hot," said the attorney with a wry smile, "but one tries to suffer with grace. While I have the ear of—ah—influential persons, I do what I can for our farmers, the forgotten heroes of this great northern county of ours."

The French doors of the solarium were open, admitting early-evening zephyrs that dissipated somewhat the impact of Penelope's perfume. Drifting in from the trio in the foyer were Cole Porter melodies that created the right touch of gaiety and sophistication.

When the butler approached with a silver tray of potables, the Goodwinters recognized the local retailing tycoon and exchanged incredulous glances, but they maintained their poise.

"Champagne, madame," Lanspeak intoned, "and Catawba grape juice."

Penelope hesitated, looked briefly at her brother, and chose the nonalcoholic beverage.

Qwilleran said, "There are mixed drinks if you prefer."

"I consider this an occasion for Champagne," Alexander said, taking a glass with a flourish. "History is made tonight. To our knowledge this if the first festive dinner ever to take place at the Klingenshoen mansion."

"The Klingenshoens were never active in the social life of Pickax," his sister said with elevated eyebrows.

The guests circulated, remarked about the size of the rubber plants, admired the Siamese, and made smalltalk.

"Hello, Koko," Roger said bravely, but the cat ignored him. Both Koko and Yum Yum were intent upon circling Penelope, sniffing ardently and occasionaly sneezing a delicate whispered *chiff.*

The guest of honor was teasing Sharon about the primitive airport.

"Don't laugh, Mr. Riker. My grandmother arrived here in a covered wagon, and that was only seventy-five years ago. Our farms didn't have electricity until 1937."

To Junior, Riker said, "You must be the world's youngest managing editor."

"I'm starting at the top and working my way down," Junior said. "My ambition is to be a copyboy for the *Daily Fluxion*."

"Copy *facilitator*," the editor corrected him.

At a signal from the hostess the butler carried a silver tray of small envelopes to the gentlemen, containing the names of the ladies they were to take into the dining room. "Dinner is served," he announced. The musicians switched to Viennese waltzes, and the guests went into dinner two by two. No one noticed Koko and Yum Yum bringing up the rear, with tails proudly erect.

Penelope, escorted by Qwilleran, whispered, "Forgive me if I sounded curt yesterday. I had received bad news, although that is no excuse. My brother sees no reason why your memorial to Tiffany Trotter should be inappropriate."

The great doors of the dining room had been rolled back, and the company gasped at the sight. Sixteen wax candles were burning in the silver candelabra, and twenty-four electric candles were aglow in the staghorn chandeliers, all of this against a rich background of linenfold paneling and drawn velvet draperies. There were comments on the magnificent centerpiece. Then the guests savored the terrine of pheasant, and Qwilleran noticed—from the corner of his eyes—two dark brown tails disappearing under the white damask.

Seated at the head of the table, he had Penelope on his right and Amanda on his left. At one point he described the incident caused by Hackpole's dog, also his decision to make a formal complaint.

Amanda said, "It's about time somebody blew the whistle on that lamebrain. If our mayor wasn't such an ass, he wouldn't let Hackpole get away with it."

Penelope promptly launched a more genteel topic. "Everyone is tremendously pleased to hear, Mr. Qwilleran, that you might present this house to the city as a museum."

"The city won't appreciate it," Amanda retorted. "They'll find it costs a few bucks to heat the place and pay the light bill, and they'll rezone the Circle and sell it for a rooming house."

It seemed to Qwilleran that the conversation at the other end of the table was progressing with more finesse. While he labored to get Roger and Junior talking, he could hear Riker telling newspaper stories, Alexander extolling the social life in Washington, Melinda describing her week in Paris, and Sharon and Mildred laughing about the naive tourists in Mooseville.

"Chfff!" The Siamese were still under the table. Yum Yum was looking for a shoelace to untie, and Koko was listening to the guests' voices with rapt concentration.

By the time the salmon croquettes were served, the host was finding it difficult to keep a dialogue alive. Junior seemed speechless with awe; no doubt he had never seen an epergne nor eaten terrine of pheasant. Roger was eating, but he seemed somewhere else. Penelope appeared preoccupied; at best her remarks were guarded, and she was not sipping her wine. As for the outspoken Amanda, she was becoming drowsier by the minute.

The waltz rhythms emanating from the foyer were soporific, Qwilleran thought, and he wished the musicians would try Mozart or Boccherini. Yet, Melinda's immediate tablemates were pleasantly animated.

In desperation he tried one subject after another. "Birch Tree's motorbike has a stereo cassette player, cruise control, and an intercom. I prefer pedaling an old-fashioned one-speed bicycle on Ittibittiwassee Road—smooth pavement, sparse traffic, and that eerie Buckshot Mine. . . . You know a lot about mining history, Roger. What were the other nine mines?"

Roger blinked his eyes and said listlessly, "Well . . . there was the Goodwinter . . . and the Big B . . . and the Dimsdale."

"And the Moosejaw," his wife called out from her place farther down the table.

"The Moosejaw . . . and the Black Creek. How many is that?"

"That's only six, dear."

"Well . . . there was the Honey Hill and . . . Did I mention Old Glory?"

"Don't forget Smith's Folly, dear."

"Smith's Folly. There, that's it!" Roger concluded with relief.

Qwilleran had been counting on his fingers. "Including the Buckshot, that's only nine."

"He forgot the Three Pines," Sharon said. "That's where they had the big cave-in a few years ago. Even the *Daily Fluxion* wrote it up."

"*Chfff!*" There was another sneeze under the table.

The lamb *bûcheronne* was served, and Penelope asked, "Are you doing any writing, Mr. Qwilleran?"

"Only letters. I get a tremendous amount of mail."

"I understand you answer each letter personally in a most gracious way. That's really very charming of you."

Qwilleran could hear a familiar yukking sound under the table and hoped Koko was only expressing an opinion of the conversation and not throwing up on Penelope's shoe. He could also hear Mildred, far down the table, telling Alexander about her talented art student who had left town without explanation and virtually disappeared.

"A great pity," she said, "because she came from a poor family, and she could have gone to college on a scholarship and achieved some kind of success."

Alexander said with authority, "Great numbers of young women escape their humdrum existence in small towns every year, and they are assimilated into urban life, sometimes with—ah—great success. Many women professionals in New York and Washington were refugees, so to speak, from rural areas. We lost this talent because we fail to provide encouragement and opportunities and rewards."

"*Chfff!*"

"It's too bad," Mildred said, "that we don't do as much for artists as we do for farmers."

Throughout the salad course Qwilleran persevered in promoting table talk, and he was relieved when the wild raspberry trifle was served. At that point he made an announcement:

"Ladies and gentlemen, absent from this table is an important member of our household who wears many hats—those of resident manager, curator of the collection, registrar, and official appraiser. And no one has a better right to wear the hat of a master chef. We are indebted to Iris Cobb for preparing this dinner tonight. I would like to ask her to join us at the table for dessert."

There were murmurs of approval as he went to the kitchen and returned with the flustered housekeeper, and there was applause when he pulled up a chair and seated Mrs. Cobb between himself and Penelope. The attorney merely stiffened her spine.

When coffee and liqueurs were served in the drawing room, Qwilleran's somnolent tablemates began to revive. A few gathered in a chatty group around the life-size portrait of a young woman with a wasp waist and bustle, circa 1880.

"She was a dance-hall girl before he married her," Amanda said. "Look at that bawdy twinkle in her eye."

"Let's hear some stories, Roger," Junior urged. "Tell us about the K Saloon."

"Tell the one about Harry," Sharon suggested.

Roger had snapped out of his malaise. "Do you think I should?"

"Why not?"

"Go ahead!"

"Well, it was like this—and it's true. . . . One of the regular customers at the K Saloon was a miner named Harry, and eventually he drank himself to death. He was laid out at the furniture store, which was also the undertaking parlor, and his buddies decided he should have one last night at his favorite watering hole. So they smuggled him out of the store and put him on a sledge—it was the dead of winter—and off they went to the K Saloon. They propped Harry up at the bar, and all the patrons paid their respects and drowned their grief. Finally, at three in the morning, Harry's friends put him on the sled again and whipped up the horses. They were singing and feeling no pain, so they didn't notice the corpse sliding off the tail of the icy sledge. When they got back to the furniture store—no Harry! They spent the rest of the night looking for him, but the snow was drifting and they didn't find Harry until spring."

There were gasps and groans and giggles, and Qwilleran said, "They were a bunch of necrophiliacs—that is, if the story is really true. I suspect it's apocryphal."

Penelope gave a small cough and said in a firm voice, "This has been a delightful evening, and I regret we must say good night."

Alexander said, "I emplane for Washington at an early hour tomorrow."

Amanda nudged Riker and said in a stage whisper, "They can't run the country without him."

The Mooseville group also departed. Riker drove Amanda home. Mrs. Cobb went upstairs to collapse. Qwilleran and Melinda had a drink in the kitchen with the butler, the footmen, and the string trio, praising them for their performances. Then, when everyone had left, host and hostess kicked off their shoes in the library and indulged in postprandial gossip.

Melinda said, "Did you notice Penelope's reaction when you brought the cook to the table? She considered it the major faux pas of the twentieth century."

"She didn't take a drink all evening. I think she wanted champagne, but her brother vetoed it."

"Alex doesn't like her to drink; she talks too freely. How did you like her perfume, lover? It's something she asked me to bring from Paris."

"Potent, to say the least," Qwilleran said. "She was sitting on my right, you know, and I lost my sense of smell. By the time the fish was served, I couldn't taste anything. Junior was sitting next to her, and he looked glassy eyed, as if he'd been smoking something. Amanda almost passed out, and Roger couldn't remember the names of the ten defunct mines. It was the perfume, I'm sure. The cats kept sneezing."

"I had to smuggle it in," Melinda confessed. "They don't allow it to be sold in this country."

"If you ask me, it's some kind of nerve gas. What's it called?"

"Fantaisie Féline. Very expensive. . . . Am I seeing things, or is that a pickax in the corner?"

"The Pickax Boosters presented it to me. I might mount it over the fireplace, or use it as a paperweight, or swing it at stray dogs when I'm biking."

At that moment Koko stalked into the library, giving Qwilleran his gimlet stare.

"By the way," Qwilleran said, "do you know anything about the Three Pines Mine?"

Melinda looked amused. "The shaft house is a notorious lovers' lair, darling. Why? Are you interested? At *your age?*"

TWELVE

THE MORNING AFTER the party Qwilleran drove Riker to the airport under threatening skies. "We're going to get the rain the farmers have been praying for and the tourist industry has been praying against."

"I hope my plane takes off before it closes in," Riker said. "Not that I'm in a hurry to get back to the *Fluxion*. I wouldn't mind living up here. Why don't you buy the *Picayune?* I'll come up here and run it for you."

"You don't mean it!"

"I do! It would be a staggering challenge."

"We'd have to fire Benjamin Franklin and spend ten million on new mechanical equipment. . . . What did you think of Melinda?"

"Remarkable young woman. Does she wear green contacts? Are those her own eyelashes?"

"Everything is absolutely real," Qwilleran assured him. "I've checked it out."

"You know, Qwill, the gold diggers will be after you now. You'd be better off to marry a girl like Melinda and settle down. Her family is well-off; she has a profession; and she thinks you're tops."

"You're generous with your advice this morning." Qwilleran never liked to be told what to do.

"Okay, here's another shot. Why don't you quit hunting for the missing housemaid? You could get a bullet in the head—like the girl on the tractor."

Watching Riker's plane gain altitude, Qwilleran recalled that his friend had always tried to discourage his investigations—and had never succeeded. This time his own discretion was telling him, however, to wait for more developments before presenting the case to Chief Brodie. All he had to offer at this moment was circumstantial evidence, speculation, a sensitive moustache, and a smart cat.

Before returning home he bought a pink cashmere sweater at Lanspeak's and had it gift-wrapped. At Diamond Jim's he selected a gold necklace and dropped it off at the clinic, where a shingle at the entrance showed signs of fresh paint:

DR. HALIFAX GOODWINTER, M.D.
DR. MELINDA GOODWINTER, M.D.

As he approached the K mansion he was first aware of a police car, then a traffic jam, then a crowd of onlookers in the street. A bell was tolling a single solemn note as a funeral procession lined up and Tiffany's casket was carried from one of the churches on the Circle.

And then it started to rain. It rained violently, almost in anger.

Qwilleran went to his desk to write a note of condolence to Steve Trotter, with an offer of an annual scholarship in Tiffany's name. As he wrote, the telephone started to jangle with thank-you calls from the dinner guests. Junior had never eaten such good food. Sharon wanted the recipes. Mildred praised everything but thought that Alexander Goodwinter was a stuffed shirt. Amanda was hung over.

"Golly, that was a good party," the designer croaked into the phone. "I've got a hangover that would kill a horse. Did I say anything I shouldn't last night?"

"You were a model of propriety, Amanda," said Qwilleran.

"Cripes! That's the last thing I ever wanted to be. I leave that to my cousins."

"I've just driven Arch to the airport. He enjoyed your company immensely."

"He's my type! Get him up here again—soon!"

When Melinda phoned to thank him for the necklace, she complained that his line had been continually busy.

"All our dinner guests have been calling," he said. "Everyone except Penelope."

"Penny won't phone. She'll write a very proper thank-you note on engraved stationery, sealed with wax. Did Arch get away before the rains came?"

"He did, and he gave me some parting advice: (a) get married and (b) forget about the Daisy Mull mystery. I plan to take at least one of his suggestions."

At lunchtime he presented his gift to Mrs. Cobb.

"Oh, Mr. Qwilleran! Pink is my favorite, and I've never had anything cashmere. You shouldn't have done it. Did they all like the food last night?"

"Your dinner will make history," he assured her, "and when you see Mrs. Fulgrove, tell her that everyone admired her handwriting."

"When she was writing the place cards," Mrs. Cobb said, "she told me something. I don't know whether I should repeat it."

"Go ahead." Qwilleran's remark was offhand, but his moustache was bristling with curiosity.

"Well, she works three times a week at the Goodwinter house, you know, and she overheard Miss Goodwinter and her brother having a terrible row—yelling and everything. She said it was kind of frightening because they're always so nice to each other."

"What were they arguing about?"

"She couldn't hear. She was cleaning the kitchen, and they were upstairs."

At that moment a particularly objectionable burst of music came from the upper regions of the K mansion. "I see our star boarder is still on the premises," Qwilleran said.

"He's almost finished, but his bill is going to be enormous, I'm afraid."

"Don't worry. The estate will pay for it, and I'll tell them to deduct for five breakfasts, eight lunches, seven gallons of coffee, a case of beer, and a visit to the ear doctor. I think my hearing is permanently impaired."

"Oh, Mr. Qwilleran, you must be joking."

It rained hard for forty-eight hours, until the stone-paved streets of Pickax were flooded. Downtown Main Street, with its hodgepodge of architectural styles, was a parody of the Grand Canal. Grudgingly Qwilleran stayed indoors.

On the third day the rain ceased, and the wet fieldstone of the K mansion sparkled like diamonds in the sunshine. A brisk breeze started to dry up the floors. The birds sang. The Siamese rolled on the solarium floor and laundered their fur in the warm rays.

It was shortly after breakfast when an unexpected visitor arrived at the back door.

Mrs. Cobb hurried to the library to find Qwilleran. "Steve Trotter is here to see you. It looks like he's had a lot to drink."

Qwilleran dropped his newspaper and went to the kitchen, where the painter in off-duty jeans and T-shirt was leaning unsteadily against the doorjamb, his face slack and his eyelids drooping.

Qwilleran pulled out two kitchen chairs. "Come in and sit down, Steve. How about a cup of coffee?"

Mrs. Cobb quickly filled two mugs from the coffee maker and set them on the table, together with a plate of doughnuts.

"Don't want no coffee," Steve said, staring at Qwilleran belligerently. "Gotcha letter."

"It's hard to express the sorrow I feel about this outrageous crime," Qwilleran said. "I met Tiffany only twice, but—"

"Quit the bull! 'S all your fault," the painter said sullenly.

"I beg your pardon?"

"Y'got her mixed up in it. If y'didn't shoot off 'bout Daisy, wouldn'ta happened."

"Now wait a minute," Qwilleran said gently but firmly. "You overheard my private conversation with a visitor and went home and told your wife, didn't you? It was her idea to come here and talk about it. Furthermore, the police suspect that some tourist drove past the farm and—"

"Ain't no tourist, and y'know it."

"I haven't the least idea what you're implying, Steve."

"The letter y'sent me . . . tryin' to buy me off. No dice."

"What do you mean?"

"Y'wanna give money away to kids. Hell, what y'gonna do for

me? Why'n'cha pay for the fun'ral?" With an angry gesture he swept the coffee mug off the table. It shattered on the stone floor.

Mrs. Cobb made a hurried exit and returned almost immediately with Birch Tree.

"Okay, Stevie-boy," Birch said, grinning and showing his big square teeth. "Let's go home and sleep it off." He hoisted the younger man from the chair and propelled him toward the door.

Glancing out the window, Qwilleran saw the painter's truck parked with one wheel in the rhododendrons. "He can't drive in that condition," he said.

"I'll drive his truck. You follow and bring me back," Birch instructed in a tone of authority. "Only a coupla miles. Terence's dairy farm. Now you'll see where the stink comes from when the wind's from the southwest. Baa-a-a-a!"

After depositing Steve in his mobile home on the farm, Birch went to the farmhouse and talked to the in-laws. Then the two men drove back to town in the two-door, Qwilleran marveling at the man's competence and self-assurance in handling the awkward situation.

"Nice day," Birch said. "We needed rain, but they sent us too much. Baa-a-a-a!"

"I'll be able to take my bike out this afternoon," Qwilleran said.

"Me, I'm gonna knock off early and get in some fishin'. Big salmon's bitin' a few miles off Purple Point."

"Do you have a boat?"

"Sure do. Forty-foot cruiser, loaded. Fish finder, automatic pilot, ship-to-shore—you name it. Y'oughta get one."

Qwilleran frowned. "Fish-finder? What's that?"

"A graph, y'know. A CGR. Sonar computer graph recorder. Traces the bottom of the lake. Tells you where the fish are, and how many. First-class way to fish!"

By noontime Birch had cleared out with his noisebox and tools, and Qwilleran enjoyed his lunch in peace.

"It's good to have the doors fixed," Mrs. Cobb said. "It was worth all the commotion."

Qwilleran agreed. "Now Koko won't be able to barge into my room at six A.M. He thinks everyone should get up at dawn."

The housekeeper served lunch in the cheerful breakfast room, where William and Mary banister-back chairs surrounded a dark oak table, and yellow and green chintz covered the walls and draped the windows.

"Best macaroni-and-cheese I ever tasted," Qwilleran announced.

"I found some really good cheddar at a little store behind the post office," Mrs. Cobb said. After a moment she added, "I also noticed a sale of ten-speeds at the hardware store." She looked at him hopefully. "Twenty percent off."

Qwilleran grunted. "When they make a dogproof bike, I may be interested."

Later that afternoon he had another interesting scrap of conversation. The mail-cat trudged into the library to deliver Penelope's thank-you note, about which there lingered a faint but heady suggestion of Fantaisie Féline.

Qwilleran studied the intelligent-looking animal. "What was Steve trying to tell us, Koko? Who killed Tiffany Trotter—and why? And what really happened to Daisy Mull? Are we wasting our time hunting for answers?"

The cat sat tall on the desk, swaying slightly as he concentrated his blue gaze on Qwilleran's forehead. Suddenly the man realized that Koko had never experienced the murals in Daisy's apartment. He grabbed him and carried him out to the garage. The sleek body was neither struggling in protest nor limp with acquiescence—just taut with anticipation.

First Koko was allowed to examine the cars, the bicycle, the garden implements. It was always better to let him take his time and follow his own inclinations. Eventually he found the flight of stairs and scampered up to the living quarters. In the freshly painted apartment he craned his neck and sniffed in every direction without any apparent pleasure. Then he wandered down the hall and into the jungle of daisies.

Koko's first reaction was to flatten himself, belly to the floor. All around him were wild, tangled, threatening forms on the walls and ceiling. Cats could not distinguish colors, Qwilleran had been told, but they could sense them. When Koko concluded that the place was safe, he started slinking around, inspecting with caution several mysterious spots on the rug, a scratch on the dresser, and a rip in the chair upholstery. As his investigation reassured him, he stretched to his full length before prancing around the room in a dance of exhilaration—as if he could hear music in colors that Qwilleran could appreciate only with his eyes.

Then something unseen alerted the cat. He looked quickly this way and that, ran a few steps, jumped and waved his paw, scurried across the room, turned and leaped through the air, twisting his lithe body into a back somersault.

Remembering Mrs. Cobb's haunted-house theory, Qwilleran shivered involuntarily until he realized the truth. It was almost August, the season of houseflies, and Koko was chasing a tiny flying insect, matching its aerial swooping with his own acrobatics. He chased it into the hallway and soon returned, chomping and licking his chops.

"Disgusting!" Qwilleran told him. "Is that all you can find to do?"

Koko was excited by the chase and the kill, and he was bent on finding another prey. He jumped onto the bed and stood on his hind legs, extending a paw up the wall. He was a yard long when he stretched to the limit. He pawed the graffiti, trying to reach one set of initials nestled in the pattern of hearts, flowers, and foliage. Then he sprang, and a fly fell down behind the bed. In a split second the cat was after it. Dead or alive, the fly had fallen between the mattress and the wall. Koko reached into the crevice with one slender foreleg and then the other, mumbling to himself in determined gutturals.

Qwilleran watched the struggle for a while before pulling the bed away from the wall. Like a hawk Koko dived into the aperture, and soon there were sounds of moist chomping.

"Revolting!" Qwilleran said. "You eat those filthy flies, but you won't eat catfood with added vitamins and minerals. Let's get out of here. We're going home."

Koko remained behind the bed. *"Chiff! Chiff!"* It was that delicate cat-sneeze.

"It's dusty back there! Get out! Let's go!"

The cat failed to respond, and Qwilleran felt the old tingling sensation on his upper lip. Once before, Koko had dredged up some telling mementoes from behind a bed. Kneeling on the mattress the man peered down into the shadows. Koko was hunched over something, sniffing it, nuzzling it, poking it with one inquisitive paw.

Qwilleran reached down and retrieved a notebook—a school notebook with torn and ruffled pages. Koko immediately jumped out of his hiding place, yowling and demanding his treasure. Some of the pages had obviously been nibbled by mice.

With the notebook in one hand and the indignant cat in the other, Qwilleran returned to the house and headed for the library. Koko was howling in high dudgeon, and Yum Yum came running from the solarium, shrieking in sympathy. They were followed by Mrs. Cobb. "What's the matter? What's going on here?"

"Give them a treat, will you? Get them out of my hair!"

"Treat!" she cried, and led the way to the kitchen like the Pied Piper.

Qwilleran closed the library door and settled down to inspect Koko's find. It was the cheapest kind of notebook, with ruled pages, some of them nibbled and all of them stained. It had a definite mousy odor.

"A diary!" he said aloud, as he thumbed through the soiled pages with distaste. He could distinguish dates, but the handwriting was completely illegible. Once upon a time he had known an artist who could make every letter of the alphabet look like a *U;* Daisy made every letter look like *O.* The cursive writing was a coil of overlapping circles. The art teacher's comment had been apt; Daisy's calligraphic invention was attractive to the eye but impossible to read.

After his bike ride, he decided, he would phone Mildred Hanstable and ask her to look at the diary—and translate it if possible. Meanwhile he added it to the growing collection in the desk drawer: the ivory elephant, a gold bracelet, a postal card, and an envelope with a thousand in cash.

Everyone of these memorabilia had been found by that phenomenal cat, he recalled. Yet Koko always made his discoveries seem so casual. This time he went through the motions of chasing a fly, pursuing it up the wall, batting it down as it tried to camouflage itself among the initials. . . . What were the initials?

Qwilleran made a dash to the garage and back. Grabbing the little telephone directory, he combed two columns of listings.

Only three subscribers had the right initials: Sam Gafner, Scott Gippel, and Senior Goodwinter.

If SG had been the object of Daisy's affection, it would have to be Gafner, he concluded. Scott Gippel was the enormous councilman who required two chairs. Junior's father—with his paper hat and bemused expression—would hardly appeal to a giddy young girl. Gafner, the real estate broker, was the most likely candidate. After his bike ride, he decided, he would do some serious research.

It was a beautiful day for biking. Warmed by the sun and caressed by light breezes, Qwilleran headed for his favorite country road. The vegetation, freshly washed, was a vibrant green. Flocks of blackbirds rose from the brush and followed the lone rider, scolding with staccato chirps. Clicks in the sprocket and rear wheel added to the chorus. He remembered Mrs. Cobb's parting words: "Be careful with that broken-down contraption, Mr. Q. You really ought to buy a ten-speed."

Everything on Ittibittiwassee Road smelled damp and clean. The sun and breezes had dried the pavement, but the roadside ditch was filled with rainwater. It was a good thirty feet from the pavement to allow for future widening of the road. This would be a major highway when the condominium development was completed. Too bad! He liked the quiet and the loneliness of the road.

Coming up on the right was the site of the old Buckshot Mine, where miners had died in a cave-in in 1913. As he pedaled past the ruins he listened intently for the eerie whistling sound said to emanate from the mineshaft. The abandoned shaft house, a weathered silver, had been drenched with rain.

Qwilleran was studying the ruins with such concentration that he was unaware of a truck approaching from the opposite direction—unaware until its motor roared. He looked ahead in time to see its burst of speed, its sudden swerve into the eastbound lane, a murderous monster bearing down upon him and his rickety bicycle. He yanked the handlebars and plunged down toward the ditch, but his front wheel hit a rock, and he went sailing over the handlebars. For an interminable moment he was airborne. . . .

When he climbed out of the ditch, dazed and wet and bleed-

ing, he staggered painfully to the deserted highway, not knowing where he was or why he was there.

Roads go somewhere. Follow the road. Move. Keep moving.

In a few minutes or a few hours a car stopped. A man jumped
out, shouting, and put him in the front seat. For a few minutes—
or hours—he sat in a speeding car. The man kept shouting.

What is he saying? I don't know—I can't—

He was wheeled into a building. Bright lights. Strange people,
talking, talking— He was tired. .

The next morning he opened his eyes and found himself in a
strange bed in a strange room.

THIRTEEN

BEFORE QWILLERAN WAS released from Pickax Hospital, he had a consultation with Dr. Melinda.

"All your tests turned out fine," she said. "You're a very healthy guy—for your age."

"And for a young chick you're a very smart doctor."

"I'm so smart, lover, that I sneaked in a Wassermann test in case you want to apply for a marriage license. I'm also writing you a prescription for a crash helmet. With your head injury you could have drowned in that drainage ditch."

"I'm sure the hit-runner thought he was leaving me for dead."

"Some strange things are happening in Moose County," Melinda said. "Amanda may be right about the tourist invasion. You should report it to the police."

"On the strength of what? My dream? Brodie would think I damaged something else beside my bicycle. No, Melinda, I'm merely going to keep a sharp lookout for a certain truck. In my dream I could see it clearly, coming at me fast, a rusty grille grinning at me, towering over me. It was one of those terrain vehicles."

"Junior was one scared kid when he brought you in. He thought you were a zombie."

"It was a strange experience, Melinda. When I opened my

eyes in a hospital bed and didn't know where I was or *who* I was, it didn't disturb me at all. It was simply a puzzle that aroused my curiosity. Glad you got Arch Riker up here to straighten me out."

Riker picked Qwilleran up at the hospital in a rental car from the airport. "I have time for a cuppa, Qwill, before I catch my plane."

"Then head north at the traffic light and we'll tune in the coffee hour at the Dismal diner. If you think the Press Club is a gossip mill, wait till you hear the boys up here."

"What did your tests show? Everything okay?"

"Everything's fine, but I have some ugly suspicions about my bike mishap. It was no mishap. It was no accident, Arch! It was a hit-run attempt on my life."

"I warned you! Why do you get mixed up in criminal investigations that are none of your business? Leave it to the authorities."

"This has nothing to do with the missing housemaid. It's something else entirely. I came to that conclusion when I was lying in that hospital bed. You know the conditions of the Klingenshoen bequest: I have to live in Pickax for five years or the estate goes to a syndicate in New Jersey. Well, what happens if I *die* before the five years are up?"

"Without knowing anything about probate law," Riker said, "I'd guess that the dough goes to New Jersey."

"So it's to their advantage if I fade out before the five years are up. In fact, the sooner the better."

Riker gave his passenger an incredulous glance. "That's a jarring thought, Qwill. Why do you suspect them?"

"It's a so-called foundation involved in some dubious venture in Atlantic City. I don't trust those people."

The editor said, "When I first heard about the Old Lady's will, I knew it was too good to be true. Forget the inheritance, Qwill. You never wanted a fortune anyway. You know you can have your job back at the *Fluxion*."

"Then the money will leave Moose County."

"Don't try to be a hero. Get out of here and save your skin. Let those forty-seven affluent Goodwinters buy some new books for the library."

Qwilleran fingered his moustache with uncertainty. "I'll figure out something. I've got an appointment with the attorney this afternoon. And maybe we'll hear some scuttlebutt at the diner."

The coffee hour was effervescing in a haze of blue smoke. A few men in feed caps nodded to Qwilleran as he and Riker helped themselves to coffee and doughnuts. The two newsmen sat at a side table, listening.

"He's handin' out cigars, but he ain't the father."

"I butcher my own hogs, make my own sausage. Only way to go."

"It says in the Bible that a fool's voice is known by its multitude of words, and that fits him all right!'

"Birds! That's my bag, and I always limit out."

"If she's a lawyer, why would she want to get married?"

"They had to shoot the whole herd. Damn shame!"

"All she wants is his dough, I betcha."

"Man, my wife makes the best rabbit stew you ever tasted."

"Never heard the name. Is it Russian or something?"

"My mother-in-law's been here goin' on three weeks."

Before heading for the airport Riker dropped Qwilleran off at his house. "Did you get any clues from all that bull?" he asked.

Qwilleran shook his head. "They know who I am. They clammed up."

If he was expecting a joyous welcome from the Siamese, he was disappointed. They could smell the hospital, and they circled him with distaste, Yum Yum hissing and Koko producing a chesty rumble that sounded like distant thunder. The situation was still a standoff when he left for his one o'clock appointment.

He walked into the law office slowly, still hampered by the wrappings on his sutured knee. Penelope also lacked her usual verve. She was wearing dark glasses and looking pale. In a shaky voice she said, "You look a trifle battered, Mr. Qwilleran, but we are all thankful it was no worse. What can I do for you?"

He stated his question about the Klingenshoen will.

"As you know," Penelope reminded him, "it was a holographic will. The dear lady insisted on writing it herself, without an attorney and without witnesses, to protect her privacy. Let me review the document again to refresh my memory."

The clerk brought the handwritten will, and Penelope read it carefully, shaking her head. "You are justified in being concerned. In the event of your death the estate would go to the alternate heirs in New Jersey. But surely you have nothing to worry about. Except for your temporary injuries, you seem extraordinarily healthy."

"Then brace yourself," Qwilleran said. He repeated his suspicion about the so-called accident and his distrust of the East Coast heirs. "Is there anyone in town who comes from that part of the country or has connections there?"

"Not to my knowledge," she said, looking pensive and withdrawn.

He refrained from mentioning his private list of suspects. Hackpole had worked in Newark. The gardener was a Princeton man. Qwilleran's own former in-laws—an obnoxious crew—pursued some questionable profession in the Garden State.

To the attorney he said, "In any event I feel strongly that the money should stay in Moose County. It belongs here, and it can do a lot of good. How can we circumvent the present situation? Are there any loopholes? May I write a will myself, assigning my claim to the Klingenshoen Foundation?"

"I'm afraid not," Penelope said. "The language of the original will fails to grant you that power. . . . Let me think. . . . This is really an unfortunate development, Mr. Qwilleran. I can only hope you are wrong in your suspicions."

"Then be advised," he said, "that I'm going to write the will anyway. If anything happens to me, you'd better demand an investigation into the cause of my death."

"I must say, Mr. Qwilleran, you are very calm and businesslike about a distressing possibility."

"I've been in hot spots before," he said, waving her comment aside. "I'll write a holographic will, so Goodwinter & Goodwinter cannot be faulted for giving me bad advice. And I'll see that all the bases are covered—the police, the prosecutor's office, the media . . ."

"What can I say? . . . Except that I'm quite upset about your allegations."

"So be it. Discuss it with your brother, if you see fit, but right or wrong, that's going to be my course of action."

As he hobbled from the office he thought, She's hung over; she needs a hair of the dog. So he hobbled back into Penelope's presence. "Your rain check is still good, Miss Goodwinter. I'd like to suggest cocktails and dinner at the Old Stone Mill tonight, if you don't mind dining with a walking accident statistic."

She hesitated briefly before saying, "Thank you, Mr. Qwilleran, but not tonight, I'm afraid."

Her telltale physiological condition surprised him more than her refusal of his invitation. Regarding the latter he decided she just didn't like frozen ravioli.

At breakfast the next morning Mrs. Cobb had more Goodwinter gossip to report.

"Sorry to be late," Qwilleran apologized as he sat down to a plate of real buttermilk pancakes and real Canadian peameal bacon. "I seem to require more sleep since my accident." He sniffed critically. "I smell lavender."

"That's English wax," the housekeeper said. "Mrs. Fulgrove is working on the dining room furniture." She tiptoed to the door of the breakfast room and closed it gently. "She told me the Goodwinters had another fight when he got home from Washington. Miss G was shouting about mosquitoes—and a woman—and a dead body, whatever that means. None of it was very clear to me. Mrs. Fulgrove is hard to understand. She also said something about a *cow* opening a restaurant in Pickax."

"It can't be any worse than the restaurants we've got," he said. "It might even be better. Any phone calls?"

"Lori Bamba called. She said her husband will drop off the first batch of letters for you to sign. Mrs. Hanstable phoned to say she's picking wild blueberries and asked if we wanted any. She sells them to raise money for the hospital."

"I hope you placed an order."

"I told her two quarts. She'll drop them off tomorrow when she comes in town to have her hair done."

"You women," he said, "structure your lives around your hair appointments."

"Oh, Mr. Q," she laughed, admonishing him with her eyes. She was acting girlish, he thought, and he soon found out why. "I've been invited out to dinner tonight," she said. "A man I met at the Historical Society."

"Good! I'll grab a hamburger somewhere."

"You don't need to do that, Mr. Qwilleran. I bought four beautiful loin chops and some big Idaho bakers, and I could put them in the oven before I go. I thought maybe you'd like to ask someone over."

"Good idea! I'll invite Junior. I owe him one."

In the afternoon Nick Bamba arrived with seventy-five beautifully typed letters. He said proudly, "Lori makes each reply a little different, so it won't seem like a form letter. She's good at writing."

Qwilleran liked the young engineer from Mooseville. He had a healthy head of black curly hair and eyes like black onyx that shone with enthusiasm, and he always had some choice tidbit of information to impart.

"Glad you weren't seriously hurt, Qwill. Lori was praying for you."

"Tell her I need all the prayers I can get. How's she feeling?"

"Okay, except mornings, but that's natural."

"Would you like a beer?"

"Got anything stronger? Lori's on the wagon for the duration, so I do my drinking away from home."

"Spoken like a considerate husband," Qwilleran remarked.

They sat in the solarium with their drinks and discussed the Trotter case, bicycles, dogs, and the coffee crowd at the Dimsdale diner.

"On the way down here," Nick said, "I stopped at the diner for lunch, and I saw something unusual. Is Alex Goodwinter your attorney?"

"Actually his sister is handling the estate."

"I hear she's pretty sharp. I wish I could say the same for Alex. He gave a talk to the Mooseville Boosters a while back, and he's the dullest speaker I ever heard. He makes a good appearance, and a good presentation, but when it's all over, what has he said? Nothing!"

"What happened at the diner?" Qwilleran asked casually, although his curiosity was rampant.

"I was sitting at a window table, eating some by-product of a sawmill called meatloaf, and I saw this Cadillac pull into the parking lot. Usually it's all pickups and vans, you know."

"You mean you could actually see through the dirt on those windows?"

"Lori says I can see through a brick wall."

"So what did you see?"

"It was Alex driving the Caddie, and he sat there at the wheel with the motor running until one of the owners of the place went out and got in the front seat with him."

"Which partner?" Qwilleran asked.

"Not the cook. The big husky one who rides around on a motorbike. The two of them sat in the car, and it looked like they were arguing. Finally Alex got out his wallet and counted out some bills. I'd like to know what that little deal was all about."

Qwilleran's suspicions were piqued, but he offered a matter-of-fact explanation. "The guy does maintenance work. Alex could have been settling an account."

"In cash? Why wouldn't he write a check?" Nick leaned forward in his chair. "You know, I've always thought they were selling something besides food at the diner. Otherwise, how could that dump stay in business?"

Qwilleran chose to taunt Nick. "Alex is a leading citizen, a pillar of the community, a genuine rockbound Goodwinter. How can you cast aspersions?"

"Alex is a genuine four-flusher," said Nick, getting a little heated. "He likes to make people think he's an important influence in Washington, but I say he's down there having a good time."

"What does Lori think about him?"

"You know women!" Nick said with disdain. "She thinks he's a dreamboat—that's her word for him. I have another word."

Nick left, taking fifty more letters for his wife to answer, and Qwilleran visited the hardware store to look at bicycles. When he returned he said to Mrs. Cobb, "Do you know what they're asking for a ten-speed? More than I paid for my first car!"

"But you can afford it, Mr. Q."

"That's not the point. . . . You look very nice this afternoon, Mrs. Cobb."

"Thank you. I had my hair done." She was wearing more makeup than usual. "You'll never guess who invited me to dinner tonight! It's that man who objected to the forty-eight star flag."

"What? Hackpole?"

"Herb Hackpole. He's really very nice. He runs a garage, and he's going to find out why my van drips oil."

Qwilleran huffed into his moustache and reserved comment.

While waiting for Junior to arrive, he prepared dinner for the Siamese. Yum Yum had forgiven him for smelling like a hospital and had even jumped onto his lap and touched his moustache with an inquisitive paw. It was one of her endearing gestures. Accustomed to stealing toothbrushes and paintbrushes, she had never been able to understand bristles attached to a face.

Koko, on the other hand, was giving Qwilleran the silent treatment. He had stopped hissing and growling but regarded the man with utter contempt. When the plate of boned chicken was placed on the floor, he refused to eat until Qwilleran had left the room. It was an attitude entirely without precedent.

Junior arrived promptly at six, with the ravenous hunger of a twenty-two-year-old. "Hey, you look good in bandages, Qwill. You ought to wear them all the time."

They ate their pork chops at the massive kitchen table. "According to Mrs. Cobb," Qwilleran pointed out, "this is probably a sixteenth-century table from a Spanish monastery."

"She's a swell cook," Junior said. "You're lucky."

"She made a fresh peach pie for our dessert. . . . Have another roll, Junior. They're sourdough. . . . She went to dinner tonight with a guy from the Historical Society. I hope he's a decent sort. She's gullible, and I feel responsible, since I brought her up here from Down Below. Do you know Herb Hackpole?"

Junior finished chewing a large mouthful. "Everybody knows that guy."

"Mrs. Cobb finds him quite likable."

"Oh sure. He can be likable if he wants something. Mostly he's a troublemaker, always calling the paper with some piddling complaint, and we can't get kids to deliver papers on his block because of his dogs. . . . Pass the butter, Qwill."

"Has he always lived here?"

"Born and raised here, Dad says. In school everybody hated his guts. He was your standard small-town bully, you know. The whole town cheered when he went east to work. Too bad he came back. . . . Is there another beer?"

"Sure, and we've got a couple more ears of corn in the pot."

Over coffee and peach pie the young editor said, "I'm supposed to ask you a favor. Do you know the secretary at G&G? She's my aunt."

"I noticed a family resemblance," Qwilleran said.

"She thinks Penny is headed for trouble—working long hours and worried about something and *drinking,* which she doesn't usually do. My aunt thought maybe you could talk her into taking a vacation—a health spa in Mexico, or something like that."

"Me? I'm only a client. She won't even go to lunch with me."

"But Penny admires you a lot, no kidding. She used to clip your columns when you were writing for the *Fluxion.* She always—" He was interrupted abruptly by the insistent sound of his beeper. He jumped up and ran to the door. "Sorry. There's a fire. Great meal!"

He barreled away in his red Jaguar as the siren at City Hall summoned the volunteer firefighters.

It had been a busy day for Qwilleran, and it was not yet over. Penelope Goodwinter phoned to ask if she could pay a visit and bring a bottle.

FOURTEEN

IN PREPARATION FOR Penelope's visit Qwilleran carried an ice bucket and other bar essentials to the library. That was when he noticed several books on the floor—part of a twelve-volume set. The morocco covers were splayed and the India paper pages rumpled. His eyes traveled upward to the shelf and found Koko squeezed into the space between volumes II and VIII, having a nap. He had always liked to sleep on bookshelves.

"Bad cat!" Qwilleran shouted as he examined the mistreated books.

Waking suddenly, Koko yawned, stretched, and jumped to the floor, and stalked out of the room without comment.

Qwilleran replaced the books carefully, and at the same time he wondered if anyone in that house had ever read the handsomely bound twelve-volume poem titled *Doomsday*.

Doomsday! Qwilleran thought. Is that a prediction or some kind of catly curse?

He expected the tan BMW to pull into the circular drive as usual. Instead, the headlights searched out the rear of the house, and Penelope knocked at the back door with a playful rat-tat-tat that was out of keeping with her accustomed reserve.

"I hope you don't mind my coming to the service entrance,"

she caroled, waving a bottle of fine old Scotch. "After all, this is a terribly informal call."

She was relaxed almost to the point of gaiety, and she looked casual and comfortable in white ducks, sandals, and a navy blue jersey. As Melinda had mentioned, a little nip did wonders for Penelope's personality. Yet, her face was haggard and her eyes looked tired. One earring was missing, and she wore no perfume.

"The ice cubes await in the library," Qwilleran said with a flourish. "I find it the friendliest room in the house."

The brown tones of bookbindings and leather upholstery absorbed the lamplight, producing a seductive glow. Penelope slid into the slippery leather sofa and crossed her knees with the grace of a long-legged woman. Qwilleran chose a lounge chair and propped his injured leg on an ottoman.

"Are you on the mend?" she asked in a solicitous tone that sounded genuine.

"Twenty-three of my stitches are beginning to itch," he said, "so that's a healthy sign. I'm glad you decided to take a break. You've been working much too hard."

"I admit my eyes are weary."

"You need a couple of wet tea bags," he said. "My mother always recommended wet tea bags for tired eyes."

"Is the remedy effective?"

"Now is an appropriate time to find out." He hoisted himself out of the chair and returned with two soggy tea bags on a Wedgewood saucer. "Rest your head back on the back of the sofa."

She slid into a loungy position and said, "Oooh!" as he pressed the tea bags on her closed eyelids.

"How long since you've had a vacation, Penelope? I'm tired of calling you Miss Goodwinter. From now on it's *Penelope* whether you like it or not."

"I like it," she murmured.

"You should take a sybaritic week or two at one of those expensive health resorts," he suggested.

"A cruise would be more to my liking. Do you like cruise ships, Mr. Qwilleran?"

"I can't say I've ever sailed strictly for pleasure. . . . And it's *Qwill*, Penelope. Please!"

"Now that you're a man of leisure, you might try it—the Greek Islands, the Norwegian Fjords—" She was waving an empty glass in his direction, and Qwilleran poured a refill. Her first drink had disappeared fast.

"Before I start goofing off and taking cruises, I hope to produce a literary masterpiece or two," he said.

"You have a wonderful writing style. I always enjoyed your column in the *Fluxion*. You were so clever when you were writing on a subject you knew nothing about."

"Trick of the trade," he said modestly.

"It was once my ambition to be a writer, but you have real talent, Qwill. I could never aspire to what you seem to do with the greatest of ease."

Qwilleran knew he was a good writer, but he liked enormously to be told so, especially by an attractive woman. While one half of his mind basked in her effusive compliments, the other half was wondering why she had come. Had she argued with her brother again and escaped his surveillance? Why did he supervise her social conduct so assiduously? How could a stuffed shirt like Alexander exert so much influence over this intelligent woman?

Penelope was being unusually agreeable. She inquired about the health of the Siamese, Amanda's progress with the redecorating, and Mrs. Cobb's cataloguing of the collection.

"Her most recent discovery," Qwilleran said, "is a pair of majolica vases that had been relegated to the attic—circa 1870 and now worth thousands. They're just outside the door here—on top of another valuable item that she found in the garage—a Pennsylvania German wardrobe. She calls it a *schrank*. Seven feet high, and Koko can sail to the top of it in a single effortless leap."

Qwilleran wondered whether she was listening. He had spent enough time at cocktail parties to know the rhythm of social drinking, and Penelope was exceeding the speed limit. She was also sliding farther down on the slippery sofa.

In a kindly voice he said, "Be careful! The drinks can hit you hard when you're tired. You've been spending too many long hours at the office. Is it really worth it?"

"A junior partner," she said hesitantly, "has to keep her grind to the nosestone." She giggled. "Nose . . . to the . . . grindstone."

Qwilleran slipped into an investigative role he had played

many times—helpful and sympathetic, but somewhat devious. "It must be gratifying, Penelope, to know that your brother is accomplishing so much for the county when he spends his valuable time in Washington. It's a worthwhile sacrifice that he's making. I understand that he made a speech recently to the Mooseville Boosters, and they're still talking about it."

Penelope discarded the tea bags and struggled to her feet, in order to pour a more generous drink of Scotch for herself. "Did he tell them about his social—his social—conquests down there?" Her voice had a bitter edge, and her tongue tangled with certain words. "It's not—not all—business, you know."

"No doubt he'll run for office one of these days," Qwilleran went on, "and then his social contacts will be useful."

Penelope stared at him through a fog and spoke slowly and carefully. "Alex couldn't . . . get elected . . . mayor of . . . Dimsdale."

"You don't mean that, Penelope. With his name and background and suave manner and striking appearance he'd be a knockout in politics. He'd make a hit with the media. That's what counts these days."

Nastiness and alcohol contorted her handsome features. "He couldn't . . . get anywhere . . . without me." Her eyes were not focusing, and when she put her glass down on the table, it missed the edge. "Sorry," she said as she scrambled about on her knees, picking up ice cubes.

Qwilleran was relentless. "I'm sure you could manage the office efficiently while the senior partner is doing great things in the Capitol."

The brilliant, articulate Penelope was pathetically struggling to make sense. "He won't . . . go down there. He'll bring . . . he'll bring her . . . up here. New partner!"

Remarks overheard at the Dimsdale Diner flashed through Qwilleran's mind. "Is she an attorney?"

Penelope gulped what remained of her melted ice cubes. "Bring her . . . into the firm, that's what . . . but over my . . . dead body! I . . . won't . . . have it. *Won't have it!*"

"Penelope," he said soothingly, "it will be a good thing for you. Another partner will relieve you of some of the pressure."

She uttered a hysterical laugh. "Goodwinter, Goodwinter & Sh—Smfska!" She stumbled over the name. "Goodwinter, Goodwinter & Smfaska! We'll be . . . laughingstock . . . of the county!"

"Have you expressed your feelings to your brother? Perhaps he'll reconsider."

She was losing control. "He'll . . . he'll marry . . . he'll marry that—that tramp! But I'll . . . I'll stop it. I can . . . stop it. *Stop it!*" She looked wild-eyed and disheveled. "I feel . . . awful!"

Qwilleran pulled her to her feet. "You need fresh air." He walked her to the solarium and through the French doors and held her sympathetically while she gave vent to tears. "Do you want black coffee, Penelope?"

She shook her head.

"Shall I take you home?"

He drove the BMW to the turreted stone residence on Goodwinter Boulevard, with Penelope crumpled on the seat beside him. He parked under the porte cochere and carried her up the steps to the carriage entrance. A housekeeper came running, and Alexander appeared in a silk dressing gown.

"She's not well," Qwilleran said. "I think she's overly tired."

Alexander looked at his sister sternly and without compassion. "Take her upstairs," he told the housekeeper. Turning to Qwilleran he said, "Where did you—ah—find her?"

"She came to the house to discuss a legal matter, and she was taken ill. I think she needs a rest—a vacation—before she has a breakdown. Put her in the hospital for a few days. She should have a checkup."

"It is unfortunate," Alexander said, "but she goes completely out of her head when she touches alcohol, and she speaks the most utter nonsense. Thank you for returning her—ah—safely. Allow me to drive you home."

"No thanks. It's only a short distance, and it's a nice night."

As he walked slowly through the moonlit streets he reflected that Mrs. Fulgrove's report about "mosquitoes" and a dead body was roughly related to the facts, and he concluded that Penelope was overreacting to the threat of Ms. Smfska as professional partner and future sister-in-law. True, it would generate merriment in Moose County, especially among the coffee-shop regulars. Anyone familiar with the Goodwinter mystique and Penelope's insufferable snobbery would be amused at the thought of

Goodwinter, Goodwinter & Smfska. Among the cackling, bleating, guffawing crowd at the Dismal Diner it would probably become Goodwinter, Goodwinter & Mosquito. Nevertheless, after hospital rest and a vacation, he decided, the junior partner would regain her perspective.

Approaching the K mansion, he glanced at the second floor. The lights were turned on in Mrs. Cobb's suite, indicating that she had returned safely after an evening with that ape! She had always been attracted to tattoos and crew cuts. Her late husband had been a brutish-looking ruffian.

There was a light in the back entry, but the rest of the service area was dark, and as Qwilleran unlocked the door he heard a scraping sound in the kitchen. He stood motionless and listened intently, trying to identify it. *Scrape* . . . pause . . . *long scrape* . . . pause . . . *two short scrapes*. He crossed the stone floor silently in his deck shoes, reached inside the kitchen door, and flicked on the lights.

There in the middle of the floor was the cats' heavy metal commode filled with kitty gravel, and behind it was Koko, preparing to give it another shove with his nose. The cat looked up with startled eyes and ears.

"You bad cat!" Qwilleran said sharply. "You're the one who's been moving things around! You could kill a person! Cut it out!"

He returned the commode to the laundry room and went upstairs to think about Penelope and compare her to Melinda. They were both handsome women with the Goodwinter features and intelligence and education. The attorney was the more striking of the two, but she lacked Melinda's equanimity and sense of humor. He was lucky to have a healthy, well-adjusted woman like Melinda who called him "lover" and managed great dinner parties and knew how to pronounce sphygmomanometer.

The next morning he found Mildred Hanstable in the kitchen delivering wild blueberries. She and Mrs. Cobb were having a cup of coffee and getting acquainted.

Qwilleran said, "Mildred, you'll be interested to know that Mrs. Cobb is a palmist."

Mildred squealed with delight. "Really? Would you be willing to read palms at the hospital bazaar? We have tarot card readings and raise quite a bit of money that way."

The housekeeper seemed flattered. "I'd be glad to, if you think I'm good enough."

Diplomatically Qwilleran steered Mildred out of the kitchen and into the library, where he seated her in a comfortable chair and handed her a grubby clutch of yellowed paper.

She shuddered and recoiled. "What's that?"

"Daisy's diary. We found it behind her bed. It's totally illegible. I can distinguish a date at the top of each page, that's all. She began writing January first and ended in May."

Mildred accepted the diary gingerly. "It looks like a mouse nest, but it's her handwriting, all right. I wonder if I can decipher it." She studied the first page. "Once you get the hang of her letter formation it's not so bad. . . . Let's see. It starts with 'Happy New Year to me,' but the spelling's atrocious. . . . Hmmm . . . She says her mother is drunk. Poor girl never knew what it was to have a decent parent. . . . She mentions Rick. They go out in the woods and throw snowballs at trees. He buys her a burger. . . . How'm I doing, Qwill?"

"You're amazing! Don't stop."

"Oh-oh! On January second she loses her job at the studio. Calls Amanda a witch. There's something about an elephant, spelled with an *f*. It's a Christmas present from Rick."

"He's the one who stole it," Qwilleran guessed. "Amanda blamed Daisy. Her friends used to hang around the studio."

Mildred scanned the pages. "Very depressing . . . until January fifteenth. She gets a job at the Goodwinter house—uniforms provided. A room of her own. Won't have to live with Della. She celebrates with Rick, Ollie, Tiff and Jim."

"Tiffany is the one who was shot on her father's farm."

"Yes, I know. I had her in home ec. Married one of the Trotter boys. Father injured in a tractor accident. . . . Now the diary skips to February. Daisy decides she doesn't like housework. Well, neither do I, to tell the truth. . . . A new boyfriend, Sandy, gives her cologne for a Valentine. Spelled *k-l-o-n-e*. See what I mean about her spelling? . . . She doesn't write much in March. . . . April is pretty well messed up. . . . Oh-oh! Lost her job again."

"That's when she started working here, according to the employment records," Qwilleran said.

"She's in love with Sandy, spelled *l-u-v*. . . . No more mention of Rick or Ollie or Jim. . . . Sounds as if she's serious. Sandy gives her a gold bracelet. . . . Let's see what else. . . . Oh-oh! Here—on April thirteenth—she thinks she's pregnant. . . . Tiff takes her to Dr. Hal. . . . Very happy now. . . . She sketches some wedding dresses. . . . Della is pleased. Knits some things for the baby. . . . Now there are pages torn out. . . . April thirtieth, she cries all night. Sandy wants her to have an abortion. No marriage. . . . He gives her money. . . . Della tells her to have the baby and make him pay. . . . That's all. That's the last entry."

"Sad story, but it confirms all our guesses."

"Where can I wash my hands, Qwill? This book is foul. And I have to go and get my hair done."

After escorting Mildred to her car, he returned to the library to lock up the diary. To his surprise the desk drawer was open. He was sure he had closed it, but now it stood a few inches ajar. The ivory elephant was there—and the gold bracelet—and the postal card. But the envelope of money had vanished.

He made a quick trip to the kitchen, where Mrs. Cobb was preparing mustard sauce for the smoked tongue. "Was anyone here in the last half hour?"

"Only Mrs. Hanstable."

"I accompanied her to her car, and when I returned, my desk drawer was open, and an important envelope was missing."

"I can't image, unless . . . I told you strange things have been going on in this house, Mr. Q."

He headed back to the library to make a thorough search of his desktop—just in time to see Koko plodding aimlessly through the foyer, his jaws clamped on the corner of a white envelope that dragged between his legs.

"Drop that!" Qwilleran shouted. "Bad cat! How did you get it?"

Koko dropped the envelope, stepped over it with unconcern, and went to sit on the third stair of the staircase.

In the library Qwilleran found scratches on the front edge of the drawer. It was a heavy drawer, and Koko had gone to some trouble to open it. Why?

Ever since the accident on Ittibittiwassee Road, Koko had been acting strangely. Prior to that episode he and Qwilleran had been good companions. They treated each other as equals.

The man talked to the cat, and the cat listened and blinked and looked wise, then answered with a "yow" that signified tolerant interest or hearty agreement or violent disapproval. They had played games together, and since moving into the K mansion Koko had been particularly attentive.

Suddenly all that had changed. Koko's attitude was one of scornful aloofness, and he committed annoying misdemeanors—like pushing his commode around the kitchen, knocking fine books off the shelf, and—now—stealing money. Something was wrong. A personality change in an animal usually signified illness, yet Koko was the acme of health. His eyes sparkled; his appetite was good; his lithe body was taut with energy; he romped with Yum Yum. Only with Qwilleran was he reserved and remote.

There were no ready answers, and Koko committed no further mischief that day, but late that night Qwilleran was reading in his upstairs sitting room when he heard prolonged wailing, shrill and mournful. Hurrying downstairs as fast as the injured knee would permit, he followed the eerie sound to the back of the house. There, in a shaft of moonlight that beamed into the solarium, was an alarming performance. Koko, his fur unnaturally ruffled, was half crouched, with his head thrown back, and he was howling an unearthly lament that made the blood run cold.

The tall case clock in the foyer bonged twice. Approaching the cat cautiously, Qwilleran spoke to him in a soothing voice and then stroked his ridged fur until he calmed down.

"You're a good cat, Koko, and a good friend," Qwilleran said, "and I'm sorry if I've been preoccupied or cross. You've been trying to get my attention. You're smarter than I am sometimes, and I should read your messages instead of flying off on a wild hunch. Will you forgive me? Can we be friends again? You and Yum Yum are all the family I've got."

Koko blinked his eyes and squeaked a faint "ik ik ik."

It was two o'clock. Four hours later Qwilleran found out what it was all about.

FIFTEEN

IT WAS SIX o'clock, but Qwilleran already was awake when the telephone startled him with its early-morning ring of urgency. His curiosity had been working overtime and disturbing his sleep ever since Penelope's unexpected visit and Koko's unexplained antics. Was the nocturnal howl a protest? A warning? Or was it something that cats do in the light of a full moon?

Then the telephone rang, and a familiar voice said in an ominous minor key, "Qwill, did I wake you? I thought you'd want to know— Penelope has taken her life!"

He was stunned into silence.

"Qwill, this is Melinda."

"I know. I heard you. I can't believe it! Yes, I *can* believe it. I knew she was on the brink of something. What a bloody shame! What a waste of brains and gorgeousness! Was there any explanation?"

"Just the usual—she'd been depressed lately. Dad is over at their house now. Alex called him first, then the police. The medical examiner is there, too."

"Did she O.D.?"

"She took a bottle of Scotch to the garage and sat in the car with the motor running. I'm due at the hospital now. I'll call you later."

"How about dinner tonight?"

"Sorry, lover. I have to attend a baby shower, but I'll drop in beforehand and you can fortify me with a gin and tonic. I may have more information by then."

When he broke the news to Mrs. Cobb, she said, "I feel terrible about it! She was such a lovely person."

Qwilleran said, "Now would be the time for me to type some catalogue cards for you. I'd welcome the distraction."

The task required even more concentration than he expected. First he had to decipher the registrar's notes. Someday he would compose a magazine piece on the subject, titled "How Not to Write Right; or, Seven Easy Ways to Total Obfuscation."

It was like cracking a secret code. As soon as he discovered that a "habimeon glooo luptii" was actually a Bohemian glass luster, the rest was easy. On each card he had to type the file number of the artifact, its name, date, description, provenance, and value. The four-digit and five-digit evaluations kept him in a state of fiscal shock.

Naturally the Siamese were on the desk, assisting in their own unhelpful way. Yum Yum was stealing pencils and pushing paper clips to the floor. Koko, friendly once more after Qwilleran's apology, was nosing about the desktop like a bloodhound. At one point he flushed out Penelope's thank-you note written after the dinner party, and Qwilleran noted her mannered handwriting and the affected *e, r* and *s* that somehow implied a classical education.

When Melinda arrived after office hours, she explained, "I'd rather go to dinner with you, lover, but my generation is always getting married or pregnant, and I have to go to cute showers with cute invitations, cute guessing games, cut table decorations, and cute refreshments. When I marry, I'm going to elope. Would you care to elope, lover?"

"Not until they take out my itching stitches. Sit down and tell me how Alexander is reacting."

Melinda curled up in one of the solarium's big wicker chairs. "Dad had to sedate him. Alex got terribly emotional. He and Penny were very close—only a year apart—and they grew up like twins. He feels guilty for spending so much time out of town. He wishes he'd stayed home last night instead of going to a bachelor party at the club. Did you know he's getting married?"

"I heard a rumor."

"She's an attorney—young—graduated top of her class."

"Do you know her name?"

"Ilya Smfska."

Qwilleran nodded. That much checked out; Penelope hadn't been merely garbling her diction. "Who found the body?"

"Alex got home just before daylight, drove into the garage, and there she was."

"Did they establish the time of death?"

"Two A.M."

"Any suicide note?"

"Not as far as I know. Everyone knows she's been overworked, but the ironic fact is that Alex's finacée could have relieved her caseload. But it's too late now."

She finished her cool drink, declined another, and prepared to leave for her social obligation. "Anyway," she said with a cynical smirk, "Penelope won't have to attend any more showers."

After dinner Qwilleran went for a slow, thoughtful walk down Goodwinter Boulevard. The old family mansion that Penelope and Alexander had shared was partly obscured by twelve-foot hedges, but several cars could be seen in the driveway. Beyond them was the five-car attached garage, obviously a modern addition to the turreted, gabled, verandaed house. Next door was another Goodwinter residence, much less pretentious, where Dr. Halifax lived with his invalid wife. It had been Melinda's childhood home.

A raucous blast from a car horn alerted Qwilleran, and he saw Amanda turning into a driveway across the boulevard.

"Come on in for a shot," she called out with gruff heartiness.

"Make it ginger ale, and I'll take two," he said.

The interior of the designer's house appeared to be furnished with clients' rejects. He wondered if the Hunzinger chair and Pennsylvania *schrank* had been headed for this eclectic aggregation. The furniture was cluttered with design magazines, wallpaper books, and fabric samples.

"Move those magazines and sit down." Amanda said. "Had a little excitement in the neighborhood last night."

"Her act was unthinkable!" Qwilleran said.

"Not to me! I knew that unholy situation was headed for an

explosion, but I didn't figure on suicide. I thought she'd blow her brother's brains out, if he has any."

"Do you think it was really suicide?"

Amanda put down her glass on a porcelain elephant table and stared at her visitor. "Golly, that's something I never thought of. Murder, you mean? You can't pin it on Alex. He was at the club all night, playing cards with Fitch and Lanspeak and those other buzzards. Or so the story goes. Now you've got me wondering."

Qwilleran stood up and looked out the front window. "You can see their driveway from here. Did you notice any other vehicle there last night?"

"Can't say that I did. What do you think could have happened?"

"Someone could have drugged her drink and then carried her out to the garage and turned on the ignition, leaving a Scotch bottle for evidence. It's an attached garage. It could be done under cover."

"Say, this is hot stuff!" Amanda said with evident relish. "Wait till I pour another."

"Of course," Qwilleran went on, "the killer would most likely park elsewhere and arrive on foot. Is there any access to the property from the rear?"

"Only through Dr. Hal's garden."

"Don't mention this to anyone," Qwilleran requested, "but let me know if you come up with a possible clue."

"Hot damn! Just call me Nora Charles."

Qwilleran walked home slowly, and as he approached the K mansion he saw a terrain vehicle pulling away and heading north.

"Whose truck was that in the drive, Mrs. Cobb?"

She was looking radiant. "Herb Hackpole was here. He went fishing this afternoon and brought us a mess of perch, boned and everything."

"You seem to have made a hit with that guy."

"Oh, he's very nice, Mr. Q. He wants to take me fishing someday, and he offered me a good trade-in on my van, if I want to switch to a small car. He even wants to take me hunting! Imagine that!"

Qwilleran grumbled something and retired to his Chippendale sitting room, taking a volume of Trollope that Koko had knocked off a library shelf, but even the measured prose of *He Knew He Was Right* could not calm an underlying restlessness. His moustache was sending him signals so violent and so bothersome that he considered shaving it off. Only a critical examination in the bathroom mirror forestalled the rash action.

After a night of fitful sleep he again busied himself with the catalogue cards, but the morning hours dragged by. He glanced at his watch every five minutes.

At long last Mrs. Cobb announced a bit of lunch in the kitchen. "Only leftover vichyssoise and a tuna sandwich," she said.

"I can eat anything," Qwilleran told her. "Leftover vichyssoise, leftover Chateaubriand, leftover strawberry shortcake—anything. I wonder how many Castilian monks sat at this table four centuries ago and had broiled open-face tuna sandwiches with Dijon mustard and capers. They're delicious, Mrs. Cobb."

"Thank you. How are you getting along with the typing? Are you getting bored?"

"Not at all. It's highly educational. I've just learned that the chest of drawers in the upstairs hall is late baroque in lignum vitae with heartwood oystering. The knowledge will enrich my life immeasurably."

"Oh, Mr. Q! You're just being funny."

"Where are the cats? They're suspiciously quiet. Can't they smell tuna?"

"When I called you for lunch, they were both in the vestibule, waiting for the mail."

"Crazy guys!"Qwilleran said. "They know it's not delivered until midafternoon." Yet, he had to admit that he too was waiting for something to happen.

After lunch he returned to his typewriter and was translating "johirgi fiwil hax" into "Fabergé jewel box" when the pitter-patter on the marble floor announced the arrival of the post. An influx of get-well cards was now added to the daily avalanche pouring through the mail slot. Next he heard sounds of swishing, skittering, and scrambling as the Siamese pounced on the pile, sliding and tumbling with joy and talking to themselves in squeaks and mumbles.

Qwilleran let them have their fun. He was busy recording a pair of Hepplewhite knife boxes with silver escutcheons, worth as much as a cabin cruiser, when Koko labored into the library

lugging a long envelope in a rich ivory color. Qwilleran knew
that stationery, and his moustache sprang to attention. Fever-
ishly he ran a letter knife across the top of the envelope. There
were three pages of single-spaced typing on Goodwinter &
Goodwinter letterhead. It was dated two days before, and the
signature had the eccentric *e* and *r* that he recognized.

He read the letter and said to himself, She was right; she
should have been a writer; she could have written gothic ro-
mances.

Dear Qwill,

If I disgraced myself last evening, please be understanding, and I implore you to read this letter with the
sympathy and compassion you evinced during my visit.

As I write this I am of sound mind—and perfectly
sober, I assure you. I am also bitter and contrite in
equal proportions. Obviously I am still among the living, but such will not be the case when you receive this
letter. Mrs. Fulgrove has instructions to drop it in the
mail in the event of my sudden demise. She is the only
person I can trust to carry out my wishes. And if I seem
calm and businesslike at this moment, it is because I am
endeavoring to emulate you. I have, and always have
had, a great deal of admiration for you, Qwill.

In writing this painful confession, my only hope is
that you are alive to read it. Otherwise a great misfor-
tune will befall the people of Moose County. If I can
save your life and prevent this—by accusing certain
parties—I shall have done penance for my transgres-
sions.

How does one begin?

I have always loved my brother with an irrational
passion. Even as a child I was enamored and possessive,
yearning for his attention and flying into a rage if he
bestowed it elsewhere. Eventually Alex went away to
prep school and I was sent to boarding school, but we
were always together weekends.

When my father begged me to study law for Alex's
sake, I put aside my ambition to be a writer and attended law school gladly. My grandfather had been a

chief justice; my father was a brilliant attorney respected in the entire state. It was intended that Alex should follow in their footsteps. Unfortunately, as my father pointed out, his only son-and-heir would never be more than a third-rate lawyer. I was elected to compensate for his shortcomings and maintain the Goodwinter reputation in the legal field.

I never regretted my role, because it meant Alex and I could be together constantly. My rude awakening occurred five years ago when I discovered he was having an affair with our live-in maid. It was a knife in my heart! Not only had be betrayed me, but he had consorted with the commonest of females—a girl from the Mull tribe. I dismissed her at once.

But worse was yet to come. It was the shattering news that she was pregnant and expected to marry her "Sandy," as she impudently called him. After a brief moment of panic, I steeled myself and devised a constructive solution. I would arrange to send her away for an abortion and pay her to relocate in another state.

But no! Her mother, a woman of dubious reputation, influenced her to decline the abortion and file a paternity suit. My God! That such a calamity should happen to our branch of the family! I was infuriated by the arrogance of these people! In desperation I approached one of Alex's boyhood acquaintances and enlisted his cooperation.

Let me explain. When Alex and I were young, Father insisted that we attend public school in Pickax, expecting democratization to shape our life attitudes. On the contrary, we were harassed by the hateful middle-class children. I used my wits to keep them in their place, but Alex was weak and an easy target for their cruelty. I was obliged to go to his rescue.

I hired the school bully—with my own money—to keep Alex's tormentors in line. He continued as bodyguard and avenger until Father saw fit to send us to better schools in the East.

Five years ago—in our new hour of trouble—I begged the same man to convince the Mull girl to submit to an abortion and leave town permanently, in return for a generous financial arrangement, of course. Lest the support payments be traced to their source, it was agreed that cash would regularly be turned over to our intermediary—to be forwarded, less his commission, to the girl. This subterfuge was my idea. How clever I thought I was! Actually, how naive!

At the time of the girl's departure there was a cave-in at Three Pines Mine, on the heels of which that thoroughly amoral and despicable man gloatingly informed us that she was buried a thousand feet underground and would make no more trouble. He pointed out, however, that we were accomplices before the fact.

The deed was done! No amount of remorse would undo the crime. It remained only to avoid scandal at all costs. The cash payments continued, increasing regularly with inflation and the man's greed. But, at least, Alex and I felt safe, and we had each other.

Then, to my horror, Qwill, you arrived on the scene and raised questions about the missing housemaid—although how your suspicions were prompted, I cannot fathom. It came to our attention that you were talking freely about the matter and interviewing possible witnesses.

The two men agreed between themselves that the two witnesses should be silenced, and I reluctantly agreed. What else could I do? But when they discussed ways to stop your meddling, Qwill, I was appalled! I pointed out that your death would mean the loss of billions of dollars in Moose County. My arguments accounted for nothing. They cared only about saving their own skins.

You have suspected a plot against your life, and you were right to do so. You have misidentified the conspirators, however. Now you know the truth.

For five years I have lived with this specter of guilt and fear. It was bearable only because I had saved the family from unthinkable scandal—and because I had Alex's love.

And then he broke the terrible news that he was bringing a "brilliant" young attorney to Pickax as a partner in the firm and—this was the crushing blow—as a wife!

It was more than I could bear. My lifetime of sacrifice and devotion was thrown aside in a moment. I had involved myself in heinous crime, only to have it end like this—only to be cast aside.

What could I do? There was only one way to stop it. In a frenzy of desperation I confronted Alex and threatened to reveal his complicity in three murders. The instant the words were out of my mouth I realized I had made a fatal mistake. My God! The hatred in my brothers' eyes! How can I describe the rage and vengeance that contorted my brother's features—the face that I had thought so beautiful!

Forgive me if I appear melodramatic, but I now fear for my life. I fear that every day may be my last. A bullet from the same rifle that killed the farm girl will be quick and merciful, or they will devise a means that will simulate an accident or suicide.

In any event, Mrs. Fulgrove will mail this letter, and I am following your example in preparing letters for the prosecutor and the media, naming the brute who killed the pregnant girl, burying her alive in a mineshaft, who arranged a friendly drink with her mother and drugged the whiskey, who fired a single perfect shot at a girl on a farm tractor.

You are not safe, and the future of Moose County is at stake, until these two men are apprehended and brought to justice.

> Yours in good faith,
> Penelope Goodwinter

SIXTEEN

🐾

THE SHRIEK OF a bomb and the boom of a cannon shattered his frightening dream of global war. He struggled to shake off sleep.

Another boom! Was it a figment of his dream, or was something battering the bedroom door?

Boom! Qwilleran rolled out of bed and groped his way to the door, staggering with sleep. He stopped, listened, reached cautiously for the doorknob. He yanked it open! And a cat hurtled into the room.

Koko had been throwing his weight against the securely latched door, trying to break it down. Now, with stentorian yowls that turned to shrieks, he raced to the staircase.

Qwilleran, not stopping for slippers or robe or light switches, followed as fast as he could while the cat rushed ahead, swooping downstairs, bounding back upstairs to scold vehemently, then flying down again in one liquid movement.

The house was in darkness, save for a dim glow from streetlights on the Circle. Qwilleran moved warily toward the rear of the house where Koko was leading him, now in stealthy silence. Reaching the library, the man heard the back door being unlocked and slowly opened, and he saw a dark bulky figure moving furtively through the entry hall. Qwilleran stepped aside, shielded by the Pennsylvania *schrank,* while a white blur rose to the top of the seven-foot wardrobe.

Unmindful of the cold stone floor under his feet but thinking wildly of baseball bats and crowbars, Qwilleran watched the intruder pass the broom closet, hesitate at the kitchen door, then enter the large square service hall where the *schrank* stood guard. There was not a sound. Qwilleran could hear his own heartbeat. Koko was somewhere overhead, crouching between two large, rare, and valuable majolica vases.

As the dark figure edged closer, Qwilleran reached for the toprail of an antique chair, but it was wobbly with age and would shatter if used as a weapon. Just then he heard a barely audible "ik-ik" on top of the *schrank,* and he remembered the pickax in the library. He slipped into the shadows to grope for it. There were only seconds to spare!

His hand was closing around the sturdy handle when a confusion of sounds broke the silence: a thump, a clatter, a man's outcry, and a loud thud—followed by the unmistakable crash of an enormous ceramic vase on a stone floor. Qwilleran sprang forward with the pickax raised, bellowing threats, towering over the figure that now lay prone.

With squeals and shrieks Mrs. Cobb rushed downstairs, and the house flooded with light.

"Call the police," Qwilleran shouted, "before I bash his brains!"

The man lay groaning, one arm twisted at a grotesque angle and one foot in the cats' spilled commode. The shards of majolica were scattered around him, and Koko was sniffing in the pocket of his old army jacket.

"Koko never ceases to amaze me," Qwilleran said to Melinda at the dinner table that evening. "He knew someone was going to break in, and he knew far enough in advance to get upstairs and wake me up. The way he threw himself against my door, it's a wonder he didn't break every bone in his body. The fantastic thing is: he pushed his commode to a spot where the guy was sure to trip over it. The majolica vase is a small price to pay for his heroism."

Qwilleran and Melinda were having dinner at Stephanie's, the Lanspeaks' new restaurant. He called for her at her father's house on Goodwinter Boulevard, where she was changing clothes after a hard day at the clinic, giving allergy shots and bandaging Little Leaguers.

Dr. Halifax greeted him at the door. "You had another narrow escape last night, Qwill. You live a charmed life. The needles and morphine they found on him were stolen from my office a short time ago."

"What's his condition?"

"Compound fracture. Dislocated shoulder. He's a heavy fellow, and he went down like a ton of bricks on your stone floor. He's a police prisoner, of course, and a broken arm is the least of his troubles."

Qwilleran and his date walked to the restaurant, which occupied an old stone residence rezoned for commercial use.

"The Lanspeaks named it after their cow," Melinda said, "and they did the whole place in dairy colors: milk white, straw beige, and butter yellow. It's a service-oriented restaurant."

Qwilleran grunted. "What this town needs is a food-oriented restaurant."

A young hostess greeted them. "My name is Vicki, and I'm your hostperson. Your waitperson is Matthew, and he'll do everything possible to make your visit enjoyable."

A young man immediately appeared. "My name is Matthew. I am your waitperson, and I am at your service."

"My name is Jim," Qwilleran replied. "I am your customer, and I am very hungry. The lady's name is Melinda. She is my guest, and she is hungry, too."

"And thirsty," Melinda added. "Okay, Qwill, tell me all about the break-in last night. How did he get into the house?"

"Birch is pretty crafty. He made an extra key for himself when he installed our new back door lock. Evidently he waited for a moonless night—there was a heavy cloud cover—and approached through the orchard behind the house. His truck was hidden in the old barn out there. I suspect he was going to haul me away to one of the mine sites and dump me down a shaft."

"Darling, how horrible!"

"I had a look at the truck this morning, and it's the same terrain-buggy that tried to run me down on Ittibittiwassee Road. I recognized the big rusty, grinning grille from my dream. We can also assume it was Birch who doped Penelope's Scotch and carried her out to the garage while Alex was establishing his alibi at the club."

Matthew arrived with Melinda's champagne and Qwilleran's mineral water. "This is your champagne cooler," he said, "and these are your chilled glasses."

"We'd also like an appetizer," Qwilleran told him. "Bring us some *pâté de caneton.*"

"That's kind of a meatloaf made of ground-up duck," the waitperson explained helpfully.

"Thank you, Matthew. It sounds delicious."

Melinda drank a toast to Qwilleran for exposing a deplorable crime.

Apologetically he said, "I'm afraid it's going to be a nasty scandal when everything comes to light."

"A lot of us guessed the relationship between Penny and Alex," she said, "but who would dream they'd collaborate in a murder plot? And who would ever imagine he'd conspire to kill his sister? He needed her! She was the mainstay of his career."

"Not anymore. He found another brilliant woman—with Washington connections—to take her place. Penelope became a threat. She knew too much, and she was too smart."

Melinda gazed at Qwilleran with admiring green eyes. "No one thought to question Daisy's disappearance before you came here, lover."

"I can't take credit. It was Koko who sniffed out the clues. A couple of days ago he rooted out Penelope's thank-you note on my desk, and I checked it against the postal card from Maryland. She had written it in a disguised hand, but some individual letter formations gave it away. It was probably mailed from a suburb in Washington when Alex was on one of his junkets."

"Poor self-inflated Alex," Melinda said. "I hate to think what a court trial will do to him—his ego, I mean. He was a wreck, Dad told me, after his session with the prosecutor today."

"Birch and Alex may have done the dirty work, but I think Penelope was the mastermind. After I started inquiring about Daisy, Birch started doing a lot of work for us. I thought he was hooked on Mrs. Cobb's cooking, but in retrospect I believe Penelope hired him to spy on us. *Someone* was in a position to know I was talking to Tiffany Trotter and was about to talk to Della

Mull. They were probably the only two who knew the identity of Daisy's Sandy."

"Didn't you ever suspect Penelope?"

"Well, she changed the subject whenever I mentioned Daisy, but I thought she considered it gauche to discuss servants. I admit I was puzzled when she repeatedly declined my invitations to lunch or whatever."

"No mystery," Melinda said. "I told her to keep hands off or I'd spread some unsavory rumors."

"Melinda, you're a nasty green-eyed monster."

"All Goodwinters have a nasty streak; it's in our genes."

After studying the menu they ordered trout *amandine*.

"That's trout with almonds," said the waitperson, eager to be of service.

"Fine. And we'd like asparagus."

"That's extra," Matthew warned.

While they waited for the entrée Melinda said to Qwilleran, "So you were wrong about the New Jersey connection. There was no sinister plot to eliminate you and grab the inheritance."

He looked sheepish. "That's what happens when I jump to my own conclusions instead of getting my signals from Koko. You know, that cat is ten pounds of bone and muscle in a fur coat, with whiskers and a long tail and a wet nose, but he's smarter than I am. Without ever visiting Daisy's apartment, *he knew* something was wrong. *He knew* Penelope's final letter was going to be delivered. *He knew* Birch was sneaking up to the house last night."

"Cats have a sixth sense."

"Six! I say Koko has sixteen!"

"If only he could communicate!"

"He communicates all right. The problem is: I'm not smart enough to read him. Let me tell you something, Melinda. When I got the notion that the whole state of New Jersey was after me, Koko was disgusted; he avoided me for days. At one point he pushed some books off a shelf in the library, and I scolded him for it. Do you know what the books were? A poem titled *Dooms-day* by a seventeenth-century Scottish poet named *Sir William Alexander!*"

The entrée was served. "This is your trout *amandine* and asparagus on heated plates," said Matthew.

Qwilleran stared at the vegetable. "This isn't asparagus. It's broccoli."

"Sorry. I'll take it back." Matthew removed the plates but soon returned with them. "The chef says its asparagus."

They ate their trout and broccoli in silence until Qwilleran said, "If Koko hadn't sniffed out the Daisy situation, and if I hadn't started investigating, Penelope and Tiffany and Della would be alive today."

"And a murderer would be at large," Melinda reminded him.

"The Goodwinter reputation would be intact, and Alexander would run for Congress. He'd marry Ilya Smfska and produce another generation of supersnobs."

"And the murderer and his accomplices would live happily every after."

"Penelope would eventually make an emotional adjustment," Qwilleran said, "and Alexander would keep on paying for Birch Tree's boats and trucks and motorcycles, but he could afford it."

"And no one would care that Dairy was buried in the Three Pines mineshaft," Melinda said.

After the tossed salad on a chilled plate with a chilled fork, and after the Ribier grapes with homemade cheese, and after coffee served with Stephanie's own cream, Qwilleran and Melinda walked back to her father's house.

Dr. Halifax met them at the door. "Prepare for some jolting news," he said. "Just heard it on the radio. A private plane crashed fifty miles south of the airport, and the pilot has just been identified."

"Alexander," Qwilleran said quietly, as his moustache bristled.

Back at the mansion he was greeted by a prancing Siamese. Koko knew it was time for the nightly house check, and he led the way to the solarium.

"Case solved," Qwilleran said to him, "but I'd like to know the real reason why you pushed those things around the kitchen. Were you trying to tell me to get that cold stone floor carpeted?"

He finished locking the French doors, and Koko preceded him to the breakfast room. While the man checked the Staffordshire figurines and German regimental steins, the cat checked for stray crumbs under the table.

"Tell me something," Qwilleran said to him. "When you found Daisy's diary, were you just chasing a fly? And if so, how come it happened to be crawling about Sandy Goodwinter's initials?"

Koko bounded ahead to the library, where he pawed a leather-bound copy of *The Physiology of Taste*. In the dining room he sniffed the carved rabbits and pheasants on the sideboard. Then he marched into the drawing room, zigzagging across the Aubusson rug to avoid the roses in the pattern. While Qwilleran gave the bronzes and porcelains a security check, Koko headed for the antique piano.

Leaping lightly to the cushioned bench, he reached up with his right paw in an indecisive way, then withdrew it. After a few tentative passes with his left paw, he planted it firmly on G and then C. He seemed pleased with the sound made by the keys. More confidently he hit the D with his right paw and finally touched the E.

Qwilleran shook his head. "No one would believe it!" He switched off the lights and strode to the kitchen, humming the tune Koko had played: *"How Dry I Am!"*

Yum Yum was asleep on her blue cushion, and Qwilleran stroked her fur before opening the refrigerator. He splashed a jigger of white grape juice in a saucer, placed it on the floor, and watched Koko lap it up with lightning-fast tongue, his tail curled high in ecstasy.

"I'll never figure you out," Qwilleran said. "You're all cat, and yet you sense the most incredible secrets. You were fascinated by Penelope, and it wasn't just her French perfume. You howled at the exact hour when she died."

Koko licked the saucer dry and started to wash up.

"Did you know she was going to be murdered?"

Koko interrupted his ablutions to give Qwilleran a penetrating stare, and the man slapped his forehead as the truth struck him. "It wasn't a homicide set up to look like a suicide. She framed those guys! It was suicide planned to look like murder!"

Koko finished his chore, with great care to wash behind his ears, between his toes, and all along his whip of a brown tail.